Frankenstein

Frankenstein

OR

THE MODERN PROMETHEUS

MARY SHELLEY

with features written by
Philip Wilkinson

LONDON, NEW YORK, MELBOURNE,
MUNICH, AND DELHI

LONDON, NEW YORK, MELBOURNE,
MUNICH, AND DELHI

Frankenstein first published 1818

This edition published in the United States in 2008 by
DK Publishing
375 Hudson Street
New York, New York 10014

07 08 09 10 11   10 9 8 7 6 5 4 3 2 1

A catalog record for this book is available from the Library of Congress.

ISBN: 978-0-7566-3330-1

DK books are available at special discounts when purchased in bulk for sales promotions, premiums,
fund-raising, or educational use. For details, contact DK Publishing Special Markets, 375 Hudson
Street, New York, New York 10014 or SpecialSales@dk.com

Color reproduction by GRB Editrice, Italy

Printed and bound in China by Leo Paper Products Ltd.

Discover more at
www.dk.com

Contents

Why Read *Frankenstein?*

Frankenstein has a gripping plot and, in Victor Frankenstein and the monster or "Creature" that Frankenstein creates, two main characters that are among the most fascinating in any novel. Once you start reading about them, you soon want to know their whole story. How will Frankenstein manage to create a living human? What will life be like for the Creature? How will other people react to the Creature and how will the story end? Questions like these make the novel difficult to put down. The book is also full of engaging minor characters, from the explorer Robert Walton, who begins and ends the story, to Elizabeth, the woman Frankenstein loves and whose sunny character throws some light on to this dark and spooky tale.

But *Frankenstein* is more than a good read. The work is one of the earliest ancestors of two very modern kinds of book: the horror story and the science fiction novel. Mary Shelley uses both her power to shock and scare her readers, and her knowledge of science to create a special fictional blend, one that has been copied in countless stories, plays, and films in the two centuries since she wrote *Frankenstein*.

Frankenstein is also one of the most thought-provoking books of its time. This is because Mary Shelley is not content to make us scared with the actions of the scientist and his Creature. She also makes us think. Like modern writers who question the right of scientists to "play God" by doing experiments in fields such as genetics, she questions the value of Frankenstein's kind of scientific work. She does not do this by preaching to her readers, but the actions of her characters and the results of these actions are obviously meant to make us think about whether Victor Frankenstein is right to do what he does.

For example, Frankenstein himself learns that he should have taken responsibility for the Creature he created, realizing that none of the deaths and disasters that plague his life would have happened if he had been more careful with his creation rather than allowing the Creature to escape from his care. The Creature himself questions Frankenstein's actions directly, when he asks his creator: "How dare you sport thus with life? Do your duty towards me, and I will do mine towards you and the rest of mankind." By the end of the book and by the time several characters have met violent deaths, the dangers of Frankenstein's actions have been made clear.

This edition has been specifically designed to make the book accessible to a modern reader. Difficult words and concepts are explained in the footnotes and in the illustrated glossary on pp.236–252. In addition, there are a number of illustrated feature pages throughout the book that explain the historical, cultural, and literary background of the novel. These pages highlight the changes in science and technology that were taking place in the period just before *Frankenstein* was written, together with information about the literary developments that influenced Mary Shelley, from the Romantic movement in poetry and fiction to the development of the horror story. These features will provide a richer and clearer understanding of a book that has been enthralling readers for nearly 200 years.

Mary Shelley
1797–1851

Mary Wollstonecraft Shelley had one of the most eventful, and one of the toughest, lives of any English writer. *Frankenstein* was her first book, and, although it was an instant success, things were never again quite so easy for Mary, because she had to cope with the early deaths of most of those she loved best.

Mary was the daughter of two famous people. Her father was William Godwin, one of the best-known writers of his time, a man famous for his radical political views. Her mother, Mary Wollstonecraft, was also a radical and a writer. Her most familiar work, *A Vindication of the Rights of Woman*, drew attention to the way in which women were treated as second-class citizens at the time. Mary was born in 1797, when her parents were at the height of their fame, but immediately tragedy struck. Mary Wollstonecraft became sick during childbirth and died soon after the baby was born.

Four years after this tragedy, Godwin married his neighbor, Mary Jane Clairmont, but Mary never got on well with her step-mother and there was little emotional warmth in the household. Mary was a solitary child until, as a teenager, she was allowed to go on a long visit to Scotland to the household of Godwin's friend William Baxter. Here she made a good friend in Baxter's daughter, Isabel.

When she returned to London in 1814, aged 16, Mary met her father's young friend, the poet Percy Bysshe Shelley. Mary and

Mary Shelley

Percy soon fell in love—even though Percy was already married. The pair caused a scandal when they ran away together in 1814. At first, they weren't especially happy. Mary had a baby girl, but the child died shortly after birth. But in 1816, Mary and Percy joined Mary's step-sister Claire Clairmont and their friends the poet Lord Byron and writer and doctor John Polidori, in Geneva, Switzerland. The weather was very cold and wet, so Byron suggested that they each write a ghost story to amuse themselves; Mary began *Frankenstein.*

Soon after this, Shelley's wife Harriet committed suicide and Mary and Percy married. Harriet's suicide turned out to be one of a series of tragedies. Several of Mary's children died in infancy, Mary herself nearly died from a miscarriage, and in 1822 Percy was killed in an accident at sea.

For nearly 30 years Mary made her living as a writer. She produced several more novels, including *The Last Man*, a story set in the 21st century about the last human survivor in a world that had been destroyed by disease. She also wrote numerous magazine articles and stories, many biographical essays about famous writers and scientists, and a travel book about the journeys she made in Germany and Italy with her son Percy Florence, her one surviving child.

In addition to all this writing, Mary found time to produce a four-volume edition of all her husband's poems, and another edition containing his essays, letters, and the translations he had made from works in other languages. She also wanted to write the story of his life, but Percy's father, still ashamed of his son's atheism and his behavior in running away with Mary, would not let her. In 1851 Mary Shelley died, having crammed many achievements into her 54-year life. Yet none of her many books was as lastingly popular as her first, *Frankenstein.*

TIMELINE OF PUBLISHED WORKS

1817
History of a Six Weeks' Tour (with Percy Bysshe Shelley)

1818
Frankenstein, or The Modern Prometheus

1819 published 1959
Mathilde

1823
Valperga: or, the Life and Adventures of Castruccio, Price of Lucca

1826
The Last Man

1830
Perkin Warbeck

1835
Lodore

1837
Falkner

1844
Rambles in Germany and Italy

Mary's mother
The author's mother, Mary Wollstonecraft, was a writer with advanced, or "radical" views. She criticized the power of the aristocracy and argued the case for women's rights.

The structure of the novel

Robert Walton's letters
VOLUME I

Letter 1	Letter 2	Letter 3	Letter 4

Robert Walton writes to his sister from St. Petersburg, where he is preparing an expedition.

Walton's ship is trapped in ice and he spots a sled steered by a gigantic creature. The next morning he encounters another sled driven by an ailing European.

Victor Frankenstein's story
VOLUME ONE continued

Chapter 1	Chapter 2	Chapter 3	Chapter 4	Chapter 5

On board ship, the European, Victor Frankenstein, begins to relate the story of his early life.

As a teenager, Victor is fascinated by the natural world.

He begins his studies of natural philosophy and alchemy at Ingolstadt University.

Victor discovers "the cause of generation and life."

Victor fashions a "horrible monster" and is disgusted by his creation.

The Creature's story
VOLUME TWO continued

Chapter 3	Chapter 4	Chapter 5	Chapter 6	Chapter 7

The Creature tells how he left Ingolstadt and took refuge in a hovel adjacent to a small cottage in the wilderness.

By listening in on the cottagers, the Creature learns how to speak.

He teaches himself to read and realizes the full force of his deformity and solitude.

After finding entries from Victor's journal, the Creature learns the history of how he was made.

Victor Frankenstein's story resumes
VOLUME THREE

Chapter 1	Chapter 2	Chapter 3	Chapter 4	Chapter 5

Victor sets up a laboratory and begins work on a female creature.

Victor destroys his second creation and becomes the suspect in a murder enquiry.

Victor discovers the murdered man is his friend, Henry Clerval. After a time in prison, Victor is exonerated.

Victor and Elizabeth get married.

The novel's structure is complex, because it is a story, within a story, within a story. The novel begins as a series of four letters written by an explorer, Robert Walton, to his sister in London. The main story, beginning with Chapter 1, is then told by Victor Frankenstein, a scientist whom Walton comes across on an expedition to the North Pole. Frankenstein narrates his life story, telling how he came to fashion a "horrible monster" from body parts. Embedded in his narration is a moving tale told by the Creature. Frankenstein resumes his story at the beginning of Volume 3 and finally, at the end of Volume 3, Walton's letters begin again, describing the fate of both Frankenstein and the Creature; hence the letters serve to frame the entire story.

VOLUME TWO

Chapter 6	Chapter 7	Chapter 8	Chapter 1	Chapter 2
Victor realizes the Creature has killed his youngest brother, William. A servant, Justine Moritz, is accused of the murder.		Justine is executed.	Victor is tormented by guilt and contemplates suicide.	At the summit of Montanvert, Victor spots the Creature and follows him to a cave.

Chapter 8	Chapter 9
The Creature recounts how he murdered William and then framed Justine.	Victor agrees to provide the Creature with a female companion.

Walton's letters continue

Chapter 6	Chapter 7	
The Creature kills Elizabeth on her wedding night and Victor vows to destroy his creation.	Victor tracks the Creature northward until he happens upon Walton and his ship.	Walton describes Victor's death and how he finds the Creature weeping over his dead creator. The Creature then leaps to his death into an icy sea.

Publisher's note on the use of England and Britain

The two kingdoms of England and Scotland were formally joined to form Great Britain in 1707. However, the characters in *Frankenstein*, like many people today, use "Britain" to refer to the whole country and also use "England" and "Scotland" to refer to the parts on either side of the border.

Author's Introduction to the Standard Novels Edition (1831)

The publishers of the Standard Novels, in selecting *Frankenstein* for one of their series, expressed a wish that I should furnish them with some account of the origin of the story. I am the more willing to comply, because I shall thus give a general answer to the question, so very frequently asked me. 'How I, then a young girl, came to think of and to dilate upon so very hideous an idea?' It is true that I am very averse to bringing myself forward in print; but as my account will only appear as an appendage to a former production, and as it will be confined to such topics as have connexion with my authorship alone, I can scarcely accuse myself of a personal intrusion.

It is not singular that, as the daughter of two persons of distinguished literary celebrity, I should very early in life have thought of writing. As a child I scribbled; and my favourite pastime during the hours given me for recreation was to 'write stories'. Still, I had a dearer pleasure than this, which was the formation of castles in the air – the indulging in waking dreams – the following up trains of thought, which had for their subject the formation of a succession of imaginary incidents. My dreams were at once more fantastic and agreeable than my writings. In the latter I was a close imitator – rather doing as others had done than putting down the suggestions of my own mind. What I wrote was intended at least for one other eye – my childhood's companion and friend; but my dreams were all my own; I accounted for them to nobody; they were my refuge when annoyed – my dearest pleasure when free.

I lived principally in the country as a girl, and passed a considerable time in Scotland. I made occasional visits to the more picturesque parts; but my habitual residence was on the blank and dreary northern shores of the **Tay**, near Dundee. Blank and dreary on retrospection I call them, they were not so to me then. They were the **eyry** of freedom, and the pleasant region where unheeded I could commune with the creatures of my fancy. I wrote then – but in a most common-place style. It was beneath the trees of the grounds belonging to our house, or on the bleak sides of the woodless mountains near, that my true compositions, the airy

Tay A river in Scotland.
eyry The nest of a bird of prey. Here, figuratively, a lofty or high-perched retreat.

flights of my imagination, were born and fostered. I did not make myself the heroine of my tales. Life appeared to me too common-place an affair as regarded myself. I could not figure to myself that romantic woes or wonderful events would ever be my lot; but I was not confined to my own identity, and I could people the hours with creations far more interesting to me at that age than my own sensations.

After this my life became busier, and reality stood in place of fiction. **My husband**, however, was from the first, very anxious that I should prove myself worthy of my parentage, and enrol myself on the page of fame. He was for ever inciting me to obtain literary reputation, which even on my own part I cared for then, though since I have become infinitely indifferent to it. At this time he desired that I should write, not so much with the idea that I could produce any thing worthy of notice, but that he might himself judge how far I possessed the promise of better things hereafter. Still I did nothing. Travelling, and the cares of a family, occupied my time; and study, in the way or reading of improving my ideas in communication with his far more cultivated mind, was all of literary employment that engaged my attention.

In the summer of 1816, we visited Switzerland and became the neighbours of **Lord Byron**. At first we spent our pleasant hours on the lake, or wandering on its shores; and Lord Byron, who was writing the third canto of *Childe Harold*, was the only one among us who put his thoughts upon paper. These, as he brought them successively to us, clothed all the light and harmony of poetry, seemed to stamp as divine the glories of heaven and earth, whose influences we partook with him.

But it proved a wet, ungenial summer, and incessant rain often confined us for days to the house. Some volumes of ghost stories, translated from the German into French, fell into our hands. There was the *History of the Inconstant Lover*, who, when he thought to clasp the bride to whom he had pledged his vows, found himself in the arms of the pale ghost of her whom he had deserted. There was the tale of the sinful founder of his race whose miserable doom it was to bestow the kiss of death on all the younger sons of his fated house, just when they reached the age of promise. His gigantic, shadowy form, clothed like the ghost in *Hamlet*, in complete armour, but with

My husband Percy Bysshe Shelley (1792–1822) a major English poet associated with the Romantic Movement.

Lord Byron George Gordon, Lord Byron (1788–1824) was a leading figure in the

Romantic Movement. Byron's best-known works include *Don Juan* and *Childe Harold's Pilgrimage*.

the **beaver** up, was seen at midnight, by the moon's fitful beams, to advance slowly along the gloomy avenue. The shape was lost beneath the shadow of the castle walls; but soon a gate swung back, a step was heard, the door of the chamber opened, and he advanced to the couch of the blooming youths, cradled in healthy sleep. Eternal sorrow sat upon his face as he bent down and kissed the forehead of the boys, who from that hour withered like flowers snapt upon the stalk. I have not seen these stories since then; but their incidents are as fresh in my mind as if I had read them yesterday.

'We will each write a ghost story,' said Lord Byron; and his proposition was acceded to. There were four of us. The noble author began a tale, a fragment of which he printed at the end of his poems of Mazeppa. Shelley, more apt to embody ideas and sentiments in the radiance of brilliant imagery, and in the music of the most melodious verse that adorns our language, than to invent the machinery of a story, commenced one founded on the experiences of his early life. Poor **Polidori** had some terrible idea about a skull-headed lady who was so punished for peeping through a keyhole – what to see I forget – something very shocking and wrong of course; but when she was reduced to a worse condition than the renowned Tom of Coventry, he did not know what to do with her and was obliged to dispatch her to the tomb of the **Capulets**, the only place for which she was fitted. The illustrious poets also, annoyed by the platitude of prose, speedily relinquished their uncongenial task.

I busied myself *to think of a story*, – a story to rival those which had excited us to this task. One which would speak to the mysterious fears of our nature and awaken thrilling horror – one to make the reader dread to look round, to curdle the blood, and quicken the beatings of the heart. If I did not accomplish these things, my ghost story would be unworthy of its name. I thought and pondered – vainly. I felt that blank incapability of invention which is the greatest misery of authorship, when dull Nothing replies to our anxious invocations. 'Have you thought of a story?' I was asked each morning, and each morning I was forced to reply with a mortifying negative.

Every thing must have a beginning, to speak in **Sanchean phrase**; and that beginning must be linked to something that went before. The Hindoos give the world an elephant to support it, but they

---

beaver Adjustable piece of armor protecting the face.

Polidori John Polidori (1795–1821), traveling companion and personal physician to Lord Byron.

Capulets From Shakespeare's *Romeo and Juliet*. The Capulets were Juliet's family.

Sanchean phrase Words like those of Sancho Panza in Miguel de Cervantes' novel *Don Quixote*.

make the elephant stand upon a tortoise. Invention, it must be humbly admitted, does not consist in creating out of void, but out of chaos; the materials must, in the first place, be afforded: it can give form to dark, shapeless substances, but cannot bring into being the substance itself. In all matters of discovery and invention, even of those that **appertain** to the imagination, we are continually reminded of the story of **Columbus and his egg**. Invention consists in the capacity of seizing on the capabilities of a subject: and in the power of moulding and fashioning ideas suggested to it.

Many and long were the conversations between Lord Byron and Shelley, to which I was a devout but nearly silent listener. During one of these, various philosophical doctrines were discussed, and among others the nature of the principle of life, and whether there was any probability of its ever being discovered and communicated. They talked of the experiments of **Dr Darwin** (I speak not of what the Doctor really did, or said that he did, but, as more to my purpose, of what was then spoken of as having been done by him), who preserved a piece of vermicelli in a glass case, till by some extraordinary means it began to move with voluntary motion. Not thus, after all, would life be given. Perhaps a corpse would be re-animated; **galvanism** had given token of such things: perhaps the component parts of a creature might be manufactured, brought together, and endued with vital warmth.

Night waned upon this talk, and even the witching hour had gone by, before we retired to rest. When I placed my head on my pillow, I did not sleep, nor could I be said to think. My imagination, unbidden, possessed and guided me, gifting the successive images that arose in my mind with a vividness far beyond the usual bounds of **reverie**. I saw – with shut eyes, but acute mental vision – I saw a pale student of unhallowed arts kneeling beside the thing he had put together. I saw the hideous **phantasm** of a man stretched out, and then, on the working of some powerful engine, show signs of life, and stir with an uneasy, half-vital motion. Frightful must it be; for supremely frightful would be the effect of any human endeavour to mock the stupendous mechanism of the Creator of the world. His success would terrify the artist; he would rush away from his odious handywork, horror-stricken. He would hope that, left to itself, the slight spark of life which he had communicated would fade; that

appertain To belong naturally or relate.
Columbus and his egg A story in Washington Irving's *Christopher Columbus* (see glossary.)
Dr Darwin Erasmus Darwin (1731–1802), scientist, and grandfather of Charles Darwin.

galvanism Electricity produced by chemical action.
reverie Daydream
phantasm Apparition or ghost.

this thing, which had received such imperfect animation would subside into dead matter; and he might sleep in the belief that the silence of the grave would quench forever the transient existence of the hideous corpse which he had looked upon as the cradle of life. He sleeps; but he is awakened; he opens his eyes; behold, the horrid thing stands at his bedside, opening his curtains and looking on him with yellow, watery, but speculative eyes.

I opened mine in terror. The idea so possessed my mind, that a thrill of fear ran through me, and I wished to exchange the ghastly image of my fancy for the realities around. I see them still; the very room, the dark **parquet**, the closed shutters, with the moonlight struggling through, and the sense I had that the glassy lake and white high Alps were beyond. I could not so easily get rid of my hideous phantom; still it haunted me. I must try to think of something else. I recurred to my ghost story – my tiresome, unlucky ghost story! O! if I could only contrive one which would frighten my reader as I myself had been frightened that night!

Swift as light and as cheering was the idea that broke in upon me. 'I have found it! What terrified me will terrify others; and I need only describe the spectre which had haunted my midnight pillow.' On the morrow I announced that I had *thought of a story*. I began that day with the words. 'It was on a dreary night of November,' making only a transcript of the grim terrors of my waking dream.

At first I thought but a few pages – of a short tale; but Shelley urged me to develop the idea at greater length. I certainly did not owe the suggestion of one incident, nor scarcely of one train of feeling, to my husband, and yet but for his incitement it would never have taken the form in which it was presented to the world. From this declaration I must except the preface. As far as I can recollect, it was entirely written by him.

And now, once again, I bid my hideous progeny go forth and prosper. I have an affection for it, for it was the offspring of happier days, when death and grief were but words, which found no true echo in my heart. Its several pages speak of many a walk, many a drive, and many a conversation, when I was not alone; and my companion was one who, in this world, I shall never see more. But this is for myself; my readers have nothing to do with these associations.

parquet Flooring made of wooden blocks laid in a pattern.

I will add but one word as to the alterations I have made. They are principally those of style. I have changed no portion of the story nor introduced any new ideas or circumstances. I have mended the language where it was so bald as to interfere with the interest of the narrative; and these changes occur almost exclusively in the beginning of the first volume. Throughout they are entirely confined to such parts as are mere adjuncts to the story, leaving the core and substance of it untouched.

M.W.S.
London, October 15th, 1831.

Preface
(by P. B. Shelley, 1818)

The event on which this fiction is founded has been supposed, by Dr Darwin and some of the physiological writers of Germany, as not of impossible occurrence. I shall not be supposed as according the remotest degree of serious faith to such an imagination; yet, in assuming it has the basis of a work of fancy, I have not considered myself as merely weaving a series of supernatural terrors. The event on which the interest of the story depends is exempt from the disadvantages of a mere tale of **spectres** or enchantment. It was recommended by the novelty of the situations which it develops, and, however impossible as a physical fact, affords a point of view to the imagination for the delineating of human passions more comprehensive and commanding than any which the ordinary relations of existing events can yield.

I have thus endeavoured to preserve the truth of the **elementary principles** of human nature, while I have not scrupled to innovate upon their combinations. The *Iliad*, the tragic poetry of Greece, – Shakespeare in *The Tempest* and *Midsummer Night's Dream*, – and most especially Milton, in *Paradise Lost,* conform to this rule; and the most humble novelist, who seeks to confer or receive amusement from his labours, may, without presumption, apply to prose fictions a licence, or rather a rule, from the adoption of which so many exquisite combinations of human feeling have resulted in the highest specimens of poetry.

The circumstance on which my story rests was suggested in casual conversation. It was commenced partly as a source of amusement, and partly as an expedient for exercising any untried resources of mind. Other motives were mingled with these as the work proceeded. I am by no means indifferent to the manner in which whatever moral tendencies exist in the sentiments or characters it contains shall affect the reader; yet my chief concern in this respect has been limited to the avoiding the **enervating** effects of the novels of the present day, and to the exhibition of the amiableness of domestic affection, and the excellence of universal virtue. The opinions which naturally spring from the character and situation

spectres Ghosts, objects of terror.
elementary principles Basic rules.
enervating Weakening, exhausting.

of the hero are by no means to be conceived as existing always in my own conviction; nor is any inference justly to be drawn from the following pages as prejudicing any philosophical doctrine of whatever kind.

It is a subject also of additional interest to the author that this story was begun in the majestic region where the scene is principally laid, and in society which cannot cease to be regretted. I passed the summer of 1816 in the environs of Geneva. The season was cold and rainy, and in the evenings we crowded around a blazing wood fire, and occasionally amused ourselves with some German stories of ghosts which happened to fall into our hands. These tales excited in us a playful desire of imitation. Two other friends (a tale from the pen of one of whom would be far more acceptable to the public than anything I can ever hope to produce) and myself agreed to write each a story founded on some supernatural occurrence.

The weather, however, suddenly became serene; and my two friends left me on a journey among the Alps and lost, in the magnificent scenes which they present, all memory of their ghostly visions. The following tale is the only one which has been completed.

Marlow
September 1817

Volume One

Letter 1

To Mrs Saville, England.

St Petersburgh, Dec. 11th, 17–.
You will rejoice to hear that no disaster has accompanied the
commencement of an enterprise which you have regarded with
such evil forebodings. I arrived here yesterday; and my first task is to
assure my dear sister of my welfare, and increasing confidence in the
success of my undertaking.

I am already far north of London; and as I walk in the streets
of Petersburgh, I feel a cold northern breeze play upon my
cheeks, which braces my nerves, and fills me with delight. Do you
understand this feeling? This breeze, which has travelled from the
regions towards which I am advancing, gives me a foretaste of
those icy climes. Inspirited by this wind of promise, my day dreams
become more **fervent** and vivid. I try in vain to be persuaded that
the pole is the seat of frost and desolation; it ever presents itself to
my imagination as the region of beauty and delight. There, Margaret,
the sun is for ever visible, its broad disk just skirting the horizon,
and diffusing a perpetual splendour. There – for with your leave,
my sister, I will put some trust in preceding navigators – there
snow and frost are banished; and, sailing over a calm sea, we may be
wafted to a land surpassing in wonders and in beauty every region
hitherto discovered on the habitable globe. Its productions and
features may be without example, as the phenomena of the heavenly
bodies undoubtedly are in those undiscovered solitudes. What may
not be expected in a country of eternal light? I may there discover
the wondrous power which attracts the needle; and may regulate
a thousand celestial observations, that require only this voyage to
render their seeming eccentricities consistent for ever. I shall satiate
my ardent curiosity with the sight of a part of the world never
before visited, and may tread a land never before imprinted by the
foot of man. These are my enticements, and they are sufficient to
conquer all fear of danger or death, and to induce me to commence
this laborious voyage with the joy a child feels when he embarks in

---

fervent Showing great warmth of feeling;
extremely devoted or earnest.

a little boat, with his holiday mates, on an expedition of discovery up his native river. But, supposing all these conjectures to be false, you cannot contest the **inestimable** benefit which I shall confer on all mankind to the last generation, by discovering a passage near the pole to those countries, to reach which at present so many months are requisite; or by ascertaining the secret of the magnet, which, if at all possible, can only be effected by an undertaking such as mine.

These reflections have dispelled the agitation with which I began my letter, and I feel my heart glow with an enthusiasm which elevates me to heaven; for nothing contributes so much to tranquillize the mind as a steady purpose – a point on which the soul may fix its intellectual eye. This expedition has been the favourite dream of my early years. I have read with ardour the accounts of the various voyages which have been made in the prospect of arriving at the North Pacific Ocean through the seas which surround the pole. You may remember that a history of all the voyages made for purposes of discovery composed the whole of our good uncle Thomas's library. My education was neglected, yet I was passionately fond of reading. These volumes were my study day and night, and my familiarity with them increased that regret which I had felt, as a child, on learning that my father's dying injunction had forbidden my uncle to allow me to embark in a seafaring life.

These visions faded when I perused, for the first time, those poets whose effusions, entranced my soul, and lifted it to heaven. I also became a poet, and for one year lived in a Paradise of my own creation; I imagined that I also might obtain a niche in the temple where the names of Homer and Shakespeare are consecrated. You are well acquainted with my failure, and how heavily I bore the disappointment. But just at that time I inherited the fortune of my cousin, and my thoughts were turned into the channel of their earlier bent.

Six years have passed since I resolved on my present undertaking. I can, even now, remember the hour from which I dedicated myself to this great enterprise. I commenced by inuring my body to hardship. I accompanied the whale-fishers on several expeditions to the North Sea; I voluntarily endured cold, famine, thirst, and want of sleep; I often worked harder than the common sailors during the day, and devoted my nights to the study of mathematics, the theory of medicine, and those branches of physical science from which a

inestimable Too great to be properly measured or appreciated.

naval adventure might derive the greatest practical advantage. Twice I actually hired myself as an under-mate in a Greenland whaler, and acquitted myself to admiration. I must own I felt a little proud, when my captain offered me the second dignity in the vessel and intreated me to remain with the greatest earnestness so valuable did he consider my services.

And now, dear Margaret, do I not deserve to accomplish some great purpose? My life might have been passed in ease and luxury; but I preferred glory to every enticement that wealth placed in my path. Oh, that some encouraging voice would answer in the affirmative! My courage and my resolution is firm; but my hopes fluctuate, and my spirits are often depressed. I am about to proceed on a long and difficult voyage, the emergencies of which will demand all my fortitude: I am required not only to raise the spirits of others, but sometimes to sustain my own, when theirs are failing.

This is the most favourable period for travelling in Russia. They fly quickly over the snow in their sledges; the motion is pleasant, and, in my opinion, far more agreeable than that of an English stage-coach. The cold is not excessive, if you are wrapped in furs – a dress which I have already adopted; for there is a great difference between walking the deck and remaining seated motionless for hours, when no exercise prevents the blood from actually freezing in your veins. I have no ambition to lose my life on the post-road between St Petersburgh and **Archangel**.

I shall depart for the latter town in a fortnight or three weeks; and my intention is to hire a ship there, which can easily be done by paying the insurance for the owner, and to engage as many sailors as I think necessary among those who are accustomed to the whale-fishing. I do not intend to sail until the month of June; and when shall I return? Ah, dear sister, how can I answer this question? If I succeed, many, many months, perhaps years, will pass before you and I may meet. If I fail, you will see me again soon, or never.

Farewell, my dear, excellent Margaret. Heaven shower down blessings on you, and save me, that I may again and again testify my gratitude for all your love and kindness.

Your affectionate brother,

R. WALTON

Archangel English form of Arhangelsk, a town on the northern coast of Russia.

Letter 2

To Mrs Saville, England.

Archangel, March 28th, 17–.
How slowly the time passes here, encompassed as I am by frost and
snow! yet a second step is taken towards my enterprise. I have hired a
vessel, and am occupied in collecting my sailors; those whom I have
already engaged, appear to be men on whom I can depend and are
certainly possessed of dauntless courage.

But I have one want which I have never yet been able to satisfy;
and the absence of the object of which I now feel as a most severe
evil. I have no friend, Margaret: when I am glowing with the
enthusiasm of success, there will be none to participate my joy; if
I am assailed by disappointment, no one will endeavour to sustain
me in dejection. I shall commit my thoughts to paper, it is true; but
that is a poor medium for the communication of feeling. I desire
the company of a man who could sympathise with me; whose eyes
would reply to mine. You may deem me **romantic**, my dear sister,
but I bitterly feel the want of a friend. I have no one near me, gentle
yet courageous, possessed of a cultivated as well as of a capacious
mind, whose tastes are like my own, to approve or amend my plans.
How would such a friend repair the faults of your poor brother! I
am too ardent in execution, and too impatient of difficulties. But it is
a still greater evil to me that I am self-educated: for the first fourteen
years of my life I ran wild on a common, and read nothing but our
uncle Thomas's books of voyages. At that age I became acquainted
with the celebrated poets of our own country; but it was only
when it had ceased to be in my power to derive its most important
benefits from such a conviction, that I perceived the necessity of
becoming acquainted with more languages than that of my native
country. Now I am twenty-eight and am in reality more illiterate
than many schoolboys of fifteen. It is true that I have thought more,
and that my day dreams are more extended and magnificent, but
they want (as the painters call it) *keeping*; and I greatly need a friend
who would have sense enough not to despise me as romantic, and

---

romantic Describing a person who values
freedom, originality, and individuality in the
arts—a follower of the Romantic movement.

keeping In painting: setting down with attention
to proper proportions and harmony.

affection enough for me to endeavour to regulate my mind.

Well, these are useless complaints; I shall certainly find no friend on the wide ocean, nor even here in Archangel, among merchants and seamen. Yet some feelings, unallied to the **dross** of human nature, beat even in these rugged bosoms. My lieutenant, for instance, is a man of wonderful courage and enterprise; he is madly desirous of glory: or rather, to word my phrase more characteristically, of advancement in his profession. He is an Englishman, and in the midst of national and professional prejudices, unsoftened by cultivation, retains some of the noblest endowments of humanity. I first became acquainted with him on board a whale vessel: finding that he was unemployed in this city, I easily engaged him to assist in my enterprise.

The master is a person of an excellent disposition, and is remarkable in the ship for his gentleness and the mildness of his discipline. This circumstance, added to his well-known **integrity** and dauntless courage, made me very desirous to engage him. A youth passed in solitude, my best years spent under your gentle and feminine fosterage, has so refined the groundwork of my character that I cannot overcome an intense distaste to the usual brutality exercised on board ship: I have never believed it to be necessary, and when I heard of a mariner equally noted for his kindliness of heart and the respect and obedience paid to him by his crew, I felt myself peculiarly fortunate in being able to secure his services. I heard of him first in rather a romantic manner, from a lady who owes to him the happiness of her life. This, briefly, is his story. Some years ago he loved a young Russian lady of moderate fortune; and having amassed a considerable sum in prize-money, the father of the girl consented to the match. He saw his mistress once before the destined ceremony; but she was bathed in tears, and, throwing herself at his feet, intreated him to spare her, confessing at the time that she loved another, but that he was poor, and that her father would never consent to the union. My generous friend reassured the **suppliant**, and on being informed of the name of her lover, instantly abandoned his pursuit. He had already bought a farm with his money, on which he had designed to pass the remainder of his life; but he bestowed the whole on his rival, together with the remains of his prize-money to purchase stock, and then himself solicited the

dross Refuse, waste matter.
integrity Uprightness; honesty; sincerity.
suppliant Person who makes a humble request.

young woman's father to consent to her marriage with her lover. But the old man decidedly refused, thinking himself bound in honour to my friend; who, when he found the father **inexorable**, quitted his country, nor returned until he heard that his former mistress was married according to her inclinations. 'What a noble fellow!' you will exclaim. He is so; but then he is wholly uneducated: he is as silent as a Turk, and a kind of ignorant carelessness attends him, which, while it renders his conduct the more astonishing, detracts from the interest and sympathy which otherwise he would command.

Yet do not suppose, because I complain a little, or because I can conceive a consolation for my toils which I may never know, that I am wavering in my resolutions. Those are as fixed as fate, and my voyage is only now delayed until the weather shall permit my embarkation. The winter has been dreadfully severe, but the spring promises well, and it is considered as a remarkably early season; so that perhaps I may sail sooner than I expected. I shall do nothing rashly: you know me sufficiently to confide in my prudence and considerateness whenever the safety of others is committed to my care.

I cannot describe to you my sensations on the near prospect of my undertaking. It is impossible to communicate to you a conception of the trembling sensation, half pleasurable and half fearful, with which I am preparing to depart. I am going to unexplored regions to 'the land of mist and snow'; but I shall kill no **albatross**, therefore do not be alarmed for my safety, or if I should come back to you as worn and woeful as the 'Ancient Mariner'. You will smile at my allusion; but I will disclose a secret. I have often attributed my attachment to, my passionate enthusiasm for, the dangerous mysteries of ocean, to that production of the most imaginative of modern poets. There is something at work in my soul, which I do not understand. I am practically industrious – painstaking; a workman to execute with perseverance and labour: – but besides this, there is a love for the marvellous, a belief in the marvellous, intertwined in all my projects, which hurries me out of the common pathways of men, even to the wild sea and unvisited regions I am about to explore.

But to return to dearer considerations. Shall I meet you again, after having traversed immense seas, and returned by the most

---

inexorable Unyielding.

albatross A reference to Samuel Taylor Coleridge's *The Rime of the Ancient Mariner* (1798). In this narrative poem, a ship is driven off course by a storm and reaches Antarctica.

An albatross leads the crew out of danger, and then a Mariner, for unknown reasons, shoots it. As a result of this action, supernatural spirits pursue the ship.

southern cape of Africa or America? I dare not expect such success, yet I cannot bear to look on the reverse of the picture. Continue for the present to write to me by every opportunity: I may receive your letters on some occasions when I need them most to support my spirits. I love you very tenderly. Remember me with affection, should you never hear from me again.

Your affectionate brother,
ROBERT WALTON

Letter 3

To Mrs Saville, England.

July 7th, 17–.

MY DEAR SISTER,

I write a few lines in haste to say that I am safe – and well advanced on my voyage. This letter will reach England by a merchantman now on its homeward voyage from Archangel; more fortunate than I, who may not see my native land, perhaps, for many years. I am, however, in good spirits: my men are bold, and apparently firm of purpose, nor do the floating sheets of ice that continually pass us, indicating the dangers of the region towards which we are advancing, appear to dismay them. We have already reached a very high latitude; but it is the height of summer, and although not so warm as in England, the southern gales, which blow us speedily towards those shores which I so ardently desire to attain, breathe a degree of renovating warmth which I had not expected.

No incidents have hitherto befallen us that would make a figure in a letter. One or two stiff gales, and the springing of a leak, are accidents which experienced navigators scarcely remember to record; and I shall be well content if nothing worse happen to us during our voyage.

Adieu, my dear Margaret. Be assured, that for my own sake, as well as yours, I will not rashly encounter danger. I will be cool, persevering and prudent.

But success *shall* crown my endeavours. Wherefore not? Thus far I have gone, tracing a secure way over the pathless seas: the very stars themselves being witnesses and testimonies of my triumph. Why not still proceed over the untamed yet obedient element? What can stop the determined heart and resolved will of man?

My swelling heart involuntarily pours itself out thus. But I must finish. Heaven bless my beloved sister!

R.W.

Letter 4

To Mrs Saville, England.

August 5th, 17–.

So strange an accident has happened to us that I cannot **forbear** recording it, although it is very probable that you will see me before these papers can come into your possession.

Last Monday (July 31st) we were nearly surrounded by ice, which closed in the ship on all sides, scarcely leaving her the searoom in which she floated. Our situation was somewhat dangerous, especially as we were compassed round by a very thick fog. We accordingly lay to, hoping that some change would take place in the atmosphere and weather.

About two o'clock the mist cleared away, and we beheld, stretched out in every direction, vast and irregular plains of ice, which seemed to have no end. Some of my comrades groaned, and my own mind began to grow watchful with anxious thoughts, when a strange sight suddenly attracted our attention, and diverted our solicitude from our own situations. We perceived a low carriage, fixed on a sledge and drawn by dogs, pass on towards the north, at the distance of half a mile; a being which had the shape of a man, but apparently of gigantic stature, sat in the sledge, and guided the dogs. We watched the rapid progress of the traveller with our telescopes until he was lost among the distant inequalities of the ice.

This appearance excited our unqualified wonder. We were, as we believed, many hundred miles from any land; but this apparition seemed to denote that it was not, in reality, so distant as we had supposed. Shut in, however, by ice, it was impossible to follow his track, which we had observed with the greatest attention.

About two hours after this occurrence we heard the **ground sea**; and before night the ice broke, and freed our ship. We, however, lay to until the morning, fearing to encounter in the dark those large loose masses which float about after the breaking up of the ice. I profited of this time to rest for a few hours.

In the morning, however, as soon as it was light, I went upon deck

forbear Refrain, hold back.
ground sea Ocean swell, which occurs in calm waters, without apparent cause.

and found all the sailors busy on one side of the vessel, apparently talking to some one in the sea. It was, in fact, a sledge, like that we had seen before, which had drifted towards us in the night on a large fragment of ice. Only one dog remained alive; but there was a human being within it, whom the sailors were persuading to enter the vessel. He was not as the other traveller seemed to be, a savage inhabitant of some undiscovered island, but an European. When I appeared on deck, the master said, 'Here is our captain, and he will not allow you to perish on the open sea.'

On perceiving me, the stranger addressed me in English, although with a foreign accent. 'Before I come on board your vessel,' said he, 'will you have the kindness to inform me whither you are bound?'

You may conceive my astonishment on hearing such a question addressed to me from a man on the brink of destruction and to whom I should have supposed that my vessel would have been a resource which he would not have exchanged for the most precious wealth the earth can afford. I replied, however, that we were on a voyage of discovery towards the northern pole.

Upon hearing this he appeared satisfied, and consented to come on board. Good God! Margaret, if you had seen the man who thus **capitulated** for his safety, your surprise would have been boundless. His limbs were nearly frozen, and his body dreadfully emaciated by fatigue and suffering. I never saw a man in so wretched a condition. We attempted to carry him into the cabin; but as soon as he had quitted the fresh air, he fainted. We accordingly brought him back to the deck, and restored him to animation by rubbing him with brandy and forcing him to swallow a small quantity. As soon as he showed signs of life, we wrapped him up in blankets and placed him near the chimney of the kitchen stove. By slow degrees he recovered, and ate a little soup which restored him wonderfully.

Two days passed in this manner before he was able to speak; and I often feared that his sufferings had deprived him of understanding. When he had in some measure recovered, I removed him to my own cabin, and attended on him as much as my duty would permit. I never saw a more interesting creature; his eyes have generally an expression of wildness, and even madness, but there are moments when, if any one performs an act of kindness towards him or does him any the most trifling service, his whole countenance is lighted

capitulated Yielded, surrendered.

up, as it were, with a beam of benevolence and sweetness that I never saw equalled. But he is generally **melancholy** and despairing; and sometimes he gnashes his teeth; as if impatient of the weight of woes that oppresses him.

When my guest was a little recovered, I had great trouble to keep off the men, who wished to ask him a thousand questions; but I would not allow him to be tormented by their idle curiosity, in a state of body and mind whose restoration evidently depended upon entire repose. Once, however, the lieutenant asked why he had come so far upon the ice in so strange a vehicle?

His countenance instantly assumed an aspect of the deepest gloom; and he replied, 'To seek one who fled from me.'

'And did the man whom you pursued travel in the same fashion?'

'Yes.'

'Then I fancy we have seen him, for the day before we picked you up, we saw some dogs drawing a sledge, with a man in it, across the ice.'

This aroused the stranger's attention, and he asked a multitude of questions concerning the route which the **daemon**, as he called him, had pursued. Soon after, when he was alone with me, he said, 'I have, doubtless, excited your curiosity, as well as that of these good people; but you are too considerate to make enquiries.'

'Certainly; it would indeed be very impertinent and inhuman in me to trouble you with any inquisitiveness of mine.'

'And yet you rescued me from a strange and perilous situation: you have benevolently restored me to life.'

Soon after this he enquired if I thought that the breaking up of the ice had destroyed the other sledge? I replied, that I could not answer with any degree of certainty, for the ice had not broken until near midnight, and the traveller might have arrived at a place of safety before that time; but of this I could not judge.

From this time a new spirit of life animated the decaying frame of the stranger. He manifested the greatest eagerness to be upon deck, to watch for the sledge which had before appeared; but I have persuaded him to remain in the cabin, for he is far too weak to sustain the rawness of the atmosphere. I have promised that some one should watch for him and give him instant notice if any new object should appear in sight.

melancholy Depressed, brooding.
daemon Evil spirit.

Such is my journal of what relates to this strange occurrence up to the present day. The stranger has gradually improved in health, but is very silent, and appears uneasy when anyone except myself enters the cabin. Yet his manners are so conciliating and gentle, that the sailors are all interested in him, although they have had very little communication with him. For my own part, I begin to love him as a brother; and his constant and deep grief fills me with sympathy and compassion. He must have been a noble creature in his better days, being even now in wreck so attractive and amiable.

I said in one of my letters, my dear Margaret, that I should find no friend on the wide ocean; yet I have found a man who, before his spirit had been broken by misery, I should have been happy to have possessed as the brother of my heart.

I shall continue my journal concerning the stranger at intervals, should I have any fresh incidents to record.

August 13th, 17–.

My affection for my guest increases every day. He excites at once my admiration and my pity to an astonishing degree. How can I see so noble a creature destroyed by misery, without feeling the most poignant grief? He is so gentle, yet so wise; his mind is so cultivated, and when he speaks, although his words are **culled with the choicest art**, yet they flow with rapidity and unparalleled eloquence.

He is now much recovered from his illness, and is continually on the deck, apparently watching for the sledge that preceded his own. Yet, although unhappy, he is not so utterly occupied by his own misery but that he interests himself deeply in the projects of others. He has frequently conversed with me on mine, which I have communicated to him without disguise. He entered attentively into all my arguments in favour of my eventual success, and into every minute detail of the measures I had taken to secure it. I was easily led by the sympathy which he **evinced**, to use the language of my heart, to give utterance to the burning ardour of my soul; and to say, with all the fevour that warmed me, how gladly I would sacrifice my fortune, my existence, my every hope, to the furtherance of my enterprise. One man's life or death were but a small price to pay for the acquirement of the knowledge which I sought for the dominion

---

culled with the choicest art Carefully selected.
evinced Displayed, exhibited.

I should acquire and transmit over the **elemental** foes of our race.
As I spoke, a dark gloom spread over my listener's countenance.
At first I perceived that he tried to suppress his emotion; he placed
his hands before his eyes, and my voice quivered and failed me as
I beheld tears trickle fast from between his fingers – a groan burst
from his heaving breast. I paused; at length he spoke, in broken
accents – 'Unhappy man! Do you share my madness? Have you
drunk also of the **intoxicating draught?** Hear me – let me reveal
my tale, and you will dash the cup from your lips!'

Such words, you may imagine, strongly excited my curiosity;
but the **paroxysm** of grief that had seized the stranger overcame
his weakened powers, and many hours of repose and tranquil
conversation were necessary to restore his composure.

Having conquered the violence of his feelings, he appeared to
despise himself for being the slave of passion; and quelling the dark
tyranny of despair, he led me again to converse concerning myself
personally. He asked me the history of my earlier years. The tale was
quickly told: but it awakened various trains of reflection. I spoke
of my desire of finding a friend – of my thirst for a more intimate
sympathy with a fellow mind than had ever fallen to my lot; and
expressed my conviction that a man could boast of little happiness,
who did not enjoy this blessing.

'I agree with you,' replied the stranger; 'we are unfashioned
creatures, but half made up, if one wiser, better, dearer than ourselves
– such a friend ought to be – do not lend his aid to **perfectionate**
our weak and faulty natures. I once had a friend, the most noble
of human creatures, and am entitled, therefore, to judge respecting
friendship. You have hope, and the world before you, and have no
cause for despair. But I – I have lost every thing and cannot begin
life anew.'

As he said this his countenance became expressive of a calm,
settled grief, that touched me to the heart. But he was silent, and
presently retired to his cabin.

Even broken in spirit as he is, no one can feel more deeply than
he does the beauties of nature. The starry sky, the sea, and every sight
afforded by these wonderful regions, seems still to have the power
of elevating his soul from earth. Such a man has a double existence:
he may suffer misery and be overwhelmed by disappointments, yet,

elemental Relating to the powers or spirits of
nature.

intoxicating draught Literally, alcoholic
drink. Figuratively, something which causes
exhilaration beyond self-control and delirium.

paroxysm Fit, sudden outburst.

perfectionate Bring to perfection.

when he has retired into himself, he will be like a celestial spirit, that has a halo around him, within whose circle no grief or folly ventures.

Will you smile at the enthusiasm I express concerning this divine wanderer? You would not, if you saw him. You have been tutored and refined by books and retirement from the world, and you are therefore somewhat **fastidious**; but this only renders you the more fit to appreciate the extraordinary merits of this wonderful man. Sometimes I have endeavoured to discover what quality it is which he possesses, that elevates him so immeasurably above any other person I ever knew. I believe it to be an **intuitive** discernment; a quick but never-failing power of judgment; a penetration into the causes of things, unequalled for clearness and precision; add to this a facility of expression, and a voice whose varied intonations are soul-subduing music.

August 19th, 17–.

Yesterday the stranger said to me, 'You may easily perceive, Captain Walton, that I have suffered great and unparalled misfortunes. I had determined, at one time, that the memory of these evils should die with me, but you have won me to alter my determination. You seek for knowledge and wisdom, as I once did; and I ardently hope that the gratification of your wishes may not be a serpent to sting you, as mine has been. I do not know that the relation of my disasters will be useful to you; yet, when I reflect that you are pursuing the same course, exposing yourself to the same dangers which have rendered me what I am, I imagine that you may deduce an apt moral from my tale; one that may direct you if you succeed in your undertaking, and console you in case of failure. Prepare to hear of occurrences which are usually deemed marvellous. Were we among the tamer scenes of nature, I might fear to encounter your unbelief, perhaps your ridicule; but many things will appear possible in these wild and mysterious regions, which would provoke the laughter of those unacquainted with the ever-varied powers of nature; – nor can I doubt but that my tale conveys in its series internal evidence of the truth of the events of which it is composed.'

You may easily imagine that I was much gratified by the offered communication, yet I could not endure that he should renew his

---

fastidious Exacting in taste, difficult to please.
intuitive Having to do with immediate or instinctive understanding

grief by a recital of his misfortunes. I felt the greatest eagerness to hear the promised narrative, partly from curiosity, and partly from a strong desire to **ameliorate** his fate, if it were in my power. I expressed these feelings in my answer.

'I thank you,' he replied, 'for your sympathy, but it is useless; my fate is nearly fulfilled. I wait but for one event, and then I shall repose in peace. I understand your feeling,' continued he, perceiving that I wished to interrupt him: 'but you are mistaken, my friend, if thus you will allow me to name you; nothing can alter my destiny; listen to my history, and you will perceive how irrevocably it is determined.'

He then told me, that he would commence his narrative the next day, when I should be at leisure. This promise drew from me the warmest thanks. I have resolved every night, when I am not imperatively occupied by my duties, to record, as nearly as possible in his own words, what he has related during the day. If I should be engaged, I will at least make notes. This manuscript will doubtless afford you the greatest pleasure: but to me, who know him and who hear it from his own lips — with what interest and sympathy shall I read it in some future day! Even now, as I commence my task, his full-toned voice swells in my ears; his lustrous eyes dwell on me with all their melancholy sweetness; I see his thin hand raised in animation, while the **lineaments** of his face are **irradiated** by the soul within. Strange and harrowing must be his story, frightful the storm which embraced the gallant vessel on its course and wrecked it — thus!

ameliorate Improve, make better.
lineaments Features.
irradiated Lit up.

Chapter 1

I am by birth a **Genevese**, and my family is one of the most distinguished of that republic. My ancestors had been for many years counsellors and **syndics**; and my father had filled several public situations with honour and reputation. He was respected by all who knew him, for his integrity and indefatigable attention to public business. He passed his younger days perpetually occupied by the affairs of his country; a variety of circumstances had prevented his marrying early, nor was it until the decline of life that he became a husband and the father of a family.

As the circumstances of his marriage illustrate his character, I cannot refrain from relating them. One of his most intimate friends was a merchant who, from a flourishing state, fell, through numerous mischances, into poverty. This man, whose name was Beaufort, was of a proud and unbending disposition and could not bear to live in poverty and oblivion in the same country where he had formerly been distinguished for his rank and magnificence. Having paid his debts, therefore, in the most honourable manner, he retreated with his daughter to the town of Lucerne, where he lived unknown and in wretchedness. My father loved Beaufort with the truest friendship, and was deeply grieved by his retreat in these unfortunate circumstances. He bitterly deplored the false pride which led his friend to a conduct so little worthy of the affection that united them. He lost no time in endeavouring to seek him out, with the hope of persuading him to begin the world again through his credit and assistance.

Beaufort had taken effectual measures to conceal himself; and it was ten months before my father discovered his abode. Overjoyed at this discovery, he hastened to the house, which was situated in a mean street near the Reuss. But when he entered, misery and despair alone welcomed him. Beaufort had saved but a very small sum of money from the wreck of his fortunes, but it was sufficient to provide him with sustenance for some months, and in the mean time he hoped to procure some respectable employment in a merchant's house. The interval was, consequently, spent in inaction; his grief

Genevese Native of Geneva, Switzerland.
syndics Government magistrates.

only became more deep and rankling, when he had leisure for reflection; and at length it took so fast hold of his mind, that at the end of three months he lay on a bed of sickness, incapable of any exertion.

His daughter attended him with the greatest tenderness; but she saw with despair that their little fund was rapidly decreasing, and that there was no other prospect of support. But Caroline Beaufort possessed a mind of an uncommon mould, and her courage rose to support her in her adversity. She procured **plain work**; she **plaited straw**; and by various means contrived to earn a pittance scarcely sufficient to support life.

Several months passed in this manner. Her father grew worse; her time was more entirely occupied in attending him; her means of subsistence decreased; and in the tenth month her father died in her arms, leaving her an orphan and a beggar. This last blow overcame her, and she knelt by Beaufort's coffin, weeping bitterly, when my father entered the chamber. He came like a protecting spirit to the poor girl, who committed herself to his care; and after the **interment** of his friend he conducted her to Geneva, and placed her under the protection of a relation. Two years after this event Caroline became his wife.

There was a considerable difference between the ages of my parents, but this circumstance seemed to unite them only closer in bonds of devoted affection. There was a sense of justice in my father's upright mind, which rendered it necessary that he should approve highly to love strongly. Perhaps during former years he had suffered from the late-discovered unworthiness of one beloved, and so was disposed to set a greater value on tried worth. There was a show of gratitude and worship in his attachment to my mother, differing wholly from the doating fondness of age, for it was inspired by reverence for her virtues and a desire to be the means of, in some degree, **recompensing** her for the sorrows she had endured, but which gave inexpressible grace to his behaviour to her. Every thing was made to yield to her wishes and her convenience. He strove to shelter her, as a fair **exotic** is sheltered by the gardener, from every rougher wind, and to surround her with all that could tend to excite pleasurable emotion in her soft and benevolent mind. Her health, and even the tranquillity of her hitherto constant spirit, had

plain work Simple needlework.

plaited straw Wove strands of straw together to be used in basket-weaving or hat-making.

interment Burial.

recompensing Compensating for a loss or injury, making amends.

exotic Plant introduced from a foreign country.

been shaken by what she had gone through. During the two years that had elapsed previous to their marriage my father had gradually relinquished all his public functions; and immediately after their union they sought the pleasant climate of Italy, and the change of scene and interest attendant on a tour through that land of wonders, as a restorative for her weakened frame.

From Italy they visited Germany and France. I, their eldest child, was born at Naples, and as an infant accompanied them in their rambles. I remained for several years their only child. Much as they were attached to each other, they seemed to draw inexhaustible stores of affection from a very mine of love to bestow them upon me. My mother's tender caresses and my father's smile of benevolent pleasure while regarding me, are my first recollections. I was their plaything and their idol, and something better – their child, the innocent and helpless creature bestowed on them by Heaven, whom to bring up to good, and whose future lot it was in their hands to direct to happiness or misery, according as they fulfilled their duties towards me. With this deep consciousness of what they owed towards the being to which they had given life, added to the active spirit of tenderness that animated both, it may be imagined that while during every hour of my infant life I received a lesson of patience, of charity, and of self-control, I was so guided by a silken cord that all seemed but one train of enjoyment to me.

For a long time I was their only care. My mother had much desire to have a daughter, but I continued their single offspring. When I was about five years old, while making an excursion beyond the frontiers of Italy, they passed a week on the shores of the Lake of Como. Their benevolent disposition often made them enter the cottages of the poor. This, to my mother, was more than a duty; it was a necessity, a passion – remembering what she had suffered, and how she had been relieved, – for her to act in her turn the guardian angel to the afflicted. During one of their walks a poor **cot** in the foldings of a **vale** attracted their notice as being singularly disconsolate, while the number of half-clothed children gathered about it spoke of **penury** in its worst shape. One day, when my father had gone by himself to Milan, my mother, accompanied by me, visited this abode. She found a peasant and his wife, hard working, bent down by care and labour, distributing a scanty meal

---

cot Cottage.
vale Dale or valley.
penury Destitution, poverty.

to five hungry babes. Among these there was one which attracted my mother far above all the rest. She appeared of a different stock. The four others were dark-eyed, hardy little vagrants; this child was thin, and very fair. Her hair was the brightest living gold, and despite the poverty of her clothing, seemed to set a crown of distinction on her head. Her brow was clear and ample, her blue eyes cloudless, and her lips and the moulding of her face so expressive of sensibility and sweetness that none could behold her without looking on her as of a distinct species, a being heaven-sent, and bearing a **celestial** stamp in all her features.

The peasant woman, perceiving that my mother fixed eyes of wonder and admiration on this lovely girl, eagerly communicated her history. She was not her child, but the daughter of a Milanese nobleman. Her mother was a German, and had died on giving her birth. The infant had been placed with these good people to nurse: they were better off then. They had not been long married, and their eldest child was but just born. The father of their charge was one of those Italians nursed in the memory of the antique glory of Italy – one among the *schiavi ognor frementi*, who exerted himself to obtain the liberty of his country. He became the victim of its weakness. Whether he had died, or still lingered in the dungeons of Austria, was not known. His property was confiscated; his child became an orphan and a beggar. She continued with her foster parents, and bloomed in their rude abode, fairer than a garden rose among dark-leaved brambles.

When my father returned from Milan, he found playing with me in the hall of our villa a child fairer than a pictured cherub – a creature who seemed to shed radiance from her looks and whose form and motions were lighter than the chamois of the hills. The apparition was soon explained. With his permission my mother prevailed on her rustic guardians to yield their charge to her. They were fond of the sweet orphan. Her presence had seemed a blessing to them, but it would be unfair to her to keep her in poverty and want, when Providence afforded her such powerful protection. They consulted their village priest, and the result was that Elizabeth Lavenza became the inmate of my parents' house – my more than sister – the beautiful and adored companion of all my occupations and my pleasures.

celestial Heavenly

schiavi ognor frementi Italian: slaves always trembling; referring to the plight of the Italian people when ruled by Austria in the 18th and 19th centuries.

Everyone loved Elizabeth. The passionate and most reverential attachment with which all regarded her became, while I shared it, my pride and my delight. On the evening previous to her being brought to my home, my mother had said playfully, 'I have a pretty present for my Victor – tomorrow he shall have it.' And when, on the morrow, she presented Elizabeth to me as her promised gift, I, with childish seriousness, interpreted her words literally and looked upon Elizabeth as mine – mine to protect, love, and cherish. All praises bestowed on her I received as made to a possession of my own. We called each other familiarly by the name of cousin. No word, no expression could body forth the kind of relation in which she stood to me – my more than sister, since till death she was to be mine only.

Chapter 2

We were brought up together; there was not quite a year difference in our ages. I need not say that we were strangers to any species of disunion or dispute. Harmony was the soul of our companionship, and the **diversity** and contrast that subsisted in our characters drew us nearer together. Elizabeth was of a calmer and more concentrated disposition; but, with all my ardour, I was capable of a more intense application, and was more deeply smitten with the thirst for knowledge. She busied herself with following the **aerial** creations of the poets; and in the majestic and wondrous scenes which surrounded our Swiss home – the **sublime** shapes of the mountains; the changes of the seasons; tempest and calm; the silence of winter, and the life and turbulence of our Alpine summers – she found ample scope for admiration and delight. While my companion contemplated with a serious and satisfied spirit the magnificent appearances of things, I delighted in investigating their causes. The world was to me a secret which I desired to **divine**. Curiosity, earnest research to learn the hidden laws of nature, gladness akin to rapture, as they were unfolded to me, are among the earliest sensations I can remember.

On the birth of a second son, my junior by seven years, my parents gave up entirely their wandering life, and fixed themselves in their native country. We possessed a house in Geneva, and a *campagne* on Belrive, the eastern shore of the lake, at the distance of rather more than a **league** from the city. We resided principally in the latter, and the lives of my parents were passed in considerable seclusion. It was my temper to avoid a crowd, and to attach myself fervently to a few. I was indifferent, therefore, to my schoolfellows in general; but I united myself in the bonds of the closest friendship to one among them. Henry Clerval was the son of a merchant of Geneva. He was a boy of singular talent and fancy. He loved enterprise, hardship, and even danger for its own sake. He was deeply read in books of chivalry and romance. He composed heroic songs, and began to write many a tale of enchantment and knightly adventure. He tried to make us act plays and to enter into **masquerades**, in which

---

diversity Quality or state of being varied.
aerial Imaginary, ideal.
sublime Inspiring awe or admiration through grandeur or beauty.

divine Discover, make known.
campagne Country house.
league A distance of about three miles.
masquerades Masked balls.

the characters were drawn from the heroes of **Roncesvalles**, of the Round Table of King Arthur, and the chivalrous train who shed their blood to redeem the holy sepulchre from the hands of the **infidels**.

No human being could have passed a happier childhood than myself. My parents were possessed by the very spirit of kindness and indulgence. We felt that they were not the tyrants to rule our lot according to their caprice, but the agents and creators of all the many delights which we enjoyed. When I mingled with other families, I distinctly discerned how peculiarly fortunate my lot was, and gratitude assisted the development of filial love.

My temper was sometimes violent, and my passions vehement; but by some law in my **temperature** they were turned not towards childish pursuits but to an eager desire to learn, and not to learn all things indiscriminately. I confess that neither the structure of languages, nor the code of governments, nor the politics of various states possessed attractions for me. It was the secrets of heaven and earth that I desired to learn; and whether it was the outward substance of things, or the inner spirit of nature and the mysterious soul of man that occupied me, still my enquiries were directed to the **metaphysical**, or in its highest sense, the physical secrets of the world.

Meanwhile Clerval occupied himself, so to speak, with the moral relations of things. The busy stage of life, the virtues of heroes, and the actions of men were his theme; and his hope and his dream was to become one among those whose names are recorded in story, as the gallant and adventurous benefactors of our species. The saintly soul of Elizabeth shone like a shrine-dedicated lamp in our peaceful home. Her sympathy was ours; her smile, her soft voice, the sweet glance of her celestial eyes, were ever there to bless and animate us. She was the living spirit of love to soften and attract: I might have become sullen in my study, rough through the ardour of my nature, but that she was there to subdue me to a semblance of her own gentleness. And Clerval – could aught ill entrench on the noble spirit of Clerval – yet he might not have been so perfectly humane, so thoughtful in his generosity – so full of kindness and tenderness amidst his passion for adventurous exploit, had she not unfolded to him the real loveliness of beneficence, and made the doing good the end and aim of his soaring ambition.

Roncesvalles A village in the Navarre province of northern Spain where Basque tribes defeated Charlemagne's troops.

infidels People who do not believe in a particular religion (here Christianity).

temperature Temperament.

metaphysical To do with the basic principles of nature.

I feel exquisite pleasure in dwelling on the recollections of childhood, before misfortune had tainted my mind, and changed its bright visions of extensive usefulness into gloomy and narrow reflections upon self. Besides, in drawing the picture of my early days, I also record those events which led, by insensible steps, to my after tale of misery: for when I would account to myself for the birth of that passion, which afterwards ruled my destiny, I find it arise, like a mountain river, from ignoble and almost forgotten sources; but, swelling as it proceeded, it became the torrent which, in its course, has swept away all my hopes and joys.

Natural philosophy is the genius that has regulated my fate; I desire, therefore, in this narration, to state those facts which led to my **predilection** for that science. When I was thirteen years of age we all went on a party of pleasure to the baths near Thonon: the inclemency of the weather obliged us to remain a day confined to the inn. In this house I chanced to find a volume of the works of **Cornelius Agrippa**. I opened it with apathy; the theory which he attempts to demonstrate, and the wonderful facts which he relates soon changed this feeling into enthusiasm. A new light seemed to dawn upon my mind, and, bounding with joy, I communicated my discovery to my father. My father looked carelessly at the titlepage of my book and said, 'Ah! Cornelius Agrippa! My dear Victor, do not waste your time upon this; it is sad trash.'

If, instead of this remark, my father had taken the pains to explain to me that the principles of Agrippa had been entirely **exploded**, and that a modern system of science had been introduced, which possessed much greater powers than the ancient, because the powers of the latter were **chimerical**, while those of the former were real and practical; under such circumstances I should certainly have thrown Agrippa aside and have contented my imagination, warmed as it was, by returning with greater ardour to my former studies. It is even possible that the train of my ideas would never have received the fatal impulse that led to my ruin. But the cursory glance my father had taken of my volume by no means assured me that he was acquainted with its contents; and I continued to read with the greatest avidity.

When I returned home my first care was to procure the whole works of this author, and afterwards of **Paracelsus** and **Albertus**

Natural philosophy Physical science—the study of nature.

predilection Preference.

Cornelius Agrippa (1486-1535) A German occult writer, astrologer, and alchemist.

exploded Brought into disrepute.

chimerical Fanciful, imaginary

Paracelsus Philippus Theophrastus Aureolus Bombastus von Hohenheim (1493–1541), a Swiss alchemist.

Magnus. I read and studied the wild fancies of these writers with delight; they appeared to me treasures known to few besides myself. I have described myself as always having been imbued with a fervent longing to penetrate the secrets of nature. In spite of the intense labour and wonderful discoveries of modern philosophers, I always came from my studies discontented and unsatisfied. **Sir Isaac Newton** is said to have avowed that he felt like a child picking up shells beside the great and unexplored ocean of truth. Those of his successors in each branch of natural philosophy with whom I was acquainted, appeared even to my boy's apprehensions, as **tyros** engaged in the same pursuit.

The untaught peasant beheld the elements around him, and was acquainted with their practical uses. The most learned philosopher knew little more. He had partially unveiled the face of Nature, but her immortal lineaments were still a wonder and a mystery. He might dissect, anatomise, and give names; but, not to speak of a final cause, causes in their secondary and tertiary grades were utterly unknown to him. I had gazed upon the fortifications and impediments that seemed to keep human beings from entering the citadel of nature, and rashly and ignorantly I had repined.

But here were books, and here were men who had penetrated deeper and knew more. I took their word for all that they averred, and I became their disciple. It may appear strange that such should arise in the eighteenth century; but while I followed the routine of education in the schools of Geneva, I was, to a great degree, self-taught with regard to my favourite studies. My father was not scientific, and I was left to struggle with a child's blindness, added to a student's thirst for knowledge. Under the guidance of my new **preceptors**, I entered with the greatest diligence into the search of the **philosopher's stone** and the **elixir of life**; but the latter soon obtained my undivided attention. Wealth was an inferior object; but what glory would attend the discovery, if I could banish disease from the human frame and render man invulnerable to any but a violent death!

Nor were these my only visions. The raising of ghosts or devils was a promise liberally accorded by my favourite authors, the fulfilment of which I most eagerly sought; and if my incantations were always unsuccessful, I attributed the failure rather to my own inexperience

Albertus Magnus (1193–1280), a theologian and natural scientist who applied Aristotle's philosophy to Christian doctrine.
Sir Isaac Newton British scientist (1642–1727) (see pp.72–73).

tyros Novices.
preceptors Tutors, teachers.
philosopher's stone Imaginary substance that alchemists hoped would enable them to transform low-value metals into gold.

and mistake, than to a want of skill or fidelity in my instructors.
And thus for a time I was occupied by exploded systems, mingling,
like an unadept, a thousand contradictory theories, and floundering
desperately in a very **slough** of multifarious knowledge, guided by
an ardent imagination and childish reasoning, till an accident again
changed the current of my ideas.

When I was about fifteen years old we had retired to our house
near Belrive, when we witnessed a most violent and terrible
thunder-storm. It advanced from behind the mountains of Jura;
and the thunder burst at once with frightful loudness from various
quarters of the heavens. I remained, while the storm lasted, watching
its progress with curiosity and delight. As I stood at the door, on
a sudden I beheld a stream of fire issue from an old and beautiful
oak, which stood about twenty yards from our house; and so
soon as the dazzling light vanished, the oak had disappeared, and
nothing remained but a blasted stump. When we visited it the next
morning, we found the tree shattered in a singular manner. It was
not splintered by the shock, but entirely reduced to thin ribbons of
wood. I never beheld anything so utterly destroyed.

Before this I was not unacquainted with the more obvious laws
of electricity. On this occasion a man of great research in natural
philosophy was with us, and, excited by this catastrophe, he entered
on the explanation of a theory which he had formed on the
subject of electricity and galvanism, which was at once new and
astonishing to me. All that he said threw greatly into the shade
Cornelius Agrippa, Albertus Magnus, and Paracelsus, the lords of
my imagination; but by some fatality the overthrow of these men
disinclined me to pursue my accustomed studies. It seemed to me
as if nothing would or could ever be known. All that had so long
engaged my attention suddenly grew despicable. By one of those
caprices of the mind, which we are perhaps most subject to in early
youth, I at once gave up my former occupations, set down natural
history and all its progeny as a deformed and abortive creation, and
entertained the greatest disdain for a would-be science which could
never even step within the threshold of real knowledge. In this
mood of mind I betook myself to the mathematics, and the branches
of study appertaining to that science, as being built upon secure
foundations, and so worthy of my consideration.

elixir of life Imaginary potion that would make
the drinker live for ever.
slough Muddy area or marsh.

Thus strangely are our souls constructed, and by such slight ligaments are we bound to prosperity or ruin. When I look back, it seems to me as if this almost miraculous change of inclination and will was the immediate suggestion of the guardian angel of my life – the last effort made by the spirit of preservation to avert the storm that was even then hanging in the stars, and ready to envelope me. Her victory was announced by an unusual tranquillity and gladness of soul, which followed the relinquishing of my ancient and latterly tormenting studies. It was thus that I was to be taught to associate evil with their prosecution, happiness with their disregard.

It was a strong effort of the spirit of good; but it was ineffectual. Destiny was too potent, and her immutable laws had decreed my utter and terrible destruction.

Chapter 3

When I had attained the age of seventeen, my parents resolved, that I should become a student at the **university of Ingolstadt**. I had hitherto attended the schools of Geneva; but my father thought it necessary, for the completion of my education, that I should be made acquainted with other customs than those of my native country. My departure was therefore fixed at an early date; but, before the day resolved upon could arrive, the first misfortune of my life occurred – an omen, as it were, of my future misery.

Elizabeth had caught the scarlet fever; her illness was severe, and she was in the greatest danger. During her illness, many arguments had been urged to persuade my mother to refrain from attending upon her. She had, at first, yielded to our intreaties, but when she heard that the life of her favourite was menaced, she could no longer control her anxiety. She attended her sickbed; – her watchful attentions triumphed over the malignity of the distemper, – Elizabeth was saved, but the consequences of this imprudence were fatal to her preserver. On the third day my mother sickened; her fever was accompanied by the most alarming symptoms, and the looks of her medical attendants **prognosticated** the worst event. On her death-bed the fortitude and benignity of this best of women did not desert her. She joined the hands of Elizabeth and myself: – 'My children,' she said, 'my firmest hopes of future happiness were placed on the prospect of your union. This expectation will now be the consolation of your father. Elizabeth, my love, you must supply my place to my younger children. Alas! I regret that I am taken from you; and, happy and beloved as I have been, is it not hard to quit you all? But these are not thoughts befitting me; I will endeavour to resign myself cheerfully to death, and will indulge a hope of meeting you in another world.'

She died calmly; and her countenance expressed affection even in death. I need not describe the feelings of those whose dearest ties are rent by that most irreparable evil; the void that presents itself to the soul; and the despair that is exhibited on the countenance. It is so long before the mind can persuade itself that she, whom we saw

university of Ingolstadt A Bavarian University (1472–1800). During the 18th century, the University was associated with the Illuminati, an Enlightenment secret society with humanist, anti-church attitudes.

prognosticated Indicated, foretold.

every day, and whose very existence appeared a part of our own, can have departed forever – that the brightness of a beloved eye can have been extinguished, and the sound of a voice so familiar and dear to the ear can be hushed, never more to be heard. These are the reflections of the first days; but when the lapse of time proves the reality of the evil, then the actual bitterness of grief commences. Yet from whom has not that rude hand rent away some dear connexion? and why should I describe a sorrow which all have felt, and must feel? The time at length arrives when grief is rather an indulgence than a necessity; and the smile that plays upon the lips, although it may be deemed a sacrilege, is not banished. My mother was dead, but we had still duties which we ought to perform; we must continue our course with the rest, and learn to think ourselves fortunate, whilst one remains whom the spoiler had not seized.

My departure for Ingolstadt, which had been deferred by these events, was now again determined upon. I obtained from my father a respite of some weeks. It appeared to me sacrilege so soon to leave the repose, akin to death, of the house of mourning and to rush into the thick of life. I was new to sorrow, but it did not the less alarm me. I was unwilling to quit the sight of those that remained to me; and above all, I desired to see my sweet Elizabeth in some degree consoled.

She indeed veiled her grief, and strove to act the comforter to us all. She looked steadily on life, and assumed its duties with courage and zeal. She devoted herself to those whom she had been taught to call her uncle and cousins. Never was she so enchanting as at this time, when she recalled the sunshine of her smiles and spent them upon us. She forgot even her own regret in her endeavours to make us forget.

The day of my departure at length arrived. Clerval spent the last evening with us. He had endeavoured to persuade his father to permit him to accompany me and to become my fellow student; but in vain. His father was a narrow-minded trader, and saw idleness and ruin in the aspirations and ambition of his son. Henry deeply felt the misfortune of being debarred from a **liberal education**. He said little; but when he spoke, I read in his kindling eye and in his animated glance a restrained but firm resolve, not to be chained to the miserable details of commerce.

liberal education Form of education designed to develop the mind for its own sake rather than to give the pupil specific knowledge.

We sat late. We could not tear ourselves away from each other, nor persuade ourselves to say the word 'Farewell!' It was said; and we retired under the pretence of seeking repose, each fancying that the other was deceived: but when at morning's dawn I descended to the carriage which was to convey me away, they were all there – my father again to bless me, Clerval to press my hand once more, my Elizabeth to renew her intreaties that I would write often, and to bestow the last feminine attentions on her playmate and friend.

I threw myself into the **chaise** that was to convey me away and indulged in the most melancholy reflections. I, who had ever been surrounded by amiable companions, continually engaged in endeavouring to bestow mutual pleasure, I was now alone. In the university, whither I was going, I must form my own friends and be my own protector. My life had hitherto been remarkably secluded and domestic; and this had given me invincible repugnance to new countenances. I loved my brothers, Elizabeth, and Clerval; these were **'old familiar faces**,' but I believed myself totally unfitted for the company of strangers. Such were my reflections as I commenced my journey; but as I proceeded, my spirits and hopes rose. I ardently desired the acquisition of knowledge. I had often, when at home, thought it hard to remain during my youth cooped up in one place, and had longed to enter the world, and take my station among other human beings. Now my desires were complied with, and it would, indeed, have been folly to repent.

I had sufficient leisure for these and many other reflections during my journey to Ingolstadt, which was long and fatiguing. At length the high white steeple of the town met my eyes. I alighted, and was conducted to my solitary apartment, to spend the evening as I pleased.

The next morning I delivered my letters of introduction, and paid a visit to some of the principal professors. Chance – or rather the evil influence, the Angel of Destruction, which asserted omnipotent sway over me from the moment I turned my reluctant steps from my father's door – led me first to M. Krempe, professor of natural philosophy. He was an uncouth man, but deeply imbued in the secrets of his science. He asked me several questions concerning my progress in the different branches of science appertaining to natural philosophy. I replied carelessly; and, partly in contempt, mentioned

chaise Lightweight open carriage.
'old familiar faces' Title of poem by Charles Lamb (1775–1834).

the names of my alchymists as the principal authors I had studied.
The professor stared. 'Have you,' he said, 'really spent your time in
studying such nonsense?'

I replied in the affirmative. 'Every minute,' continued M. Krempe
with warmth, 'every instant that you have wasted on those books
is utterly and entirely lost. You have burdened your memory with
exploded systems and useless names. Good God! In what desert land
have you lived, where no one was kind enough to inform you that
these fancies which you have so greedily imbibed are a thousand
years old and as musty as they are ancient? I little expected, in
this enlightened and scientific age, to find a disciple of Albertus
Magnus and Paracelsus. My dear sir, you must begin your studies
entirely anew.'

So saying, he stept aside, and wrote down a list of several books
treating of natural philosophy, which he desired me to procure;
and dismissed me after mentioning that in the beginning of the
following week he intended to commence a course of lectures upon
natural philosophy in its general relations, and that M. Waldman, a
fellow-professor, would lecture upon chemistry the alternate days
that he omitted.

I returned home, not disappointed, for I have said that I had long
considered those authors useless whom the professor reprobated; but
I returned, not at all the more inclined to recur to these studies in
any shape. M. Krempe was a little squat man, with a gruff voice and
a repulsive countenance; the teacher, therefore, did not prepossess me
in favour of his pursuits. In rather a too philosophical and connected
a strain, perhaps, I have given an account of the conclusions I had
come to concerning them in my early years. As a child, I had not
been content with the results promised by the modern professors
of natural science. With a confusion of ideas only to be accounted
for by my extreme youth, and my want of a guide on such matters,
I had **retrod** the steps of knowledge along the paths of time, and
exchanged the discoveries of recent enquirers for the dreams of
forgotten alchymists. Besides, I had a contempt for the uses of
modern natural philosophy. It was very different, when the masters
of the science sought immortality and power; such views, although
futile, were grand; but now the scene was changed. The ambition
of the enquirer seemed to limit itself to the annihilation of those

---

retrod Literally, retraced. Thus, figuratively, re-
investigated.

visions on which my interest in science was chiefly founded. I was required to exchange **chimeras** of boundless grandeur for realities of little worth.

Such were my reflections during the first two or three days of my residence at Ingolstadt, which were chiefly spent in becoming acquainted with the localities, and the principal residents in my new abode. But as the ensuing week commenced, I thought of the information which M. Krempe had given me concerning the lectures. And although I could not consent to go and hear that little conceited fellow deliver sentences out of a pulpit, I recollected what he had said of M. Waldman, whom I had never seen, as he had hither to been out of town.

Partly from curiosity, and partly from idleness, I went into the lecturing room, which M. Waldman entered shortly after. This professor was very unlike his colleague. He appeared about fifty years of age, but with an aspect expressive of the greatest benevolence; a few grey hairs covered his temples, but those at the back of his head were nearly black. His person was short, but remarkably erect; and his voice the sweetest I had ever heard. He began his lecture by a **recapitulation** of the history of chemistry and the various improvements made by different men of learning, pronouncing with fervour the names of the most distinguished discoverers. He then took a cursory view of the present state of the science, and explained many of its elementary terms. After having made a few preparatory experiments, he concluded with a **panegyric** upon modern chemistry, the terms of which I shall never forget: –

'The ancient teachers of this science,' said he, 'promised impossibilities, and performed nothing. The modern masters promise very little; they know that metals cannot be transmuted, and that the elixir of life is a chimera. But these philosophers, whose hands seem only made to dabble in dirt, and their eyes to pore over the microscope or crucible, have indeed performed miracles. They penetrate into the recesses of nature, and show how she works in her hiding-places. They ascend into the heavens: they have discovered how the blood circulates, and the nature of the air we breathe. They have acquired new and almost unlimited powers; they can command the thunders of heaven, mimic the earthquake, and even mock the invisible world with its own shadows.'

chimeras From Greek mythology, fire-breathing monsters. Thus, figuratively, unreal creatures or fantasies.

recapitulation Summary, brief repetition of main points.

panegyric Speech of praise.

Such were the professor's words – rather let me say such the words
of the fate – **enounced** to destroy me. As he went on I felt as if
my soul were grappling with a **palpable** enemy; one by one the
various keys were touched which formed the mechanism of my
being: chord after chord was sounded, and soon my mind was filled
with one thought, one conception, one purpose. So much has been
done, exclaimed the soul of Frankenstein, – more, far more, will I
achieve: treading in the steps already marked, I will pioneer a new
way, explore unknown powers, and unfold to the world the deepest
mysteries of creation.

I closed not my eyes that night. My internal being was in a state
of insurrection and turmoil; I felt that order would thence arise, but
I had no power to produce it. By degrees, after the morning's dawn,
sleep came. I awoke, and my yesternight's thoughts were as a dream.
There only remained a resolution to return to my ancient studies
and to devote myself to a science for which I believed myself to
possess a natural talent. On the same day, I paid M. Waldman a visit.
His manners in private were even more mild and attractive than in
public; for there was a certain dignity in his **mien** during his lecture,
which in his own house was replaced by the greatest **affability**
and kindness. I gave him pretty nearly the same account of my
former pursuits as I had given to his fellow-professor. He heard with
attention the little narration concerning my studies, and smiled at
the names of Cornelius Agrippa and Paracelsus, but without the
contempt that M. Krempe had exhibited. He said that 'these were
men to whose indefatigable zeal modern philosophers were indebted
for most of the foundations of their knowledge. They had left to
us, as an easier task to give new names, and arrange in connected
classifications the facts which they in a great degree had been the
instruments of bringing to light. The labours of men of genius,
however erroneously directed, scarcely ever fail in ultimately turning
to the solid advantage of mankind.' I listened to his statement, which
was delivered without any presumption or affectation; and then
added that his lecture had removed any prejudices against modern
chemists; I expressed myself in measured terms, with the modesty
and deference due from a youth to his instructor, without letting
escape (inexperience in life would have made me ashamed) any of
the enthusiasm which stimulated my intended labours. I requested

---

enounced Uttered.

palpable Tangible, something that can be
touched or handled.

mien Appearance, demeanor.

affability Courteousness, openness of manner.

his advice concerning the books I ought to procure.

'I am happy,' said M. Waldman, 'to have gained a disciple; and if your application equals your ability, I have no doubt of your success. Chemistry is that branch of natural philosophy in which the greatest improvements have been and may be made: it is on that account that I have made it my peculiar study; but at the same time, I have not neglected the other branches of science. A man would make but a very sorry chemist if he attended to that department of human knowledge alone. If your wish is to become really a man of science, and not merely a petty experimentalist, I should advise you to apply to every branch of natural philosophy, including mathematics.'

He then took me into his laboratory and explained to me the uses of his various machines; instructing me as to what I ought to procure, and promising me the use of his own when I should have advanced far enough in the science not to **derange** their mechanism. He also gave me the list of books which I had requested; and I took my leave.

Thus ended a day memorable to me: it decided my future destiny.

derange Disturb or destroy the order of.

Mary Shelley's circle

Frankenstein is one of the few classic novels written by a teenager—
Mary Shelley was just 19 years old when she wrote it. This amazing
achievement was possible partly because Mary was the talented
daughter of two writers, William Godwin and Mary Wollstonecraft.
She must have inherited their abilities and when she was growing up,
her father encouraged her love of reading by giving her many of the
best books of the time to read. But Mary also became a great writer
because she was encouraged and stimulated by other people around
her, especially her husband, the poet Percy Bysshe Shelley, and their
friend Lord Byron, who was perhaps the most famous poet of the age.

Percy Shelley

Mary got to know Percy Shelley (1792–1822) because he was a friend and
admirer of her father. Shelley was a frequent visitor to Godwin's house and
helped Mary's father when he was short of money. Like Mary, Shelley began
writing in his teens, and his early poems and stories show a love of horror and
the Gothic (see pp.122–123), which Mary shared. She was also interested
in his radical views—he was an atheist, a vegetarian, and
thought that the British monarchy should be replaced
with a republic. When Mary began her story about

Frankenstein, Percy encouraged her to extend it into a full-length novel. Some of the natural descriptions in the novel may be influenced by similar passages in Percy's poetry, as well as by the sights the couple had seen on their travels through Europe together.

Lord Byron

George Gordon, Lord Byron, (1788–1824) was nine years older than Mary and had already had an eventful life by the time he shared a house with the Shelleys in Geneva. His first book of poems, called *Hours of Idleness*, was published in 1807. Several other books of his poetry had appeared by the time he went to Switzerland, the best known being the first two cantos (sections)

George Gordon, Lord Byron
*In 1814 artist Thomas Phillips
painted Byron wearing a costume
from Albania.*

of *Childe Harold's Pilgrimage*, published in 1812. They made Byron famous. Byron was also a restless traveler, journeying to Portugal, Spain, Greece, and the eastern Mediterranean in 1809–11. In the early-19th century it was rare for a British person to travel to these places. Byron's fascination with characters that were social outcasts (see pp.172–173) and his knowledge of remote places must have been stimulating for Mary. Traveling with Byron was his personal physician, Dr. John Polidori (1795–1821). Polidori had ambitions as a writer and published numerous poems and essays. He adapted Byron's idea for a ghost story into a tale called *The Vampyre* and this work began the fashion for stories about vampires that is still current today.

A group of friends

The company of other people was vital to Mary, and it is not surprising that one of her novel's most sympathetic characters, Robert Walton, finds friendship so important. When they were not traveling, Mary and her friends occupied their time reading, sometimes reading out loud to one another. The books they read influenced Mary's writing. As well as devouring ghost stories, Mary was influenced by books on other topics. One topic was Greek mythology, in which she read about Prometheus, the Greek god who created humanity and who stole fire from the other gods, to help his creations to keep warm and cook their food. Victor Frankenstein tries to imitate the god by manufacturing a human being, and the parallel is close enough for Mary Shelley to remind us of it in her title, *Frankenstein, or The Modern Prometheus*.

Percy Bysshe Shelley
*Painter Joseph Servern portrayed Shelley in a
typically Romantic setting in front of an ancient
ruin in a craggy landscape.*

Chapter 4

From this day natural philosophy, and particularly chemistry, in the most comprehensive sense of the term, became nearly my sole occupation. I read with ardour those works, so full of genius and discrimination, which modern enquirers have written on these subjects. I attended the lectures, and cultivated the acquaintance, of the men of science of the university; and I found even in M. Krempe a great deal of sound sense and real information, combined, it is true, with a repulsive **physiognomy** and manners, but not on that account the less valuable. In M. Waldman I found a true friend. His gentleness was never tinged by **dogmatism**, and his instructions were given with an air of frankness and good nature, that banished every idea of **pedantry**. In a thousand ways he smoothed for me the path of knowledge, and made the most abstruse enquiries clear and facile to my apprehension. My application was at first fluctuating and uncertain; it gained strength as I proceeded, and soon became so ardent and eager, that the stars often disappeared in the light of morning whilst I was yet engaged in my laboratory.

As I applied so closely, it may be easily conceived that my progress was rapid. My ardour was indeed the astonishment of the students, and my proficiency that of the masters. Professor Krempe often asked me, with a sly smile, how Cornelius Agrippa went on? whilst M. Waldman expressed the most heartfelt exultation in my progress. Two years passed in this manner, during which I paid no visit to Geneva, but was engaged, heart and soul, in the pursuit of some discoveries which I hoped to make. None but those who have experienced them can conceive of the enticements of science. In other studies you go as far as others have gone before you, and there is nothing more to know; but in a scientific pursuit there is continual food for discovery and wonder. A mind of moderate capacity, which closely pursued one study must infallibly arrive at great proficiency in that study; and I, who continually sought the attainment of one object of pursuit and was solely wrapt up in this, improved so rapidly, that, at the end of two years, I made some discoveries in the improvement of some chemical instruments, which procured me

physiognomy Physical appearance, especially of the face.
dogmatism Stubborn or arrogant assertion of an opinion.
pedantry Showy display of learning.

great esteem and admiration at the university. When I had arrived at this point and had become as well acquainted with the theory and practice of natural philosophy as depended on the lessons of any of the professors at Ingolstadt, my residence there being no longer conducive to my improvements, I thought of returning to my friends and my native town, when an incident happened that protracted my stay.

One of the phenomena which had peculiarly attracted my attention was the structure of the human frame, and, indeed, any animal endued with life. Whence, I often asked myself, did the principle of life proceed? It was a bold question, and one which has ever been considered as a mystery; yet with how many things are we upon the brink of becoming acquainted, if cowardice or carelessness did not restrain our enquiries. I revolved these circumstances in my mind, and determined thenceforth to apply myself more particularly to those branches of natural philosophy which relate to **physiology**. Unless I had been animated by an almost supernatural enthusiasm, my application to this study would have been irksome, and almost intolerable. To examine the causes of life, we must first have recourse to death. I became acquainted with the science of anatomy: but this was not sufficient; I must also observe the natural decay and corruption of the human body. In my education my father had taken the greatest precautions that my mind should be impressed with no supernatural horrors. I do not ever remember to have trembled at a tale of superstition, or to have feared the apparition of a spirit. Darkness had no effect upon my fancy; and a churchyard was to me merely the receptacle of bodies deprived of life, which, from being the seat of beauty and strength, had become food for the worm. Now I was led to examine the cause and progress of this decay, and forced to spend days and nights in vaults and **charnel-houses**. My attention was fixed upon every object the most insupportable to the delicacy of the human feelings. I saw how the fine form of man was degraded and wasted; I beheld the corruption of death succeed to the blooming cheek of life; I saw how the worm inherited the wonders of the eye and brain. I paused, examining and analysing all the **minutiae** of **causation**, as exemplified in the change from life to death, and death to life, until from the midst of this darkness a sudden light broke in upon me – a light so brilliant and wondrous,

physiology Science of living things and their parts.

charnel-houses Places where corpses are stored.

minutiae Small details.

causation The bringing-about of effects.

yet so simple, that while I became dizzy with the immensity of the prospect which it illustrated, I was surprised, that among so many men of genius who had directed their enquiries towards the same science, that I alone should be reserved to discover so astonishing a secret.

Remember, I am not recording the vision of a madman. The sun does not more certainly shine in the heavens, than that which I now affirm is true. Some miracle might have produced it, yet the stages of the discovery were distinct and probable. After days and nights of incredible labour and fatigue, I succeeded in discovering the cause of generation and life; nay, more, I became myself capable of **bestowing animation** upon lifeless matter.

The astonishment which I had at first experienced on this discovery soon gave place to delight and rapture. After so much time spent in painful labour, to arrive at once at the summit of my desires, was the most gratifying consummation of my toils. But this discovery was so great and overwhelming, that all the steps by which I had been progressively led to it were obliterated, and I beheld only the result. What had been the study and desire of the wisest men since the creation of the world was now within my grasp. Not that, like a magic scene, it all opened upon me at once: the information I had obtained was of a nature rather to direct my endeavours so soon as I should point them towards the object of my search, than to exhibit that object already accomplished. I was like the Arabian who had been **buried with the dead** and found a passage to life, aided only by one glimmering and seemingly ineffectual light.

I see by your eagerness and the wonder and hope which your eyes express, my friend, that you expect to be informed of the secret with which I am acquainted; that cannot be: listen patiently until the end of my story, and you will easily perceive why I am reserved upon that subject. I will not lead you on, unguarded and ardent as I then was, to your destruction and infallible misery. Learn from me, if not by my **precepts**, at least by my example, how dangerous is the acquirement of knowledge and how much happier that man is who believes his native town to be the world, than he who aspires to become greater than his nature will allow.

When I found so astonishing a power placed within my hands, I hesitated a long time concerning the manner in which I should

---

bestowing Giving.
animation Life.
buried with the dead In *The Thousand and One Nights*, Sinbad the Sailor is trapped in a communal tomb during one of his voyages.

precepts Rules of conduct.

employ it. Although I possessed the capacity of bestowing animation, yet to prepare a frame for the reception of it, with all its intricacies of fibres, muscles, and veins, still remained a work of inconceivable difficulty and labour. I doubted at first whether I should attempt the creation of a being like myself, or one of simpler organisation; but my imagination was too much exalted by my first success to permit me to doubt of my ability to give life to an animal as complex and wonderful as man. The materials at present within my command hardly appeared adequate to so arduous an undertaking; but I doubted not that I should ultimately succeed. I prepared myself for a multitude of reverses; my operations might be incessantly baffled, and at last my work be imperfect: yet, when I considered the improvement which every day takes place in science and mechanics, I was encouraged to hope my present attempts would at least lay the foundations of future success. Nor could I consider the magnitude and complexity of my plan as any argument of its impracticability. It was with these feelings that I began the creation of a human being. As the minuteness of the parts formed a great hindrance to my speed, I resolved, contrary to my first intention, to make the being of a gigantic stature; that is to say, about eight feet in height, and proportionally large. After having formed this determination and having spent some months in successfully collecting and arranging my materials, I began.

No one can conceive the variety of feelings which bore me onwards, like a hurricane, in the first enthusiasm of success. Life and death appeared to me ideal bounds, which I should first break through, and pour a torrent of light into our dark world. A new species would bless me as its creator and source; many happy and excellent natures would owe their being to me. No father could claim the gratitude of his child so completely as I should deserve theirs. Pursuing these reflections, I thought, that if I could bestow animation upon lifeless matter, I might in process of time (although I now found it impossible) renew life where death had apparently devoted the body to corruption.

These thoughts supported my spirits, while I pursued my undertaking with unremitting ardour. My cheek had grown pale with study, and my person had become **emaciated** with confinement. Sometimes, on the very brink of certainty, I failed; yet

emaciated Thin, wasted away.

still I clung to the hope which the next day or the next hour might realise. One secret which I alone possessed was the hope to which I had dedicated myself; and the moon gazed on my midnight labours, while, with unrelaxed and breathless eagerness, I pursued nature to her hiding-places. Who shall conceive the horrors of my secret toil as I dabbled among the unhallowed damps of the grave or tortured the living animal to animate the lifeless clay? My limbs now tremble, and my eyes swim with the remembrance; but then a resistless, and almost frantic impulse, urged me forward; I seemed to have lost all soul or sensation but for this one pursuit. It was indeed but a passing trance, that only made me feel with renewed acuteness so soon as, the unnatural stimulus ceasing to operate, I had returned to my old habits. I collected bones from charnel-houses and disturbed, with profane fingers, the tremendous secrets of the human frame. In a solitary chamber, or rather cell, at the top of the house, and separated from all the other apartments by a gallery and staircase, I kept my workshop of filthy creation: my eyeballs were starting from their sockets in attending to the details of my employment. The dissecting room and the slaughter-house furnished many of my materials; and often did my human nature turn with loathing from my occupation, whilst, still urged on by an eagerness which perpetually increased, I brought my work near to a conclusion.

The summer months passed while I was thus engaged, heart and soul, in one pursuit. It was a most beautiful season; never did the fields bestow a more plentiful harvest, or the vines yield a more luxuriant vintage: but my eyes were insensible to the charms of nature. And the same feelings which made me neglect the scenes around me caused me also to forget those friends who were so many miles absent, and whom I had not seen for so long a time. I knew my silence disquieted them; and I well remembered the words of my father: 'I know that while you are pleased with yourself, you will think of us with affection, and we shall hear regularly from you. You must pardon me if I regard any interruption in your correspondence as a proof that your other duties are equally neglected.'

I knew well therefore what would be my father's feelings; but I could not tear my thoughts from my employment, loathsome in itself, but which had taken an irresistible hold of my imagination. I wished, as it were, to procrastinate all that related to my feelings of affection until the great object, which swallowed up every habit of my nature, should be completed.

I then thought that my father would be unjust if he ascribed my neglect to vice, or faultiness on my part, but I am now convinced that he was justified in conceiving that I should not be altogether free from blame. A human being in perfection ought always to preserve a calm and peaceful mind, and never to allow passion or a transitory desire to disturb his tranquillity. I do not think that the pursuit of knowledge is an exception to this rule. If the study to which you apply yourself has a tendency to weaken your affections, and to destroy your taste for those simple pleasures in which no **alloy** can possibly mix, then that study is certainly unlawful, that is to say, not befitting the human mind. If this rule were always observed; if no man allowed any pursuit whatsoever to interfere with the tranquillity of his domestic affections, Greece had not been enslaved; Caesar would have spared his country; America would have been discovered more gradually; and the empires of Mexico and Peru had not been destroyed.

But I forget that I am moralising in the most interesting part of my tale, and your looks remind me to proceed.

My father made no reproach in his letters, and only took notice of my silence by enquiring into my occupations more particularly than before. Winter, spring, and summer passed away during my labours; but I did not watch the blossom or the expanding leaves – sights which before always yielded me supreme delight – so deeply was I engrossed in my occupation. The leaves of that year had withered before my work drew to a close; and now every day showed me more plainly how well I had succeeded. But my enthusiasm was checked by my anxiety, and I appeared rather like one doomed by slavery to toil in the mines, or any other unwholesome trade than an artist occupied by his favourite employment. Every night I was oppressed by a slow fever, and I became nervous to a most painful degree; the fall of a leaf startled me, and I shunned my fellow-creatures as if I had been guilty of a crime. Sometimes I grew alarmed at the wreck I perceived that I had become; the energy of my purpose alone sustained me: my labours would soon end, and I believed that exercise and amusement would then drive away incipient disease; and I promised myself both of these when my creation should be complete.

alloy Literally, a mixture of two metals, or of metal with nonmetal. More generally, an adulterated substance.

Chapter 5

It was on a dreary night of November, that I beheld the accomplishment of my toils. With an anxiety that almost amounted to agony, I collected the instruments of life around me, that I might infuse a spark of being into the lifeless thing that lay at my feet. It was already one in the morning; the rain pattered dismally against the panes, and my candle was nearly burnt out, when, by the glimmer of the half-extinguished light, I saw the dull yellow eye of the creature open; it breathed hard, and a convulsive motion agitated its limbs.

How can I describe my emotions at this catastrophe, or how **delineate** the wretch whom with such infinite pains and care I had endeavoured to form? His limbs were in proportion, and I had selected his features as beautiful. Beautiful! – Great God! His yellow skin scarcely covered the work of muscles and arteries beneath; his hair was of a lustrous black, and flowing; his teeth of pearly whiteness; but these luxuriances only formed a more horrid contrast with his watery eyes, that seemed almost of the same colour as the **dun-white** sockets in which they were set, his shrivelled complexion and straight black lips.

The different accidents of life are not so changeable as the feelings of human nature. I had worked hard for nearly two years, for the sole purpose of infusing life into an inanimate body. For this I had deprived myself of rest and health. I had desired it with an ardour that far exceeded moderation; but now that I had finished, the beauty of the dream vanished, and breathless horror and disgust filled my heart. Unable to endure the aspect of the being I had created, I rushed out of the room, and continued a long time traversing my bedchamber, unable to compose my mind to sleep. At length **lassitude** succeeded to the tumult I had before endured; and I threw myself on the bed in my clothes, endeavouring to seek a few moments of forgetfulness. But it was in vain: I slept, indeed, but I was disturbed by the wildest dreams. I thought I saw Elizabeth, in the bloom of health, walking in the streets of Ingolstadt. Delighted and surprised, I embraced her, but as I imprinted the first kiss on her

delineate Describe or portray.
dun-white A dull or dingy shade of white.
lassitude Weariness.

lips, they became livid with the hue of death; her features appeared to change, and I thought that I held the corpse of my dead mother in my arms; a shroud enveloped her form, and I saw the grave-worms crawling in the folds of flannel. I started from my sleep with horror; a cold dew covered my forehead, my teeth chattered, and every limb became convulsed: when, by the dim and yellow light of the moon, as it forced its way through the window shutters, I beheld the wretch – the miserable monster whom I had created. He held up the curtain of the bed; and his eyes, if eyes they may be called, were fixed on me. His jaws opened, and he muttered some inarticulate sounds, while a grin wrinkled his cheeks. He might have spoken, but I did not hear; one hand was stretched out, seemingly to detain me, but I escaped, and rushed downstairs. I took refuge in the courtyard belonging to the house which I inhabited; where I remained during the rest of the night, walking up and down in the greatest agitation, listening attentively, catching and fearing each sound as if it were to announce the approach of the **demoniacal** corpse to which I had so miserably given life.

Oh! no mortal could support the horror of that countenance. A mummy again endued with animation could not be so hideous as that wretch. I had gazed on him while unfinished; he was ugly then; but when those muscles and joints were rendered capable of motion, it became a thing such as even **Dante** could not have conceived.

I passed the night wretchedly. Sometimes my pulse beat so quickly and hardly that I felt the **palpitation** of every artery; at others, I nearly sank to the ground through languor and extreme weakness. Mingled with this horror, I felt the bitterness of disappointment; dreams that had been my food and pleasant rest for so long a space were now become a hell to me; and the change was so rapid, the overthrow so complete!

Morning, dismal and wet, at length dawned, and discovered to my sleepless and aching eyes the church of Ingolstadt, its white steeple and clock, which indicated the sixth hour. The porter opened the gates of the court, which had that night been my asylum, and I issued into the streets, pacing them with quick steps, as if I sought to avoid the wretch whom I feared every turning of the street would present to my view. I did not dare return to the apartment which I inhabited, but felt impelled to hurry on, although drenched by the

demoniacal Like a demon or evil spirit.

Dante Dante Alighieri (1265–1321), Italian poet, writer of the *Divine Comedy*, the most famous part of which, the *Inferno*, describes the torments of the damned in hell.

palpitation Quivering, throbbing.

rain which poured from a black and comfortless sky.

I continued walking in this manner for some time, endeavouring by bodily exercise to ease the load that weighed upon my mind. I traversed the streets without any clear conception of where I was or what I was doing. My heart palpitated in the sickness of fear, and I hurried on with irregular steps, not daring to look about me:

> Like one, on a lonesome road who,
> Doth walk in fear and dread,
> And, having once turned round, walks on,
> And turns no more his head;
> Because he knows a frightful friend
> Doth close behind him tread. *

Continuing thus, I came at length opposite to the inn at which the various **diligences** and carriages usually stopped. Here I paused, I knew not why; but I remained some minutes with my eyes fixed on a coach that was coming towards me from the other end of the street. As it drew nearer I observed that it was the Swiss diligence: it stopped just where I was standing; and, on the door being opened, I perceived Henry Clerval, who, on seeing me, instantly sprung out. 'My dear Frankenstein,' exclaimed he, 'how glad I am to see you! how fortunate that you should be here at the very moment of my alighting!'

Nothing could equal my delight on seeing Clerval; his presence brought back to my thoughts my father, Elizabeth, and all those scenes of home so dear to my recollection. I grasped his hand, and in a moment forgot my horror and misfortune; I felt suddenly, and for the first time during many months, calm and serene joy. I welcomed my friend, therefore, in the most cordial manner, and we walked towards my college. Clerval continued talking for some time about our mutual friends and his own good fortune in being permitted to come to Ingolstadt. 'You may easily believe,' said he, 'how great was the difficulty to persuade my father that all necessary knowledge was not comprised in the noble art of book-keeping; and, indeed, I believe I left him **incredulous** to the last, for his constant answer to my unwearied intreaties was the same as that to the Dutch schoolmaster in *The Vicar of Wakefield*: "I have ten thousand **florins**

---

* Coleridge's *Ancient Mariner* [Author's footnote.]
diligences Stage coaches.
incredulous Unbelieving, skeptical.

The Vicar of Wakefield A novel by Oliver Goldsmith (1766). It is most often described as a "sentimental novel" promoting belief in the innate goodness of all human beings.
florins Dutch coins each worth one guilder.

a year without Greek, I eat heartily without Greek." But his affection for me at length overcame his dislike of learning, and he has permitted me to undertake a voyage of discovery to the land of knowledge.'

'It gives me the greatest delight to see you; but tell me how you left my father, brothers, and Elizabeth.'

'Very well, and very happy, only a little uneasy that they hear from you so seldom. By the by, I mean to lecture you a little upon their account myself – But, my dear Frankenstein,' continued he, stopping short and gazing full in my face, 'I did not before remark how very ill you appear; so thin and pale; and look as if you had been watching for several nights.'

'You have guessed right; I have lately been so deeply engaged in one occupation, that I have not allowed myself sufficient rest, as you see; but I hope, I sincerely hope, that all these employments are now at an end, and that I am at length free.'

I trembled excessively; I could not endure to think of, and far less to allude to, the occurrences of the preceding night. I walked with a quick pace, and we soon arrived at my college. I then reflected, and the thought made me shiver, that the creature whom I had left in my apartment might still be there, alive and walking about. I dreaded to behold this monster; but I feared still more that Henry should see him. Intreating him, therefore, to remain a few minutes at the bottom of the stairs, I darted up towards my own room. My hand was already on the lock of the door before I recollected myself. I then paused; and a cold shivering came over me. I threw the door forcibly open, as children are accustomed to do when they expect a spectre to stand in waiting for them on the other side; but nothing appeared. I stepped fearfully in: the apartment was empty; and my bedroom was also freed from its hideous guest. I could hardly believe that so great a good fortune could have befallen me; but when I became assured that my enemy had indeed fled, I clapped my hands for joy and ran down to Clerval.

We ascended into my room, and the servant presently brought breakfast; but I was unable to contain myself. It was not joy only that possessed me; I felt my flesh tingle with excess of sensitiveness, and my pulse beat rapidly. I was unable to remain for a single instant in the same place; I jumped over the chairs, clapped my hands, and laughed aloud. Clerval at first attributed my unusual spirits to joy on his arrival, but when he observed me more attentively, he saw a wildness in my eyes for which he could not account; and my loud, unrestrained, heartless laughter frightened and astonished him.

'My dear Victor,' cried he, 'what, for God's sake, is the matter? do not laugh in that manner. How ill you are! What is the cause of all this?'

'Do not ask me,' cried I, putting my hands before my eyes, for I thought I saw the dreaded spectre glide into the room; 'he can tell. – Oh, save me! save me!' I imagined that the monster seized me; I struggled furiously and fell down in a fit.

Poor Clerval! what must have been his feelings? A meeting, which he anticipated with such joy, so strangely turned to bitterness. But I was not the witness of his grief; for I was lifeless, and did not recover my senses for a long, long time.

This was the commencement of a nervous fever, which confined me for several months. During all that time Henry was my only nurse. I afterwards learned that, knowing my father's advanced age, and unfitness for so long a journey, and how wretched my sickness would make Elizabeth, he spared them this grief by concealing the extent of my disorder. He knew that I could not have a more kind and attentive nurse than himself; and, firm in the hope he felt of my recovery, he did not doubt that, instead of doing harm, he performed the kindest action that he could towards them.

But I was in reality very ill; and surely nothing but the unbounded and unremitting attentions of my friend could have restored me to life. The form of the monster on whom I had bestowed existence was forever before my eyes, and I raved incessantly concerning him. Doubtless my words surprised Henry; he at first believed them to be the wanderings of my disturbed imagination; but the **pertinacity** with which I continually recurred to the same subject, persuaded him that my disorder indeed owed its origin to some uncommon and terrible event.

By very slow degrees, and with frequent relapses that alarmed and grieved my friend, I recovered. I remember the first time I became capable of observing outward objects with any kind of pleasure, I perceived that the fallen leaves had disappeared and that the young buds were shooting forth from the trees that shaded my window.

pertinacity Obstinacy.

It was a divine spring; and the season contributed greatly to my convalescence. I felt also sentiments of joy and affection revive in my bosom; my gloom disappeared, and in a short time I became as cheerful as before I was attacked by the fatal passion.

'Dearest Clerval,' exclaimed I, 'how kind, how very good you are to me. This whole winter, instead of being spent in study, as you promised yourself, has been consumed in my sick room. How shall I ever repay you? I feel the greatest remorse for the disappointment of which I have been the occasion; but you will forgive me.'

'You will repay me entirely, if you do not discompose yourself, but get well as fast as you can; and since you appear in such good spirits, I may speak to you on one subject, may I not?'

I trembled. One subject! What could it be? Could he allude to an object on whom I dared not even think?

'Compose yourself,' said Clerval, who observed my change of colour, 'I will not mention it if it agitates you; but your father and cousin would be very happy if they received a letter from you in your own handwriting. They hardly know how ill you have been, and are uneasy at your long silence.'

'Is that all, my dear Henry? How could you suppose that my first thought would not fly towards those dear, dear friends whom I love, and who are so deserving of my love?'

'If this is your present temper, my friend, you will perhaps be glad to see a letter that has been lying here some days for you: it is from your cousin, I believe.'

The Enlightenment

Frankenstein is set in the 18th century, a time when many writers and thinkers were caught up in a powerful intellectual movement called the Enlightenment, which rejected many of the scientific and religious ideas of previous ages. Instead of believing things were true because ancient writers said so, the thinkers of the Enlightenment aimed to base their ideas on logical reasoning, human understanding, and the evidence of their own eyes and ears. In doing this they turned their backs on major fields of study such as alchemy, the science that was supposed to be able to turn base metals into gold. Alchemy had once fascinated scientists but was now thought to be no more than superstition. The scientists and philosophers of the Enlightenment, with their emphasis on reason and rationality, were so influential that the 18th century is often known as the Age of Reason. Mary Shelley was deeply interested in these ideas—partly through the influence of her father, the writer William Godwin (1756–1836), a leading exponent of the Enlightenment in Britain.

The beginnings

The Enlightenment had its beginnings in the 17th century. This was the time when British scientist Isaac Newton (1642–1727) made his key discoveries in optics, mathematics, and gravity and when Frenchman René Descartes (1596–1650) transformed the methods used in philosophy by going back to its simplest and most basic ideas—the rigorous use of logic and the belief that we exist because we have consciousness. The thinkers of the 18th century built on the work of Newton and Descartes, using their logical methods to test their own theories.

Frontispiece from Diderot's Encyclopedia
This illustration shows the figures of Reason, Philosophy, and Truth surrounded by bright light, a symbol of the Enlightenment.

Diderot's Encyclopedia

One of the most amazing products of the Enlightenment was the Encyclopédie, a huge work in 28 volumes that aimed to cover every field of knowledge, from artistic to scientific. The work was edited by the French writers Denis Diderot (1713–84) and Jean d'Alembert (1717–83) and the text was written by many of France's most eminent authors. For the first time it seemed that the whole of human knowledge had been set down in a clear, rational, and organized way. Although the work includes articles on religion by theologians, a number of the other articles criticized superstition, so many churchmen were suspicious of the *Encyclopédie*, which was even banned for a while. The *Encyclopédie* showed that knowledge, expressed rationally, could be both powerful and subversive.

The Enlightenment in Britain

British writers such as William Godwin were hugely influenced by the thinkers of the Enlightenment. In one of his best-known books, *An Enquiry Concerning Political Justice*, Godwin concludes that reason, properly followed, will always lead people to make the best political judgments. Both Mary Shelley and her husband Percy were attracted to Godwin's ideas, and the ideas of the Enlightenment also influenced English writers such as the poet and illustrator William Blake (1757–1827) author of famous poems such as *Jerusalem* and *Milton* and the novelist Maria Edgeworth (1768–1849), author of the novel *Castle Rackrent*.

William Godwin
Mary Shelley's father was a leading figure in the Enlightenment in Britain.

Knowledge and learning in *Frankenstein*

When Victor Frankenstein leaves home to study at the University of Ingolstadt, he tells his teachers about his enthusiasm for the 15th- and 16th-century alchemists Paracelsus and Cornelius Agrippa. At Ingolstadt he soon realizes that one of the teachers, M. Krempe, has no time for such old-fashioned and superstitious writers. His other teacher, M. Waldman takes a more tolerant view, saying that writers like Agrippa and Paracelsus laid the foundations for the work of later scientists. He goes on to show Victor how to make proper chemical experiments and encourages him to make discoveries of his own, adding to the work of earlier scientists. In one sense, Waldman is introducing Victor to the values of the Enlightenment, in which you believe the evidence of your own senses, rather than the writings of ancient alchemists. Victor quickly becomes a follower of Waldman's scientific method, which does take him in a new direction, the creation of a living creature. Things go wrong in part because Frankenstein isolates himself from the world, working in solitude, so that no other scientists can test his work or ask reasonable questions about it. Robert Walton, on the other hand, makes a very different voyage of discovery, surrounding himself with experienced sailors and navigators, and learning much about what he encounters—including the story of Frankenstein himself.

Chapter 6

Clerval then put the following letter into my hands. It was from my own Elizabeth: –

MY DEAREST COUSIN,

You have been ill, very ill, and even the constant letters of dear kind Henry are not sufficient to reassure me on your account. You are forbidden to write – to hold a pen; yet one word from you, dear Victor, is necessary to calm our apprehensions. For a long time I have thought that each post would bring this line, and my persuasions have restrained my uncle from undertaking a journey to Ingolstadt. I have prevented his encountering the inconveniences and perhaps dangers of so long a journey, yet how often have I regretted not being able to perform it myself! I figure to myself that the task of attending on your sickbed has devolved on some mercenary old nurse, who could never guess your wishes, nor minister to them with the care and affection of your poor cousin. Yet that is over now: Clerval writes that indeed you are getting better. I eagerly hope that you will confirm this intelligence soon in your own handwriting.

Get well – and return to us. You will find a happy, cheerful home, and friends who love you dearly. Your father's health is vigorous, and he asks but to see you, but to be assured that you are well; and not a care will ever cloud his benevolent countenance. How pleased you would be to remark the improvement of our Ernest! He is now sixteen, and full of activity and spirit. He is desirous to be a **true Swiss**, and to enter into **foreign service**, but we cannot part with him, at least until his elder brother return to us. My uncle is not pleased with the idea of a military career in a distant country, but Ernest never had your powers of application. He looks upon study as an odious **fetter**; his time is spent in the open air, climbing the hills or rowing on the lake. I fear that he will become an idler, unless we yield the point, and permit him to enter on the profession which he has selected.

Little alteration, except the growth of our dear children, has taken place since you left us. The blue lake, and snow-clad mountains

true Swiss A patriotic citizen of Switzerland.
foreign service Diplomatic or military service.
fetter Restraint.

– they never change; and I think our placid home and our contented hearts are regulated by the same **immutable** laws. My trifling occupations take up my time and amuse me, and I am rewarded for any exertions by seeing none but happy, kind faces around me. Since you left us, but one change has taken place in our little household. Do you remember on what occasions Justine Moritz entered our family? Probably you do not; I will relate her history, therefore, in a few words. Madame Moritz, her mother, was a widow with four children, of whom Justine was the third. This girl had always been the favourite of her father; but, through a strange perversity, her mother could not endure her, and after the death of M. Moritz, treated her very ill. My aunt observed this, and when Justine was twelve years of age, prevailed on her mother to allow her to live at our house. The **republican institutions** of our country have produced simpler and happier manners than those which prevail in the great monarchies that surround it. Hence there is less distinction between the several classes of its inhabitants; and the lower orders, being neither so poor nor so despised, their manners are more refined and moral. A servant in Geneva does not mean the same thing as a servant in France and England. Justine, thus received in our family, learned the duties of a servant; a condition which, in our fortunate country, does not include the idea of ignorance, and a sacrifice of the dignity of a human being.

Justine, you may remember, was a great favourite of yours; and I recollect you once remarked that if you were in an ill humour, one glance from Justine could dissipate it, for the same reason that **Ariosto** gives concerning the beauty of **Angelica** – she looked so frank-hearted and happy. My aunt conceived a great attachment for her, by which she was induced to give her an education superior to that which she had at first intended. This benefit was fully repaid; Justine was the most grateful little creature in the world: I do not mean that she made any **professions**; I never heard one pass her lips, but you could see by her eyes that she almost adored her protectress. Although her disposition was gay, and in many respects inconsiderate, yet she paid the greatest attention to every gesture of my aunt. She thought her the model of all excellence and endeavoured to imitate her phraseology and manners, so that even now she often reminds me of her.

---

immutable Unchangeable.
republican institutions At this time, Switzerland had no centralized government. There was a Confederation composed of semi-independent regions called cantons.

Ariosto Ludovico Ariosto (1474–1533) an Italian poet.
Angelica Heroine of Ariosto's epic poem, *Orlando Furioso* (1516).
professions Declarations of love or friendship.

When my dearest aunt died, every one was too much occupied in their own grief to notice poor Justine, who had attended her illness with the most anxious affection. Poor Justine was very ill, but other trials were reserved for her.

One by one, her brothers and sister died; and her mother, with the exception of her neglected daughter, was left childless. The conscience of the woman was troubled; she began to think that the deaths of her favourites were a judgment from heaven to **chastise** her **partiality**. She was a Roman catholic; and I believe her **confessor** confirmed the idea which she had conceived. Accordingly, a few months after your departure for Ingolstadt, Justine was called home by her repentant mother. Poor girl! she wept when she quitted our house; she was much altered since the death of my aunt; grief had given softness and a winning mildness to her manners which had before been remarkable for vivacity. Nor was her residence at her mother's house of a nature to restore her gaiety. The poor woman was very **vacillating** in her repentance. She sometimes begged Justine to forgive her unkindness but much oftener accused her of having caused the deaths of her brothers and sister. Perpetual fretting at length threw Madame Moritz into a decline, which at first increased her irritability, but she is now at peace forever. She died on the first approach of cold weather, at the beginning of this last winter. Justine has returned to us, and I assure you I love her tenderly. She is very clever and gentle, and extremely pretty; as I mentioned before, her mien and her expressions continually remind me of my dear aunt.

I must say also a few words to you, my dear cousin, of little darling William. I wish you could see him; he is very tall of his age, with sweet laughing blue eyes, dark eyelashes, and curling hair. When he smiles, two little dimples appear on each cheek, which are rosy with health. He has already had one or two little *wives*, but Louisa Biron is his favourite, a pretty little girl of five years of age.

Now, dear Victor, I dare say you wish to be indulged in a little gossip concerning the good people of Geneva. The pretty Miss Mansfield has already received the congratulatory visits on her approaching marriage with a young Englishman, John Melbourne, Esq. Her ugly sister, Manon, married M. Duvillard, the rich banker, last autumn. Your favourite school-fellow, Louis Manoir, has suffered

---

chastise Punish.

partiality Bias; taking one person's side over another.

confessor In the Catholic Church, the priest who hears a person's confession of their sins.

vacillating Unsteady.

misfortunes since the departure of Clerval from Geneva. But he has already recovered his spirits and is reported to be on the point of marrying a very lively, pretty Frenchwoman, Madame Tavernier. She is a widow, and much older than Manoir; but she is very much admired and a favourite with every body.

I have written myself into better spirits, dear cousin; but my anxiety returns upon me as I conclude. Write, dearest Victor – one line – one word will be a blessing to us. Ten thousand thanks to Henry for his kindness, his affection, and his many letters: we are sincerely grateful. Adieu! my cousin, take care of yourself; and, I intreat you, write!

ELIZABETH LAVENZA

Geneva, March 18th, 17–.

'Dear, dear Elizabeth!' I exclaimed, when I had read her letter, 'I will write instantly, and relieve them from the anxiety they must feel.' I wrote, and this exertion greatly fatigued me; but my convalescence had commenced, and proceeded regularly. In another fortnight I was able to leave my chamber.

One of my first duties on my recovery was to introduce Clerval to the several professors of the university. In doing this, I underwent a kind of rough usage, ill befitting the wounds that my mind had sustained. Ever since the fatal night, the end of my labours, and the beginning of my misfortunes, I had conceived a violent **antipathy** even to the name of natural philosophy. When I was otherwise quite restored to health, the sight of a chemical instrument would renew all the agony of my nervous symptoms. Henry saw this and had removed all my apparatus from my view. He had also changed my apartment, for he perceived that I had acquired a dislike for the room which had previously been my laboratory. But these cares of Clerval were made of no avail when I visited the professors. M. Waldman inflicted torture when he praised, with kindness and warmth, the astonishing progress I had made in the sciences. He soon perceived that I disliked the subject; but not guessing the real cause, he attributed my feelings to modesty and changed the subject from my improvement to the science itself, with a desire, as I evidently saw, of drawing me out. What could I do? He meant to please, and he tormented me. I felt as if he had placed carefully, one

---

antipathy Aversion, strong dislike.

by one, in my view those instruments which were to be afterwards used in putting me to a slow and cruel death. I writhed under his words, yet dared not exhibit the pain I felt. Clerval, whose eyes and feelings were always quick in discerning the sensations of others, declined the subject, alleging, in excuse, his total ignorance; and the conversation took a more general turn. I thanked my friend from my heart, but I did not speak. I saw plainly that he was surprised, but he never attempted to draw my secret from me; and although I loved him with a mixture of affection and reverence that knew no bounds, yet I could never persuade myself to confide to him that event which was so often present to my recollection, but which I feared the detail to another would only impress more deeply.

M. Krempe was not equally docile; and in my condition at that time, of almost insupportable sensitiveness, his harsh, blunt **encomiums** gave me even more pain than the benevolent approbation of M. Waldman, 'D–n the fellow!' cried he; 'why, M. Clerval, I assure you he has outstript us all. Ay, stare if you please; but it is nevertheless true. A youngster who, but a few years ago, believed in Cornelius Agrippa as firmly as in the Gospel, has now set himself at the head of the university; and if he is not soon pulled down, we shall all be out of countenance. – Ay, ay,' continued he, observing my face expressive of suffering, 'M. Frankenstein is modest, an excellent quality in a young man. Young men should be diffident of themselves, you know, M. Clerval: I was myself when young, but that wears out in a very short time.'

M. Krempe had now commenced a **eulogy** on himself, which happily turned the conversation from a subject that was so annoying to me.

Clerval had never sympathised in my tastes for natural science; and his literary pursuits differed wholly from whose which had occupied me. He came to the university with the design of making himself complete master of the Oriental languages, as thus he should open a field for the plan of life he had marked out for himself. Resolved to pursue no **inglorious** career, he turned his eyes towards the East as affording scope for his spirit of enterprise. The Persian, Arabic, and **Sanscrit** languages engaged his attention, and I was easily induced to enter on the same studies. Idleness had ever been irksome to me, and now that I wished to fly from reflection and hated my former

encomiums Praise.
eulogy Speech in praise of someone or something.
inglorious Disgraceful, shameful.

Sanscrit Ancient literary language of India; now usually spelled *Sanskrit*.

studies, I felt great relief in being the fellow pupil with my friend, and found not only instruction but consolation in the works of the Orientalists. I did not, like him, attempt a critical knowledge of their dialects, for I did not contemplate making any other use of them than temporary amusement. I read merely to understand their meaning, and they well repaid my labours. Their melancholy is soothing, and their joy elevating, to a degree I never experienced in studying the authors of any other country. When you read their writings, life appears to consist in a warm sun and a garden of roses, in the smiles and frowns of a fair enemy, and the fire that consumes your own heart. How different from the manly and heroical poetry of Greece and Rome!

Summer passed away in these occupations, and my return to Geneva was fixed for the latter end of autumn; but being delayed by several accidents, winter and snow arrived, the roads were deemed impassable, and my journey was retarded until the ensuing spring. I felt this delay very bitterly; for I longed to see my native town and my beloved friends. My return had only been delayed so long from an unwillingness to leave Clerval in a strange place before he had become acquainted with any of its inhabitants. The winter, however, was spent cheerfully, and although the spring was uncommonly late, when it came its beauty compensated for its **dilatoriness**.

The month of May had already commenced, and I expected the letter daily which was to fix the date of my departure, when Henry proposed a pedestrian tour in the environs of Ingolstadt, that I might bid a personal farewell to the country I had so long inhabited. I acceded with pleasure to this proposition: I was fond of exercise, and Clerval had always been my favourite companion in the rambles of this nature that I had taken among the scenes of my native country.

We passed a fortnight in these **perambulations:** my health and spirits had long been restored, and they gained additional strength from the **salubrious** air I breathed, the natural incidents of our progress, and the conversation of my friend. Study had before secluded me from the intercourse of my fellow-creatures, and rendered me unsocial, but Clerval called forth the better feelings of my heart; he again taught me to love the aspect of nature, and the cheerful faces of children. Excellent friend! how sincerely did you love me and endeavour to elevate my mind until it was on a

dilatoriness Tardiness.
perambulations Strolls, leisurely walks.
salubrious Healthful.

level with your own! A selfish pursuit had cramped and narrowed me, until your gentleness and affection warmed and opened my senses; I became the same happy creature who, a few years ago, loved and beloved by all, had no sorrow or care. When happy, inanimate nature had the power of bestowing on me the most delightful sensations. A serene sky and verdant fields filled me with ecstasy. The present season was indeed divine; the flowers of spring bloomed in the hedges, while those of summer were already in bud. I was undisturbed by thoughts which during the preceding year had pressed upon me, notwithstanding my endeavours to throw them off, with an invincible burden.

Henry rejoiced in my gaiety, and sincerely sympathised in my feelings: he exerted himself to amuse me, while he expressed the sensations that filled his soul. The resources of his mind on this occasion were truly astonishing: his conversation was full of imagination; and very often, in imitation of the Persian and Arabic writers, he invented tales of wonderful fancy and passion. At other times, he repeated my favourite poems, or drew me out into arguments, which he supported with great ingenuity.

We returned to our college on a Sunday afternoon: the peasants were dancing, and everyone we met appeared gay and happy. My own spirits were high, and I bounded along with feelings of unbridled joy and hilarity.

Chapter 7

O n my return, I found the following letter from my father: –

MY DEAR VICTOR,

You have probably waited impatiently for a letter to fix the date of your return to us; and I was at first tempted to write only a few lines, merely mentioning the day on which I should expect you. But that would be a cruel kindness, and I dare not do it. What would be your surprise, my son, when you expect a happy and glad welcome, to behold, on the contrary, tears and wretchedness? And how, Victor, can I relate our misfortune? Absence cannot have rendered you callous to our joys and griefs; and how shall I inflict pain on my long-absent son? I wish to prepare you for the woeful news, but I know it is impossible; even now your eye skims over the page, to seek the words which are to convey to you the horrible tidings.

William is dead! – that sweet child, whose smiles delighted and warmed my heart, who was so gentle, yet so gay! Victor, he is murdered!

I will not attempt to console you; but will simply relate the circumstances of the transaction.

Last Thursday (May 7th) I, my niece, and your two brothers went to walk in **Plainpalais**. The evening was warm and serene, and we prolonged our walk farther than usual. It was already dusk before we thought of returning; and then we discovered that William and Ernest, who had gone on before, were not to be found. We accordingly rested on a seat until they should return. Presently Ernest came, and enquired if we had seen his brother: he said that he had been playing with him, that William had run away to hide himself, and that he vainly sought for him, and afterwards waited for him a long time, but he did not return.

This account rather alarmed us, and we continued to search for him until night fell, when Elizabeth conjectured that he might have returned to the house. He was not there. We returned again, with torches, for I could not rest when I thought that my sweet boy had lost himself and was exposed to all the damps and dews

Plainpalais A promenade south of Geneva.

of night; Elizabeth also suffered extreme anguish. About five in the morning I discovered my lovely boy, whom the night before I had seen blooming and active in health, stretched on the grass livid and motionless: the print of the murderer's finger was on his neck.

He was conveyed home, and the anguish that was visible in my countenance betrayed the secret to Elizabeth. She was very earnest to see the corpse. At first I attempted to prevent her, but she persisted, and entering the room where it lay, hastily examined the neck of the victim, and clasping her hands, exclaimed, 'Oh, God! I have murdered my darling child!'

She fainted, and was restored with extreme difficulty. When she again lived, it was only to weep and sigh. She told me that that same evening William had teased her to let him wear a very valuable **miniature** that she possessed of your mother. This picture is gone, and was doubtless the temptation which urged the murderer to the deed. We have no trace of him at present, although our exertions to discover him are unremitted; but they will not restore my beloved William!

Come, dearest Victor; you alone can console Elizabeth. She weeps continually and accuses herself unjustly as the cause of his death; her words pierce my heart. We are all unhappy, but will not that be an additional motive for you, my son, to return and be our comforter? Your dear mother! Alas, Victor! I now say, Thank God she did not live to witness the cruel, miserable death of her youngest darling!

Come, Victor; not brooding thoughts of vengeance against the assassin, but with feelings of peace and gentleness, that will heal, instead of festering, the wounds of our minds. Enter the house of mourning, my friend, but with kindness and affection for those who love you, and not with hatred for your enemies.

Your affectionate and afflicted father,
ALPHONSE FRANKENSTEIN
Geneva, May 12th, 17–.

Clerval, who had watched my countenance as I read this letter, was surprised to observe the despair that succeeded to the joy I at first expressed on receiving news from my friends. I threw the letter on the table, and covered my face with my hands.

'My dear Frankenstein,' exclaimed Henry, when he perceived me

miniature A very small portrait, often painted on ivory.

weep with bitterness, 'are we always to be unhappy? My dear friend, what has happened?'

I motioned to him to take up the letter, while I walked up and down the room in the extremest agitation. Tears also gushed from the eyes of Clerval, as he read the account of my misfortune.

'I can offer you no consolation, my friend,' said he; 'your disaster is irreparable. What do you intend to do?'

'To go instantly to Geneva: come with me, Henry, to order the horses.'

During our walk Clerval endeavoured to say a few words of consolation; he could only express his heartfelt sympathy. 'Poor William!' said he. 'Dear lovely child, he now sleeps with his angel mother! Who that had seen him bright and joyous in his young beauty, but must weep over his untimely loss! To die so miserably; to feel the murderer's grasp! How much more a murderer, that could destroy such radiant innocence! Poor little fellow! one only consolation have we; his friends mourn and weep, but he is at rest. The pang is over, his sufferings are at an end forever. A sod covers his gentle form, and he knows no pain. He can no longer be a subject for pity; we must reserve that for his miserable survivors.'

Clerval spoke thus as we hurried through the streets; the words impressed themselves on my mind, and I remembered them afterwards in solitude. But now, as soon as the horses arrived, I hurried into a **cabriolet** and bade farewell to my friend.

My journey was very melancholy. At first I wished to hurry on, for I longed to console and sympathise with my loved and sorrowing friends; but when I drew near my native town, I slackened my progress. I could hardly sustain the multitude of feelings that crowded into my mind. I passed through scenes familiar to my youth, but which I had not seen for nearly six years. How altered every thing might be during that time! One sudden and desolating change had taken place; but a thousand little circumstances might have by degrees worked other alterations, which, although they were done more tranquilly, might not be the less decisive. Fear overcame me; I dared not advance, dreading a thousand nameless evils that made me tremble, although I was unable to define them.

I remained two days at **Lausanne**, in this painful state of mind. I contemplated the lake: the waters were placid: all around was

cabriolet Two-wheeled, one-horse carriage with two seats and a folding roof.

Lausanne Capital of the Vaud canton on the northern shore of Lake Geneva.

calm; and the snowy mountains, 'the palaces of nature', were not changed. By degrees the calm and heavenly scene restored me, and I continued my journey towards Geneva.

The road ran by the side of the lake, which became narrower as I approached my native town. I discovered more distinctly the black sides of **Jura**, and the bright summit of **Mont Blanc**. I wept like a child. 'Dear mountains! My own beautiful lake! How do you welcome your wanderer? Your summits are clear; the sky and lake are blue and placid. Is this to prognosticate peace, or to mock at my unhappiness?'

I fear, my friend, that I shall render myself tedious by dwelling on these preliminary circumstances; but they were days of comparative happiness, and I think of them with pleasure. My country, my beloved country! who but a native can tell the delight I took in again beholding thy streams, thy mountains, and, more than all, thy lovely lake!

Yet, as I drew nearer home, grief and fear again overcame me. Night also closed around; and when I could hardly see the dark mountains, I felt still more gloomily. The picture appeared a vast and dim scene of evil, and I foresaw obscurely that I was destined to become the most wretched of human beings. Alas! I prophesied truly, and failed only in one single circumstance, that in all the misery I imagined and dreaded, I did not conceive the hundredth part of the anguish I was destined to endure.

It was completely dark when I arrived in the environs of Geneva; the gates of the town were already shut; and I was obliged to pass the night at Secheron, a village at the distance of half a league from the city. The sky was serene; and as I was unable to rest, I resolved to visit the spot where my poor William had been murdered. As I could not pass through the town, I was obliged to cross the lake in a boat to arrive at Plainpalais. During this short voyage I saw the lightnings playing on the summit of Mont Blanc in the most beautiful figures. The storm appeared to approach rapidly; and, on landing, I ascended a low hill, that I might observe its progress. It advanced; the heavens were clouded, and I soon felt the rain coming slowly in large drops, but its violence quickly increased.

I quitted my seat and walked on, although the darkness and storm increased every minute and the thunder burst with a terrific crash

---

'**palaces of nature**' Quotation from Lord Byron's poem *Childe Harold's Pilgrimage*.

Jura Heavily forested mountains that run along the border between France and Switzerland.

Mont Blanc The highest peak in Europe; it marks the border between France and Italy. Mary and Percy Shelley visited Mont Blanc in 1816 and Percy Shelley wrote a poem about it.

over my head. It was echoed from Salêve, the Juras, and the Alps of Savoy; vivid flashes of lightning dazzled my eyes, illuminating the lake, making it appear like a vast sheet of fire; then for an instant every thing seemed of a pitchy darkness, until the eye recovered itself from the preceding flash. The storm, as is often the case in Switzerland, appeared at once in various parts of the heavens. The most violent storm hung exactly north of the town, over that part of the lake which lies between the promontory of Belrive and the village of Copêt. Another storm enlightened Jura with faint flashes; and another darkened and sometimes disclosed the Môle, a peaked mountain to the east of the lake.

While I watched the tempest, so beautiful yet terrific, I wandered on with a hasty step. This noble war in the sky elevated my spirits; I clasped my hands and exclaimed aloud, 'William, dear angel! this is thy funeral, this thy dirge!' As I said these words, I perceived in the gloom a figure which stole from behind a clump of trees near me; I stood fixed, gazing intently: I could not be mistaken. A flash of lightning illuminated the object, and discovered its shape plainly to me; its gigantic stature, and the deformity of its aspect, more hideous than belongs to humanity, instantly informed me that it was the wretch, the filthy daemon to whom I had given life. What did he there? Could he be (I shuddered at the conception) the murderer of my brother? No sooner did that idea cross my imagination, than I became convinced of its truth; my teeth chattered, and I was forced to lean against a tree for support. The figure passed me quickly, and I lost it in the gloom. Nothing in human shape could have destroyed that fair child. *He* was the murderer! I could not doubt it. The mere presence of the idea was an irresistible proof of the fact. I thought of pursuing the devil; but it would have been in vain, for another flash discovered him to me hanging among the rocks of the nearly perpendicular ascent of Mount Salêve, a hill that bound Plainpalais on the south. He soon reached the summit, and disappeared.

I remained motionless. The thunder ceased, but the rain still continued, and the scene was enveloped in an impenetrable darkness. I revolved in my mind the events which I had until now sought to forget: the whole train of my progress towards the creation; the appearance of the work of my own hands alive at my bedside; its departure. Two years had now nearly elapsed since the night on which he first received life; and was this his first crime? Alas! I had turned loose into the world a depraved wretch, whose delight was in carnage and misery; had he not murdered my brother?

No one can conceive the anguish I suffered during the remainder of the night, which I spent, cold and wet, in the open air. But I did not feel the inconvenience of the weather; my imagination was busy in scenes of evil and despair. I considered the being whom I had cast among mankind, and endowed with the will and power to effect purposes of horror, such as the deed which he had now done, nearly in the light of my own vampire, my own spirit let loose from the grave, and forced to destroy all that was dear to me.

Day dawned; and I directed my steps towards the town. The gates were open, and I hastened to my father's house. My first thought was to discover what I knew of the murderer, and cause instant pursuit to be made. But I paused when I reflected on the story that I had to tell. A being whom I myself had formed, and endued with life, had met me at midnight among the precipices of an inaccessible mountain. I remembered also the nervous fever with which I had been seized just at the time that I dated my creation, and which would give an air of delirium to a tale otherwise so utterly improbable. I well knew that if any other had communicated such a relation to me, I should have looked upon it as the ravings of insanity. Besides, the strange nature of the animal would elude all pursuit, even if I were so far credited as to persuade my relatives to commence it. And then of what use would be pursuit? Who could arrest a creature capable of scaling the overhanging sides of Mont Salêve? These reflections determined me, and I resolved to remain silent.

It was about five in the morning when I entered my father's house. I told the servants not to disturb the family, and went into the library to attend their usual hour of rising.

Six years had elapsed, passed as a dream but for one indelible trace, and I stood in the same place where I had last embraced my father before my departure for Ingolstadt. Beloved and venerable parent! He still remained to me. I gazed on the picture of my mother which stood over the mantel-piece. It was an historical subject, painted at my father's desire, and represented Caroline Beaufort in an agony of despair, kneeling by the coffin of her dead father. Her

garb was **rustic**, and her cheek pale; but there was an air of dignity and beauty, that hardly permitted the sentiment of pity. Below this picture was a miniature of William; and my tears flowed when I looked upon it. While I was thus engaged, Ernest entered: he had heard me arrive, and hastened to welcome me. He expressed a sorrowful delight to see me. 'Welcome, my dearest Victor,' said he. 'Ah! I wish you had come three months ago, and then you would have found us all joyous and delighted. You come to us now to share a misery which nothing can alleviate; yet your presence will, I hope, revive our father, who seems sinking under his misfortune; and your persuasions will induce poor Elizabeth to cease her vain and tormenting self-accusations. – Poor William! he was our darling and our pride!'

Tears, unrestrained, fell from my brother's eyes; a sense of mortal agony crept over my frame. Before, I had only imagined the wretchedness of my desolated home; the reality came on me as a new and a not less terrible disaster. I tried to calm Ernest; I enquired more minutely concerning my father, and her I named my cousin.

'She most of all,' said Ernest, 'requires consolation; she accused herself of having caused the death of my brother, and that made her very wretched. But since the murderer has been discovered –'

'The murderer discovered! Good God! how can that be? who could attempt to pursue him? It is impossible; one might as well try to overtake the winds or confine a mountain-stream with a straw. I saw him too; he was free last night!'

'I do not know what you mean,' replied my brother, in accents of wonder, 'but to us the discovery we have made completes our misery. No one would believe it at first; and even now Elizabeth will not be convinced, notwithstanding all the evidence. Indeed, who would credit that Justine Moritz, who was so amiable and fond of all the family, could suddenly become capable of so frightful, so appalling a crime?'

'Justine Moritz! Poor, poor girl, is she the accused? But it is wrongfully; every one knows that; no one believes it, surely, Ernest?'

'No one did at first; but several circumstances came out that have almost forced conviction upon us; and her own behaviour has been so confused as to add to the evidence of facts a weight that, I fear, leaves no hope for doubt. But she will be tried today, and you will

garb Clothing.
rustic Typical of country people or the countryside.

then hear all.'

He related that, the morning on which the murder of poor William had been discovered, Justine had been taken ill, and confined to her bed for several days. During this interval one of the servants, happening to examine the apparel she had worn on the night of the murder, had discovered in her pocket the picture of my mother, which had been judged to be the temptation of the murderer. The servant instantly showed it to one of the others, who, without saying a word to any of the family, went to a magistrate; and, upon their deposition, Justine was apprehended. On being charged with the fact, the poor girl confirmed the suspicion in a great measure by her extreme confusion of manner.

This was a strange tale, but it did not shake my faith, and I replied earnestly, 'You are all mistaken; I know the murderer. Justine, poor, good Justine, is innocent.'

At that instant my father entered. I saw unhappiness deeply impressed on his countenance, but he endeavoured to welcome me cheerfully; and after we had exchanged our mournful greeting, would have introduced some other topic than that of our disaster, had not Ernest exclaimed, 'Good God, Papa! Victor says that he knows who was the murderer of poor William.'

'We do also, unfortunately,' replied my father; 'for indeed I had rather have been forever ignorant than have discovered so much depravity and ingratitude in one I valued so highly.'

'My dear father, you are mistaken; Justine is innocent.'

'If she is, God forbid that she should suffer as guilty. She is to be tried today, and I hope, I sincerely hope, that she will be acquitted.'

This speech calmed me. I was firmly convinced in my own mind that Justine, and indeed every human being, was guiltless of this murder. I had no fear, therefore, that any **circumstantial evidence** could be brought forward strong enough to convict her. My tale was not one to announce publicly; its astounding horror would be looked upon as madness by the vulgar. Did any one indeed exist, except I, the creator, who would believe, unless his senses convinced him, in the existence of the living monument of presumption and rash ignorance which I had let loose upon the world?

We were soon joined by Elizabeth. Time had altered her since I last beheld her; it had endowed her with loveliness surpassing the

circumstantial evidence Indirect evidence that
is not conclusive.

beauty of her childish years. There was the same candour, the same **vivacity**, but it was allied to an expression more full of sensibility and intellect. She welcomed me with the greatest affection. 'Your arrival, my dear cousin,' said she, 'fills me with hope. You perhaps will find some means to justify my poor guiltless Justine. Alas! who is safe, if she be convicted of crime? I rely on her innocence as certainly as I do upon my own. Our misfortune is doubly hard to us; we have not only lost that lovely darling boy, but this poor girl, whom I sincerely love, is to be torn away by even a worse fate. If she is condemned, I never shall know joy more. But she will not, I am sure she will not; and then I shall be happy again, even after the sad death of my little William.'

'She is innocent, my Elizabeth,' said I, 'and that shall be proved; fear nothing, but let your spirits be cheered by the assurance of her acquittal.'

'How kind and generous you are! every one else believes in her guilt, and that made me wretched, for I knew that it was impossible: and to see every one else prejudiced in so deadly a manner rendered me hopeless and despairing.' She wept.

'Dearest niece,' said my father, 'dry your tears. If she is, as you believe, innocent, rely on the justice of our laws, and the activity with which I shall prevent the slightest shadow of partiality.'

vivacity Spiritual or mental vigor; liveliness.

Chapter 8

W e passed a few sad hours, until eleven o'clock, when the trial was to commence. My father and the rest of the family being obliged to attend as witnesses, I accompanied them to the court. During the whole of this wretched mockery of justice I suffered living torture. It was to be decided, whether the result of my curiosity and lawless devices would cause the death of my fellow-beings: one a smiling babe full of innocence and joy; the other far more dreadfully murdered, with every aggravation of infamy that could make the murder memorable in horror. Justine also was a girl of merit, and possessed qualities which promised to render her life happy; now all was to be obliterated in an ignominious grave, and I the cause! A thousand times rather would I have confessed myself guilty of the crime ascribed to Justine; but I was absent when it was committed, and such a declaration would have been considered as the ravings of a madman, and would not have **exculpated** her who suffered through me.

The appearance of Justine was calm. She was dressed in mourning; and her countenance, always engaging, was rendered, by the solemnity of her feelings, exquisitely beautiful. Yet she appeared confident in innocence and did not tremble, although gazed on and execrated by thousands; for all the kindness which her beauty might otherwise have excited was obliterated in the minds of the spectators by the imagination of the enormity she was supposed to have committed. She was tranquil, yet her tranquillity was evidently constrained; and as her confusion had before been adduced as a proof of her guilt, she worked up her mind to an appearance of courage. When she entered the court she threw her eyes round it, and quickly discovered where we were seated. A tear seemed to dim her eye when she saw us; but she quickly recovered herself, and a look of sorrowful affection seemed to attest her utter guiltlessness.

The trial began; and after the advocate against her had stated the charge, several witnesses were called. Several strange facts combined against her, which might have staggered any one who had not such proof of her innocence as I had. She had been out the whole of

exculpated Freed from blame.

the night on which the murder had been committed, and towards morning had been perceived by a market-woman not far from the spot where the body of the murdered child had been afterwards found. The woman asked her what she did there; but she looked very strangely, and only returned a confused and unintelligible answer. She returned to the house about eight o'clock; and when one enquired where she had passed the night, she replied that she had been looking for the child and demanded earnestly if any thing had been heard concerning him. When shown the body, she fell into violent hysterics, and kept her bed for several days. The picture was then produced, which the servant had found in her pocket; and when Elizabeth, in a faltering voice, proved that it was the same which, an hour before the child had been missed, she had placed round his neck, a murmur of horror and indignation filled the court.

Justine was called on for her defence. As the trial proceeded, her countenance had altered. Surprise, horror, and misery were strongly expressed. Sometimes she struggled with her tears; but when she was desired to plead, she collected her powers, and spoke in an audible although variable voice.

'God knows,' she said, 'how entirely I am innocent. But I do not pretend that my protestations should acquit me: I rest my innocence on a plain and simple explanation of the facts which have been adduced against me; and I hope the character I have always borne will incline my judges to a favourable interpretation, where any circumstance appears doubtful or suspicious.'

She then related that, by the permission of Elizabeth, she had passed the evening of the night on which the murder had been committed at the house of an aunt at Chêne, a village situated at about a league from Geneva. On her return, at about nine o'clock, she met a man who asked her if she had seen any thing of the child who was lost. She was alarmed by this account, and passed several hours in looking for him, when the gates of Geneva were shut, and she was forced to remain several hours of the night in a barn belonging to a cottage, being unwilling to call up the inhabitants, to whom she was well known. Most of the night she spent here watching; towards morning she believed that she slept for a few minutes; some steps disturbed her, and she awoke. It was dawn, and she quitted her **asylum**, that she might again endeavour to find

asylum Place of refuge.

my brother. If she had gone near the spot where his body lay, it was without her knowledge. That she had been bewildered when questioned by the market-woman was not surprising, since she had passed a sleepless night and the fate of poor William was yet uncertain. Concerning the picture she could give no account.

'I know,' continued the unhappy victim, 'how heavily and fatally this one circumstance weighs against me, but I have no power of explaining it; and when I have expressed my utter ignorance, I am only left to conjecture concerning the probabilities by which it might have been placed in my pocket. But here also I am checked. I believe that I have no enemy on earth, and none surely would have been so wicked as to destroy me wantonly. Did the murderer place it there? I know of no opportunity afforded him for so doing; or, if I had, why should he have stolen the jewel, to part with it again so soon?

'I commit my cause to the justice of my judges, yet I see no room for hope. I beg permission to have a few witnesses examined concerning my character; and if their testimony shall not overweigh my supposed guilt, I must be condemned, although I would pledge my salvation on my innocence.'

Several witnesses were called who had known her for many years, and they spoke well of her; but fear and hatred of the crime of which they supposed her guilty rendered them **timorous**, and unwilling to come forward. Elizabeth saw even this last resource, her excellent dispositions and irreproachable conduct, about to fail the accused, when, although violently agitated, she desired permission to address the court.

'I am,' said she, 'the cousin of the unhappy child who was murdered, or rather his sister, for I was educated by and have lived with his parents ever since and even long before, his birth. It may therefore be judged indecent in me to come forward on this occasion; but when I see a fellow creature about to perish through the cowardice of her pretended friends, I wish to be allowed to speak, that I may say what I know of her character. I am well acquainted with the accused. I have lived in the same house with her, at one time for five, and at another for nearly two years. During all that period she appeared to me the most amiable and benevolent of human creatures. She nursed Madame Frankenstein, my aunt, in

timorous Frightened, apprehensive.

her last illness, with the greatest affection and care, and afterwards attended her own mother during a tedious illness, in a manner that excited the admiration of all who knew her; after which she again lived in my uncle's house, where she was beloved by all the family. She was warmly attached to the child who is now dead, and acted towards him like a most affectionate mother. For my own part, I do not hesitate to say that, notwithstanding all the evidence produced against her, I believe and rely on her perfect innocence. She had no temptation for such an action: as to the bauble on which the chief proof rests, if she had earnestly desired it, I should have willingly given it to her; so much do I esteem and value her.'

A murmur of **approbation** followed Elizabeth's simple and powerful appeal; but it was excited by her generous interference, and not in favour of poor Justine, on whom the public indignation was turned with renewed violence, charging her with the blackest ingratitude. She herself wept as Elizabeth spoke, but she did not answer. My own agitation and anguish was extreme during the whole trial. I believed in her innocence; I knew it. Could the daemon who had (I did not for a minute doubt) murdered my brother also in his hellish sport have betrayed the innocent to death and ignominy? I could not sustain the horror of my situation, and when I perceived that the popular voice and the countenances of the judges had already condemned my unhappy victim, I rushed out of the court in agony. The tortures of the accused did not equal mine; she was sustained by innocence, but the fangs of **remorse** tore my bosom and would not forego their hold.

I passed a night of unmingled wretchedness. In the morning I went to the court; my lips and throat were parched. I dared not ask the fatal question; but I was known, and the officer guessed the cause of my visit. The **ballots** had been thrown; they were all black, and Justine was condemned.

I cannot pretend to describe what I then felt. I had before experienced sensations of horror; and I have endeavoured to bestow upon them adequate expressions, but words cannot convey an idea of the heart-sickening despair that I then endured. The person to whom I addressed myself added, that Justine had already confessed her guilt. 'That evidence,' he observed, 'was hardly required in so glaring a case, but I am glad of it; and, indeed, none of our judges

---

approbation Approval.
remorse Deep regret or guilt felt for a wrong one has done.
ballots Here, counters used in a court to indicate the judges' or jurors' decision; black

ballots indicated a verdict of guilty.

like to condemn a criminal upon circumstantial evidence, be it ever so decisive.'

This was strange and unexpected intelligence; what could it mean? Had my eyes deceived me? And was I really as mad as the whole world would believe me to be, if I disclosed the object of my suspicions? I hastened to return home, and Elizabeth eagerly demanded the result.

'My cousin,' replied I, 'it is decided as you may have expected; all judges had rather that ten innocent should suffer than that one guilty should escape. But she has confessed.'

This was a dire blow to poor Elizabeth, who had relied with firmness upon Justine's innocence. 'Alas!' said she. 'How shall I ever again believe in human goodness? Justine, whom I loved and esteemed as my sister, how could she put on those smiles of innocence only to betray? her mild eyes seemed incapable of any severity or **guile**, and yet she has committed a murder.'

Soon after we heard that the poor victim had expressed a desire to see my cousin. My father wished her not to go, but said that he left it to her own judgment and feelings to decide. 'Yes,' said Elizabeth, 'I will go, although she is guilty; and you, Victor, shall accompany me: I cannot go alone.' The idea of this visit was torture to me, yet I could not refuse.

We entered the gloomy prison chamber and beheld Justine sitting on some straw at the farther end; her hands were manacled, and her head rested on her knees. She rose on seeing us enter; and when we were left alone with her, she threw herself at the feet of Elizabeth, weeping bitterly. My cousin wept also.

'Oh, Justine!' said she. 'Why did you rob me of my last consolation? I relied on your innocence, and although I was then very wretched, I was not so miserable as I am now.'

'And do you also believe that I am so very, very wicked? Do you also join with my enemies to crush me, to condemn me as a murderer?' Her voice was suffocated with sobs.

'Rise, my poor girl,' said Elizabeth; 'why do you kneel, if you are innocent? I am not one of your enemies; I believed you guiltless, notwithstanding every evidence, until I heard that you had yourself declared your guilt. That report, you say, is false; and be assured, dear Justine, that nothing can shake my confidence in you for a moment, but your own confession.'

guile Deceit, treachery.

'I did confess; but I confessed a lie. I confessed, that I might obtain **absolution**; but now that falsehood lies heavier at my heart than all my other sins. The God of heaven forgive me! Ever since I was condemned, my confessor has besieged me; he threatened and menaced, until I almost began to think that I was the monster that he said I was. He threatened **excommunication** and hell fire in my last moments if I continued **obdurate**. Dear lady, I had none to support me; all looked on me as a wretch doomed to ignominy and **perdition**. What could I do? In an evil hour I subscribed to a lie; and now only am I truly miserable.'

She paused, weeping, and then continued – 'I thought with horror, my sweet lady, that you should believe your Justine, whom your blessed aunt had so highly honoured and whom you loved, was a creature capable of a crime which none but the devil himself could have perpetrated. Dear William! Dearest blessed child! I soon shall see you again in heaven, where we shall all be happy; and that consoles me, going as I am to suffer ignominy and death.'

'Oh, Justine! Forgive me for having for one moment distrusted you. Why did you confess? But do not mourn, dear girl. Do not fear. I will proclaim, I will prove your innocence. I will melt the stony hearts of your enemies by my tears and prayers. You shall not die! You, my playfellow, my companion, my sister, perish on the scaffold! No! No! I never could survive so horrible a misfortune.'

Justine shook her head mournfully. 'I do not fear to die,' she said; 'that pang is past. God raises my weakness and gives me courage to endure the worst. I leave a sad and bitter world; and if you remember me and think of me as of one unjustly condemned, I am resigned to the fate awaiting me. Learn from me, dear lady, to submit in patience to the will of heaven!'

During this conversation I had retired to the corner of the prison room, where I could conceal the horrid anguish that possessed me. Despair! Who dared talk of that? The poor victim, who on the morrow was to pass the awful boundary between life and death, felt not, as I did, such deep and bitter agony. I gnashed my teeth and ground them together, uttering a groan that came from my inmost soul. Justine started. When she saw who it was, she approached me and said, 'Dear sir, you are very kind to visit me; you, I hope, do not believe that I am guilty?'

---

absolution Release from punishment for a person's sins; in the Roman Catholic Church, a priest may declare absolution after sins have been confessed.

excommunication Exclusion from a religious community; especially, banning from Christian Holy Communion.

obdurate Stubborn.

perdition Spiritual damnation, hell.

I could not answer. 'No, Justine,' said Elizabeth; 'he is more convinced of your innocence than I was; for even when he heard that you had confessed, he did not credit it.'

'I truly thank him. In these last moments I feel the sincerest gratitude towards those who think of me with kindness. How sweet is the affection of others to such a wretch as I am! It removes more than half my misfortune; and I feel as if I could die in peace, now that my innocence is acknowledged by you, dear lady, and your cousin.'

Thus the poor sufferer tried to comfort others and herself. She indeed gained the resignation she desired. But I, the true murderer, felt the never-dying worm alive in my bosom, which allowed of no hope or consolation. Elizabeth also wept and was unhappy; but hers also was the misery of innocence, which, like a cloud that passes over the fair moon, for a while hides but cannot tarnish its brightness. Anguish and despair had penetrated into the core of my heart; I bore a hell within me which nothing could extinguish. We stayed several hours with Justine; and it was with great difficulty that Elizabeth could tear herself away. 'I wish,' cried she, 'that I were to die with you; I cannot live in this world of misery.'

Justine assumed an air of cheerfulness, while she with difficulty repressed her bitter tears. She embraced Elizabeth and said, in a voice of half-suppressed emotion, 'Farewell, sweet lady, dearest Elizabeth, my beloved and only friend; may Heaven, in its bounty, bless and preserve you; may this be the last misfortune that you will ever suffer! Live, and be happy, and make others so.'

And on the morrow Justine died. Elizabeth's heart-rending eloquence failed to move the judges from their settled conviction in the criminality of the saintly sufferer. My passionate and indignant appeals were lost upon them. And when I received their cold answers and heard the harsh, unfeeling reasoning of these men, my purposed avowal died away on my lips. Thus I might proclaim myself a madman, but not revoke the sentence passed upon my wretched victim. She perished on the scaffold as a murderess!

From the tortures of my own heart, I turned to contemplate the deep and voiceless grief of my Elizabeth. This also was my doing! And my father's woe, and the desolation of that late so smiling home – all was the work of my thrice-accursed hands! Ye weep,

unhappy ones; but these are not your last tears! Again shall you raise
the funeral wail, and the sound of your lamentations shall again and
again be heard! Frankenstein, your son, your kinsman, your early,
much-loved friend; he who would spend each vital drop of blood
for your sakes – who has no thought nor sense of joy, except as it
is mirrored also in your dear countenances – who would fill the air
with blessings and spend his life in serving you – he bids you weep
– to shed countless tears; happy beyond his hopes, if thus inexorable
fate be satisfied, and if the destruction pause before the peace of the
grave have succeeded to your sad torments!

Thus spoke my prophetic soul, as, torn by remorse, horror, and
despair, I beheld those I loved spend vain sorrow upon the graves
of William and Justine, the first hapless victims to my **unhallowed
arts.**

END OF VOLUME ONE

unhallowed arts Ungodly or unnatural scientific
activities.

Lightning
*People have
always been
fascinated by
thunderstorms,
but in the
18th century
scientists first
realized that
lightning is
caused by
electricity.*

Science in Mary Shelley's time

What was the secret of life? What was it that made the difference between a living thing and something lifeless? In Mary Shelley's time, scientists thought a lot about these questions and so does Victor Frankenstein, whose research begins with the question, "Whence…did the principle of life proceed?" One answer that the scientists of the 18th century came up with was electricity. Although they had not yet discovered how to generate electricity, they knew that lightning was an electrical phenomenon. In 1800, the Italian scientist Alessandro Volta (1745–1827) created the first battery.

Animal electricity

In the late 18th century, another Italian, Luigi Galvani (1737–98) carried out some experiments with dead frogs. He found that when he touched the frogs' legs with metal rods, the legs twitched. Galvani thought that the reason for this was that the bodies of the frogs contained "animal electricity." We now know that animals do produce electricity, but not in the way Galvani supposed. What was probably happening with Galvani's frogs was that contact with the metal rods was causing a chemical reaction in the legs and this reaction produced electricity. In other words, the metal rods turned the frogs' legs into a simple battery.

Galvanism

Volta called the magical movement of the frogs' legs "galvanism." Many people believed Galvani's explanation of it, and thought that electricity was the mysterious force that gave animals the spark of life. Some even believed that if electricity was the "vital spark," then applying an electric current to a dead creature would

A GALVANISED CORPSE

Galvanism

Angry devils look on as a 19th-century scientist uses electricity to bring a corpse back to life in this engraving.

bring the corpse back to life. Galvani's nephew Giovanni Aldini (1762–1834), was a keen supporter of the idea. He used one of Volta's batteries to apply a current to the bodies of dead animals. When their muscles twitched like the frogs' legs, he went on to try the experiment with human corpses, sometimes in public demonstrations of his work. The same thing happened. It looked as if the dead bodies were on the point of coming back to life. Aldini also used electrical currents to try to treat people with mental illnesses, and sometimes he was successful.

Erasmus Darwin

In Britain, one of the most famous scientists to show an interest in galvanism was Erasmus Darwin (1731–1802). Some of his ideas about the development of living species were surprisingly close to those his grandson, Charles Darwin, developed in his famous theory of evolution. Erasmus Darwin carried out experiments with galvanism, and also wrote about how creatures such as worms might be created from non-living material. The scientist was one of the many friends of Mary Shelley's father, William Godwin, and he was also much admired by Mary's husband, Percy Shelley. She recalls in her Introduction to *Frankenstein* how she and her friends discussed Darwin's work, and wondered whether a corpse could be brought back to life with a "powerful engine," in other words an electrical device such as one of Volta's batteries.

Frankenstein's science

In the novel, Victor Frankenstein is fascinated by electricity and its power. In Volume One, Chapter 2 he watches a tree being struck by lightning and afterwards a scientist friend explains to him the exciting theories of galvanism. Frankenstein uses these ideas when he gives life to his Creature, discovering how to do so after days and nights of solitary, obsessive work. Although many scientists did not believe in theories of "animal electricity," such ideas were well known at the time and would not have seemed quite as odd to Mary Shelley and her friends as they do to us. They would have shared some of Frankenstein's fascination with the power of electricity and its apparent ability to bring the dead to life.

Volume Two

Chapter 1

Nothing is more painful to the human mind than, after the
feelings have been worked up by a quick succession of events,
the dead calmness of inaction and certainty which follows and
deprives the soul both of hope and fear. Justine died; she rested;
and I was alive. The blood flowed freely in my veins, but a weight
of despair and remorse pressed on my heart, which nothing could
remove. Sleep fled from my eyes; I wandered like an evil spirit, for
I had committed deeds of mischief beyond description horrible,
and more, much more (I persuaded myself) was yet behind. Yet my
heart overflowed with kindness, and the love of virtue. I had begun
life with benevolent intentions, and thirsted for the moment when
I should put them in practice and make myself useful to my fellow
beings. Now all was blasted: instead of that serenity of conscience
which allowed me to look back upon the past with self-satisfaction,
and from thence to gather promise of new hopes, I was seized by
remorse and the sense of guilt, which hurried me away to a hell of
intense tortures, such as no language can describe.

This state of mind preyed upon my health, which had perhaps
never entirely recovered from the first shock it had sustained. I
shunned the face of man; all sound of joy or complacency was
torture to me; solitude was my only consolation – deep, dark,
deathlike solitude.

My father observed with pain the alteration perceptible in my
disposition and habits, and endeavoured by arguments, deduced from
the feelings of his serene conscience and guiltless life, to inspire me
with fortitude, and awaken in me the courage to dispel the dark
cloud which brooded over me. 'Do you think, Victor,' said he, 'that
I do not suffer also? No one could love a child more than I loved
your brother' – tears came into his eyes as he spoke – 'but is it not a
duty to the survivors that we should refrain from augmenting their
unhappiness by an appearance of immoderate grief? It is also a duty
owed to yourself; for excessive sorrow prevents improvement or
enjoyment, or even the discharge of daily usefulness, without which
no man is fit for society.'

This advice, although good, was totally inapplicable to my case; I should have been the first to hide my grief and console my friends, if remorse had not mingled its bitterness, and terror its alarm, with my other sensations. Now I could only answer my father with a look of despair, and endeavour to hide myself from his view.

About this time we retired to our house at Belrive. This change was particularly agreeable to me. The shutting of the gates regularly at ten o'clock and the impossibility of remaining on the lake after that hour, had rendered our residence within the walls of Geneva very irksome to me. I was now free. Often, after the rest of the family had retired for the night, I took the boat and passed many hours upon the water. Sometimes, with my sails set, I was carried by the wind; and sometimes, after rowing into the middle of the lake, I left the boat to pursue its own course, and gave way to my own miserable reflections. I was often tempted, when all was at peace around me, and I the only unquiet thing that wandered restless in a scene so beautiful and heavenly – if I except some bat, or the frogs, whose harsh and interrupted croaking was heard only when I approached the shore – often, I say, I was tempted to plunge into the silent lake, that the waters might close over me and my **calamities** forever. But I was restrained, when I thought of the heroic and suffering Elizabeth, whom I tenderly loved, and whose existence was bound up in mine. I thought also of my father and surviving brother: should I by my base desertion leave them exposed and unprotected to the malice of the fiend whom I had let loose among them?

At these moments I wept bitterly, and wished that peace would revisit my mind only that I might afford them consolation and happiness. But that could not be. Remorse extinguished every hope. I had been the author of unalterable evils, and I lived in daily fear lest the monster whom I had created should perpetrate some new wickedness. I had an obscure feeling that all was not over, and that he would still commit some signal crime, which by its enormity should almost **efface** the recollection of the past. There was always scope for fear, so long as anything I loved remained behind. My abhorrence of this fiend cannot be conceived. When I thought of him I gnashed my teeth, my eyes became inflamed, and I ardently wished to extinguish that life which I had so thoughtlessly bestowed. When I reflected on his crimes and malice, my hatred and revenge

calamities Troubles, misfortunes.
efface Obliterate, wipe out.

burst all bounds of moderation. I would have made a pilgrimage to the highest peak of the Andes, could I, when there, have precipitated him to their base. I wished to see him again, that I might wreak the utmost extent of abhorrence on his head, and avenge the deaths of William and Justine.

Our house was the house of mourning. My father's health was deeply shaken by the horror of the recent events. Elizabeth was sad and **desponding**; she no longer took delight in her ordinary occupations; all pleasure seemed to her sacrilege toward the dead; eternal woe and tears she then thought was the just tribute she should pay to innocence so blasted and destroyed. She was no longer that happy creature who in earlier youth wandered with me on the banks of the lake, and talked with ecstasy of our future prospects. The first of these sorrows which are sent to wean us from the earth, had visited her, and its dimming influence quenched her dearest smiles.

'When I reflect, my dear cousin,' said she, 'on the miserable death of Justine Moritz, I no longer see the world and its works as they before appeared to me. Before, I looked upon the accounts of vice and injustice, that I read in books or heard from others as tales of ancient days or imaginary evils; at least they were remote and more familiar to reason than to the imagination; but now misery has come home, and men appear to me as monsters thirsting for each other's blood. Yet I am certainly unjust. Every body believed that poor girl to be guilty; and if she could have committed the crime for which she suffered, assuredly she would have been the most depraved of human creatures. For the sake of a few jewels, to have murdered the son of her benefactor and friend, a child whom she had nursed from its birth, and appeared to love as if it had been her own! I could not consent to the death of any human being; but certainly I should have thought such a creature unfit to remain in the society of men. But she was innocent. I know, I feel, she was innocent; you are of the same opinion, and that confirms me. Alas! Victor, when falsehood can look so like the truth, who can assure themselves of certain happiness? I feel as if I were walking on the edge of a precipice, towards which thousands are crowding, and endeavouring to plunge me into the abyss. William and Justine were assassinated, and the murderer escapes: he walks about the world free, and perhaps

desponding Dejected, lacking in hope.

respected. But even if I were condemned to suffer on the scaffold for the same crimes, I would not change places with such a wretch.'

I listened to this discourse with the extremest agony. I, not in deed, but in effect, was the true murderer. Elizabeth read my anguish in my countenance, and kindly taking my hand, said, 'My dearest friend, you must calm yourself. These events have affected me, God knows how deeply; but I am not so wretched as you are. There is an expression of despair, and sometimes of revenge, in your countenance that makes me tremble. Dear Victor, banish these dark passions. Remember the friends around you, who centre all their hopes in you. Have we lost the power of rendering you happy? Ah! while we love – while we are true to each other, here in this land of peace and beauty, your native country, we may reap every tranquil blessing – what can disturb our peace?'

And could not such words from her whom I fondly prized before every other gift of fortune, suffice to chase away the fiend that lurked in my heart? Even as she spoke I drew near to her, as if in terror; lest at that very moment the destroyer had been near to rob me of her.

Thus not the tenderness of friendship, nor the beauty of earth, nor of heaven, could redeem my soul from woe: the very accents of love were ineffectual. I was encompassed by a cloud which no beneficial influence could penetrate. The wounded deer dragging its fainting limbs to some untrodden **brake**, there to gaze upon the arrow which had pierced it, and to die – was but a type of me.

Sometimes I could cope with the sullen despair that overwhelmed me: but sometimes the whirlwind passions of my soul drove me to seek, by bodily exercise and by change of place, some relief from my intolerable sensations. It was during an **access** of this kind that I suddenly left my home, and bending my steps towards the near Alpine valleys, sought in the magnificence, the eternity of such scenes, to forget myself and my **ephemeral**, because human, sorrows. My wanderings were directed towards the valley of **Chamounix**. I had visited it frequently during my boyhood. Six years had passed since then: *I* was a wreck – but nought had changed in those savage and enduring scenes.

I performed the first part of my journey on horseback. I afterwards hired a mule, as the more sure-footed and least liable to receive

brake Overgrown area or thicket.
access Passionate outburst.
ephemeral Short-lived, transitory.
Chamounix A valley at the foot of Mont Blanc.

Percy Shelley describes the valley in *History of a Six Weeks' Tour.*

injury on these rugged roads. The weather was fine: it was about the middle of the month of August, nearly two months after the death of Justine; that miserable epoch from which I dated all my woe. The weight upon my spirit was sensibly lightened as I plunged yet deeper in the ravine of Arve. The immense mountains and precipices that overhung me on every side – the sound of the river raging among the rocks, and the dashing of the waterfalls around, spoke of a power mighty as Omnipotence – and I ceased to fear, or to bend before any being less almighty than that which had created and ruled the elements, here displayed in their most terrific guise. Still, as I ascended higher, the valley assumed a more magnificent and astonishing character. Ruined castles hanging on the precipices of piny mountains; the impetuous Arve, and cottages every here and there peeping forth from among the trees, formed a scene of singular beauty. But it was augmented and rendered sublime by the mighty Alps, whose white and shining pyramids and domes towered above all, as belonging to another earth, the habitations of another race of beings.

I passed the bridge of Pélissier, where the ravine, which the river forms, opened before me, and I began to ascend the mountain that overhangs it. Soon after I entered the valley of Chamounix. This valley is more wonderful and sublime, but not so beautiful and picturesque, as that of Servox, through which I had just passed. The high and snowy mountains were its immediate boundaries; but I saw no more ruined castles and fertile fields. Immense glaciers approached the road; I heard the rumbling thunder of the falling avalanche and marked the smoke of its passage. Mont Blanc, the supreme and magnificent Mont Blanc, raised itself from the surrounding *aiguilles*, and its tremendous **dôme** overlooked the valley.

A tingling long-lost sense of pleasure often came across me during this journey. Some turn in the road, some new object suddenly **perceived** and recognised, reminded me of days gone by, and were associated with the light-hearted gaiety of boyhood. The very winds whispered in soothing accents, and maternal nature bade me weep no more. Then again the kindly influence ceased to act – I found myself fettered again to grief and indulging in all the misery of reflection. Then I spurred on my animal, striving so to forget the

aiguilles French: peaks (literally: needles).
dôme French: summit of a mountain or hill.
perceived Grasped mentally; observed.

world, my fears, and more than all, myself – or, in a more desperate
fashion, I alighted and threw myself on the grass, weighed down by
horror and despair.

At length I arrived at the village of Chamounix. Exhaustion
succeeded to the extreme fatigue both of body and of mind which
I had endured. For a short space of time I remained at the window,
watching the pallid lightnings that played above Mont Blanc, and
listening to the rushing of the Arve, which pursued its noisy way
beneath. The same lulling sounds acted as a lullaby to my too keen
sensations: when I placed my head upon my pillow, sleep crept over
me; I felt it as it came and blest the giver of oblivion.

Chapter 2

I spent the following day roaming through the valley. I stood beside the sources of the **Arveiron**, which take their rise in a glacier, that with slow pace is advancing down from the summit of the hills, to barricade the valley. The abrupt sides of vast mountains were before me; the icy wall of the glacier overhung me; a few shattered pines were scattered around; and the solemn silence of this glorious presence-chamber of imperial Nature was broken only by the brawling waves or the fall of some vast fragment, the thunder sound of the avalanche or the cracking, reverberated along the mountains, of the accumulated ice, which, through the silent working of immutable laws, was ever and anon rent and torn, as if it had been but a plaything in their hands. These sublime and magnificent scenes afforded me the greatest consolation that I was capable of receiving. They elevated me from all littleness of feeling; and although they did not remove my grief, they subdued and tranquillised it. In some degree, also, they diverted my mind from the thoughts over which it had brooded for the last month. I retired to rest at night; my slumbers, as it were, waited on and ministered to by the assemblance of grand shapes which I had contemplated during the day. They congregated round me; the unstained snowy mountain-top, the glittering pinnacle, the pine woods, and ragged bare ravine, the eagle, soaring amidst the clouds – they all gathered round me and bade me be at peace.

Where had they fled when the next morning I awoke? All of soul-inspiriting fled with sleep, and dark melancholy clouded every thought. The rain was pouring in torrents, and thick mists hid the summits of the mountains, so that I even saw not the faces of those mighty friends. Still I would penetrate their misty veil and seek them in their cloudy retreats. What were rain and storm to me? My mule was brought to the door, and I resolved to ascend to the summit of Montanvert. I remembered the effect that the view of the tremendous and ever-moving glacier had produced upon my mind when I first saw it. It had then filled me with a sublime ecstasy, that gave wings to the soul, and allowed it to soar from the obscure world

Arveiron A river near Mont Blanc.

to light and joy. The sight of the awful and majestic in nature had indeed always the effect of solemnising my mind and causing me to forget the passing cares of life. I determined to go without a guide, for I was well acquainted with the path, and the presence of another would destroy the solitary grandeur of the scene.

The ascent is precipitous, but the path is cut into continual and short windings, which enable you to surmount the perpendicularity of the mountain. It is a scene terrifically desolate. In a thousand spots the traces of the winter avalanche may be perceived, where trees lie broken and strewed on the ground; some entirely destroyed, others bent, leaning upon the jutting rocks of the mountain or transversely upon other trees. The path, as you ascend higher, is intersected by ravines of snow, down which stones continually roll from above; one of them is particularly dangerous, as the slightest sound, such as even speaking in a loud voice, produces a concussion of air sufficient to draw destruction upon the head of the speaker. The pines are not tall or luxuriant, but they are sombre and add an air of severity to the scene. I looked on the valley beneath; vast mists were rising from the rivers which ran through it and curling in thick wreaths around the opposite mountains, whose summits were hid in the uniform clouds, while rain poured from the dark sky, and added to the melancholy impression I received from the objects around me. Alas! why does man boast of sensibilities superior to those apparent in the brute; it only renders them more necessary beings. If our impulses were confined to hunger, thirst, and desire, we might be nearly free; but now we are moved by every wind that blows and a chance word or scene that that word may convey to us.

> We rest; a dream has power to poison sleep.
> We rise; one wand'ring thought pollutes the day.
> We feel, conceive, or reason; laugh or weep,
> Embrace fond woe, or cast our cares away;
> It is the same: for, be it joy or sorrow,
> The path of its departure still is free.
> Man's yesterday may ne'er be like his morrow;
> Nought may endure but **mutability**!

It was nearly noon when I arrived at the top of the ascent. For

---

mutability Changeability; the quotation is the last part of Percy Bysshe Shelley's poem *Mutability*.

some time I sat upon the rock that overlooks the sea of ice. A mist covered both that and the surrounding mountains. Presently a breeze dissipated the cloud, and I descended upon the glacier. The surface is very uneven, rising like the waves of a troubled sea, descending low, and interspersed by rifts that sink deep. The field of ice is almost a league in width, but I spent nearly two hours in crossing it. The opposite mountain is a bare perpendicular rock. From the side where I now stood Montanvert was exactly opposite, at the distance of a league; and above it rose Mont Blanc, in awful majesty. I remained in a recess of the rock, gazing on this wonderful and stupendous scene. The sea, or rather the vast river of ice, wound among its dependent mountains, whose aerial summits hung over its recesses. Their icy and glittering peaks shone in the sunlight over the clouds. My heart, which was before sorrowful, now swelled with something like joy; I exclaimed – 'Wandering spirits, if indeed ye wander, and do not rest in your narrow beds, allow me this faint happiness, or take me, as your companion, away from the joys of life.'

As I said this, I suddenly beheld the figure of a man, at some distance, advancing towards me with superhuman speed. He bounded over the crevices in the ice, among which I had walked with caution; his stature, also, as he approached, seemed to exceed that of man. I was troubled: a mist came over my eyes, and I felt a faintness seize me; but I was quickly restored by the cold gale of the mountains. I perceived, as the shape came nearer (sight tremendous and abhorred!) that it was the wretch whom I had created. I trembled with rage and horror, resolving to wait his approach, and then close with him in mortal combat. He approached; his countenance bespoke bitter anguish, combined with disdain and **malignity**, while its unearthly ugliness rendered it almost too horrible for human eyes. But I scarcely observed this; rage and hatred had at first deprived me of utterance, and I recovered only to overwhelm him with words expressive of furious detestation and contempt.

'Devil,' I exclaimed, 'do you dare approach me? and do not you fear the fierce vengeance of my arm wreaked on your miserable head? Begone, vile insect! or rather, stay, that I may trample you to dust! and, oh! that I could, with the extinction of your miserable existence, restore those victims whom you have so

malignity Deep-rooted ill will, hatred.

diabolically murdered!'

'I expected this reception,' said the daemon. 'All men hate the wretched; how, then, must I be hated, who am miserable beyond all living things! Yet you, my creator, detest and spurn me, thy creature, to whom thou art bound by ties only dissoluble by the annihilation of one of us. You purpose to kill me. How dare you sport thus with life? Do your duty towards me, and I will do mine towards you and the rest of mankind. If you will comply with my conditions, I will leave them and you at peace; but if you refuse, I will **glut the maw** of death, until it be **satiated** with the blood of your remaining friends.'

'Abhorred monster! fiend that thou art! the tortures of hell are too mild a vengeance for thy crimes. Wretched devil! you reproach me with your creation; come on, then, that I may extinguish the spark which I so negligently bestowed.'

My rage was without bounds; I sprang on him, impelled by all the feelings which can arm one being against the existence of another.

He easily eluded me, and said –

'Be calm! I intreat you to hear me, before you give vent to your hatred on my devoted head. Have I not suffered enough, that you seek to increase my misery? Life, although it may only be an accumulation of anguish, is dear to me, and I will defend it. Remember, thou hast made me more powerful than thyself; my height is superior to thine, my joints more supple. But I will not be tempted to set myself in opposition to thee. I am thy creature, and I will be even mild and docile to my natural lord and king, if thou wilt also perform thy part, the which thou owest me. Oh, Frankenstein, be not equitable to every other and trample upon me alone, to whom thy justice, and even thy **clemency** and affection, is most due. Remember, that I am thy creature; I ought to be thy Adam, but I am rather the fallen angel, whom thou drivest from joy for no misdeed. Everywhere I see bliss, from which I alone am **irrevocably** excluded. I was benevolent and good; misery made me a fiend. Make me happy, and I shall again be virtuous.'

'Begone! I will not hear you. There can be no community between you and me; we are enemies. Begone, or let us try our strength in a fight in which one must fall.'

'How can I move thee? Will no intreaties cause thee to turn a

glut the maw Overfeed the stomach; the creature is imagining death as a living being who he is feeding with his murder victims.

satiated Satisfied fully or to excess.

clemency Mercy, leniency.

irrevocably In a way that cannot be undone; unalterably.

favourable eye upon thy creature, who implores thy goodness and compassion? Believe me, Frankenstein: I was benevolent; my soul glowed with love and humanity; but am I not alone, miserably alone? You, my creator, abhor me; what hope can I gather from your fellow-creatures, who owe me nothing? they spurn and hate me. The desert mountains and dreary glaciers are my refuge. I have wandered here many days; the caves of ice, which I only do not fear, are a dwelling to me, and the only one which man does not grudge. These bleak skies I hail, for they are kinder to me than your fellow beings. If the multitude of mankind knew of my existence, they would do as you do, and arm themselves for my destruction. Shall I not then hate them who abhor me? I will keep no terms with my enemies. I am miserable, and they shall share my wretchedness. Yet it is in your power to recompense me, and deliver them from an evil which it only remains for you to make so great, that not only you and your family, but thousands of others, shall be swallowed up in the whirlwinds of its rage. Let your compassion be moved, and do not disdain me. Listen to my tale: when you have heard that, abandon or commiserate me, as you shall judge that I deserve. But hear me. The guilty are allowed, by human laws, bloody as they are, to speak in their own defence before they are condemned. Listen to me, Frankenstein. You accuse me of murder, and yet you would, with a satisfied conscience, destroy your own creature. Oh, praise the eternal justice of man! Yet I ask you not to spare me: listen to me; and then, if you can, and if you will, destroy the work of your hands.'

'Why do you call to my remembrance,' I rejoined, 'circumstances, of which I shudder to reflect, that I have been the miserable origin and author? Cursed be the day, abhorred devil, in which you first saw light! Cursed (although I curse myself) be the hands that formed you! You have made me wretched beyond expression. You have left me no power to consider whether I am just to you, or not. Begone! relieve me from the sight of your detested form.'

'Thus I relieve thee, my creator,' he said, and placed his hated hands before my eyes, which I flung from me with violence; 'thus I take from thee a sight which you abhor. Still thou canst listen to me and grant me thy compassion. By the virtues that I once possessed, I demand this from you. Hear my tale; it is long and strange, and the temperature of this place is not fitting to your fine sensations; come to the hut upon the mountain. The sun is yet high in the heavens; before it descends to hide itself beyond yon snowy precipices, and illuminate another world, you will have heard my story and can decide. On you it rests, whether I quit forever the neighbourhood of man and lead a harmless life, or become the scourge of your fellow creatures, and the author of your own speedy ruin.'

As he said this, he led the way across the ice: I followed. My heart was full, and I did not answer him; but as I proceeded, I weighed the various arguments that he had used, and determined at least to listen to his tale. I was partly urged by curiosity, and compassion confirmed my resolution. I had hitherto supposed him to be the murderer of my brother, and I eagerly sought a confirmation or denial of this opinion. For the first time, also, I felt what the duties of a creator towards his creature were, and that I ought to render him happy before I complained of his wickedness. These motives urged me to comply with his demand. We crossed the ice, therefore, and ascended the opposite rock. The air was cold, and the rain again began to descend: we entered the hut, the fiend with an air of exultation, I with a heavy heart and depressed spirits. But I consented to listen, and seating myself by the fire which my odious companion had lighted, he thus began his tale.

Chapter 3

'It is with considerable difficulty that I remember the original era of my being: all the events of that period appear confused and indistinct. A strange multiplicity of sensations seized me, and I saw, felt, heard, and smelt at the same time; and it was, indeed, a long time before I learned to distinguish between the operations of my various senses. By degrees, I remember, a stronger light pressed upon my nerves, so that I was obliged to shut my eyes. Darkness then came over me, and troubled me; but hardly had I felt this when, by opening my eyes, as I now suppose, the light poured in upon me again. I walked and, I believe, descended; but I presently found a great alteration in my sensations. Before, dark and opaque bodies had surrounded me, impervious to my touch or sight; but I now found that I could wander on at liberty, with no obstacles which I could not either surmount or avoid. The light became more and more oppressive to me; and the heat wearying me as I walked, I sought a place where I could receive shade. This was the forest near Ingolstadt; and here I lay by the side of a brook resting from my fatigue, until I felt tormented by hunger and thirst. This roused me from my nearly dormant state, and I ate some berries which I found hanging on the trees or lying on the ground. I **slaked** my thirst at the brook; and then lying down, was overcome by sleep.

'It was dark when I awoke; I felt cold also, and half frightened, as it were, instinctively, finding myself so desolate. Before I had quitted your apartment, on a sensation of cold, I had covered myself with some clothes; but these were insufficient to secure me from the dews of night. I was a poor, helpless, miserable wretch; I knew, and could distinguish, nothing; but feeling pain invade me on all sides, I sat down and wept.

'Soon a gentle light stole over the heavens, and gave me a sensation of pleasure. I started up and beheld a radiant form rise from among the trees.* I gazed with a kind of wonder. It moved slowly, but it enlightened my path, and I again went out in search of berries. I was still cold when under one of the trees I found a huge cloak, with which I covered myself, and sat down upon the ground. No distinct

slaked Quenched or satisfied.
* The moon [author's footnote].

ideas occupied my mind; all was confused. I felt light, and hunger, and thirst, and darkness; **innumerable** sounds rang in my ears, and on all sides various scents saluted me: the only object that I could distinguish was the bright moon, and I fixed my eyes on that with pleasure.

'Several changes of day and night passed, and the orb of night had greatly lessened, when I began to distinguish my sensations from each other. I gradually saw plainly the clear stream that supplied me with drink, and the trees that shaded me with their foliage. I was delighted when I first discovered that a pleasant sound, which often saluted my ears, proceeded from the throats of the little winged animals who had often intercepted the light from my eyes. I began also to observe, with greater accuracy, the forms that surrounded me, and to perceive the boundaries of the radiant roof of light which canopied me. Sometimes I tried to imitate the pleasant songs of the birds, but was unable. Sometimes I wished to express my sensations in my own mode, but the uncouth and inarticulate sounds which broke from me frightened me into silence again.

'The moon had disappeared from the night, and again, with a lessened form, showed itself, while I still remained in the forest. My sensations had by this time become distinct, and my mind received every day additional ideas. My eyes became accustomed to the light and to perceive objects in their right forms; I distinguished the insect from the herb, and by degrees, one herb from another. I found that the sparrow uttered none but harsh notes, whilst those of the blackbird and thrush were sweet and enticing.

'One day, when I was oppressed by cold, I found a fire which had been left by some wandering beggars, and was overcome with delight at the warmth I experienced from it. In my joy I thrust my hand into the live embers, but quickly drew it out again with a cry of pain. How strange, I thought, that the same cause should produce such opposite effects! I examined the materials of the fire, and to my joy found it to be composed of wood. I quickly collected some branches; but they were wet and would not burn. I was pained at this; and sat still watching the operation of the fire. The wet wood which I had placed near the heat dried, and itself became inflamed. I reflected on this; and by touching the various branches, I discovered the cause, and busied myself in collecting a great quantity of wood,

innumerable Too many to be counted.

that I might dry it and have a plentiful supply of fire. When night
came on and brought sleep with it, I was in the greatest fear lest my
fire should be extinguished. I covered it carefully with dry wood
and leaves, and placed wet branches upon it; and then, spreading my
cloak, I lay on the ground, and sunk into sleep.

'It was morning when I awoke, and my first care was to visit the
fire. I uncovered it, and a gentle breeze quickly fanned it into a
flame. I observed this also and contrived a fan of branches, which
roused the embers when they were nearly extinguished. When
night came again I found, with pleasure, that the fire gave light as
well as heat; and that the discovery of this element was useful to
me in my food, for I found some of the offals that the travellers
had left had been roasted, and tasted much more savoury than the
berries I gathered from the trees. I tried, therefore, to dress my food
in the same manner, placing it on the live embers. I found that the
berries were spoiled by this operation, and the nuts and roots
much improved.

'Food, however, became scarce; and I often spent the whole day
searching in vain for a few acorns to assuage the pangs of hunger.
When I found this, I resolved to quit the place that I had hitherto
inhabited, to seek for one where the few wants I experienced would
be more easily satisfied. In this emigration, I exceedingly lamented
the loss of the fire which I had obtained through accident, and
knew not how to reproduce it. I gave several hours to the serious
consideration of this difficulty; but I was obliged to relinquish all
attempts to supply it; and, wrapping myself up in my cloak, I struck
across the wood towards the setting sun. I passed three days in these
rambles, and at length discovered the open country. A great fall of
snow had taken place the night before, and the fields were of one
uniform white; the appearance was disconsolate, and I found my feet
chilled by the cold damp outside that covered the ground.

'It was about seven in the morning, and I longed to obtain
food and shelter; at length I perceived a small hut, on a rising
ground, which had doubtless been built for the convenience of
some shepherd. This was a new sight to me; and I examined the
structure; with great curiosity. Finding the door open, I entered.
An old man sat in it, near a fire, over which he was preparing
his breakfast. He turned on hearing a noise; and perceiving me,

shrieked loudly, and quitting the hut, ran across the fields with a speed of which his debilitated form hardly appeared capable. His appearance, different from any I had ever before seen, and his flight, somewhat surprised me. But I was enchanted by the appearance of the hut: here the snow and rain could not penetrate; the ground was dry; and it presented to me then as exquisite and divine a retreat as **Pandaemonium** appeared to the daemons of hell after their sufferings in the lake of fire. I greedily devoured the remnants of the shepherd's breakfast, which consisted of bread, cheese, milk, and wine; the latter, however, I did not like. Then, overcome by fatigue, I lay down among some straw, and fell asleep.

'It was noon when I awoke; and, allured by the warmth of the sun, which shone brightly on the white ground, I determined to recommence my travels; and, depositing the remains of the peasant's breakfast in a wallet I found, I proceeded across the fields for several hours, until at sunset I arrived at a village. How miraculous did this appear! the huts, the neater cottages, and stately houses engaged my admiration by turns. The vegetables in the gardens, the milk and cheese that I saw placed at the windows of some of the cottages, allured my appetite. One of the best of these I entered; but I had hardly placed my foot within the door before the children shrieked, and one of the women fainted. The whole village was roused; some fled, some attacked me, until, grievously bruised by stones and many other kinds of missile weapons, I escaped to the open country and fearfully took refuge in a low hovel, quite bare, and making a wretched appearance after the palaces I had beheld in the village. This hovel, however, joined a cottage of a neat and pleasant appearance; but, after my late dearly bought experience, I dared not enter it. My place of refuge was constructed of wood, but so low that I could with difficulty sit upright in it. No wood, however, was placed on the earth which formed the floor, but it was dry; and although the wind entered it by innumerable chinks, I found it an agreeable asylum from the snow and rain.

'Here then I retreated, and lay down happy to have found a shelter, however miserable, from the inclemency of the season, and still more from the barbarity of man.

'As soon as morning dawned, I crept from my kennel, that I might view the adjacent cottage and discover if I could remain in the

---

Pandaemonium Reference to John Milton's epic poem, *Paradise Lost*. Pandaemonium is the capital of hell, a palace built by fallen angels.

habitation I had found. It was situated against the back of the cottage and surrounded on the sides which were exposed by a pig-sty and a clear pool of water. One part was open, and by that I had crept in; but now I covered every crevice by which I might be perceived with stones and wood, yet in such a manner that I might move them on occasion to pass out: all the light I enjoyed came through the sty, and that was sufficient for me.

'Having thus arranged my dwelling and carpeted it with clean straw, I retired; for I saw the figure of a man at a distance, and I remembered too well my treatment the night before, to trust myself in his power. I had first, however, provided for my sustenance for that day by a loaf of coarse bread, which I **purloined**, and a cup with which I could drink, more conveniently than from my hand, of the pure water which flowed by my retreat. The floor was a little raised, so that it was kept perfectly dry, and by its vicinity to the chimney of the cottage it was tolerably warm.

'Being thus provided, I resolved to reside in this hovel until something should occur which might alter my determination. It was indeed a paradise compared to the bleak forest, my former residence, the rain-dropping branches, and dank earth. I ate my breakfast with pleasure and was about to remove a plank to procure myself a little water when I heard a step, and looking through a small chink, I beheld a young creature, with a pail on her head, passing before my hovel. The girl was young and of gentle demeanour, unlike, what I have since found cottagers and farm-house servants to be. Yet she was meanly dressed, a coarse blue petticoat and a linen jacket being her only grab; her fair hair was plaited, but not adorned: she looked patient, yet sad. I lost sight of her; and in about a quarter of an hour she returned bearing the pail, which was now partly filled with milk. As she walked along, seemingly **incommoded** by the burden, a young man met her, whose countenance expressed a deeper despondence. Uttering a few sounds with an air of melancholy, he took the pail from her head and bore it to the cottage himself. She followed, and they disappeared. Presently I saw the young man again, with some tools in his hand, cross the field behind the cottage; and the girl was also busied, sometimes in the house and sometimes in the yard.

'On examining my dwelling, I found that one of the windows of

purloined Stole.
incommoded Troubled.

the cottage had formerly occupied a part of it, but the panes had been filled up with wood. In one of these was a small and almost imperceptible chink, through which the eye could just penetrate. Through this crevice a small room was visible, whitewashed and clean, but very bare of furniture. In one corner, near a small fire, sat an old man, leaning his head on his hands in a disconsolate attitude. The young girl was occupied in arranging the cottage; but presently she took something out of a drawer, which employed her hands, and she sat down beside the old man, who, taking up an instrument, began to play, and to produce sounds sweeter than the voice of the thrush or the nightingale. It was a lovely sight, even to me, poor wretch! who had never beheld aught beautiful before. The silver hair and benevolent countenance of the aged cottager won my reverence, while the gentle manners of the girl enticed my love. He played a sweet mournful air, which I perceived drew tears from the eyes of his **amiable** companion, of which the old man took no notice, until she sobbed audibly; he then pronounced a few sounds, and the fair creature, leaving her work, knelt at his feet. He raised her, and smiled with such kindness and affection that I felt sensations of a peculiar and overpowering nature: they were a mixture of pain and pleasure, such as I had never before experienced, either from hunger or cold, warmth or food; and I withdrew from the window, unable to bear these emotions.

'Soon after this the young man returned, bearing on his shoulders a load of wood. The girl met him at the door, helped to relieve him of his burden, and taking some of the fuel into the cottage, placed it on the fire; then she and the youth went apart into a nook of the cottage, and he showed her a large loaf and a piece of cheese. She seemed pleased, and went into the garden for some roots and plants, which she placed in water, and then upon the fire. She afterwards continued her work, whilst the young man went into the garden, and appeared busily employed in digging and pulling up roots. After he had been employed thus about an hour, the young woman joined him, and they entered the cottage together.

'The old man had, in the mean time, been **pensive**; but on the appearance of his companions he assumed a more cheerful air, and they sat down to eat. The meal was quickly dispatched. The young woman was again occupied in arranging the cottage; the old man

---

amiable Good-natured; having a pleasant and friendly disposition.

pensive In deep thought.

walked before the cottage in the sun for a few minutes, leaning on the arm of the youth. Nothing could exceed in beauty the contrast between these two excellent creatures. One was old, with silver hairs and a countenance beaming with benevolence and love: the younger was slight and graceful in his figure, and his features were moulded with the finest symmetry; yet his eyes and attitude expressed the utmost sadness and **despondency**. The old man returned to the cottage; and the youth, with tools different from those he had used in the morning, directed his steps across the fields.

'Night quickly shut in; but to my extreme wonder, I found that the cottagers had a means of prolonging light by the use of **tapers**, and was delighted to find that the setting of the sun did not put an end to the pleasure I experienced in watching my human neighbours. In the evening, the young girl and her companion were employed in various occupations which I did not understand; and the old man again took up the instrument which produced the divine sounds that had enchanted me in the morning. So soon as he had finished the youth began, not to play, but to utter sounds that were monotonous, and neither resembling the harmony of the old man's instrument nor the songs of the birds: I since found that he read aloud, but at that time I knew nothing of the science of words or letters.

'The family, after having been thus occupied for a short time, extinguished their lights and retired, as I conjectured, to rest.'

---

despondency Dejection; feeling of hopelessness.
tapers Wax candles.

Horror stories

Frankenstein's sinister plot, its concern with dead bodies, and its accounts of weird scientific experiments, make it seem more like a modern horror story than a 19th-century novel. But in fact Mary Shelley's book was part of a vogue for stories about ghosts, the supernatural, and the uncanny that began in the 1760s and carried on for several decades. These books are usually known as Gothic novels. None of them are now as famous as *Frankenstein,* but many were very popular when they were first published.

Gothic novels
Gothic novels deal mostly with ghosts and the supernatural and they are set among castles, graveyards, and in dramatic, often mountainous scenery. The first Gothic novel to appear was *The Castle of Otranto,* which was written by English author Horace Walpole (1717–97), a rich man who was the son of the British Prime Minister, Robert Walpole. Its characters include ghastly apparitions, giants, and a statue that seems to come to life. The book was published in 1765 and was immediately popular, and over the next few decades, other writers wrote Gothic stories. The most successful examples included *The Monk,* by M. G. Lewis (1775–1818), in which a monk breaks his vows and ends up sentenced to death and damnation for his sins, and *Vathek,* by William Beckford (1759–1844), a story set in Arabia about a sultan who has the power to kill people just by looking at them.

The Gothic setting
Many of the Gothic novels were set in castles, abbeys, and similar buildings of the medieval period. The architectural style of these buildings—using pointed arches, stone vaults, and features such as stained-glass windows—was itself known as Gothic. The style had been current between the 13th and 15th centuries, and it became fashionable again in the 18th. Both Horace Walpole and William Beckford lived in elaborate Gothic-style houses that they built to satisfy their passion for the medieval period. Beckford's house, called Fonthill Abbey, was

modeled on the kind of church in which some Gothic novels were set. *Frankenstein*, with its graveyards and charnel houses, has a similar kind of setting. Its use of dramatic mountain scenery (see pp.234–235) is also typical of the work of the other Gothic writers.

Why Gothic novels?

Many writers liked the Gothic style for the same reason that some movie-makers like to produce horror films today—because it enabled them to explore all kinds of subjects that were outside the scope of ordinary, realistic stories. Readers liked the style because Gothic tales were usually gripping and included lots of moments that were surprising or scary. But not everyone admired Gothic fiction. Some people thought the characters unbelievable and the stories silly. Two prominent novelists, Jane Austen (1775–1817), in *Northanger Abbey*, and Thomas Love Peacock (1785–1866) in *Nightmare Abbey*, had a good time mocking the Gothic novel, all its horrific props and devices, and the people who read this kind of fiction so enthusiastically.

Grotesque
Medieval sculptors, and their later imitators, liked to carve grotesque monsters on the outsides of their churches—a perfect inspiration for writers of horror stories.

Frankenstein and the Gothic

Mary Shelley does not mock the Gothic mode in *Frankenstein*. Like her husband and friends, she was a keen reader of the ghost stories by German writers that she discovered during her stay in Switzerland. As a result, she rose to the challenge when Lord Byron suggested that all the members of their group should write a ghost story of their own. She proved to be at least as good at shocks and surprises as any other writer of her time. She includes vivid, atmospheric descriptions of "Gothic" scenery, such as the towering castles by the Rhine River in Germany, and powerfully depicts the horrific appearance of the Creature as a hideous, mummy-like being, so sinister that it must have magical powers. Victor Frankenstein himself turns into a broken, Gothic character who describes himself as "a restless spectre," in other words, little more than a ghost.

Gothic ruin
18th-century horror stories were often set among ruins like this, their tall pointed arches typical of Gothic architecture.

Chapter 4

' I lay on my straw, but I could not sleep. I thought of the occurrences of the day. What chiefly struck me was the gentle manners of these people; and I longed to join them, but dared not. I remembered too well the treatment I had suffered the night before from the barbarous villagers, and resolved, whatever course of conduct I might hereafter think it right to pursue, that for the present I would remain quietly in my hovel, watching, and endeavouring to discover the motives which influenced their actions.

'The cottagers arose the next morning before the sun. The young woman arranged the cottage and prepared the food; and the youth departed after the first meal.

'This day was passed in the same routine as that which preceded it. The young man was constantly employed out of doors, and the girl in various laborious occupations within. The old man, whom I soon perceived to be blind, employed his leisure hours on his instrument or in contemplation. Nothing could exceed the love and respect which the younger cottagers exhibited towards their venerable companion. They performed towards him every little office of affection and duty with gentleness; and he rewarded them by his benevolent smiles.

'They were not entirely happy. The young man and his companion often went apart, and appeared to weep. I saw no cause for their unhappiness; but I was deeply affected by it. If such lovely creatures were miserable, it was less strange that I, an imperfect and solitary being, should be wretched. Yet why were these gentle beings unhappy? They possessed a delightful house (for such it was in my eyes) and every luxury; they had a fire to warm them when chill, and delicious **viands** when hungry; they were dressed in excellent clothes; and, still more, they enjoyed one another's company and speech, interchanging each day looks of affection and kindness. What did their tears imply? Did they really express pain? I was at first unable to solve these questions; but perpetual attention and time explained to me many appearances which were at first enigmatic.

'A considerable period elapsed before I discovered one of the causes of the uneasiness of this amiable family: it was poverty, and

---

viands Provisions, items of food.

they suffered that evil in a very distressing degree. Their nourishment consisted entirely of the vegetables of their garden and the milk of one cow, which gave very little during the winter, when its masters could scarcely procure food to support it. They often, I believe, suffered the pangs of hunger very poignantly, especially the two younger cottagers; for several times they placed food before the old man when they reserved none for themselves.

'This trait of kindness moved me sensibly. I had been accustomed, during the night, to steal a part of their store for my own consumption; but when I found that in doing this I inflicted pain on the cottagers, I abstained, and satisfied myself with berries, nuts, and roots, which I gathered from a neighbouring wood.

'I discovered also another means through which I was enabled to assist their labours. I found that the youth spent a great part of each day in collecting wood for the family fire; and, during the night I often took his tools, the use of which I quickly discovered, and brought home firing sufficient for the consumption of several days.

'I remember, the first time that I did this, the young woman, when she opened the door in the morning, appeared greatly astonished on seeing a great pile of wood on the outside. She uttered some words in a loud voice, and the youth joined her, who also expressed surprise. I observed, with pleasure, that he did not go to the forest that day, but spent it in repairing the cottage and cultivating the garden.

'By degrees I made a discovery of still greater moment. I found that these people possessed a method of communicating their experience and feelings to one another by articulate sounds. I perceived that the words they spoke sometimes produced pleasure or pain, smiles or sadness, in the minds and countenances of the hearers. This was indeed a godlike science, and I ardently desired to become acquainted with it. But I was baffled in every attempt I made for this purpose. Their pronunciation was quick; and the words they uttered, not having any apparent connection with visible objects, I was unable to discover any clue by which I could unravel the mystery of their reference. By great application, however, and after having remained during the space of several revolutions of the moon in my hovel, I discovered the names that were given to some of the most familiar objects of discourse; I learned and applied the words, "fire", "milk", "bread", and "wood". I learned also the names of the cottagers themselves. The youth and his companion had each of them several names, but the old man had only one, which was "father". The girl was called "sister", or "Agatha", and the youth "Felix", "brother", or "son". I cannot describe the delight I felt when I learned the ideas appropriated to each of these sounds, and was able to pronounce them. I distinguished several other words without being able as yet to understand or apply them; such as "good", "dearest", "unhappy".

'I spent the winter in this manner. The gentle manners and beauty of the cottagers greatly endeared them to me: when they were unhappy, I felt depressed; when they rejoiced, I sympathised in their joys. I saw few human beings besides them; and if any other happened to enter the cottage, their harsh manners and rude gait only enhanced to me the superior accomplishments of my friends. The old man, I could perceive, often endeavoured to encourage his children, as sometimes I found that he called them, to cast off their melancholy. He would talk in a cheerful accent, with an expression of goodness that bestowed pleasure even upon me. Agatha listened with respect, her eyes sometimes filled with tears, which she endeavoured to wipe away unperceived; but I generally found that her countenance and tone were more cheerful after having listened to the exhortations of her father. It was not thus with Felix. He was always the saddest of the group, and, even to my unpractised senses, he appeared to have suffered more deeply than his friends. But if his countenance was more sorrowful, his voice was more cheerful than that of his sister, especially when he addressed the old man.

'I could mention innumerable instances which, although slight, marked the dispositions of these amiable cottagers. In the midst of poverty and want, Felix carried with pleasure to his sister the first little white flower that peeped out from beneath the snowy ground. Early in the morning, before she had risen, he cleared away the snow that obstructed her path to the milk-house, drew water from the well, and brought the wood from the out-house, where, to his perpetual astonishment, he found his store always replenished by an invisible hand. In the day, I believe, he worked sometimes for a neighbouring farmer, because he often went forth and did not return until dinner, yet brought no wood with him. At other times he worked in the garden; but as there was little to do in the frosty season, he read to the old man and Agatha.

'This reading had puzzled me extremely at first; but, by degrees, I discovered that he uttered many of the same sounds when he read, as when he talked. I conjectured, therefore, that he found on the paper signs for speech which he understood, and I ardently longed to comprehend these also; but how was that possible when I did not even understand the sounds for which they stood as signs? I improved, however, sensibly in this science, but not sufficiently to follow up any kind of conversation, although I applied my whole mind to the endeavour: for I easily perceived that, although I eagerly longed to **discover** myself to the cottagers, I ought not to make the attempt until I had first become master of their language; which knowledge might enable me to make them overlook the deformity of my figure; for with this also the contrast perpetually presented to my eyes had made me acquainted. *fear of the unknown*

'I had admired the perfect forms of my cottagers – their grace, beauty, and delicate complexions: but how was I terrified, when I viewed myself in a transparent pool! At first I started back, unable to believe that it was indeed I who was reflected in the mirror; and when I became fully convinced that I was in reality the monster that I am, I was filled with the bitterest sensations of despondence and mortification. Alas! I did not yet entirely know the fatal effects of this miserable deformity.

'As the sun became warmer, and the light of day longer, the snow vanished, and I beheld the bare trees and the black earth. From this time Felix was more employed; and the heart-moving indications of impending famine disappeared. Their food, as I afterwards found, was coarse, but it was wholesome; and they procured a sufficiency of it. Several new kinds of plants sprang up in the garden, which they dressed; and these signs of comfort increased daily as the season advanced.

'The old man, leaning on his son, walked each day at noon, when it did not rain, as I found it was called when the heavens poured forth its water. This frequently took place; but a high wind quickly dried the earth, and the season became far more pleasant than it had been.

'My mode of life in my hovel was uniform. During the morning I attended the motions of the cottagers; and when they were dispersed in various occupations, I slept: the remainder of the day was spent

discover Reveal, expose to view.

in observing my friends. When they had retired to rest, if there was any moon or the night was star-light, I went into the woods and collected my own food and fuel for the cottage. When I returned, as often as it was necessary, I cleared their path from the snow and performed those offices that I had seen done by Felix. I afterwards found that these labours, performed by an invisible hand, greatly astonished them; and once or twice I heard them, on these occasions, utter the words "good spirit", "wonderful"; but I did not then understand the signification of these terms.

'My thoughts now became more active, and I longed to discover the motives and feelings of these lovely creatures; I was inquisitive to know why Felix appeared so miserable and Agatha so sad. I thought (foolish wretch!) that it might be in my power to restore happiness to these deserving people. When I slept or was absent, the forms of the venerable blind father, the gentle Agatha, and the excellent Felix, flitted before me. I looked upon them as superior beings, who would be the **arbiters** of my future destiny. I formed in my imagination a thousand pictures of presenting myself to them, and their reception of me. I imagined that they would be disgusted, until, by my gentle demeanour and conciliating words, I should first win their favour, and afterwards their love.

'These thoughts exhilarated me and led me to apply with fresh ardour to the acquiring the art of language. My organs were indeed harsh, but supple; and although my voice was very unlike the soft music of their tones, yet I pronounced such words as I understood with tolerable ease. It was as the **ass and the lap-dog**; yet surely the gentle ass whose intentions were affectionate, although his manners were rude, deserved better treatment than blows and **execration**.

'The pleasant showers and genial warmth of spring greatly altered the aspect of the earth. Men, who before this change seemed to have been hid in caves, dispersed themselves, and were employed in various arts of cultivation. The birds sang in more cheerful notes, and the leaves began to bud forth on the trees. Happy, happy earth! fit habitation for gods, which, so short a time before, was bleak, damp, and unwholesome. My spirits were elevated by the enchanting appearance of nature; the past was blotted from my memory, the present was tranquil, and the future gilded by bright rays of hope, and anticipations of joy.' —

arbiters Judges, those whose opinions are authoritative.

ass and the lap-dog A reference to one of the *Fables* of the French poet Jean de La Fontaine (1621–95), in which an ass (donkey) tries to copy the affectionate behavior of his master's dog, but gets beaten rather than rewarded.

execration Utterance of curses, expression of hatred.

Chapter 5

'I now hasten to the more moving part of my story. I shall relate
events, that impressed me with feelings which, from what I had
been, have made me what I am.

'Spring advanced rapidly; the weather became fine and the skies
cloudless. It surprised me, that what before was desert and gloomy
should now bloom with the most beautiful flowers and verdure. My
senses were gratified and refreshed by a thousand scents of delight,
and a thousand sights of beauty.

'It was on one of these days, when my cottagers periodically rested
from labour – the old man played on his guitar, and the children
listened to him – that I observed the countenance of Felix was
melancholy beyond expression; he sighed frequently; and once his
father paused in his music, and I conjectured by his manner that he
enquired the cause of his son's sorrow. Felix replied in a cheerful
accent, and the old man was recommencing his music when someone tapped at the door.

'It was a lady on horseback, accompanied by a countryman as a
guide. The lady was dressed in a dark suit, and covered with a thick
black veil. Agatha asked a question, to which the stranger only
replied by pronouncing, in a sweet accent, the name of Felix. Her
voice was musical but unlike that of either of my friends. On hearing
this word, Felix came up hastily to the lady, who, when she saw him,
threw up her veil, and I beheld a countenance of angelic beauty and
expression. Her hair of a shining raven black, and curiously braided;
her eyes were dark, but gentle, although animated; her features of a
regular proportion, and her complexion wondrously fair, each cheek
tinged with a lovely pink.

'Felix seemed ravished with delight when he saw her, every trait
of sorrow vanished from his face, and it instantly expressed a degree
of ecstatic joy, of which I could hardly have believed it capable; his
eyes sparkled, as his cheek flushed with pleasure; and at that moment
I thought him as beautiful as the stranger. She appeared affected
by different feelings; wiping a few tears from her lovely eyes, she
held out her hand to Felix, who kissed it rapturously and called

her, as well as I could distinguish, his sweet Arabian. She did not appear to understand him, but smiled. He assisted her to dismount, and dismissing her guide, conducted her into the cottage. Some conversation took place between him and his father; and the young stranger knelt at the old man's feet and would have kissed his hand, but he raised her, and embraced her affectionately.

'I soon perceived, that although the stranger uttered articulate sounds, and appeared to have a language of her own, she was neither understood by, nor herself understood, the cottagers. They made many signs which I did not comprehend; but I saw that her presence diffused gladness through the cottage, dispelling their sorrow as the sun dissipates the morning mists. Felix seemed peculiarly happy, and with smiles of delight welcomed his Arabian. Agatha, the ever-gentle Agatha, kissed the hands of the lovely stranger; and pointing to her brother, made signs which appeared to me to mean that he had been sorrowful until she came. Some hours passed thus, while they, by their countenances, expressed joy, the cause of which I did not comprehend. Presently I found, by the frequent recurrence of some sound which the stranger repeated after them, that she was endeavouring to learn their language; and the idea instantly occurred to me that I should make use of the same instructions to the same end. The stranger learned about twenty words at the first lesson, most of them, indeed, were those which I had before understood, but I profited by the others.

'As night came on, Agatha and the Arabian retired early. When they separated, Felix kissed the hand of the stranger and said, "Good night, sweet Safie." He sat up much longer, conversing with his father; and by the frequent repetition of her name, I conjectured that their lovely guest was the subject of their conversation. I ardently desired to understand them, and bent every faculty towards that purpose, but found it utterly impossible.

'The next morning Felix went out to his work; and, after the usual occupations of Agatha were finished, the Arabian sat at the feet of the old man, and taking his guitar, played some airs so entrancingly beautiful that they at once drew tears of sorrow and delight from my eyes. She sang, and her voice flowed in a rich cadence, swelling or dying away, like a nightingale of the woods.

'When she had finished, she gave the guitar to Agatha, who at first declined it. She played a simple air, and her voice accompanied it in sweet accents, but unlike the wondrous strain of the stranger. The old man appeared enraptured and said some words, which Agatha endeavoured to explain to Safie, and by which he appeared to wish to express that she bestowed on him the greatest delight by her music.

'The days now passed as peaceably as before, with the sole alteration that joy had taken place of sadness in the countenances of my friends. Safie was always gay and happy; she and I improved rapidly in the knowledge of language, so that in two months I began to comprehend most of the words uttered by my protectors.

'In the meanwhile also the black ground was covered with herbage, and the green banks interspersed with innumerable flowers, sweet to the scent and the eyes, stars of pale radiance among the moonlight woods; the sun became warmer, the nights clear and balmy; and my nocturnal rambles were an extreme pleasure to me, although they were considerably shortened by the late setting and early rising of the sun, for I never ventured abroad during daylight, fearful of meeting with the same treatment I had formerly endured in the first village which I entered.

'My days were spent in close attention, that I might more speedily master the language; and I may boast that I improved more rapidly than the Arabian, who understood very little and conversed in broken accents, whilst I comprehended and could imitate almost every word that was spoken.

'While I improved in speech, I also learned the science of letters as it was taught to the stranger; and this opened before me a wide field for wonder and delight.   *pursuit of knowledge*

'The book from which Felix instructed Safie was **Volney's *Ruins of Empires.*** I should not have understood the purport of this book had not Felix, in reading it, given very minute explanations. He had chosen this work, he said, because the **declamatory** style was framed in imitation of the eastern authors. Through this work I obtained a cursory knowledge of history and a view of the several empires at present existing in the world; it gave me an insight into the manners, governments, and religions of the different nations of the earth. I heard of the slothful Asiatics; of the stupendous genius and mental activity of the Grecians; of the wars and wonderful virtue

Volney's *Ruins of Empires* Constantin François de Chasseboeuf, Comte de Volney (1757–1820), a French historian. His *Ruins of Empires* (1791) describes the rise and fall of ancient empires and advances the idea that all religions share an underlying common truth.

declamatory Having the elaborate quality of a public speech.

of the early Romans – of their subsequent degenerating – of the decline of that mighty empire, of chivalry, Christianity, and kings. I heard of the discovery of the American hemisphere and wept with Safie over the hapless fate of its original inhabitants.

'These wonderful narrations inspired me with strange feelings. Was man, indeed, at once so powerful, so virtuous, and magnificent, yet so vicious and base? He appeared at one time a mere **scion** of the evil principle, and at another as all that can be conceived as noble and godlike. To be a great and virtuous man appeared the highest honour that can befall a sensitive being; to be base and vicious, as many on record have been, appeared the lowest degradation, a condition more abject than that of the blind mole or harmless worm. For a long time I could not conceive how one man could go forth to murder his fellow, or even why there were laws and governments; but when I heard details of vice and bloodshed, my wonder ceased, and I turned away with disgust and loathing.

'Every conversation of the cottagers now opened new wonders to me. While I listened to the instructions which Felix bestowed upon the Arabian, the strange system of human society was explained to me. I heard of the division of property, of immense wealth and squalid poverty; of rank, descent, and noble blood.

'The words induced me to turn towards myself. I learned that the possessions most esteemed by your fellow creatures were, high and unsullied descent united with riches. A man might be respected with only one of these advantages; but without either he was considered, except in very rare instances, as a vagabond and a slave, doomed to waste his powers for the profits of the chosen few! And what was I? Of my creation and creator I was absolutely ignorant, but I knew that I possessed no money, no friends, no kind of property. I was, besides, endued with a figure hideously deformed and loathsome; I was not even of the same nature as man. I was more agile than they and could subsist upon coarser diet; I bore the extremes of heat and cold with less injury to my frame; my stature far exceeded theirs. When I looked around I saw and heard of none like me. Was I, then, a monster, a blot upon the earth, from which all men fled and whom all men disowned?

'I cannot describe to you the agony that these reflections inflicted upon me: I tried to dispel them, but sorrow only increased with

scion Heir, descendant.

knowledge. Oh, that I had forever remained in my native wood, nor known nor felt beyond the sensations of hunger, thirst and heat!

'Of what a strange nature is knowledge! It clings to the mind, when it has once seized on it, like a lichen on the rock. I wished sometimes to shake off all thought and feeling; but I learned that there was but one means to overcome the sensation of pain, and that was death – a state which I feared yet did not understand. I admired virtue and good feelings and loved the gentle manners and amiable qualities of my cottagers, but I was shut out from intercourse with them, except through means which I obtained by stealth, when I was unseen and unknown, and which rather increased than satisfied the desire I had of becoming one among my fellows. The gentle words of Agatha and the animated smiles of the charming Arabian, were not for me. The mild exhortations of the old man, and the lively conversation of the loved Felix were not for me. Miserable, unhappy wretch!

'Other lessons were impressed upon me even more deeply. I heard of the difference of sexes; and the birth and growth of children; how the father **doted** on the smiles of the infant, and the lively **sallies** of the older child; how all the life and cares of the mother were wrapped up in the precious charge; how the mind of youth expanded and gained knowledge; of brother, sister, and all the various relationships which bind one human being to another in mutual bonds.

'But where were my friends and relations? No father had watched my infant days, no mother had blessed me with smiles and caresses; or if they had, all my past life was now a blot, a blind vacancy in which I distinguished nothing. From my earliest remembrance I had been as I then was in height and proportion. I had never yet seen a being resembling me, or who claimed any intercourse with me. What was I? The question again recurred, to be answered only with groans.

'I will soon explain to what these feeling tended; but allow me now to return to the cottagers, whose story excited in me such various feelings of indignation, delight, and wonder, but which all terminated in additional love and reverence for my protectors (for so I loved, in an innocent, half-painful self-deceit, to call them).'

---

doted Bestowed love or fondness.
sallies Bounding leaps. Alternatively, clever remarks.

Chapter 6

'Some time elapsed before I learned the history of my friends. It was one which could not fail to impress itself deeply on my mind, unfolding as it did a number of circumstances, each interesting and wonderful to one so utterly inexperienced as I was.

'The name of the old man was De Lacey. He was descended from a good family in France, where he had lived for many years in affluence, respected by his superiors and beloved by his equals. His son was bred in the service of his country; and Agatha had ranked with ladies of the highest distinction. A few months before my arrival they had lived in a large and luxurious city called Paris, surrounded by friends and possessed of every enjoyment which virtue, refinement of intellect, or taste, accompanied by a moderate fortune, could afford.

'The father of Safie had been the cause of their ruin. He was a Turkish merchant, and had inhabited Paris for many years, when, for some reason which I could not learn, he became obnoxious to the government. He was seized and cast into prison the very day that Safie arrived from **Constantinople** to join him. He was tried and condemned to death. The injustice of his sentence was very flagrant; all Paris was indignant; and it was judged that his religion and wealth rather than the crime alleged against him had been the cause of his condemnation.

'Felix had accidentally been present at the trial; his horror and indignation were uncontrollable when he heard the decision of the court. He made, at that moment, a solemn vow to deliver him and then looked around for the means. After many fruitless attempts to gain admittance to the prison, he found a strongly **grated** window in an unguarded part of the building, which lighted the dungeon of the unfortunate **Mahometan**; who, loaded with chains, waited in despair the execution of the barbarous sentence. Felix visited the grate at night and made known to the prisoner his intentions in his favour. The Turk, amazed and delighted, endeavoured to kindle the zeal of his deliverer by promises of reward and wealth. Felix rejected his offers with contempt; yet when he saw the lovely Safie, who was

Constantinople Former name of the city of Istanbul, Turkey.
grated Here, fitted with bars.
Mahometan Muslim.

allowed to visit her father and who, by her gestures, expressed her
lively gratitude, the youth could not help owning to his own mind
that the captive possessed a treasure which would fully reward his
toil and hazard.

'The Turk quickly perceived the impression that his daughter had
made on the heart of Felix and endeavoured to secure him more
entirely in his interests by the promise of her hand in marriage, so
soon as he should be conveyed to a place of safety. Felix was too
delicate to accept his offer; yet he looked forward to the probability
of the event as to the consummation of his happiness.

'During the ensuing days, while the preparations were going
forward for the escape of the merchant, the zeal of Felix was
warmed by several letters that he received from this lovely girl, who
found means to express her thoughts in the language of her lover
by the aid of an old man, a servant of her father who understood
French. She thanked him in the most ardent terms for his intended
services towards her parent; and at the same time she gently deplored
her own fate.

'I have copies of these letters; for I found means, during my
residence in the hovel, to procure the implements of writing; and the
letters were often in the hands of Felix or Agatha. Before I depart,
I will give them to you, they will prove the truth of my tale; but at
present, as the sun is already far declined, I shall only have time to
repeat the substance of them to you.

'Safie related that her mother was a Christian Arab, seized and
made a slave by the Turks; recommended by her beauty, she had
won the heart of the father of Safie, who married her. The young
girl spoke in high and enthusiastic terms of her mother, who, born
in freedom, spurned the bondage to which she was now reduced.
She instructed her daughter in the tenets of her religion and taught
her to aspire to higher powers of intellect and an independence of
spirit forbidden to the female followers of **Mahomet**. This lady
died; but her lessons were indelibly impressed on the mind of Safie,
who sickened at the prospect of again returning to Asia and being
immured within the walls of a **harem**, allowed only to occupy
herself with infantile amusements, ill-suited to the temper of her
soul, now accustomed to grand ideas and a noble emulation of
virtue. The prospect of marrying a Christian and remaining in a

Mahomet Muhammad, the great prophet of the
Islamic religion.
immured Walled in.
harem Women's quarters in the palace of a
Turkish sultan.

country where women were allowed to take a rank in society was enchanting to her.

'The day for the execution of the Turk was fixed; but on the night previous to it he quitted his prison, and before morning was distant many leagues from Paris. Felix had procured passports in the name of his father, sister, and himself. He had previously communicated his plan to the former, who aided the deceit by quitting his house, under the pretence of a journey and concealing himself, with his daughter, in an obscure part of Paris.

'Felix conducted the fugitives through France to Lyons and across Mont Cenis to **Leghorn**, where the merchant had decided to wait a favourable opportunity of passing into some part of the Turkish dominions.

'Safie resolved to remain with her father until the moment of his departure, before which time the Turk renewed his promise that she should be united to her deliverer; and Felix remained with them in expectation of that event; and in the mean time he enjoyed the society of the Arabian, who exhibited towards him the simplest and tenderest affection. They conversed with one another through the means of an interpreter, and sometimes with the interpretation of looks; and Safie sang to him the divine airs of her native country.

'The Turk allowed this intimacy to take place, and encouraged the hopes of the youthful lovers, while in his heart he had formed far other plans. He loathed the idea that his daughter should be united to a Christian; but he feared the resentment of Felix if he should appear lukewarm; for he knew that he was still in the power of his deliverer if he should choose to betray him to the Italian state which they inhabited. He revolved a thousand plans by which he should be enabled to prolong the deceit until it might be no longer necessary, and secretly to take his daughter with him when he departed. His plans were facilitated by the news which arrived from Paris.

'The government of France were greatly enraged at the escape of their victim and spared no pains to detect and punish his deliverer. The plot of Felix was quickly discovered, and De Lacey and Agatha were thrown into prison. The news reached Felix and roused him from his dream of pleasure. His blind and aged father and his gentle sister lay in a **noisome** dungeon while he enjoyed the free air and the society of her whom he loved. This idea was torture to him.

Leghorn Old-fashioned English name for the town of Livorno, on the north-western coast of Italy.

noisome Foul-smelling, disagreeable.

He quickly arranged with the Turk that if the latter should find a favourable opportunity for escape before Felix could return to Italy, Safie should remain as a boarder at a convent at Leghorn; and then, quitting the lovely Arabian, he hastened to Paris, and delivered himself up to the vengeance of the law, hoping to free De Lacey and Agatha by this proceeding.

'He did not succeed. They remained confined for five months before the trial took place; the result of which deprived them of their fortune and condemned them to a perpetual exile from their native country.

'They found a miserable asylum in the cottage in Germany, where I discovered them. Felix soon learned that the treacherous Turk, for whom he and his family endured such unheard-of oppression, on discovering that his deliverer was thus reduced to poverty and ruin, became a traitor to good feeling and honour and had quitted Italy with his daughter, insultingly sending Felix a pittance of money to aid him, as he said, in some plan of future maintenance.

'Such were the events that preyed on the heart of Felix and rendered him, when I first saw him, the most miserable of his family. He could have endured poverty; and while this distress had been the **meed** of his virtue, he gloried in it; but the ingratitude of the Turk and the loss of his beloved Safie, were misfortunes more bitter and irreparable. The arrival of the Arabian now infused new life into his soul.

'When the news reached Leghorn that Felix was deprived of his wealth and rank, the merchant commanded his daughter to think no more of her lover, but to prepare to return to her native country. The generous nature of Safie was outraged by this command; she attempted to **expostulate** with her father, but he left her angrily, reiterating his tyrannical **mandate**.

'A few days after, the Turk entered his daughter's apartment and told her hastily that he had reason to believe that his residence at Leghorn had been divulged and that he should speedily be delivered up to the French government; he had, consequently, hired a vessel to convey him to Constantinople, for which city he should sail in a few hours. He intended to leave his daughter under the care of a confidential servant, to follow at her leisure with the greater part of his property, which had not yet arrived at Leghorn.

meed Reward, result.
expostulate Argue, plead, or remonstrate.
mandate Right to rule or wield power.

'When alone, Safie resolved in her own mind the plan of conduct that it would become her to pursue in this emergency. A residence in Turkey was abhorrent to her; her religion and her feelings were alike averse to it. By some papers of her father which fell into her hands she heard of the exile of her lover and learnt the name of the spot where he then resided. She hesitated some time, but at length she formed her determination. Taking with her some jewels that belonged to her and a sum of money, she quitted Italy with an attendant, a native of Leghorn, but who understood the common language of Turkey, and departed for Germany.

'She arrived in safety at a town about twenty leagues from the cottage of De Lacey, when her attendant fell dangerously ill. Safie nursed her with the most devoted affection; but the poor girl died, and the Arabian was left alone, unacquainted with the language of the country and utterly ignorant of the customs of the world. She fell, however, into good hands. The Italian had mentioned the name of the spot for which they were bound; and after her death, the woman of the house in which they had lived took care that Safie should arrive in safety at the cottage of her lover.'

Chapter 7

'Such was the history of my beloved cottagers. It impressed me deeply. I learned, from the views of social life which it developed, to admire their virtues and to deprecate the vices of mankind.

'As yet I looked upon crime as a distant evil; benevolence and generosity were ever present before me, inciting within me a desire to become an actor in the busy scene where so many admirable qualities were called forth and displayed. But in giving an account of the progress of my intellect, I must not omit a circumstance which occurred in the beginning of the month of August of the same year.

'One night, during my accustomed visit to the neighbouring wood, where I collected my own food and brought home firing for my protectors, I found on the ground a leathern **portmanteau**, containing several articles of dress and some books. I eagerly seized the prize, and returned with it to my hovel. Fortunately the books were written in the language, the elements of which I had acquired at the cottage; they consisted of *Paradise Lost*, a volume of **Plutarch's Lives**, and the *Sorrows of Werter*. The possession of these treasures gave me extreme delight; I now continually studied and exercised my mind upon these histories, whilst my friends were employed in their ordinary occupations.

'I can hardly describe to you the effect of these books. They produced in me an infinity of new images and feelings, that sometimes raised me to ecstasy, but more frequently sunk me into the lowest dejection. In the *Sorrows of Werter*, besides the interest of its simple and affecting story, so many opinions are canvassed, and so many lights thrown upon what had hitherto been to me obscure subjects, that I found in it a never-ending source of speculation and astonishment. The gentle and domestic manners it described, combined with lofty sentiments and feelings, which had for their object something out of self, accorded well with my experience among my protectors, and with the wants which were forever alive in my own bosom. But I thought Werter himself a more divine being than I had ever beheld or imagined; his character contained

---

portmanteau Traveling bag.
Paradise Lost An epic poem in blank verse by John Milton (1608–1674) (see Glossary).
Plutarch's Lives Written by Mestrius Plutarchus (46–127), *Parallel Lives* contains biographies of
famous Greeks and Romans.
Sorrows of Werter Influential Romantic novel (see Glossary).

no pretension, but it sunk deep. The **disquisitions** upon death and suicide were calculated to fill me with wonder. I did not pretend to enter into the merits of the case, yet I inclined towards the opinions of the hero, whose extinction I wept, without precisely understanding it.

'As I read, however, I applied much personally to my own feelings and condition. I found myself similar, yet at the same time strangely unlike to the beings concerning whom I read, and to whose conversation I was a listener. I sympathised with and partly understood them, but I was unformed in mind; I was dependent on none, and related to none. "The path of my departure was free," and there was none to lament my annihilation. My person was hideous and my stature gigantic. What did this mean? Who was I? What was I? Whence did I come? What was my destination? These questions continually recurred, but I was unable to solve them.

'The volume of Plutarch's *Lives* which I possessed, contained the histories of the first founders of the ancient republics. This book had a far different effect upon me from the *Sorrows of Werter*. I learned from Werter's imaginations despondency and gloom: but Plutarch taught me high thoughts; he elevated me above the wretched sphere of my own reflections, to admire and love the heroes of past ages. Many things I read surpassed my understanding and experience. I had a very confused knowledge of kingdoms, wide extents of country, mighty rivers, and boundless seas. But I was perfectly unacquainted with towns, and large assemblages of men. The cottage of my protectors had been the only school in which I had studied human nature; but this book developed new and mightier scenes of action. I read of men concerned in public affairs, governing or massacring their species. I felt the greatest ardour for virtue rise within me, and abhorrence for vice, as far as I understood the signification of those terms, relative as they were, as I applied them, to pleasure and pain alone. Induced by these feelings, I was of course led to admire peaceable lawgivers, **Numa**, **Solon**, and **Lycurgus**, in preference to **Romulus** and **Theseus**. The patriarchal lives of my protectors caused these impressions to take a firm hold on my mind; perhaps, if my first introduction to humanity had been made by a young soldier, burning for glory and slaughter, I should have been imbued with different sensations.

disquisitions Carefully written accounts.
Numa The second king of Rome (c.715–673 BCE).
Solon (c.638–c.558 BCE) an Athenian statesman.

Lycurgus (c.700–c.630 BCE) A lawmaker from Sparta.
Romulus (c.771–c.717 BCE) Legendary founder of Rome and creator of the Roman Senate and Legions.

'But *Paradise Lost* excited different and far deeper emotions. I read it, as I had read the other volumes which had fallen into my hands, as a true history. It moved every feeling of wonder and awe, that the picture of an omnipotent God warring with his creatures was capable of exciting. I often referred the several situations, as their similarity struck me, to my own. Like Adam, I was apparently united by no link to any other being in existence; but his state was far different from mine in every other respect. He had come forth from the hands of God a perfect creature, happy and prosperous, guarded by the especial care of his Creator; he was allowed to converse with and acquire knowledge from beings of a superior nature: but I was wretched, helpless, and alone. Many times I considered Satan as the fitter emblem of my condition; for often, like him, when I viewed the bliss of my protectors, the bitter gall of envy rose within me.

'Another circumstance strengthened and confirmed these feelings. Soon after my arrival in the hovel, I discovered some papers in the pocket of the dress which I had taken from your laboratory. At first I had neglected them; but now that I was able to decipher the characters in which they were written, I began to study them with diligence. It was your journal of the four months that preceded my creation. You minutely described in these papers every step you took in the progress of your work; this history was mingled with accounts of domestic occurrences. You doubtless recollect these papers. Here they are. Every thing is related in them which bears reference to my accursed origin; the whole detail of that series of disgusting circumstances which produced it is set in view; the minutest description of my odious and loathsome person is given, in language which painted your own horrors and rendered mine indelible. I sickened as I read. "Hateful day when I received life!" I exclaimed in agony. "Accursed creator! Why did you form a monster so hideous that even *you* turned from me in disgust? God, in pity, made man beautiful and alluring, after his own image; but my form is a filthy type of yours, more horrid even from the very resemblance. Satan had his companions, fellow-devils, to admire and encourage him; but I am solitary and abhorred."

'These were the reflections of my hours of despondency and solitude; but when I contemplated the virtues of the cottagers, their amiable and benevolent dispositions, I persuaded myself that

Theseus A legendary king of Athens credited with slaying the Minotaur, a mythological creature part man, part bull.

when they should become acquainted with my admiration of their virtues, they would compassionate me and overlook my personal deformity. Could they turn from their door one, however monstrous, who solicited their compassion and friendship? I resolved, at least, not to despair, but in every way to fit myself for an interview with them, which would decide my fate. I postponed this attempt for some months longer; for the importance attached to its success inspired me with a dread lest I should fail. Besides, I found that my understanding improved so much with every day's experience that I was unwilling to commence this undertaking until a few more months should have added to my sagacity.

'Several changes, in the mean time, took place in the cottage. The presence of Safie diffused happiness among its inhabitants; and I also found that a greater degree of plenty reigned there. Felix and Agatha spent more time in amusement and conversation, and were assisted in their labours by servants. They did not appear rich, but they were contented and happy; their feelings were serene and peaceful, while mine became every day more tumultuous. Increase of knowledge only discovered to me more clearly what a wretched outcast I was. I cherished hope, it is true; but it vanished when I beheld my person reflected in water, or my shadow in the moonshine, even as that frail image and that inconstant shade.

'I endeavoured to crush these fears, and to fortify myself for the trial which in a few months I resolved to undergo; and sometimes I allowed my thoughts, unchecked by reason, to ramble in the fields of Paradise, and dared to fancy amiable and lovely creatures sympathising with my feelings and cheering my gloom; their angelic countenances breathed smiles of consolation. But it was all a dream; no Eve soothed my sorrows nor shared my thoughts; I was alone. I remembered Adam's supplication to his Creator. But where was mine? He had abandoned me, and in the bitterness of my heart I cursed him.

'Autumn passed thus. I saw, with surprise and grief, the leaves decay and fall, and nature again assume the barren and bleak appearance it had worn when I first beheld the woods and the lovely moon. Yet I did not heed the bleakness of the weather; I was better fitted by my conformation for the endurance of cold than heat. But my chief delights were the sight of the flowers, the birds, and all the gay apparel of summer; when those deserted me, I turned with more attention towards the cottagers. Their happiness was not decreased by the absence of summer. They loved and sympathised with one another; and their joys, depending on each other, were not interrupted by the casualties that took place around them. The more I saw of them, the greater became my desire to claim their protection and kindness; my heart yearned to be known and loved by these amiable creatures; to see their sweet looks directed towards me with affection was the utmost limit of my ambition. I dared not think that they would turn them from me with disdain and horror. The poor that stopped at their door were never driven away. I asked, it is true, for greater treasures than a little food or rest: I required kindness and sympathy; but I did not believe myself unworthy of it.

'The winter advanced, and an entire revolution of the seasons had taken place since I awoke into life. My attention, at this time, was solely directed towards my plan of introducing myself into the cottage of my protectors. I revolved many projects; but that on which I finally fixed was, to enter the dwelling when the blind old man should be alone. I had sagacity enough to discover, that the unnatural hideousness of my person was the chief object of horror with those who had formerly beheld me. My voice, although harsh, had nothing terrible in it; I thought, therefore, that if in the absence of his children, I could gain the good-will and mediation of the old De Lacey, I might by his means be tolerated by my younger protectors.

'One day, when the sun shone on the red leaves that strewed the ground, and diffused cheerfulness, although it denied warmth, Safie, Agatha, and Felix departed on a long country walk, and the old man, at his own desire, was left alone in the cottage. When his children had departed, he took up his guitar, and played several mournful but sweet airs, more sweet and mournful than I had ever heard him play before. At first his countenance was illuminated with pleasure, but, as he continued, thoughtfulness and sadness succeeded; at length, laying aside the instrument, he sat absorbed in reflection.

'My heart beat quick; this was the hour and moment of trial, which would decide my hopes, or realise my fears. The servants were gone to a neighbouring fair. All was silent in and around the cottage: it was an excellent opportunity; yet, when I proceeded to execute my plan, my limbs failed me, and I sank to the ground. Again I rose; and, exerting all the firmness of which I was master, removed the planks which I had placed before my hovel to conceal my retreat. The fresh air revived me, and, with renewed determination, I approached the door of their cottage.

'I knocked. "Who is there?" said the old man – "Come in."

'I entered; "Pardon this intrusion", said I; "I am a traveller in want of a little rest; you would greatly oblige me if you would allow me to remain a few minutes before the fire."

'"Enter," said De Lacey, "and I will try in what manner I can to relieve your wants; but, unfortunately, my children are from home, and as I am blind, I am afraid I shall find it difficult to procure food for you."

'"Do not trouble yourself, my kind host; I have food; it is warmth and rest only that I need."

'I sat down, and a silence ensued. I knew that every minute was precious to me, yet I remained irresolute in what manner to commence the interview; when the old man addressed me. "By your language, stranger, I suppose you are my countryman; – are you French?"

'"No, but I was educated by a French family, and understand that language only. I am now going to claim the protection of some friends, whom I sincerely love, and of whose favour I have some hopes."

'"Are they Germans?"

'"No, they are French. But let us change the subject. I am an unfortunate and deserted creature; I look around, and I have no relation or friend upon earth. These amiable people to whom I go have never seen me, and know little of me. I am full of fears, for if I fail there, I am an outcast in the world forever."

'"Do not despair. To be friendless is indeed to be unfortunate; but the hearts of men, when unprejudiced by any obvious self-interest, are full of brotherly love and charity. Rely, therefore, on your hopes; and if these friends are good and amiable, do not despair."

'"They are kind – they are the most excellent creatures in the world; but unfortunately, they are prejudiced against me. I have good dispositions; my life has been hitherto harmless and in some degree beneficial; but a fatal prejudice clouds their eyes, and where they ought to see a feeling and kind friend, they behold only a detestable monster."

"'That is indeed unfortunate; but if you are really blameless, cannot you undeceive them?"

"'I am about to undertake that task; and it is on that account that I feel so many overwhelming terrors. I tenderly love these friends; I have, unknown to them, been for many months in the habits of daily kindness towards them; but they believe that I wish to injure them, and it is that prejudice which I wish to overcome."

"'Where do these friends reside?"

"'Near this spot."

'The old man paused and then continued, "If you will unreservedly confide to me the particulars of your tale, I perhaps may be of use in undeceiving them. I am blind and cannot judge of your countenance, but there is something in your words which persuades me that you are sincere. I am poor and an exile, but it will afford me true pleasure to be in any way serviceable to a human creature."

"'Excellent man! I thank you and accept your generous offer. You raise me from the dust by this kindness; and I trust that, by your aid, I shall not be driven from the society and sympathy of your fellow-creatures."

"'Heaven forbid! Even if you were really criminal, for that can only drive you to desperation, and not instigate you to virtue. I also am unfortunate; I and my family have been condemned, although innocent; judge, therefore, if I do not feel for your misfortunes."

"'How can I thank you, my best and only benefactor? From your lips first have I heard the voice of kindness directed towards me; I shall be forever grateful; and your present humanity assures me of success with those friends whom I am on the point of meeting."

"'May I know the names and residence of those friends?"

'I paused. This, I thought, was the moment of decision, which was to rob me of, or bestow happiness on me forever. I struggled vainly for firmness sufficient to answer him, but the effort destroyed all my remaining strength; I sank on the chair and sobbed aloud. At that moment I heard the steps of my younger protectors. I had not a moment to lose, but, seizing the hand of the old man, I cried, "Now is the time! Save and protect me! You and your family are the friends whom I seek. Do not you desert me in the hour of trial!"

"'Great God!" exclaimed the old man, "who are you?"

'At that instant the cottage door was opened, and Felix, Safie, and Agatha entered. Who can describe their horror and consternation on beholding me? Agatha fainted, and Safie, unable to attend to her friend, rushed out of the cottage. Felix darted forward, and with supernatural force tore me from his father, to whose knees I clung: in a transport of fury, he dashed me to the ground and struck me violently with a stick. I could have torn him limb from limb, as the lion rends the antelope. But my heart sunk within me as with bitter sickness, and I refrained. I saw him on the point of repeating his blow, when, overcome by pain and anguish, I quitted the cottage, and in the general tumult escaped unperceived to my hovel.'

Chapter 8

'Cursed, cursed creator! Why did I live? Why, in that instant, did I not extinguish the spark of existence which you had so wantonly bestowed? I know not; despair had not yet taken possession of me; my feelings were those of rage and revenge. I could with pleasure have destroyed the cottage and its inhabitants, and have glutted myself with their shrieks and misery.

'When night came I quitted my retreat and wandered in the wood; and now, no longer restrained by the fear of discovery, I gave vent to my anguish in fearful howlings. I was like a wild beast that had broken the toils, destroying the objects that obstructed me and ranging through the wood with a staglike swiftness. O! what a miserable night I passed! the cold stars shone in mockery, and the bare trees waved their branches above me: now and then the sweet voice of a bird burst forth amidst the universal stillness. All, save I, were at rest or in enjoyment: I, like the **archfiend**, bore a hell within me, and finding myself unsympathised with, wished to tear up the trees, spread havoc and destruction around me, and then to have sat down and enjoyed the ruin.

'But this was a luxury of sensation that could not endure; I became fatigued with excess of bodily exertion, and sank on the damp grass in the sick impotence of despair. There was none among the **myriads** of men that existed who would pity or assist me; and should I feel kindness towards my enemies? No: from that moment I declared ever-lasting war against the species, and, more than all, against him who had formed me, and sent me forth to this insupportable misery.

'The sun rose; I heard the voices of men and knew that it was impossible to return to my retreat during that day. Accordingly I hid myself in some thick underwood, determining to devote the ensuing hours to reflection on my situation.

'The pleasant sunshine, and the pure air of day, restored me to some degree of tranquillity; and when I considered what had passed at the cottage, I could not help believing that I had been too hasty in my conclusions. I had certainly acted imprudently. It was apparent

archfiend Principal devil, in other words, Satan, the former angel who rebels against God and who is one of the main characters of John Milton's epic poem *Paradise Lost*.

myriads Countless numbers, hordes.

that my conversation had interested the father in my behalf, and I was a fool in having exposed my person to the horror of his children. I ought to have familiarised the old De Lacey to me, and by degrees to have discovered myself to the rest of his family, when they should have been prepared for my approach. But I did not believe my errors to be irretrievable, and after much consideration I resolved to return to the cottage, seek the old man, and by my representations win him to my party.

'These thoughts calmed me, and in the afternoon I sank into a profound sleep; but the fever of my blood did not allow me to be visited by peaceful dreams. The horrible scene of the preceding day was forever acting before my eyes; the females were flying, and the enraged Felix tearing me from his father's feet. I awoke exhausted; and finding that it was already night, I crept forth from my hiding-place, and went in search of food.

'When my hunger was appeased, I directed my steps towards the well-known path that conducted to the cottage. All there was at peace. I crept into my hovel, and remained in silent expectation of the accustomed hour when the family arose. That hour passed, the sun mounted high in the heavens, but the cottagers did not appear. I trembled violently, apprehending some dreadful misfortune. The inside of the cottage was dark, and I heard no motion; I cannot describe the agony of this suspense.

'Presently two countrymen passed by; but pausing near the cottage, they entered into conversation, using violent gesticulations; but I did not understand what they said, as they spoke the language of the country, which differed from that of my protectors. Soon after, however, Felix approached with another man; I was surprised, as I knew that he had not quitted the cottage that morning, and waited anxiously to discover, from his discourse, the meaning of these unusual appearances.

'"Do you consider," said his companion to him, "that you will be obliged to pay three months' rent and to lose the produce of your garden? I do not wish to take any unfair advantage, and I beg therefore that you will take some days to consider of your determination."

'"It is utterly useless," replied Felix; "we can never again inhabit your cottage. The life of my father is in the greatest danger, owing to the dreadful circumstance that I have related. My wife and my sister will never recover from their horror. I intreat you not to reason with me any more. Take possession of your tenement, and let me fly from this place."

'Felix trembled violently as he said this. He and his companion entered the cottage, in which they remained for a few minutes, and then departed. I never saw any of the family of De Lacey more.

'I continued for the remainder of the day in my hovel in a state of utter and stupid despair. My protectors had departed, and had broken the only link that held me to the world. For the first time the feelings of revenge and hatred filled my bosom, and I did not strive to control them; but allowing myself to be borne away by the stream, I bent my mind towards injury and death. When I thought of my friends, of the mild voice of De Lacey, the gentle eyes of Agatha, and the exquisite beauty of the Arabian, these thoughts vanished and a gush of tears somewhat soothed me. But again when I reflected that they had spurned and deserted me, anger returned, a rage of anger, and unable to injure anything human, I turned my fury towards inanimate objects. As night advanced I placed a variety of combustibles around the cottage; and, after having destroyed every vestige of cultivation in the garden, I waited with forced impatience until the moon had sunk to commence my operations.

'As the night advanced, a fierce wind arose from the woods, and quickly dispersed the clouds that had loitered in the heavens; the blast tore along like a mighty avalanche and produced a kind of insanity in my spirits, that burst all bounds of reason and reflection. I lighted the dry branch of a tree and danced with fury around the devoted cottage, my eyes still fixed on the western horizon, the edge of which the moon nearly touched. A part of its orb was at length hid, and I waved my brand; it sank, and with a loud scream I fired the straw, and heath, and bushes, which I had collected. The wind fanned the fire, and the cottage was quickly enveloped by the flames, which clung to it and licked it with their forked and destroying tongues.

'As soon as I was convinced that no assistance could save any part of the habitation, I quitted the scene, and sought for refuge in the woods.

'And now, with the world before me, whither should I bend my steps? I resolved to fly far from the scene of my misfortunes; but to me, hated and despised, every country must be equally horrible. At length the thought of you crossed my mind. I learned from your papers that you were my father, my creator; and to whom could I apply with more fitness than to him who had given me life? Among the lessons that Felix had bestowed upon Safie, geography had not been omitted: I had learned from these the relative situations of the different countries of the earth. You had mentioned Geneva as the name of your native town; and towards this place I resolved to proceed.

'But how was I to direct myself? I knew that I must travel in a south-westerly direction to reach my destin¬ation; but the sun was my only guide. I did not know the names of the towns that I was to pass through, nor could I ask information from a single human being; but I did not despair. From you only could I hope for **succour**, although towards you I felt no sentiment but that of hatred. Unfeeling, heartless creator! You had endowed me with perceptions and passions and then cast me abroad an object for the scorn and horror of mankind. But on you only had I any claim for pity and redress, and from you I determined to seek that justice which I vainly attempted to gain from any other being that wore the human form.

'My travels were long, and the sufferings I endured intense. It was late in autumn when I quitted the district where I had so long resided. I travelled only at night, fearful of encountering the visage of a human being. Nature decayed around me, and the sun became heatless; rain and snow poured around me; mighty rivers were frozen; the surface of the earth was hard and chill, and bare, and I found no shelter. Oh, earth! how often did I imprecate curses on the cause of my being! The mildness of my nature had fled, and all within me was turned to gall and bitterness. The nearer I approached to your habitation, the more deeply did I feel the spirit of revenge enkindled in my heart. Snow fell, and the waters were hardened, but I rested not. A few incidents now and then directed me, and I possessed a map of the country; but I often wandered wide from my path. The agony of my feelings allowed me no respite: no incident occurred from which my rage and misery could not extract its food; but a circumstance that happened when I arrived on the confines of

succour Help, assistance.

Switzerland, when the sun had recovered its warmth and the earth again began to look green, confirmed in an especial manner the bitterness and horror of my feelings.

'I generally rested during the day, and travelled only when I was secured by night from the view of man. One morning, however, finding that my path lay through a deep wood, I ventured to continue my journey after the sun had risen; the day, which was one of the first of spring, cheered even me by the loveliness of its sunshine and the balminess of the air. I felt emotions of gentleness and pleasure, that had long appeared dead, revive within me. Half surprised by the novelty of these sensations, I allowed myself to be borne away by them, and, forgetting my solitude and deformity, dared to be happy. Soft tears again bedewed my cheeks, and I even raised my humid eyes with thankfulness towards the blessed sun, which bestowed such joy upon me.

'I continued to wind among the paths of the wood, until I came to its boundary, which was skirted by a deep and rapid river, into which many of the trees bent their branches, now budding with the fresh spring. Here I paused, not exactly knowing what path to pursue, when I heard the sound of voices, that induced me to conceal myself under the shade of a cypress. I was scarcely hid, when a young girl came running towards the spot where I was concealed, laughing, as if she ran from some one in sport. She continued her course along the precipitous sides of the river, when suddenly her foot slipt, and she fell into the rapid stream. I rushed from my hiding-place, and, with extreme labour from the force of the current, saved her, and dragged her to shore. She was senseless; and I endeavoured, by every means in my power, to restore animation, when I was suddenly interrupted by the approach of a rustic, who was probably the person from whom she had playfully fled. On seeing me, he darted towards me, and tearing the girl from my arms, hastened towards the deeper parts of the wood. I followed speedily, I hardly knew why; but when the man saw me draw near, he aimed a gun, which he carried, at my body, and fired. I sank to the ground, and my injurer, with increased swiftness, escaped into the wood.

'This was then the reward of my benevolence! I had saved a human being from destruction, and as a recompense I now writhed under the miserable pain of a wound which shattered the flesh

and bone. The feelings of kindness and gentleness, which I had
entertained but a few moments before, gave place to hellish rage
and gnashing of teeth. Inflamed by pain, I vowed eternal hatred and
vengeance to all mankind. But the agony of my wound overcame
me; my pulses paused, and I fainted.

'For some weeks I led a miserable life in the woods, endeavouring
to cure the wound which I had received. The ball had entered my
shoulder, and I knew not whether it had remained there or passed
through; at any rate I had no means of extracting it. My sufferings
were **augmented** also by the oppressive sense of the injustice and
ingratitude of their infliction. My daily vows rose for revenge – a
deep and deadly revenge, such as would alone compensate for the
outrages and anguish I had endured.

'After some weeks my wound healed, and I continued my journey.
The labours I endured were no longer to be alleviated by the bright
sun or gentle breezes of spring; all joy was but a mockery which
insulted my desolate state, and made me feel more painfully that I
was not made for the enjoyment of pleasure.

'But my toils now drew near a close, and in two months from this
time, I reached the environs of Geneva.

'It was evening when I arrived, and I retired to a hiding-place
among the fields that surround it, to meditate in what manner I
should apply to you. I was oppressed by fatigue and hunger, and far
too unhappy to enjoy the gentle breezes of evening, or the prospect
of the sun setting behind the stupendous mountains of Jura.

'At this time a slight sleep relieved me from the pain of reflection,
which was disturbed by the approach of a beautiful child, who
came running into the recess I had chosen, with all the sportiveness
of infancy. Suddenly, as I gazed on him, an idea seized me that this
little creature was unprejudiced, and had lived too short a time to
have imbibed a horror of deformity. If, therefore, I could seize him
and educate him as my companion and friend, I should not be so
desolate in this peopled earth.

'Urged by this impulse, I seized on the boy as he passed and drew
him towards me. As soon as he beheld my form, he placed his hands
before his eyes, and uttered a shrill scream; I drew his hand forcibly
from his face and said, "Child, what is the meaning of this? I do not
intend to hurt you; listen to me."

augmented Made greater.

'He struggled violently. "Let me go," he cried; "monster! ugly wretch! you wish to eat me and tear me to pieces – You are an ogre – Let me go, or I will tell my papa."

'"Boy, you will never see your father again; you must come with me."

'"Hideous monster! let me go. My papa is a syndic – he is M. Frankenstein – he will punish you. You dare not keep me."

'"Frankenstein! you belong then to my enemy – to him towards whom I have sworn eternal revenge; you shall be my first victim."

'The child still struggled, and loaded me with **epithets** which carried despair to my heart; I grasped his throat to silence him, and in a moment he lay dead at my feet.

'I gazed on my victim, and my heart swelled with exultation and hellish triumph; clapping my hands, I exclaimed, "I too can create desolation; my enemy is not invulnerable; this death will carry despair to him, and a thousand other miseries shall torment and destroy him."

'As I fixed my eyes on the child, I saw something glittering on his breast. I took it; it was a portrait of a most lovely woman. In spite of my malignity, it softened and attracted me. For a few moments I gazed with delight on her dark eyes, fringed by deep lashes, and her lovely lips; but presently my rage returned: I remembered that I was forever deprived of the delights that such beautiful creatures could bestow; and that she whose resemblance I contemplated would, in regarding me, have changed that air of divine **benignity** to one expressive of disgust and affright.

'Can you wonder that such thoughts transported me with rage? I only wonder that at that moment, instead of venting my sensations in exclamations and agony, I did not rush among mankind, and perish in the attempt to destroy them.

'While I was overcome by these feelings, I left the spot where I had committed the murder, and seeking a more secluded hiding-place, I entered a barn which had appeared to me to be empty. A woman was sleeping on some straw; she was young: not indeed so beautiful as her whose portrait I held; but of an agreeable aspect and blooming in the loveliness of youth and health. Here, I thought, is one of those whose joy-imparting smiles are bestowed on all but me. And then I bent over her, and whispered, "Awake, fairest, thy

epithets Descriptive words or phrases.
benignity Kindness, generosity.

lover is near – he who would give his life but to obtain one look of affection from thine eyes: my beloved, awake!"

'The sleeper stirred; a thrill of terror ran through me. Should she indeed awake, and see me, and curse me, and denounce the murderer? Thus would she assuredly act, if her darkened eyes opened, and she beheld me. The thought was madness; it stirred the fiend within me – not I, but she, shall suffer; the murder I have committed because I am forever robbed of all that she could give me, she shall atone. The crime had its source in her: be hers the punishment! Thanks to the lessons of Felix and the **sanguinary** laws of man, I had learned how to work mischief. I bent over her and placed the portrait securely in one of the folds of her dress. She moved again, and I fled.

'For some days I haunted the spot where these scenes had taken place; sometimes wishing to see you, sometimes resolved to quit the world and its miseries forever. At length I wandered towards these mountains, and have ranged through their immense recesses, consumed by a burning passion which you alone can gratify. We may not part until you have promised to comply with my **requisition**. I am alone, and miserable; man will not associate with me; but one as deformed and horrible as myself would not deny herself to me. My companion must be of the same species, and have the same defects. This being you must create.'

---

sanguinary Bloody, bloodthirsty.
requisition Demand, request.

Chapter 9

The being finished speaking, and fixed his looks upon me in the expectation of a reply. But I was bewildered, perplexed, and unable to arrange my ideas sufficiently to understand the full extent of his proposition. He continued.

'You must create a female for me, with whom I can live in the interchange of those sympathies necessary for my being. This you alone can do; and I demand it of you as a right which you must not refuse to concede.'

The latter part of his tale had kindled anew in me the anger that had died away while he narrated his peaceful life among the cottagers, and, as he said this, I could no longer suppress the rage that burned within me.

'I do refuse it,' I replied; 'and no torture shall ever extort a consent from me. You may render me the most miserable of men, but you shall never make me base in my own eyes. Shall I create another like yourself, whose joint wickedness might desolate the world? Begone! I have answered you; you may torture me, but I will never consent.'

'You are in the wrong,' replied the fiend; 'and, instead of threatening, I am content to reason with you. I am malicious because I am miserable. Am I not shunned and hated by all mankind? You, my creator, would tear me to pieces, and triumph; remember that, and tell me why I should pity man more than he pities me? You would not call it murder, if you could **precipitate** me into one of those ice-rifts, and destroy my frame, the work of your own hands. Shall I respect man when he contemns me? Let him live with me in the interchange of kindness; and, instead of injury I would bestow every benefit upon him with tears of gratitude at his acceptance. But that cannot be; the human senses are insurmountable barriers to our union. Yet mine shall not be the submission of abject slavery. I will revenge my injuries: if I cannot inspire love, I will cause fear, and chiefly towards you my arch-enemy, because my creator, do I swear inextinguishable hatred. Have a care: I will work at your destruction, nor finish until I desolate your heart, so that you shall curse the hour of your birth.'

precipitate Cast down violently, throw over.

A fiendish rage animated him as he said this; his face was wrinkled into contortions too horrible for human eyes to behold; but presently he calmed himself and proceeded.

'I intended to reason. This passion is detrimental to me; for you do not reflect that *you* are the cause of its excess. If any being felt emotions of benevolence towards me, I should return them an hundred and an hundredfold; for that one creature's sake I would make peace with the whole kind! But I now indulge in dreams of bliss that cannot be realised. What I ask of you is reasonable and moderate; I demand a creature of another sex, but as hideous as myself; the gratification is small, but it is all that I can receive, and it shall content me. It is true, we shall be monsters, cut off from all the world; but on that account we shall be more attached to one another. Our lives will not be happy, but they will be harmless, and free from the misery I now feel. Oh! my creator, make me happy; let me feel gratitude towards you for one benefit! Let me see that I excite the sympathy of some existing thing; do not deny me my request!'

I was moved. I shuddered when I thought of the possible consequences of my consent, but I felt that there was some justice in his argument. His tale, and the feelings he now expressed, proved him to be a creature of fine sensations; and did I not as his maker, owe him all the portion of happiness that it was in my power to bestow? He saw my change of feeling and continued.

'If you consent, neither you nor any other human being shall ever see us again: I will go to the vast wilds of South America. My food is not that of man; I do not destroy the lamb and the kid to glut my appetite; acorns and berries afford me sufficient nourishment. My companion will be of the same nature as myself, and will be content with the same fare. We shall make our bed of dried leaves; the sun will shine on us as on man, and will ripen our food. The picture I present to you is peaceful and human, and you must feel that you could deny it only in the wantonness of power and cruelty. Pitiless as you have been towards me, I now see compassion in your eyes; let me seize the favourable moment and persuade you to promise what I so ardently desire.'

'You propose,' replied I, 'to fly from the habitations of man, to dwell in those wilds where the beasts of the field will be your only companions. How can you, who long for the love and sympathy of man, persevere in this exile? You will return, and again seek their kindness, and you will meet with their detestation; your evil passions will be renewed, and you will then have a companion to aid you in the task of destruction. This may not be: cease to argue the point, for I cannot consent.'

'How inconstant are your feelings! but a moment ago you were moved by my representations, and why do you again harden yourself to my complaints? I swear to you, by the earth which I inhabit, and by you that made me, that with the companion you bestow I will quit the neighbourhood of man, and dwell, as it may chance, in the most savage of places. My evil passions will have fled, for I shall meet with sympathy! my life will flow quietly away, and in my dying moments I shall not curse my maker.'

His words had a strange effect upon me. I compassionated him and sometimes felt a wish to console him; but when I looked upon him, when I saw the filthy mass that moved and talked, my heart sickened and my feelings were altered to those of horror and hatred. I tried to stifle these sensations; I thought, that as I could not sympathise with him, I had no right to withhold from him the small portion of happiness which was yet in my power to bestow.

'You swear,' I said, 'to be harmless; but have you not already shown a degree of malice that should reasonably make me distrust you? May not even this be a **feint** that will increase your triumph by affording a wider scope for your revenge?'

'How is this? I must not be trifled with: and I demand an answer. If I have no ties and no affections, hatred and vice must be my portion; the love of another will destroy the cause of my crimes, and I shall become a thing of whose existence every one will be ignorant. My vices are the children of a forced solitude that I abhor; and my virtues will necessarily arise when I live in communion with an equal. I shall feel the affections of a sensitive being, and become linked to the chain of existence and events, from which I am now excluded.'

I paused some time to reflect on all he had related, and the various arguments which he had employed. I thought of the promise of virtues which he had displayed on the opening of his existence, and the subsequent blight of all kindly feeling by the loathing and

feint Deceptive action.

scorn which his protectors had manifested towards him. His power and threats were not omitted to my calculations: a creature who could exist in the ice-caves of the glaciers, and hide himself from pursuit among the ridges of inaccessible precipices, was a being possessing faculties it would be vain to cope with. After a long pause of reflection, I concluded that the justice due both to him and my fellow creatures demanded of me that I should comply with his request. Turning to him, therefore, I said –

'I consent to your demand, on your solemn oath to quit Europe forever, and every other place in the neighbourhood of man, as soon as I shall deliver into your hands a female who will accompany you in your exile.'

'I swear,' he cried, 'by the sun, and by the blue sky of Heaven, and by the fire of love that burns my heart, that if you grant my prayer, while they exist you shall never behold me again. Depart to your home, and commence your labours: I shall watch their progress with unutterable anxiety; and fear not but that when you are ready I shall appear.'

Saying this, he suddenly quitted me, fearful, perhaps, of any change in my sentiments. I saw him descend the mountain with greater speed than the flight of an eagle, and quickly lost among the **undulations** of the sea of ice.

His tale had occupied the whole day, and the sun was upon the verge of the horizon when he departed. I knew that I ought to hasten my descent towards the valley, as I should soon be encompassed in darkness; but my heart was heavy, and my steps slow. The labour of winding among the little paths of the mountain and fixing my feet firmly as I advanced, perplexed me, occupied as I was by the emotions which the occurrences of the day had produced. Night was far advanced when I came to the half way resting-place and seated myself beside the fountain. The stars shone at intervals, as the clouds passed from over them; the dark pines rose before me, and every here and there a broken tree lay on the ground: it was a scene of wonderful solemnity and stirred strange thoughts within me. I wept bitterly; and clasping my hands in agony, I exclaimed, 'Oh! stars and clouds and winds, ye are all about to mock me: if ye really pity me, crush sensation and memory; let me become as nought; but if not, depart, depart, and leave me in darkness.'

undulations Wave-like movements, rising and
falling.

These were wild and miserable thoughts; but I cannot describe to you how the eternal twinkling of the stars weighed upon me, and how I listened to every blast of wind, as if it were a dull ugly **siroc** on its way to consume me.

Morning dawned before I arrived at the village of Chamounix; I took no rest, but returned immediately to Geneva. Even in my own heart I could give no expression to my sensations – they weighed on me with a mountain's weight, and their excess destroyed my agony beneath them. Thus I returned home, and entering the house, presented myself to the family. My haggard and wild appearance awoke intense alarm; but I answered no questions, scarcely did I speak. I felt as if I were placed under a ban – as if I had no right to claim their sympathies – as if never more might I enjoy companionship with them. Yet even thus I loved them to adoration; and to save them, I resolved to dedicate myself to my most abhorred task. The prospect of such an occupation made every other circumstance of existence pass before me like a dream, and that thought only had to me the reality of life.

END OF VOLUME TWO

siroc A hot, dust-laden, wind blowing from North Africa.

The Industrial Revolution

The 18th century saw one of the biggest-ever changes in the way people lived and worked. Before this time, most people lived in the countryside and worked on farms. But in the mid-18th century, large-scale industry was established, offering ways of making an endless variety of products by using machines. Soon, most people lived in towns and cities and worked in factories manufacturing goods. The industrial revolution had arrived.

A big leap forward

This kind of large-scale industry was made possible because a number of inventions and changes had all happened in Britain at around the same time. One was the development of the steam engine, perfected by the Scottish engineer James Watt (1736–1819) in the 1760s. One steam engine could power lots of machinery, and could keep going continuously—all it needed was a steady supply of coal, and engineers were busy building a network of canals up and down the country, so that this heavy fuel could be transported easily and cheaply to the factories. At the same time, inventors were devising all kinds of machines that could be powered by steam. The textile industry, for example, had previously employed thousands of home-workers, who spun thread and wove cloth by hand using spinning wheels and hand looms. By Mary Shelley's time, this work was being done by steam-powered machinery. One person could operate several machines, each of which did the work of many home-workers.

James Watt
Scotsman James Watt's improvements to steam engines made them efficient power sources for industrial machinery.

Social changes

All this meant huge changes for working people. Thousands moved to the cities to work in the factories. The conditions were unpleasant—the machinery was noisy, the factories were dark, and the hours were long. It was dangerous, too. Many people lost arms or hands that got caught in the machinery. And the housing provided by factory owners for their workers was often cramped and inadequate. But people came to the factories because that was where the jobs were. Old-fashioned craftworkers, by contrast, were no longer in demand.

The scenery of industry
In industrial Britain, huge factories with their tall chimneys transformed the landscape and the flames from furnaces lit up the sky.

Making a protest

Although he was a member of the upper class and did not have to work himself, Mary Shelley's friend Lord Byron knew all about the problems faced by traditional workers. In his home county of Nottinghamshire, many people had made their living by knitting socks and stockings by hand at home. Now this work was done by machinery and the knitters had no money. Some of them rioted, destroyed the factory machines, and faced the death penalty, or prison, for their vandalism. Byron stood up for them, and made a speech in the House of Lords, arguing that the authorities should be merciful because the people had lost their livelihoods. But he could not turn back the tide—the factories were here to stay.

A world of possibilities

Mary Shelley would have heard a lot about the developments in industry— not only from Byron but also from her father's friend, the scientist Erasmus Darwin (see pp.98–99). Darwin was one of a group of thinkers, scientists, and industrialists who met regularly in the Birmingham house of Matthew Boulton (1728–1809), manufacturer of steam engines. The group, which included Boulton's business partner, the engineer James Watt, and scientists such as Joseph Priestley (1733–1804), one of the discoverers of oxygen, discussed a range of subjects, including both scientific discoveries and the progress of industry. They saw the new technologies of the industrial revolution as opening up all kinds of opportunities. Anything seemed to be possible. Mary Shelley must have caught some of this enthusiasm, and this sense that anything was possible, even something as amazing as making a living "human" being from body parts, makes the story of *Frankenstein* believable. By the time the third edition was published in 1831, railways hauled by steam locomotives were being built and the possibilities of technology seemed endless. People would soon be joking that ingenious inventors would make machines that would be able to manufacture young children by means of steam power.

Volume Three

Chapter 1

D ay after day, week after week, passed away on my return to
Geneva; and I could not collect the courage to recommence
my work. I feared the vengeance of the disappointed fiend, yet I
was unable to overcome my repugnance to the task which was
enjoined me. I found that I could not compose a female without
again devoting several months to profound study and laborious
disquisition. I had heard of some discoveries having been made by
an English philosopher, the knowledge of which was material to my
success, and I sometimes thought of obtaining my father's consent
to visit England for this purpose; but I clung to every pretence
of delay, and shrank from taking the first step in an undertaking
whose immediate necessity began to appear less absolute to me. A
change indeed had taken place in me: my health, which had hitherto
declined, was now much restored; and my spirits, when unchecked
by the memory of my unhappy promise, rose proportionably. My
father saw this change with pleasure, and he turned his thoughts
towards the best method of eradicating the remains of my
melancholy, which every now and then would return by fits, and
with a devouring blackness overcast the approaching sunshine. At
these moments I took refuge in the most perfect solitude. I passed
whole days on the lake alone in a little boat, watching the clouds,
and listening to the rippling of the waves, silent and listless. But the
fresh air and bright sun seldom failed to restore me to some degree
of composure; and, on my return, I met the salutations of my friends
with a readier smile and a more cheerful heart.

It was after my return from one of these rambles that my father,
calling me aside, thus addressed me –

'I am happy to remark, my dear son, that you have resumed your
former pleasures, and seem to be returning to yourself. And yet you
are still unhappy, and still avoid our society. For some time I was lost
in conjecture as to the cause of this; but yesterday an idea struck me,
and if it is well founded, I conjure you to avow it. Reserve on such a
point would be not only useless, but draw down treble misery on
us all.'

I trembled violently at his **exordium**, and my father continued –
'I confess, my son, that I have always looked forward to your
marriage with our dear Elizabeth as the tie of our domestic comfort,
and the stay of my declining years. You were attached to each other
from your earliest infancy; you studied together, and appeared, in
dispositions and tastes, entirely suited to one another. But so blind is
the experience of man, that what I conceived to be the best assistants
to my plan may have entirely destroyed it. You, perhaps, regard her
as your sister, without any wish that she might become your wife.
Nay, you may have met with another whom you may love; and
considering yourself as bound in honour to Elizabeth, this struggle
may occasion the poignant misery which you appear to feel.'

'My dear father, re-assure yourself. I love my cousin tenderly and
sincerely. I never saw any woman who excited, as Elizabeth does, my
warmest admiration and affection. My future hopes and prospects
are entirely bound up in the expectation of our union.'

'The expression of your sentiments of this subject, my dear Victor,
gives me more pleasure than I have for some time experienced. If
you feel thus, we shall assuredly be happy, however present events
may cast a gloom over us. But it is this gloom which appears to have
taken so strong a hold of your mind, that I wish to dissipate. Tell
me, therefore, whether you object to an immediate **solemnisation**
of the marriage. We have been unfortunate, and recent events have
drawn us from that everyday tranquillity befitting my years and
infirmities. You are younger; yet I do not suppose, possessed as
you are of a competent fortune, that an early marriage would at
all interfere with any future plans of honour and utility that you
may have formed. Do not suppose, however, that I wish to dictate
happiness to you, or that a delay on your part would cause me any
serious uneasiness. Interpret my words with candour and answer me,
I conjure you, with confidence and sincerity.'

I listened to my father in silence, and remained for some time
incapable of offering any reply. I revolved rapidly in my mind
a multitude of thoughts, and endeavoured to arrive at some
conclusion. Alas! to me the idea of an immediate union with my
Elizabeth was one of horror and dismay. I was bound by a solemn
promise, which I had not yet fulfilled, and dared not break; or if I
did, what manifold miseries might not impend over me and my

---

exordium Introductory part of a speech.
solemnisation Performance of a ceremony or rite.

devoted family! Could I enter into a festival with this deadly weight yet hanging round my neck, and bowing me to the ground? I must perform my engagement, and let the monster depart with his mate, before I allowed myself to enjoy the delight of a union from which I expected peace.

I remembered also the necessity imposed upon me of either journeying to England, or entering into a long correspondence with those philosophers of that country, whose knowledge and discoveries were of indispensable use to me in my present undertaking. The latter method of obtaining the desired intelligence was **dilatory** and unsatisfactory: besides, I had an insurmountable aversion to the idea of engaging myself in my loathsome task in my father's house, while in habits of familiar intercourse with those I loved. I knew that a thousand fearful accidents might occur, the slightest of which would disclose a tale to thrill all connected with me with horror. I was aware also that I should often lose all self-command, all capacity of hiding the harrowing sensations that would possess me during the progress of my unearthly occupation. I must absent myself from all I loved while thus employed. Once commenced, it would quickly be achieved, and I might be restored to my family in peace and happiness. My promise fulfilled, the monster would depart forever. Or (so my fond fancy imaged) some accident might meanwhile occur to destroy him, and put an end to my slavery forever.

These feelings dictated my answer to my father. I expressed a wish to visit England; but concealing the true reasons of this request, I clothed my desires under a guise which excited no suspicion, while I urged my desire with an earnestness that easily induced my father to comply. After so long a period of an absorbing melancholy, that resembled madness in its intensity and effects, he was glad to find that I was capable of taking pleasure in the idea of such a journey, and he hoped that change of scene and varied amusement would, before my return, have restored me entirely to myself.

The duration of my absence was left to my own choice; a few months, or at most a year, was the period contemplated. One paternal kind precaution he had taken to ensure my having a companion. Without previously communicating with me, he had, in concert with Elizabeth, arranged that Clerval should join me in Strasburgh. This interfered with the solitude I coveted for the

dilatory Slow, tending to cause delay.

prosecution of my task; yet at the commencement of my journey the presence of my friend could in no way be an impediment, and truly I rejoiced that thus I should be saved many hours of lonely, maddening reflection. Nay, Henry might stand between me and the intrusion of my foe. If I were alone, would he not at times force his abhorred presence on me, to remind me of my task or to contemplate its progress?

To England, therefore, I was bound, and it was understood that my union with Elizabeth should take place immediately on my return. My father's age rendered him extremely averse to delay. For myself, there was one reward I promised myself from my detested toils – one consolation for my unparalleled sufferings; it was the prospect of that day when, enfranchised from my miserable slavery, I might claim Elizabeth, and forget the past in union with her.

I now made arrangements for my journey; but one feeling haunted me, which filled me with fear and agitation. During my absence I should leave my friends unconscious of the existence of their enemy, and unprotected from his attacks, exasperated as he might be by my departure. But he had promised to follow me wherever I might go; and would he not accompany me to England? This imagination was dreadful in itself, but soothing, inasmuch as it supposed the safety of my friends. I was agonised with the idea of the possibility that the reverse of this might happen. But through the whole period during which I was the slave of my creature I allowed myself to be governed by the impulses of the moment; and my present sensations strongly intimated that the fiend would follow me, and exempt my family from the danger of his **machinations**.

It was in the latter end of August that I again quitted my native country. My journey had been my own suggestion, and Elizabeth, therefore, acquiesced; but she was filled with disquiet at the idea of my suffering, away from her, the inroads of misery and grief. It had been her care which provided me a companion in Clerval – and yet a man is blind to a thousand minute circumstances, which call forth a woman's **sedulous** attention. She longed to bid me hasten my return – a thousand conflicting emotions rendered her mute, as she bade me a tearful, silent farewell.

I threw myself into the carriage that was to convey me away, hardly knowing whither I was going, and careless of what was

machinations Plots or schemes, usually with evil intent.
sedulous Diligent, persistent.

passing around. I remembered only, and it was with a bitter anguish that I reflected on it, to order that my chemical instruments should be packed to go with me. Filled with dreary imaginations, I passed through many beautiful and majestic scenes, but my eyes were fixed and unobserving. I could only think of the **bourne** of my travels, and the work which was to occupy me whilst they endured.

After some days spent in listless **indolence**, during which I traversed many leagues, I arrived at Strasburgh where I waited two days for Clerval. He came. Alas, how great was the contrast between us! He was alive to every new scene; joyful when he saw the beauties of the setting sun, and more happy when he beheld it rise and recommence a new day. He pointed out to me the shifting colours of the landscape, and the appearances of the sky. 'This is what it is to live,' he cried; 'now I enjoy existence! But you, my dear Frankenstein, wherefore are you desponding and sorrowful?' In truth, I was occupied by gloomy thoughts, and neither saw the descent of the evening star, nor the golden sunrise reflected in the Rhine. – And you, my friend, would be far more amused with the journal of Clerval, who observed the scenery with an eye of feeling and delight, than in listening to my reflections. I, a miserable wretch, haunted by a curse that shut up every avenue to enjoyment.

We had agreed to descend the Rhine in a boat from Strasburgh to Rotterdam, whence we might take shipping for London. During this voyage we passed many willowy islands, and saw several beautiful towns. We stayed a day at Mannheim, and, on the fifth from our departure from Strasburgh, arrived at Mayence. The course of the Rhine below Mayence becomes much more picturesque. The river descends rapidly, and winds between hills, not high, but steep, and of beautiful forms. We saw many ruined castles standing on the edges of precipices, surrounded by black woods, high and inaccessible. This part of the Rhine, indeed, presents a singularly variegated landscape. In one spot you view rugged hills, ruined castles overlooking tremendous precipices, with the dark Rhine rushing beneath; and, on the sudden turn of a promontory, flourishing vineyards with green sloping banks and a meandering river and populous towns occupy the scene.

We travelled at the time of the vintage, and heard the song of the labourers, as we glided down the stream. Even I, depressed in

bourne Literally, stream; here used figuratively to mean the course of Frankenstein's travels.

indolence A state of torpor or ease without pleasure or pain.

mind, and my spirits continually agitated by gloomy feelings, even
I was pleased. I lay at the bottom of the boat, and, as I gazed on the
cloudless blue sky, I seemed to drink in a tranquillity to which I
had long been a stranger. And if these were my sensations, who can
describe those of Henry? He felt as if he had been transported to
Fairy-land and enjoyed a happiness seldom tasted by man. 'I have
seen,' he said, 'the most beautiful scenes of my own country; I have
visited the lakes of Lucerne and Uri, where the snowy mountains
descend almost perpendicularly to the water, casting black and
impenetrable shades, which would cause a gloomy and mournful
appearance were it not for the most verdant islands that relieve
the eye by their gay appearance; I have seen this lake agitated by a
tempest, when the wind tore up whirlwinds of water and gave you
an idea of what the waterspout must be on the great ocean; and the
waves dash with fury the base of the mountain, where the priest
and his mistress were overwhelmed by an avalanche and where their
dying voices are still said to be heard amid the pauses of the nightly
wind; I have seen the mountains of La Valais, and the Pays de Vaud:
but this country, Victor, pleases me more than all those wonders. The
mountains of Switzerland are more majestic and strange; but there
is a charm in the banks of this divine river, that I never before saw
equalled. Look at that castle which overhangs yon precipice; and that
also on the island, almost concealed amongst the foliage of those
lovely trees; and now that group of labourers coming from among
their vines; and that village half hid in the recess of the mountain.
Oh, surely the spirit that inhabits and guards this place has a soul
more in harmony with man than those who pile the glacier, or retire
to the inaccessible peaks of the mountains of our own country.'

Clerval! beloved friend! Even now it delights me to record your
words, and to dwell on the praise of which you are so eminently
deserving. He was a being formed in the '**very poetry of nature**'.
His wild and enthusiastic imagination was chastened by the
sensibility of his heart. His soul overflowed with ardent affections,
and his friendship was of that devoted and wondrous nature that
the worldly-minded teach us to look for only in the imagination.
But even human sympathies were not sufficient to satisfy his eager
mind. The scenery of external nature, which others regard only with
admiration, he loved with ardour: –

'**very poetry of nature**' Quotation from *The
Story of Rimini* by English poet Leigh Hunt
(1784–1859).

> The sounding cataract
> Haunted him like a passion: the tall rock,
> The mountain, and the deep and gloomy wood,
> Their colours and their forms, were then to him
> An appetite; a feeling, and a love,
> That had no need of a remoter charm,
> By thought supplied, or any interest
> Unborrow'd from the eye.★

And where does he now exist? Is this gentle and lovely being lost forever? Has this mind, so **replete** with ideas, imaginations fanciful and magnificent, which formed a world, whose existence depended on the life of its creator – has this mind perished? Does it now only exist in my memory? No, it is not thus; your form so divinely wrought, and beaming with beauty, has decayed, but your spirit still visits and consoles your unhappy friend.

Pardon this gush of sorrow; these ineffectual words are but a slight tribute to the unexampled worth of Henry, but they soothe my heart, overflowing with the anguish which his remembrance creates. I will proceed with my tale.

Beyond Cologne we descended to the plains of Holland; and we resolved to post the remainder of our way; for the wind was contrary, and the stream of the river was too gentle to aid us.

Our journey here lost the interest arising from beautiful scenery, but we arrived in a few days at Rotterdam; whence we proceeded by sea to England. It was on a clear morning, in the latter days of September, that I first saw the white cliffs of Britain. The banks of the Thames presented a new scene; they were flat, but fertile, and almost every town was marked by the remembrance of some story. We saw **Tilbury Fort**, and remembered the **Spanish Armada**; Gravesend, Woolwich, and Greenwich – places which I had heard of even in my country.

At length we saw the numerous steeples of London, **St Paul's** towering above all, and the **Tower**, famed in English history.

---

* Wordsworth's *Tintern Abbey* [author's footnote].

replete Plentifully supplied.

Tilbury Fort A fort built on the bank of the Thames River to protect London from invasion.

Spanish Armada Fleet of ships sent by King Philip II of Spain to invade England in 1588.

St Paul's St Paul's Cathedral, London.

Tower The Tower of London.

Individuals and outcasts

The Romantic writers of early-19th-century England (see pp.234–235) placed a huge emphasis on the individual. In doing this they were reacting against the values of the previous generation of thinkers and writers, who prized rational discussion and who often seemed to be more interested in the collective good than in personal emotions. The Romantics' interest in the individual was so strong that the typical "Romantic hero" was an isolated person or a social outcast, often waging a personal war on the beliefs or values of the rest of society.

Emotion and imagination

Unlike the thinkers of the Enlightenment (see pp.72–73), the Romantics valued the irrational side of the human character and, above all, the imagination. They often wrote about people struggling to make a living in a harsh environment. They saw the writer as an isolated person too, whose emotions and imagination could best be expressed in poetry. The idea of the artist expressing his or her own emotions seems commonplace today, but in the Romantic period this stress on individual feelings was quite new. It turned the writer into a kind of hero, struggling to put complex ideas and emotions on paper, and suffering because this was so difficult and because readers did not always understand the results.

The outcast

The Romantic writers' fascination with outcasts from society probably resulted from many of them being outcasts themselves. Rebelling against social norms, supporting political revolutions, and traveling to places considered to be remote and uncivilized—all of these were typical of the rebellious Romantic writers. Scandals in his personal life forced Lord Byron, for instance, to leave Britain for continental Europe. Percy Shelley was expelled from Oxford University because he wrote and published a pamphlet called The Necessity of Atheism at a time when all members of the university were required not only to be Christians but also members of the Church of England. Also, Mary Shelley made herself into a social outcast by

Remote castles
Ancient strongholds on isolated crags, like Lichtenstein Castle in Germany, were favorite settings for the outcast heroes of the Romantic period.

running away with Percy and living with him before they were married. Lord Byron, especially, put outcasts at the center of his work. Several of his long poems—*Childe Harold's Pilgrimage, Manfred,* and *Don Juan*—have heroes who live apart from mainstream society, just as their author did. Harold and Don Juan travel restlessly, while Manfred lives on his own in a castle in the Alps, in a setting similar to that of *Frankenstein*.

The ultimate outcast

Victor Frankenstein is perhaps the greatest of all these Romantic outcasts. He begins as a clever young man who promises to do well in his scientific studies. But because he takes the wrong course he isolates himself. He pursues his secret research in a lonely room, and is forced to haunt graveyards and charnel houses to find the body parts he needs for his work. When things go wrong, and his creation turns against him, he isolates himself further because he is unable to tell other people what he has done. The Creature he gives life to becomes an outcast, too, in spite of his attempt to make friends with humanity. When those around Frankenstein begin to suffer as a result of his actions, he is more and more cut off from the world. His promise to create a second being as a companion for the Creature sends him to Orkney in the far North, one of the loneliest places in Europe. Although Mary Shelley does not actually spell this out, it is as if Victor has taken the Romantic ideal of isolated striving to too great an extreme. He turns what could have been the worthwhile endeavor of scientific research into something hideous, and has to face the terrible consequences. In this he is contrasted with Walton, who repeatedly says that his journey of exploration would be easier if he had a friend to accompany him.

Orkney
Frankenstein travels to the Orkney Islands off the northern coast of Scotland in search of complete isolation.

Chapter 2

L ondon was our present point of rest; we determined to
remain several months in this wonderful and celebrated city.
Clerval desired the intercourse of the men of genius and talent
who flourished at this time; but this was with me a secondary
object; I was principally occupied with the means of obtaining
the information necessary for the completion of my promise,
and quickly availed myself of the letters of introduction that I
had brought with me, addressed to the most distinguished
natural philosopher.

If this journey had taken place during my days of study and
happiness, it would have afforded me inexpressible pleasure. But a
blight had come over my existence, and I only visited these people
for the sake of the information they might give me on the subject in
which my interest was so terribly profound. Company was irksome
to me; when alone, I could fill my mind with the sights of heaven
and earth; the voice of Henry soothed me, and I could thus cheat
myself into a **transitory** peace. But busy, uninteresting, joyous faces
brought back despair to my heart. I saw an insurmountable barrier
placed between me and my fellow-men; this barrier was sealed
with the blood of William and Justine, and to reflect on the events
connected with those names filled my soul with anguish.

But in Clerval I saw the image of my former self; he was
inquisitive, and anxious to gain experience and instruction.
The difference of manners which he observed was to him an
inexhaustible source of instruction and amusement. He was also
pursuing an object he had long had in view. His design was to
visit India, in the belief that he had in his knowledge of its various
languages, and in the views he had taken of its society, the means of
materially assisting the progress of European colonisation and trade.
In Britain only could he further the execution of his plan. He was
forever busy; and the only check to his enjoyments was my sorrowful
and dejected mind. I tried to conceal this as much as possible, that
I might not debar him from the pleasures natural to one, who was
entering on a new scene of life, undisturbed by any care or bitter

transitory Short-lived.

recollection. I often refused to accompany him, alleging another engagement, that I might remain alone. I now also began to collect the materials necessary for my new creation, and this was to me like the torture of single drops of water continually falling on the head. Every thought that was devoted to it was an extreme anguish, and every word that I spoke in allusion to it caused my lips to quiver, and my heart to palpitate.

After passing some months in London, we received a letter from a person in Scotland, who had formerly been our visitor at Geneva. He mentioned the beauties of his native country, and asked us if those were not sufficient allurements to induce us to prolong our journey as far north as Perth, where he resided. Clerval eagerly desired to accept this invitation; and I, although I abhorred society, wished to view again mountains and streams, and all the wondrous works with which Nature adorns her chosen dwelling-places.

We had arrived in England at the beginning of October, and it was now February. We accordingly determined to commence our journey towards the north at the expiration of another month. In this expedition we did not intend to follow the great road to Edinburgh, but to visit Windsor, Oxford, Matlock, and the **Cumberland lakes**, resolving to arrive at the completion of this tour about the end of July. I packed up my chemical instruments and the materials I had collected, resolving to finish my labours in some obscure nook in the northern highlands of Scotland.

We quitted London on the 27th of March and remained a few days at Windsor, rambling in its beautiful forest. This was a new scene to us mountaineers; the majestic oaks, the quantity of game, and the herds of stately deer, were all novelties to us.

From thence we proceeded to Oxford. As we entered this city, our minds were filled with the remembrance of the events that had been transacted there more than a century and a half before. It was here that **Charles I** had collected his forces. This city had remained faithful to him, after the whole nation had forsaken his cause to join the standard of parliament and liberty. The memory of that unfortunate king, and his companions, the amiable **Falkland**, the insolent **Goring**, his queen and son, gave a peculiar interest to every part of the city, which they might be supposed to have inhabited. The spirit of elder days found a dwelling here, and we

---

Cumberland lakes Group of lakes in north-western England dear to the Romantic poets.
Charles I (1600–1649), King of England, Scotland, and Ireland from 1625 until his execution for high treason in 1649.

Falkland Lucius Cary, second Viscount Falkland (c. 1610-1643) Secretary of State to Charles I.
Goring Lord George Goring (1608–1657), (see glossary).

delighted to trace its footsteps. If these feelings had not found an imaginary gratification, the appearance of the city had yet in itself sufficient beauty to obtain our admiration. The colleges are ancient and picturesque; the streets are almost magnificent; and the lovely **Isis**, which flows beside it through meadows of exquisite verdure, is spread forth into a placid expanse of waters, which reflects its majestic assemblage of towers, and spires, and domes, embosomed among aged trees.

I enjoyed this scene; and yet my enjoyment was embittered both by the memory of the past, and the anticipation of the future. I was formed for peaceful happiness. During my youthful days discontent never visited my mind; and if I was ever overcome by *ennui*, the sight of what is beautiful in nature, or the study of what is excellent and sublime in the productions of man, could always interest my heart, and communicate elasticity to my spirits. But I am a blasted tree; the bolt has entered my soul; and I felt then that I should survive to exhibit what I shall soon cease to be – a miserable spectacle of wrecked humanity, pitiable to others, and intolerable to myself.

We passed a considerable period at Oxford, rambling among its environs, and endeavouring to identify every spot which might relate to the most animating epoch of English history. Our little voyages of discovery were often prolonged by the successive objects that presented themselves. We visited the tomb of the illustrious **Hampden**, and the field on which that patriot fell. For a moment my soul was elevated from its debasing and miserable fears, to contemplate the divine ideas of liberty and self-sacrifice, of which these sights were the monuments and the remembrancers. For an instant I dared to shake off my chains, and look around me with a free and lofty spirit; but the iron had eaten into my flesh, and I sank again, trembling and hopeless, into my miserable self.

We left Oxford with regret, and proceeded to Matlock, which was our next place of rest. The country in the neighbourhood of this village resembled, to a greater degree, the scenery of Switzerland; but every thing is on a lower scale, and the green hills want the crown of distant white Alps, which always attend on the piny mountains of my native country. We visited the wondrous cave, and the little cabinets of natural history, where the curiosities are disposed in the same

Isis Alternative name for the Thames River where it passes through Oxford.

ennui French for boredom or dissatisfaction.

Hampden John Hampden (1594–1643), a statesman and central figure at the start of the English Civil War. He fought for the Parliamentary cause and was mortally wounded at the Battle of Chalgrove.

manner as in the collections at Servox and Chamounix. The latter
name made me tremble when pronounced by Henry; and I hastened
to quit Matlock, with which that terrible scene was thus associated.

From Derby, still journeying northwards, we passed two months
in Cumberland and Westmorland. I could now almost fancy myself
among the Swiss mountains. The little patches of snow which yet
lingered on the northern sides of the mountains, the lakes, and the
dashing of the rocky streams, were all familiar and dear sights to me.
Here also we made some acquaintances, who almost contrived to
cheat me into happiness. The delight of Clerval was proportionably
greater than mine; his mind expanded in the company of men
of talent, and he found in his own nature greater capacities and
resources than he could have imagined himself to have possessed
while he associated with his inferiors. 'I could pass my life here,'
said he to me; 'and among these mountains I should scarcely regret
Switzerland and the Rhine.'

But he found that a traveller's life is one that includes much pain
amidst its enjoyments. His feelings are forever on the stretch; and
when he begins to sink into repose, he finds himself obliged to quit
that on which he rests in pleasure for something new, which again
engages his attention, and which also he forsakes for other novelties.

We had scarcely visited various lakes of Cumberland and
Westmorland, and conceived an affection for some of the inhabitants,
when the period of our appointment with our Scotch friend
approached, and we left them to travel on. For my own part I was
not sorry. I had now neglected my promise for some time, and I
feared the effects of the daemon's disappointment. He might remain
in Switzerland, and wreak his vengeance on my relatives. This idea
pursued me, and tormented me at every moment from which I
might otherwise have snatched repose and peace. I waited for my
letters with feverish impatience: if they were delayed, I was miserable,
and overcome by a thousand fears; and when they arrived and I saw
the superscription of Elizabeth or my father, I hardly dared to read
and ascertain my fate. Sometimes I thought that the fiend followed
me, and might expedite my remissness by murdering my companion.
When these thoughts possessed me, I would not quit Henry for a
moment, but followed him as his shadow, to protect him from the
fancied rage of his destroyer. I felt as if I had committed some great

crime, the consciousness of which haunted me. I was guiltless, but I had indeed drawn down a horrible curse upon my head, as mortal as that of crime.

I visited Edinburgh with languid eyes and mind; and yet that city might have interested the most unfortunate being. Clerval did not like it so well as Oxford: for the antiquity of the latter city was more pleasing to him. But the beauty and regularity of the new town of Edinburgh, its romantic castle and its environs, the most delightful in the world, **Arthur's Seat**, **St Bernard's Well**, and the Pentland Hills, compensated him for the change, and filled him with cheerfulness and admiration. But I was impatient to arrive at the termination of my journey.

We left Edinburgh in a week, passing through Coupar, St Andrew's, and along the banks of the Tay, to Perth, where our friend expected us. But I was in no mood to laugh and talk with strangers, or enter into their feelings or plans with the good humour expected from a guest; and accordingly I told Clerval that I wished to make the tour of Scotland alone. 'Do you,' said I, 'enjoy yourself, and let this be our rendezvous. I may be absent a month or two; but do not interfere with my motions, I intreat you: leave me to peace and solitude for a short time; and when I return, I hope it will be with a lighter heart, more congenial to your own temper.'

Henry wished to dissuade me; but seeing me bent on this plan, ceased to remonstrate. He intreated me to write often. 'I had rather be with you,' he said, 'in your solitary rambles, than with these Scotch people, whom I do not know: hasten, then, my dear friend, to return, that I may again feel myself somewhat at home, which I cannot do in your absence.'

Having parted from my friend, I determined to visit some remote spot of Scotland, and finish my work in solitude. I did not doubt but that the monster followed me, and would discover himself to me when I should have finished, that he might receive his companion.

With this resolution I traversed the northern highlands, and fixed on one of the remotest of the **Orkneys** as the scene of my labours. It was a place fitted for such a work, being hardly more than a rock, whose high sides were continually beaten upon by the waves. The soil was barren, scarcely affording pasture for a few miserable cows, and oatmeal for its inhabitants, which consisted of five persons,

---

Arthur's Seat Hill in the city of Edinburgh, giving panoramic views of the city and Scottish coast.

St Bernard's Well Elegant building housing a pump that brings up water from a hot spring near the Water of Leith, a river that flows through Edinburgh, Scotland.

Orkneys A group of about 70 islands off the coast of northern Scotland.

whose gaunt and scraggy limbs gave tokens of their miserable fare.
Vegetables and bread, when they indulged in such luxuries, and even
fresh water, was to be procured from the mainland, which was about
five miles distant.

On the whole island there were but three miserable huts, and one
of these was vacant when I arrived. This I hired. It contained but two
rooms, and these exhibited all the squalidness of the most miserable
penury. The thatch had fallen in, the walls were unplastered, and
the door was off its hinges. I ordered it to be repaired, bought some
furniture, and took possession; an incident which would, doubtless,
have occasioned some surprise had not all the senses of the cottagers
been benumbed by want and squalid poverty. As it was, I lived
ungazed at and unmolested, hardly thanked for the pittance of food
and clothes which I gave; so much does suffering blunt even the
coarsest sensations of men.

In this retreat I devoted the morning to labour; but in the evening,
when the weather permitted, I walked on the stony beach of the sea
to listen to the waves as they roared and dashed at my feet. It was
a monotonous yet everchanging scene. I thought of Switzerland; it
was far different from this desolate and appalling landscape. Its hills
are covered with veins, and its cottages are scattered thickly in the
plains. Its fair lakes reflect a blue and gentle sky; and, when troubled
by the winds, their tumult is but as the play of a lively infant, when
compared to the roarings of the giant ocean.

In this manner I distributed my occupations when I first arrived;
but as I proceeded in my labour, it became every day more horrible
and irksome to me. Sometimes I could not prevail on myself to enter
my laboratory for several days; and at other times I toiled day and
night in order to complete my work. It was, indeed, a filthy process
in which I was engaged. During my first experiment, a kind of
enthusiastic frenzy had blinded me to the horror of my employment;
my mind was intently fixed on the consummation of my labour, and
my eyes shut to the horror of my proceedings. But now I went to it
in cold blood, and my heart often sickened at the work of my hands.

Thus situated, employed in the most detestable occupation,
immersed in a solitude where nothing could for an instant call my
attention from the actual scene in which I was engaged, my spirits
became unequal; I grew restless and nervous. Every moment I feared

penury Poverty, destitution.

to meet my persecutor. Sometimes I sat with my eyes fixed on the ground, fearing to raise them, lest they should encounter the object which I so much dreaded to behold. I feared to wander from the sight of my fellow-creatures, lest when alone he should come to claim his companion.

In the mean time I worked on, and my labour was already considerably advanced. I looked towards its completion with a tremulous and eager hope, which I dared not trust myself to question, but which was intermixed with obscure forebodings of evil, that made my heart sicken in my bosom.

Chapter 3

I sat one evening in my laboratory; the sun had set, and the
moon was just rising from the sea; I had not sufficient light for
my employment, and I remained idle, in a pause of consideration
of whether I should leave my labour for the night, or hasten its
conclusion by an unremitting attention to it. As I sat, a train of
reflection occurred to me, which led me to consider the effects of
what I was now doing. Three years before I was engaged in the same
manner, and had created a fiend whose unparalleled barbarity had
desolated my heart, and filled it forever with the bitterest remorse.
I was now about to form another being, of whose dispositions I
was alike ignorant; she might become ten thousand times more
malignant than her mate, and delight, for its own sake, in murder
and wretchedness. He had sworn to quit the neighbourhood of
man, and hide himself in deserts; but she had not; and she, who in all
probability was to become a thinking and reasoning animal, might
refuse to comply with a compact made before her creation. They
might even hate each other; the creature who already lived loathed
his own deformity, and might he not conceive a greater abhorrence
for it when it came before his eyes in the female form? She also
might turn with disgust from him to the superior beauty of man;
she might quit him, and he be again alone, exasperated by the fresh
provocation of being deserted by one of his own species.

Even if they were to leave Europe, and inhabit the deserts of the
new world, yet one of the first results of those sympathies for which
the daemon thirsted would be children, and a race of devils would
be propagated upon the earth, who might make the very existence
of the species of man a condition precarious and full of terror. Had
I a right, for my own benefit, to inflict this curse upon everlasting
generations? I had before been moved by the **sophisms** of the being
I had created; I had been struck senseless by his fiendish threats: but
now, for the first time, the wickedness of my promise burst upon me;
I shuddered to think that future ages might curse me as their pest,
whose selfishness had not hesitated to buy its own peace at the price,
perhaps, of the existence of the whole human race.

sophisms Deceptive, misleading arguments.

I trembled, and my heart failed within me, when, on looking up, I saw, by the light of the moon, the daemon at the casement. A ghastly grin wrinkled his lips as he gazed on me, where I sat fulfilling the task which he had allotted to me. Yes, he had followed me in my travels; he had loitered in forests, hid himself in caves, or taken refuge in wide and desert heaths; and he now came to mark my progress, and claim the fulfilment of my promise.

As I looked on him, his countenance expressed the utmost extent of malice and treachery. I thought with a sensation of madness on my promise of creating another like to him, and trembling with passion, tore to pieces the thing on which I was engaged. The wretch saw me destroy the creature on whose future existence he depended for happiness, and, with a howl of devilish despair and revenge, withdrew.

I left the room, and, locking the door, made a solemn vow in my own heart never to resume my labours; and then, with trembling steps, I sought my own apartment. I was alone; none were near me to dissipate the gloom, and relieve me from the sickening oppression of the most terrible reveries.

Several hours passed, and I remained near my window gazing on the sea; it was almost motionless, for the winds were hushed, and all nature reposed under the eye of the quiet moon. A few fishing vessels alone specked the water, and now and then the gentle breeze wafted the sound of voices as the fishermen called to one another. I felt the silence, although I was hardly conscious of its extreme profundity, until my ear was suddenly arrested by the paddling of oars near the shore, and a person landed close to my house.

In a few minutes after, I heard the creaking of my door, as if some one endeavoured to open it softly. I trembled from head to foot; I felt a presentiment of who it was, and wished to rouse one of the peasants who dwelt in a cottage not far from mine; but I was overcome by the sensation of helplessness, so often felt in frightful dreams, when you in vain endeavour to fly from an impending danger, and was rooted to the spot.

Presently I heard the sound of footsteps along the passage; the door opened, and the wretch whom I dreaded appeared. Shutting the door, he approached me and said in a smothered voice –

'You have destroyed the work which you began; what is it that you intend? Do you dare to break your promise? I have endured toil and misery: I left Switzerland with you; I crept along the shores of the Rhine, among its willow islands, and over the summits of its hills. I have dwelt many months in the heaths of England, and among the deserts of Scotland. I have endured incalculable fatigue, and cold, and hunger, do you dare destroy my hopes?'

'Begone! I do break my promise; never will I create another like yourself, equal in deformity and wickedness.'

'Slave, I before reasoned with you, but you have proved yourself unworthy of my **condescension**. Remember that I have power; you believe yourself miserable, but I can make you so wretched that the light of day will be hateful to you. You are my creator, but I am your master – obey!'

'The hour of my **irresolution** is past, and the period of your power is arrived. Your threats cannot move me to do an act of wickedness; but they confirm me in a determination of not creating you a companion in vice. Shall I, in cool blood, set loose upon the earth a daemon, whose delight is in death and wretchedness? Begone! I am firm, and your words will only exasperate my rage.'

The monster saw my determination in my face, and gnashed his teeth in the impotence of anger. 'Shall each man,' cried he, 'find a wife for his bosom, and each beast have his mate, and I be alone? I had feelings of affection, and they were requited by detestation and scorn. Man! you may hate, but beware! your hours will pass in dread and misery, and soon the bolt will fall which must ravish from you your happiness forever. Are you to be happy, while I grovel in the intensity of my wretchedness? You can blast my other passions, but revenge remains – revenge, henceforth dearer than light or food! I may die, but first you, my tyrant and tormentor, shall curse the sun that gazes on your misery. Beware; for I am fearless, and therefore powerful. I will watch with the wiliness of a snake, that I may sting with its venom. Man, you shall repent of the injuries you inflict.'

'Devil, cease; and do not poison the air with these sounds of malice. I have declared my resolution to you, and I am no coward to bend beneath words. Leave me; I am inexorable.'

'It is well. I go; but remember, I shall be with you on your wedding-night.'

I started forward, and exclaimed, 'Villain! Before you sign my

---

condescension Here, acting kindly toward one's inferiors.

irresolution Indecisiveness.

death-warrant, be sure that you are yourself safe.'

I would have seized him; but he eluded me, and quitted the house with precipitation. In a few moments I saw him in his boat, which shot across the waters with an arrowy swiftness, and was soon lost amidst the waves.

All was again silent; but his words rang in my ears. I burned with rage to pursue the murderer of my peace, and precipitate him into the ocean. I walked up and down my room hastily and perturbed, while my imagination conjured up a thousand images to torment and sting me. Why had I not followed him, and closed with him in mortal strife? But I had suffered him to depart, and he had directed his course towards the mainland. I shuddered to think who might be the next victim sacrificed to his **insatiate** revenge. And then I thought again of his words – '*I will be with you on your wedding-night.*' That then was the period fixed for the fulfilment of my destiny. In that hour I should die, and at once satisfy and extinguish his malice. The prospect did not move me to fear; yet when I thought of my beloved Elizabeth, – of her tears and endless sorrow, when she should find her lover so barbarously snatched from her, – tears, the first I had shed for many months, streamed from my eyes, and I resolved not to fall before my enemy without a bitter struggle.

The night passed away, and the sun rose from the ocean; my feelings became calmer, if it may be called calmness, when the violence of rage sinks into the depths of despair. I left the house, the horrid scene of the last night's contention, and walked on the beach of the sea, which I almost regarded as an insuperable barrier between me and my fellow-creatures; nay, a wish that such should prove the fact stole across me. I desired that I might pass my life on that barren rock, wearily, it is true, but uninterrupted by any sudden shock of misery. If I returned, it was to be sacrificed, or to see those whom I most loved die under the grasp of a daemon whom I had myself created.

I walked about the isle like a restless spectre, separated from all it loved, and miserable in the separation. When it became noon, and the sun rose higher, I lay down on the grass, and was overpowered by a deep sleep. I had been awake the whole of the preceding night, my nerves were agitated, and my eyes inflamed by watching and misery. The sleep into which I now sunk refreshed me; and when I awoke, I again felt as if I belonged to a race of human beings like myself, and

insatiate Incapable of being satisfied.

I began to reflect upon what had passed with greater composure; yet still the words of the fiend rung in my ears like a death-knell; they appeared like a dream, yet distinct and oppressive as a reality.

The sun had far descended, and I still sat on the shore, satisfying my appetite, which had become ravenous, with an oaten cake, when I saw a fishing-boat land close to me, and one of the men brought me a packet; it contained letters from Geneva, and one from Clerval entreating me to join him. He said that he was wearing away his time fruitlessly where he was; that letters from the friends he had formed in London desired his return to complete the negotiation they had entered into for his Indian enterprise. He could not any longer delay his departure; but as his journey to London might be followed, even sooner than he now conjectured, by his longer voyage, he entreated me to bestow as much of my society on him as I could spare. He besought me, therefore, to leave my solitary isle, and to meet him at Perth, that we might proceed southwards together. This letter in a degree recalled me to life, and I determined to quit my island at the expiration of two days.

Yet, before I departed, there was a task to perform, on which I shuddered to reflect: I must pack up my chemical instruments; and for that purpose I must enter the room which had been the scene of my odious work, and I must handle those utensils, the sight of which was sickening to me. The next morning, at daybreak, I summoned sufficient courage, and unlocked the door of my laboratory. The remains of the half-finished creature, whom I had destroyed, lay scattered on the floor, and I almost felt as if I had mangled the living flesh of a human being. I paused to collect myself, and then entered the chamber. With trembling hand I conveyed the instruments out of the room; but I reflected that I ought not to leave the relics of my work to excite the horror and suspicion of the peasants; and I accordingly put them into a basket, with a great quantity of stones, and, laying them up, determined to throw them into the sea that very night; and in the mean time I sat upon the beach, employed in cleaning and arranging my chemical apparatus.

Nothing could be more complete than the alteration that had taken place in my feelings since the night of the appearance of the daemon. I had before regarded my promise with a gloomy despair, as a thing that, with whatever consequences, must be fulfilled; but I now felt as if a film had been taken from before my eyes, and that I, for the first time, saw clearly. The idea of renewing my labours did not for one instant occur to me; the threat I had heard weighed on my thoughts, but I did not reflect that a voluntary act of mine could avert it. I had resolved in my own mind, that to create another like the fiend I had first made would be an act of the basest and most atrocious selfishness; and I banished from my mind every thought that could lead to a different conclusion.

Between two and three in the morning the moon rose; and I then, putting my basket aboard a little skiff, sailed out about four miles from the shore. The scene was perfectly solitary: a few boats were returning towards land, but I sailed away from them. I felt as if I was about the commission of a dreadful crime, and avoided with shuddering anxiety any encounter with my fellow-creatures. At one time the moon, which had before been clear, was suddenly overspread by a thick cloud, and I took advantage of the moment of darkness and cast my basket into the sea: I listened to the gurgling sound as it sunk, and then sailed away from the spot. The sky became clouded; but the air was pure, although chilled by the north-east breeze that was then rising. But it refreshed me, and filled me with such agreeable sensations, that I resolved to prolong my stay on the water; and, fixing the rudder in a direct position, stretched myself at the bottom of the boat. Clouds hid the moon, every-thing was obscure, and I heard only the sound of the boat, as its keel cut through the waves; the murmur lulled me, and in a short time I slept soundly.

I do not know how long I remained in this situation, but when I awoke I found that the sun had already mounted considerably. The wind was high, and the waves continually threatened the safety of my little skiff. I found that the wind was north-east, and must have driven me far from the coast from which I had embarked. I endeavoured to change my course, but quickly found that if I again made the attempt, the boat would be instantly filled with water.

Thus situated, my only resource was to drive before the wind. I confess that I felt a few sensations of terror. I had no compass with me, and was so slenderly acquainted with the geography of this part of the world, that the sun was of little benefit to me. I might be driven into the wide Atlantic, and feel all the tortures of starvation, or be swallowed up in the immeasurable waters that roared and

buffeted around me. I had already been out many hours, and felt
the torment of a burning thirst, a prelude to my other sufferings.
I looked on the heavens, which were covered by clouds that flew
before the wind, only to be replaced by others: I looked upon the
sea, it was to be my grave. 'Fiend,' I exclaimed, 'your task is already
fulfilled!' I thought of Elizabeth, of my father, and of Clerval; all
left behind, on whom the monster might satisfy his sanguinary and
merciless passions. This idea plunged me into a reverie, so despairing
and frightful, that even now, when the scene is on the point of
closing before me forever, I shudder to reflect on it.

Some hours passed thus; but by degrees, as the sun declined
towards the horizon, the wind died away into a gentle breeze, and
the sea became free from breakers. But these gave place to a heavy
swell; I felt sick, and hardly able to hold the rudder, when suddenly I
saw a line of high land towards the south.

Almost spent, as I was, by fatigue, and the dreadful suspense I
endured for several hours, this sudden certainty of life rushed like a
flood of warm joy to my heart, and tears gushed from my eyes.

How **mutable** are our feelings, and how strange is that clinging
love we have of life even in the excess of misery! I constructed
another sail with a part of my dress, and eagerly steered my course
towards the land. It had a wild and rocky appearance, but, as I
approached nearer, I easily perceived the traces of cultivation. I saw
vessels near the shore, and found myself suddenly transported back to
the neighbourhood of civilised man. I carefully traced the windings
of the land, and hailed a steeple which I at length saw issuing from
behind a small promontory. As I was in a state of extreme **debility**,
I resolved to sail directly towards the town, as a place where I could
most easily procure nourishment. Fortunately I had money with
me. As I turned the promontory, I perceived a small neat town and
a good harbour, which I entered, my heart bounding with joy at my
unexpected escape.

As I was occupied in fixing the boat and arranging the sails, several
people crowded towards the spot. They seemed much surprised at
my appearance, but instead of offering me any assistance, whispered
together with gestures that at any other time might have produced
in me a slight sensation of alarm. As it was, I merely remarked that
they spoke English; and I therefore addressed them in that language.

mutable Changeable.
debility Infirmity, weakness.

'My good friends,' said I, 'will you be so kind as to tell me the name of this town, and inform me where I am?'

'You will know that soon enough,' replied a man with a hoarse voice. 'May be you are come to a place that will not prove much to your taste; but you will not be consulted as to your quarters, I promise you.'

I was exceedingly surprised on receiving so rude an answer from a stranger; and I was also disconcerted on perceiving the frowning and angry countenances of his companions. 'Why do you answer me so roughly?' I replied; 'surely it is not the custom of Englishmen to receive strangers so inhospitably.'

'I do not know,' said the man, 'what the custom of the English may be; but it is the custom of the Irish to hate villains.'

While this strange dialogue continued, I perceived the crowd rapidly increase. Their faces expressed a mixture of curiosity and anger, which annoyed, and in some degree alarmed me. I enquired the way to the inn; but no one replied. I then moved forward, and a murmuring sound arose from the crowd as they followed and surrounded me; when an ill-looking man approaching, tapped me on the shoulder, and said, 'Come, sir, you must follow me to Mr Kirwin's, to give an account of yourself.'

'Who is Mr Kirwin? Why am I to give an account of myself? Is not this a free country?'

'Ay, sir, free enough for honest folks. Mr Kirwin is a magistrate; and you are to give an account of the death of a gentleman who was found murdered here last night.'

This answer startled me; but I presently recovered myself. I was innocent; that could easily be proved: accordingly I followed my conductor in silence and was led to one of the best houses in the town. I was ready to sink from fatigue and hunger; but, being surrounded by a crowd, I thought it politic to rouse all my strength, that no physical debility might be construed into apprehension or conscious guilt. Little did I then expect the calamity that was in a few moments to overwhelm me, and extinguish in horror and despair all fear of ignominy or death.

I must pause here; for it requires all my fortitude to recall the memory of the frightful events which I am about to relate, in proper detail, to my recollection.

Chapter 4

I was soon introduced into the presence of the magistrate, an old **benevolent** man, with calm and mild manners. He looked on me, however, with some degree of severity; and then, turning towards my conductors, he asked who appeared as witnesses on this occasion.

About half a dozen men came forward; and, one being selected by the magistrate, he **deposed**, that he had been out fishing the night before with his son and brother-in-law, Daniel Nugent, when, about ten o'clock, they observed a strong northerly blast rising, and they accordingly put in for port. It was a very dark night, as the moon had not yet risen; they did not land at the harbour, but, as they had been accustomed, at a creek about two miles below. He walked on first, carrying a part of the fishing tackle, and his companions followed him at some distance. As he was proceeding along the sands, he struck his foot against something, and fell at his length on the ground. His companions came up to assist him; and, by the light of their lantern, they found that he had fallen on the body of a man, who was to all appearance dead. Their first supposition was, that it was the corpse of some person who had been drowned, and was thrown on shore by the waves, but, on examination, they found that the clothes were not wet, and even that the body was not then cold. They instantly carried it to the cottage of an old woman near the spot, and endeavoured, but in vain, to restore it to life. It appeared to be a handsome young man, about five and twenty years of age. He had apparently been strangled; for there was no sign of any violence, except the black mark of fingers on his neck.

The first part of his deposition did not in the least interest me; but when the mark of the fingers was mentioned, I remembered the murder of my brother and felt myself extremely agitated; my limbs trembled, and a mist came over my eyes, which obliged me to lean on a chair for support. The magistrate observed me with a keen eye, and of course drew an unfavourable **augury** from my manner.

The son confirmed his father's account: but when Daniel Nugent was called, he swore positively that just before the fall of his companion, he saw a boat, with a single man in it, at a short distance

benevolent Kindly; charitable.
deposed Gave testimony; told his story.
augury Knowledge of future or hidden things.

from the shore; and, as far as he could judge by the light of a few stars, it was the same boat in which I had just landed.

A woman deposed, that she lived near the beach, and was standing at the door of her cottage, waiting for the return of the fishermen, about an hour before she heard of the discovery of the body, when she saw a boat with only one man in it push off from that part of the shore where the corpse was afterwards found.

Another woman confirmed the account of the fishermen having brought the body into her house; it was not cold. They put it into a bed and rubbed it; and Daniel went to the town for an **apothecary**, but life was quite gone.

Several other men were examined concerning my landing; and they agreed that, with the strong north wind that had arisen during the night, it was very probable that I had beaten about for many hours, and had been obliged to return nearly to the same spot from which I had departed. Besides, they observed that it appeared that I had brought the body from another place, and it was likely, that as I did not appear to know the shore, I might have put into the harbour ignorant of the distance of the town of ★★★ from the place where I had deposited the corpse.

Mr Kirwin, on hearing this evidence, desired that I should be taken into the room where the body lay for interment, that it might be observed what effect the sight of it would produce upon me. This idea was probably suggested by the extreme agitation I had exhibited when the mode of the murder had been described. I was accordingly conducted, by the magistrate and several other persons, to the inn. I could not help being struck by the strange coincidences that had taken place during this eventful night; but, knowing that I had been conversing with several persons in the island I had inhabited about the time that the body had been found, I was perfectly tranquil as to the consequences of the affair.

I entered the room where the corpse lay, and was led up to the coffin. How can I describe my sensations of beholding it? I feel yet parched with horror, nor can I reflect on that terrible moment without shuddering and agony. The examination, the presence of the magistrate and witnesses, passed like a dream from my memory, when I saw the lifeless form of Henry Clerval stretched before me. I gasped for breath; and throwing myself on the body, I exclaimed,

apothecary A druggist or pharmacist. Or, more generally, one who keeps a shop selling items such as drugs and spices.

'Have my murderous machinations deprived you also, my dearest
Henry, of life? Two I have already destroyed; other victims await their
destiny: but you, Clerval, my friend, my benefactor –'

The human frame could no longer support the agonies that I
endured, and I was carried out of the room in strong convulsions.

A fever succeeded to this. I lay for two months on the point of
death: my ravings, as I afterwards heard, were frightful; I called myself
the murderer of William, of Justine, and of Clerval. Sometimes I
intreated my attendants to assist me in the destruction of the fiend
by whom I was tormented; and at others, I felt the fingers of the
monster already grasping my neck, and screamed aloud with agony
and terror. Fortunately, as I spoke my native language, Mr Kirwin
alone understood me; but my gestures and bitter cries were sufficient
to affright the other witnesses.

Why did I not die? More miserable than man ever was before, why
did I not sink into forgetfulness and rest? Death snatches away many
blooming children, the only hopes of their doating parents: how
many brides and youthful lovers have been one day in the bloom of
health and hope, and the next a prey for worms and the decay of the
tomb! Of what materials was I made, that I could thus resist so many
shocks, which, like the turning of the wheel, continually renewed
the torture?

But I was doomed to live; and in two months, found myself as
awaking from a dream, in a prison, stretched on a wretched bed,
surrounded by gaolers, turnkeys, bolts, and all the miserable apparatus
of a dungeon. It was morning, I remember, when I thus awoke to
understanding: I had forgotten the particulars of what had happened,
and only felt as if some great misfortune had suddenly overwhelmed
me; but when I looked around, and saw the barred windows, and
the squalidness of the room in which I was, all flashed across my
memory, and I groaned bitterly.

This sound disturbed an old woman who was sleeping in a chair
beside me. She was a hired nurse, the wife of one of the turnkeys,
and her countenance expressed all those bad qualities which often
characterise that class. The lines of her face were hard and rude, like that
of persons accustomed to see without sympathising in sights of misery.
Her tone expressed her entire indifference; she addressed me in English,
and the voice struck me as one that I had heard during my sufferings: –

'Are you better now, sir?' said she.

I replied in the same language, with a feeble voice, 'I believe I am; but if it all be true, if indeed I did not dream, I am sorry that I am still alive to feel this misery and horror.'

'For that matter,' replied the old woman, 'if you mean about the gentleman you murdered, I believe that it were better for you if you were dead, for I fancy it will go hard for you! However, that's none of my business; I am sent to nurse you and get you well; I do my duty with a safe conscience; it were well if everybody did the same.'

I turned with loathing from the woman who could utter so unfeeling a speech to a person just saved, on the very edge of death; but I felt **languid**, and unable to reflect on all that had passed. The whole series of my life appeared to me as a dream; I sometimes doubted if indeed it were all true, for it never presented itself to my mind with the force of reality.

As the images that floated before me became more distinct, I grew feverish; a darkness pressed around me: no one was near me who soothed me with the gentle voice of love; no dear hand supported me. The physician came and prescribed medicines, and the old woman prepared them for me; but utter carelessness was visible in the first, and the expression of brutality was strongly marked in the visage of the second. Who could be interested in the fate of a murderer, but the hangman who would gain his fee?

These were my first reflections; but I soon learned that Mr Kirwin had shown me extreme kindness. He had caused the best room in the prison to be prepared for me (wretched indeed was the best); and it was he who had provided a physician and a nurse. It is true, he seldom came to see me, for although he ardently desired to relieve the sufferings of every human creature, he did not wish to be present at the agonies and miserable ravings of a murderer. He came, therefore, sometimes to see that I was not neglected; but his visits were short, and with long intervals.

One day, while I was gradually recovering, I was seated in a chair, my eyes half open, and my cheeks livid like those in death. I was overcome by gloom and misery, and often reflected I had better seek death than desire to remain in a world which to me was replete with wretchedness. At one time I considered whether I should not declare myself guilty, and suffer the penalty of the law, less innocent

---

languid Weak with fatigue.

than poor Justine had been. Such were my thoughts, when the
door of my apartment was opened, and Mr Kirwin entered. His
countenance expressed sympathy and compassion; he drew a chair
close to mine and addressed me in French –

'I fear that this place is very shocking to you; can I do anything to
make you more comfortable?'

'I thank you, but all that you mention is nothing to me: on the
whole earth there is no comfort which I am capable of receiving.'

'I know that the sympathy of a stranger can be but of little relief to
one borne down as you are by so strange a misfortune. But you will,
I hope, soon quit this melancholy abode; for, doubtless, evidence can
easily be brought to free you from the criminal charge.'

'That is my least concern: I am, by a course of strange events,
become the most miserable of mortals. Persecuted and tortured as I
am and have been, can death be any evil to me?'

'Nothing indeed could be more unfortunate and agonising than
the strange chances that have lately occurred. You were thrown, by
some surprising accident, on this shore, renowned for its hospitality;
seized immediately, and charged with murder. The first sight that was
presented to your eyes was the body of your friend, murdered in so
unaccountable a manner, and placed, as it were, by some fiend across
your path.'

As Mr Kirwin said this, notwithstanding the agitation I endured
on this retrospect of my sufferings, I also felt considerable surprise
at the knowledge he seemed to possess concerning me. I suppose
some astonishment was exhibited in my countenance; for Mr Kirwin
hastened to say –

'Immediately upon your being taken ill, all the papers that were
on your person were brought me, and I examined them that I might
discover some trace by which I could send to your relations an
account of your misfortune and illness. I found several letters, and,
among others, one which I discovered from its commencement to
be from your father. I instantly wrote to Geneva: nearly two months
have elapsed since the departure of my letter: – But you are ill, even
now you tremble: you are unfit for agitation of any kind.'

'This suspense is a thousand times worse than the most horrible
event: tell me what new scene of death has been acted, and whose I
am now to lament?'

'Your family is perfectly well,' said Mr Kirwin, with gentleness: 'and some one, a friend, is come to visit you.'

I know not by what chain of thought, the idea presented itself, but it instantly darted into my mind that the murderer had come to mock at my misery, and taunt me with the death of Clerval, as a new incitement for me to comply with his hellish desires. I put my hand before my eyes, and cried out in agony –

'Oh! Take him away! I cannot see him; for God's sake, do not let him enter!'

Mr Kirwin regarded me with a troubled countenance. He could not help regarding my exclamation as a presumption of my guilt, and said, in rather a severe tone –

'I should have thought, young man, that the presence of your father would have been welcome instead of inspiring such violent repugnance.'

'My father!' cried I, while every feature and every muscle was relaxed from anguish to pleasure: 'is my father indeed come? How kind, how very kind! But where is he, why does he not hasten to me?'

My change of manner surprised and pleased the magistrate; perhaps he thought that my former exclamation was a momentary return of delirium, and now he instantly resumed his former benevolence. He rose, and quitted the room with my nurse, and in a moment my father entered it.

Nothing, at this moment, could have given me greater pleasure than the arrival of my father. I stretched out my hand to him and cried –

'Are you, then, safe – and Elizabeth – and Ernest?'

My father calmed me with assurances of their welfare, and endeavoured, by dwelling on these subjects so interesting to my heart, to raise my desponding spirits; but he soon felt that a prison cannot be the abode of cheerfulness. 'What a place is this that you inhabit, my son!' said he, looking mournfully at the barred windows, and wretched appearance of the room. 'You travelled to seek happiness, but a fatality seems to pursue you. And poor Clerval –'

The name of my unfortunate and murdered friend was an agitation too great to be endured in my weak state; I shed tears.

'Alas! yes, my father,' replied I; 'some destiny of the most horrible kind hangs over me, and I must live to fulfil it, or surely I should have died on the coffin of Henry.'

We were not allowed to converse for any length of time, for the **precarious** state of my health rendered every precaution necessary that could ensure tranquillity. Mr Kirwin came in, and insisted that my strength should not be exhausted by too much exertion. But the appearance of my father was to me like that of my good angel, and I gradually recovered my health.

As my sickness quitted me, I was absorbed by a gloomy and black melancholy, that nothing could dissipate. The image of Clerval was forever before me, ghastly and murdered. More than once the agitation into which these reflections threw me made my friends dread a dangerous relapse. Alas! why did they preserve so miserable and detested a life? It was surely that I might fill my destiny, which is now drawing to a close. Soon, oh! very soon, will death extinguish these throbbings, and relieve me from the mighty weight of anguish that bears me to the dust; and, in executing the award of justice, I shall also sink to rest. Then the appearance of death was distant, although the wish was ever present to my thoughts; and I often sat for hours motionless and speechless, wishing for some mighty revolution that might bury me and my destroyer in its ruins.

The season of the assizes approached. I had already been three months in prison; and although I was still weak and in continual danger of a relapse, I was obliged to travel nearly a hundred miles to the county-town, where the court was held. Mr Kirwin charged himself with every care of collecting witnesses, and arranging my defence. I was spared the disgrace of appearing publicly as a criminal, as the case was not brought before the court that decides on life and death. The grand jury rejected the bill, on its being proved that I was on the Orkney Islands at the hour the body of my friend was found; and a fortnight after my removal I was liberated from prison.

My father was enraptured on finding me freed from the vexations of a criminal charge, that I was again allowed to breathe the fresh atmosphere, and permitted to return to my native country. I did not participate in these feelings; for to me the walls of a dungeon or a palace were alike hateful. The cup of life was poisoned for ever; and although the sun shone upon me, as upon the happy and gay of heart, I saw around me nothing but a dense and frightful darkness,

precarious Insecure, uncertain

penetrated by no light but the glimmer of two eyes that glared upon me. Sometimes they were the expressive eyes of Henry, languishing in death, the dark orbs nearly covered by the lids, and the long black lashes that fringed them; sometimes it was the watery, clouded eyes of the monster, as I first saw them in my chamber at Ingolstadt.

My father tried to awaken in me the feelings of affection. He talked of Geneva, which I should soon visit – of Elizabeth and Ernest; but these words only drew deep groans from me. Sometimes, indeed, I felt a wish for happiness; and thought, with melancholy delight of my beloved cousin; or longed, with a devouring *maladie du pays*, to see once more the blue lake and rapid Rhone, that had been so dear to me in early childhood: but my general state of feeling was a **torpor**, in which a prison was as welcome a residence as the divinest scene in nature; and these fits were seldom interrupted but by paroxysms of anguish and despair. At these moments I often endeavoured to put an end to the existence I loathed; and it required unceasing attendance and vigilance to restrain me from committing some dreadful act of violence.

Yet one duty remained to me, the recollection of which finally triumphed over my selfish despair. It was necessary that I should return without delay to Geneva, there to watch over the lives of those I so fondly loved; and to lie in wait for the murderer, that if any chance led me to the place of his concealment, or if he dared again to blast me by his presence, I might, with unfailing aim, put an end to the existence of the monstrous Image which I had endued with the mockery of a soul still more monstrous. My father still desired to delay our departure, fearful that I could not sustain the fatigues of a journey: for I was a shattered wreck – the shadow of a human being. My strength was gone. I was a mere skeleton; and fever night and day preyed upon my wasted frame.

Still, as I urged our leaving Ireland with such inquietude and impatience, my father thought it best to yield. We took our passage on board a vessel bound for **Havre-de-Grâce**, and sailed with a fair wind from the Irish shores. It was midnight. I lay on the deck, looking at the stars, and listening to the dashing of the waves. I hailed the darkness that shut Ireland from my sight; and my pulse beat with a feverish joy when I reflected that I should soon see Geneva. The past appeared to me in the light of a frightful dream;

---

maladie du pays French for homesickness.
torpor sluggishness.
Havre-de-Grâce A fortified harbor in Normandy, France.

yet the vessel in which I was, the wind that blew me from the detested shore of Ireland, and the sea which surrounded me, told me too forcibly that I was deceived by no vision, and that Clerval, my friend and dearest companion, had fallen a victim to me and the monster of my creation. I repassed, in my memory, my whole life – my quiet happiness while residing with my family in Geneva, the death of my mother, and my departure for Ingolstadt. I remembered, shuddering, the mad enthusiasm that hurried me on to the creation of my hideous enemy, and I called to mind the night in which he first lived. I was unable to pursue the train of thought; a thousand feelings pressed upon me, and I wept bitterly.

Ever since my recovery from the fever, I had been in the custom of taking every night a small quantity of **laudanum**; for it was by means of this drug only that I was enabled to gain the rest necessary for the preservation of life. Oppressed by the recollection of my various misfortunes, I now swallowed double my usual quantity, and soon slept profoundly. But sleep did not afford me respite from thought and misery; my dreams presented a thousand objects that scared me. Towards morning I was possessed by a kind of nightmare; I felt the fiend's grasp in my neck; and could not free myself from it; groans and cries rang in my ears. My father, who was watching over me, perceiving my restlessness, awoke me; the dashing waves were around: the cloudy sky above; the fiend was not here: a sense of security, a feeling that a truce was established between the present hour and the irresistible, disastrous future, imparted to me a kind of calm forgetfulness, of which the human mind is by its structure peculiarly susceptible.

laudanum A narcotic consisting of an alcohol solution of opium.

Chapter 5

The voyage came to an end. We landed, and proceeded to Paris. I soon found that I had overtaxed my strength, and that I must repose before I could continue my journey. My father's care and attentions were **indefatigable**; but he did not know the origin of my sufferings, and sought erroneous methods to remedy the incurable ill. He wished me to seek amusement in society. I abhorred the face of man. Oh, not abhorred! they were my brethren, my fellow beings, and I felt attracted even to the most repulsive among them, as to creatures of an angelic nature and celestial mechanism. But I felt that I had no right to share their intercourse. I had unchained an enemy among them, whose joy it was to shed their blood, and to revel in their groans. How they would, each and all, abhor me, and hunt me from the world, did they know my unhallowed acts and the crimes which had their source in me!

My father yielded at length to my desire to avoid society, and strove by various arguments to banish my despair. Sometimes he thought that I felt deeply the degradation of being obliged to answer a charge of murder, and he endeavoured to prove to me the futility of pride.

'Alas! my father,' said I, 'how little do you know me. Human beings, their feelings and passions, would indeed be degraded if such a wretch as I felt pride. Justine, poor unhappy Justine, was as innocent as I, and she suffered the same charge; she died for it; and I am the cause of this – I murdered her. William, Justine, and Henry – they all died by my hands.'

My father had often, during my imprisonment, heard me make the same assertion; when I thus accused myself, he sometimes seemed to desire an explanation, and at others he appeared to consider it as the offspring of delirium, and that, during my illness, some idea of this kind had presented itself to my imagination, the remembrance of which I preserved in my convalescence. I avoided explanation, and maintained a continual silence concerning the wretch I had created. I had a persuasion that I should be supposed mad; and this in itself would forever have chained my tongue. But, besides, I could

indefatigable Untiring.

not bring myself to disclose a secret which would fill my hearer with consternation, and make fear and unnatural horror the inmates of his breast. I checked, therefore, my impatient thirst for sympathy, and was silent when I would have given the world to have confided that fatal secret. Yet still words like those I have recorded would burst uncontrollably from me. I could offer no explanation of them; but their truth in part relieved the burden of my mysterious woe.

Upon this occasion my father said, with an expression of unbounded wonder, 'My dearest Victor, what infatuation is this? My dear son, I entreat you never to make such an assertion again.'

'I am not mad,' I cried energetically; 'the sun and the heavens, who have viewed my operations, can bear witness of my truth. I am the assassin of those most innocent victims; they died by my machinations. A thousand times would I have shed my own blood, drop by drop, to have saved their lives; but I could not, my father, indeed I could not sacrifice the whole human race.'

The conclusion of this speech convinced my father that my ideas were deranged, and he instantly changed the subject of our conversation, and endeavoured to alter the course of my thoughts. He wished as much as possible to obliterate the memory of the scenes that had taken place in Ireland, and never alluded to them, or suffered me to speak of my misfortunes.

As time passed away I became more calm; misery had her dwelling in my heart, but I no longer talked in the same incoherent manner of my own crimes; sufficient for me was the consciousness of them. By the utmost self-violence I curbed the **imperious** voice of wretchedness, which sometimes desired to declare itself to the whole world; and my manners were calmer and more composed than they had ever been since my journey to the sea of ice.

A few days before we left Paris on our way to Switzerland, I received the following letter from Elizabeth: –

MY DEAR FRIEND,

It gave me the greatest pleasure to receive a letter from my uncle dated at Paris; you are no longer at a formidable distance, and I may hope to see you in less than a fortnight. My poor cousin, how much you must have suffered! I expect to see you looking even more ill than when you quitted Geneva. This winter has been passed more

imperious Urgent, overbearing.

miserably, tortured as I have been by anxious suspense; yet I hope to see peace in your countenance, and to find that your heart is not totally void of comfort and tranquillity.

Yet I fear that the same feelings now exist that made you so miserable a year ago, even perhaps augmented by time. I would not disturb you at this period, when so many misfortunes weigh upon you; but a conversation that I had with my uncle previous to his departure renders some explanation necessary before we meet.

Explanation! You may possibly say; what can Elizabeth have to explain? If you really say this, my questions are answered, and all my doubts satisfied. But you are distant from me, and it is possible that you may dread, and yet be pleased with this explanation; and, in a probability of this being the case, I dare not any longer postpone writing what, during your absence, I have often wished to express to you, but have never had the courage to begin.

You well know, Victor, that our union had been the favourite plan of your parents ever since our infancy. We were told this when young, and taught to look forward to it as an event that would certainly take place. We were affectionate playfellows during childhood, and, I believe, dear and valued friends to one another as we grew older. But as brother and sister often entertain a lively affection towards each other, without desiring a more intimate union, may not such also be our case? Tell me, dearest Victor. Answer me, I conjure you, by our mutual happiness, with simple truth – Do you not love another?

You have travelled: you have spent several years of your life at Ingolstadt; and I confess to you, my friend, that when I saw you last autumn so unhappy, flying to solitude, from the society of every creature, I could not help supposing that you might regret our connection, and believe yourself bound in honour to fulfil the wishes of your parents, although they opposed themselves to your inclinations. But this is false reasoning. I confess to you, my friend, that I love you, and that in my airy dreams of futurity you have been my constant friend and companion. But it is your happiness I desire as well as my own, when I declare to you that our marriage would render me eternally miserable, unless it were the dictate of your own free choice. Even now I weep to think that, borne down as you are by the cruellest misfortunes, you may stifle, by the word 'honour', all hope of that love and happiness which would alone restore you to yourself. I, who have so disinterested an affection for you, may increase your miseries tenfold by being an obstacle to your wishes. Ah! Victor, be assured that your cousin and playmate has too sincere a love for you not to be made miserable by this supposition. Be happy, my friend; and if you obey me in this one request, remain satisfied that nothing on earth will have the power to interrupt my tranquillity.

Do not let this letter disturb you; do not answer tomorrow, or the next day, or even until you come, if it will give you pain. My uncle will send me news of your health; and if I see but one smile on your lips when we meet, occasioned by this or any other exertion of mine, I shall need no other happiness.

ELIZABETH LAVENZA
Geneva, May 18th, 17–.

This letter revived in my memory what I had before forgotten, the threat of the fiend – '*I will be with you on your wedding-night!*' Such was my sentence, and on that night would the daemon employ every art to destroy me, and tear me from the glimpse of happiness which promised partly to console my sufferings. On that night he had determined to consummate his crimes by my death. Well, be it so; a deadly struggle would then assuredly take place, in which if he were victorious I should be at peace, and his power over me be at an end. If he were vanquished, I should be a free man. Alas! what freedom? Such as the peasant enjoys when his family have been massacred before his eyes, his cottage burnt, his lands laid waste, and he is turned adrift, homeless, penniless, and alone, but free. Such would be my liberty, except that in my Elizabeth I possessed a treasure; alas! balanced by those horrors of remorse and guilt, which would pursue me until death.

Sweet and beloved Elizabeth! I read and re-read her letter, and some softened feelings stole into my heart, and dared to whisper **paradisiacal** dreams of love and joy; but the apple was already eaten, and the angel's arm bared to drive me from all hope. Yet I would die to make her happy. If the monster executed his threat, death was inevitable; yet, again, I considered whether my marriage would hasten my fate. My destruction might indeed arrive a few

paradisiacal Heavenly.

months sooner; but if my torturer should suspect that I postponed it, influenced by his menaces, he would surely find other and perhaps more dreadful means of revenge. He had vowed *to be with me on my wedding-night*, yet he did not consider that threat as binding him to peace in the mean time, for as if to show me that he was not yet satiated with blood, he had murdered Clerval immediately after the **enunciation** of his threats. I resolved, therefore, that if my immediate union with my cousin would conduce either to hers or my father's happiness, my adversary's designs against my life should not retard it a single hour.

In this state of mind I wrote to Elizabeth. My letter was calm and affectionate. 'I fear, my beloved girl,' I said, 'little happiness remains for us on earth; yet all that I may one day enjoy is centred in you. Chase away your idle fears; to you alone do I consecrate my life, and my endeavours for contentment. I have one secret, Elizabeth, a dreadful one; when revealed to you, it will chill your frame with horror, and then, far from being surprised at my misery, you will only wonder that I survive what I have endured. I will confide this tale of misery and terror to you the day after our marriage shall take place, for, my sweet cousin, there must be perfect confidence between us. But until then, I conjure you, do not mention or allude to it. This I most earnestly intreat, and I know you will comply.'

In about a week after the arrival of Elizabeth's letter, we returned to Geneva. The sweet girl welcomed me with warm affection; yet tears were in her eyes; as she beheld my emaciated frame and feverish cheeks. I saw a change in her also. She was thinner, and had lost much of that heavenly vivacity that had before charmed me; but her gentleness, and soft looks of compassion, made her a more fit companion for one blasted and miserable as I was.

The tranquillity which I now enjoyed did not endure. Memory brought madness with it; and when I thought of what had passed, a real insanity possessed me; sometimes I was furious and burnt with rage; sometimes low and despondent. I neither spoke, nor looked at any one, but sat motionless, bewildered by the multitude of miseries that overcame me.

Elizabeth alone had the power to draw me from these fits; her gentle voice would soothe me when transported by passion, and inspire me with human feelings when sunk in torpor. She wept

enunciation Utterance.

with me, and for me. When reason returned, she would remonstrate, and endeavour to inspire me with resignation. Ah! it is well for the unfortunate to be resigned, but for the guilty there is no peace. The agonies of remorse poison the luxury there is otherwise sometimes found in indulging the excess of grief.

Soon after my arrival, my father spoke of my immediate marriage with Elizabeth. I remained silent.

'Have you, then, some other attachment?'

'None on earth. I love Elizabeth and look forward to our union with delight. Let the day therefore be fixed; and on it I will consecrate myself, in life or death, to the happiness of my cousin.'

'My dear Victor, do not speak thus. Heavy misfortunes have befallen us, but let us only cling closer to what remains, and transfer our love for those whom we have lost to those who yet live. Our circle will be small, but bound close by the ties of affection and mutual misfortune. And when time shall have softened your despair, new and dear objects of care will be born to replace those of whom we have been so cruelly deprived.'

Such were the lessons of my father. But to me the remembrance of the threat returned: nor can you wonder that, omnipotent as the fiend had yet been in his deeds of blood, I should almost regard him as invincible; and that when he had pronounced the words '*I shall be with you on your wedding-night*', I should regard the threatened fate as unavoidable. But death was no evil to me, if the loss of Elizabeth were balanced with it; and I therefore, with a contented and even cheerful countenance, agreed with my father, that if my cousin would consent, the ceremony should take place in ten days, and thus put, as I imagined, the seal to my fate.

Great God! if for one instant I had thought what might be the hellish intention of my fiendish adversary, I would rather have banished myself for ever from my native country, and wandered a friendless outcast over the earth, than have consented to this miserable marriage. But, as if possessed of magic powers, the monster had blinded me to his real intentions; and when I thought that I had prepared only my own death, I hastened that of a far dearer victim.

As the period fixed for our marriage drew nearer, whether from cowardice or a prophetic feeling, I felt my heart sink within me. But I concealed my feelings by an appearance of hilarity, that brought smiles and joy to the countenance of my father, but hardly deceived the ever-watchful and **nicer** eye of Elizabeth. She looked forward to our union with placid contentment, not unmingled with a little fear, which past misfortunes had impressed, that what now appeared certain and tangible happiness, might soon dissipate into an airy dream, and leave no trace but deep and everlasting regret.

Preparations were made for the event, congratulatory visits were received, and all wore a smiling appearance. I shut up, as well as I could, in my own heart the anxiety that preyed there, and entered with seeming earnestness into the plans of my father, although they might only serve as the decorations of my tragedy. Through my father's exertions, a part of the inheritance of Elizabeth had been restored to her by the Austrian government. A small possession on the shores of Como belonged to her. It was agreed that, immediately after our union, we should proceed to Villa Lavenza, and spend our first days of happiness beside the beautiful lake near which it stood.

In the mean time I took every precaution to defend my person, in case the fiend should openly attack me. I carried pistols and a dagger constantly about me, and was ever on the watch to prevent artifice; and by these means gained a greater degree of tranquillity. Indeed, as the period approached, the threat appeared more as a delusion, not to be regarded as worthy to disturb my peace, while the happiness I hoped for in my marriage wore a greater appearance of certainty, as the day fixed for its solemnisation drew nearer, and I heard it continually spoken of as an occurrence which no accident could possibly prevent.

Elizabeth seemed happy; my tranquil demeanour contributed greatly to calm her mind. But on the day that was to fulfil my wishes and my destiny, she was melancholy, and a presentiment of evil pervaded her; and perhaps also she thought of the dreadful secret which I had promised to reveal to her on the following day. My father was in the mean time overjoyed, and in the bustle of preparation only recognised in the melancholy of his niece the diffidence of a bride.

After the ceremony was performed, a large party assembled at my father's; but it was agreed that Elizabeth and I should commence our journey by water, sleeping that night at Evian, and continuing our voyage on the following day. The day was fair, the wind favourable,

---

nicer More careful, discriminating, perceptive.

all smiled on our nuptial embarkation.

Those were the last moments of my life during which I enjoyed the feeling of happiness. We passed rapidly along: the sun was hot, but we were sheltered from its rays by a kind of canopy, while we enjoyed the beauty of the scene, sometimes on one side of the lake, where we saw Mont Salêve, the pleasant banks of Montalègre, and at a distance, surmounting all, the beautiful Mont Blanc, and the assemblage of snowy mountains that in vain endeavour to emulate her; sometimes coasting the opposite banks, we saw the mighty Jura opposing its dark side to the ambition that would quit its native country, and an almost insurmountable barrier to the invader who should wish to enslave it.

I took the hand of Elizabeth. 'You are sorrowful, my love. Ah! if you knew what I have suffered, and what I may yet endure, you would endeavour to let me taste the quiet and freedom from despair that this one day at least permits me to enjoy.'

'Be happy, my dear Victor,' replied Elizabeth; 'there is, I hope, nothing to distress you; and be assured that if a lively joy is not painted in my face, my heart is contented. Something whispers to me not to depend too much on the prospect that is opened before us, but I will not listen to such a sinister voice. Observe how fast we move along, and how the clouds, which sometimes obscure and sometimes rise above the dome of Mont Blanc, render this scene of beauty still more interesting. Look also at the innumerable fish that are swimming in the clear waters, where we can distinguish every pebble that lies at the bottom. What a divine day! how happy and serene all nature appears!'

Thus Elizabeth endeavoured to divert her thoughts and mine from all reflection upon melancholy subjects. But her temper was fluctuating; joy for a few instants shone in her eyes, but it continually gave place to distraction and reverie.

The sun sank lower in the heavens; we passed the river Drance, and observed its path through the chasms of the higher, and the glens of the lower hills. The Alps here come closer to the lake, and we approached the amphitheatre of mountains which forms its eastern boundary. The spire of Evian shone under the woods that surrounded it, and the range of mountain above mountain by which it was overhung.

The wind, which had hitherto carried us along with amazing rapidity, sunk at sunset to a light breeze; the soft air just ruffled the water, and caused a pleasant motion among the trees as we approached the shore, from which it wafted the most delightful scent of flowers and hay. The sun sunk beneath the horizon as we landed; and as I touched the shore, I felt those cares and fears revive, which soon were to clasp me, and cling to me forever.

Chapter 6

It was eight o'clock when we landed; we walked for a short time
on the shore, enjoying the transitory light, and then retired to
the inn, and contemplated the lovely scene of waters, woods,
and mountains, obscured in darkness, yet still displaying their
black outlines.

The wind, which had fallen in the south, now rose with great
violence in the west. The moon had reached her summit in the
heavens and was beginning to descend; the clouds swept across it
swifter than the flight of the vulture and dimmed her rays, while
the lake reflected the scene of the busy heavens, rendered still busier
by the restless waves that were beginning to rise. Suddenly a heavy
storm of rain descended.

I had been calm during the day; but so soon as night obscured the
shapes of objects, a thousand fears arose in my mind. I was anxious
and watchful, while my right hand grasped a pistol which was
hidden in my bosom; every sound terrified me; but I resolved that I
would sell my life dearly, and not shrink from the conflict until my
own life, or that of my adversary, was extinguished.

Elizabeth observed my agitation for some time in timid and fearful
silence, but there was something in my glance which communicated
terror to her, and trembling, she asked, 'What is it that agitates you,
my dear Victor? What is it you fear?'

'Oh! peace, peace, my love,' replied I; 'this night, and all will be safe:
but this night is dreadful, very dreadful.'

I passed an hour in this state of mind, when suddenly, I reflected
how fearful the combat which I momentarily expected would be to
my wife, and I earnestly intreated her to retire, resolving not to join
her until I had obtained some knowledge as to the situation of
my enemy.

She left me, and I continued some time walking up and down the
passages of the house, and inspecting every corner that might afford
a retreat to my adversary. But I discovered no trace of him, and was
beginning to conjecture that some fortunate chance had intervened
to prevent the execution of his menaces; when suddenly I heard

a shrill and dreadful scream. It came from the room into which
Elizabeth had retired. As I heard it, the whole truth rushed into my
mind, my arms dropped, the motion of every muscle and fibre was
suspended; I could feel the blood trickling in my veins, and tingling
in the extremities of my limbs. This state lasted but for an instant; the
scream was repeated, and I rushed into the room.

Great God! why did I not then expire! Why am I here to relate
the destruction of the best hope, and the purest creature of earth?
She was there, lifeless and inanimate, thrown across the bed, her head
hanging down, and her pale and distorted features half covered by
her hair. Every where I turn I see the same figure – her bloodless
arms and relaxed form flung by the murderer on its bridal bier.
Could I behold this, and live? Alas! life is obstinate, and clings closest
where it is most hated. For a moment only did I lose recollection: I
fell senseless on the ground.

When I recovered, I found myself surrounded by the people of the
inn; their countenances expressed a breathless terror: but the horror
of others appeared only as a mockery, a shadow of the feelings that
oppressed me. I escaped from them to the room where lay the body
of Elizabeth, my love, my wife, so lately living, so dear, so worthy.
She had been moved from the posture in which I had first beheld
her; and now, as she lay, her head upon her arm, and a handkerchief
thrown across her face and neck, I might have supposed her asleep.
I rushed towards her, and embraced her with ardour; but the deadly
langour and coldness of the limbs told me, that what I now held
in my arms had ceased to be the Elizabeth whom I had loved and
cherished. The murderous mark of the fiend's grasp was on her neck,
and the breath had ceased to issue from her lips.

While I still hung over her in the agony of despair, I happened to
look up. The windows of the room had before been darkened, and
I felt a kind of panic on seeing the pale yellow light of the moon
illuminate the chamber. The shutters had been thrown back; and,
with a sensation of horror not to be described, I saw at the open
window a figure the most hideous and abhorred. A grin was on the
face of the monster; he seemed to jeer, as with his fiendish finger
he pointed towards the corpse of my wife. I rushed towards the
window, and drawing a pistol from my bosom, fired: but he eluded
me, leaped from his station, and, running with the swiftness of

lightning, plunged into the lake.

The report of the pistol brought a crowd into the room. I pointed to the spot where he had disappeared, and we followed the track with boats; nets were cast, but in vain. After passing several hours, we returned hopeless, most of my companions believing it to have been a form conjured up by my fancy. After having landed, they proceeded to search the country, parties going in different directions among the woods and vines.

I attempted to accompany them, and proceeded a short distance from the house; but my head whirled round, my steps were like those of a drunken man, I fell at last in a state of utter exhaustion; a film covered my eyes, and my skin was parched with the heat of fever. In this state I was carried back, and placed on a bed, hardly conscious of what had happened; my eyes wandered round the room, as if to seek something that I had lost.

After an interval I arose, and, as if by instinct, crawled into the room where the corpse of my beloved lay. There were women weeping around; – I hung over it, and joined my sad tears to theirs – all this time no distinct idea presented itself to my mind; but my thoughts rambled to various subjects, reflecting confusedly on my misfortunes and their cause. I was bewildered, in a cloud of wonder and horror. The death of William, the execution of Justine, the murder of Clerval, and lastly of my wife; even at that moment I knew not that my only remaining friends were safe from the malignity of the fiend; my father even now might be writhing under his grasp, and Ernest might be dead at his feet. This idea made me shudder, and recalled me to action. I started up, and resolved to return to Geneva with all possible speed.

There were no horses to be procured, and I must return by the lake; but the wind was unfavourable and the rain fell in torrents. However, it was hardly morning, and I might reasonably hope to arrive by night. I hired men to row and took an oar myself; for I had always experienced relief from mental torment in bodily exercise. But the overflowing misery I now felt, and the excess of agitation that I endured, rendered me incapable of any exertion. I threw down the oar; and leaning my head upon my hands, gave way to every gloomy idea that arose. If I looked up, I saw scenes which were familiar to me in my happier time, and which I had contemplated but the day before in the company of her who was now but a shadow and a recollection. Tears streamed from my eyes. The rain had ceased for a moment, and I saw the fish play in the waters as they had done a few hours before; they had then been observed by Elizabeth. Nothing is so painful to the human mind as a great and sudden change. The sun might shine, or the clouds might lower: but nothing could appear to me as it had done the day before. A fiend had snatched from me every hope of future happiness: no creature had ever been so miserable as I was; so frightful an event is single in the history of man.

But why should I dwell upon the incidents that followed this last overwhelming event? Mine has been a tale of horrors; I have reached their *acme*, and what I must now relate can but be tedious to you. Know that, one by one, my friends were snatched away; I was left desolate. My own strength is exhausted; and I must tell, in a few words, what remains of my hideous narration.

I arrived at Geneva. My father and Ernest yet lived; but the former sunk under the tidings that I bore. I see him now, excellent and venerable old man! his eyes wandered in vacancy, for they had lost their charm and their delight – his Elizabeth, his more than daughter, whom he doated on with all that affection which a man feels, who in the decline of life, having few affections, clings more earnestly to those that remain. Cursed, cursed be the fiend that brought misery on his grey hairs, and doomed him to waste in wretchedness! He could not live under the horrors that were accumulated around him; the springs of existence suddenly gave way: he was unable to rise from his bed, and in a few days he died in my arms.

What then became of me? I know not; I lost sensation and chains and darkness were the only objects that pressed upon me. Sometimes, indeed, I dreamt that I wandered in flowery meadows and pleasant vales with the friends of my youth, but I awoke, and found myself in a dungeon. Melancholy followed, but by degrees I gained a clear conception of my miseries and situation, and was then released from my prison. For they had called me mad; and during many months, as I understood, a solitary cell had been my habitation.

Liberty, however, had been an useless gift to me, had I not, as I awakened to reason, at the same time awakened to revenge. As the memory of past misfortunes pressed upon me, I began to reflect

acme Highest point.

on their cause – the monster whom I had created, the miserable
daemon whom I had sent abroad into the world for my destruction.
I was possessed by a maddening rage when I thought of him, and
desired and ardently prayed that I might have him within my grasp
to wreak a great and signal revenge on his cursed head.

Nor did my hate long confine itself to useless wishes; I began
to reflect on the best means of securing him; and for this purpose,
about a month after my release, I repaired to a criminal judge in the
town, and told him that I had an accusation to make; that I knew the
destroyer of my family; and that I required him to exert his whole
authority for the apprehension of the murderer.

The magistrate listened to me with attention and kindness: – 'Be
assured sir,' said he, 'no pains or exertions on my part shall be spared
to discover the villain.'

'I thank you,' replied I; 'listen, therefore, to the deposition that I
have to make. It is indeed a tale so strange, that I should fear you
would not credit it were there not something in truth which,
however wonderful, forces conviction. The story is too connected
to be mistaken for a dream, and I have no motive for falsehood.'
My manner, as I thus addressed him, was impressive, but calm; I
had formed in my own heart a resolution to pursue my destroyer
to death; and this purpose quieted my agony, and for an interval
reconciled me to life. I now related my history, briefly, but with
firmness and precision, marking the dates with accuracy, and never
deviating into invective or exclamation.

The magistrate appeared at first perfectly incredulous, but
as I continued he became more attentive and interested; I saw
him sometimes shudder with horror; at others a lively surprise,
unmingled with disbelief, was painted on his countenance.

When I had concluded my narration I said, 'This is the being
whom I accuse, and for whose seizure and punishment I call upon
you to exert your whole power. It is your duty as a magistrate, and I
believe and hope that your feelings as a man will not revolt from the
execution of those functions on this occasion.'

This address caused a considerable change in the **physiognomy** of
my own auditor. He had heard my story with that half kind of belief
that is given to a tale of spirits and supernatural events; but when
he was called upon to act officially in consequence, the whole tide

physiognomy Facial features or expression.

of his incredulity returned. He, however, answered mildly, 'I would willingly afford you every aid in your pursuit; but the creature of whom you speak appears to have powers which would put all my exertions to defiance. Who can follow an animal which can traverse the sea of ice, and inhabit caves and dens where no man would venture to intrude? Besides, some months have elapsed since the commission of his crimes, and no one can conjecture to what place he has wandered, or what region he may now inhabit.

'I do not doubt that he hovers near the spot which I inhabit; and if he has indeed taken refuge in the Alps, he may be hunted like the **chamois**, and destroyed as a beast of prey. But I perceive your thoughts: you do not credit my narrative, and do not intend to pursue my enemy with the punishment which is his desert.'

As I spoke, rage sparkled in my eyes; the magistrate was intimidated: – 'You are mistaken,' said he. 'I will exert myself; and if it is in my power to seize the monster, be assured that he shall suffer punishment proportionate to his crimes. But I fear, from what you have yourself described to be his properties, that this will prove impracticable; and thus, while every proper measure is pursued, you should make up your mind to disappointment.'

'That cannot be; but all that I can say will be of little avail. My revenge is of no moment to you; yet, while I allow it to be a vice, I confess that it is the devouring and only passion of my soul. My rage is unspeakable, when I reflect that the murderer, whom I have turned loose upon society, still exists. You refuse my just demand: I have but one resource; and I devote myself, either in my life or death, to his destruction.'

I trembled with excess of agitation as I said this; there was a frenzy in my manner, and something, I doubt not, of that haughty fierceness which the martyrs of old are said to have possessed. But to a Genevan magistrate, whose mind was occupied by far other ideas than those of devotion and heroism, this elevation of mind had much the appearance of madness. He endeavoured to soothe me as a nurse does a child, and reverted to my tale as the effects of delirium.

'Man,' I cried, 'how ignorant art thou in thy pride of wisdom! Cease; you know not what it is you say.'

I broke from the house angry and disturbed, and retired to meditate on some other mode of action.

chamois Wild antelope that inhabits the highest parts of the Alps and other mountain ranges of Europe and Asia.

Chapter 7

M y present situation was one in which all voluntary thought was swallowed up and lost. I was hurried away by fury; revenge alone endowed me with strength and composure; it moulded my feelings, and allowed me to be calculating and calm, at periods when otherwise delirium or death would have been my portion.

My first resolution was to quit Geneva forever; my country, which, when I was happy and beloved, was dear to me, now, in my adversity, became hateful. I provided myself with a sum of money, together with a few jewels which had belonged to my mother, and departed.

And now my wanderings began, which are to cease but with life. I have traversed a vast portion of the earth, and have endured all the hardships which travellers, in deserts and barbarous countries, are wont to meet. How I have lived I hardly know; many times have I stretched my failing limbs upon the sandy plain, and prayed for death. But revenge kept me alive; I dared not die, and leave my adversary in being.

When I quitted Geneva, my first labour was to gain some clue by which I might trace the steps of my fiendish enemy. But my plan was unsettled; and I wandered many hours round the confines of the town, uncertain what path I should pursue. As night approached, I found myself at the entrance of the cemetery where William, Elizabeth, and my father reposed. I entered it, and approached the tomb which marked their graves. Every thing was silent, except the leaves of the trees, which were gently agitated by the wind; the night was nearly dark; and the scene would have been solemn and affecting even to an uninterested observer. The spirits of the departed seemed to flit around, and to cast a shadow, which was felt but not seen, around the head of the mourner.

The deep grief which this scene had at first excited quickly gave way to rage and despair. They were dead, and I lived; their murderer also lived, and to destroy him I must drag out my weary existence. I knelt on the grass, and kissed the earth, and with quivering lips exclaimed, 'By the sacred earth on which I kneel, by the shades that wander near me, by the deep and eternal grief that I feel, I swear; and by thee, O Night, and the spirits that preside over thee, to pursue the daemon, who caused this misery, until he or I shall perish in mortal conflict. For this purpose I will preserve my life: to execute this dear revenge will I again behold the sun, and tread the green herbage of earth, which otherwise should vanish from my eyes forever. And I call on you, spirits of the dead; and on you, wandering ministers of vengeance, to aid and conduct me in my work. Let the cursed and hellish monster drink deep of agony; let him feel the despair that now torments me.'

I had begun my **adjuration** with solemnity, and an awe which almost assured me that the shades of my murdered friends heard and approved my devotion; but the furies possessed me as I concluded, and rage choked my utterance.

I was answered through the stillness of night by a loud and fiendish laugh. It rang on my ears long and heavily; the mountains re-echoed it, and I felt as if all hell surrounded me with mockery and laughter. Surely in that moment I should have been possessed by frenzy, and have destroyed my miserable existence, but that my vow was heard, and that I was reserved for vengeance. The laughter died away; when a well-known and abhorred voice, apparently close to my ear, addressed me in an audible whisper, 'I am satisfied: miserable wretch! you have determined to live, and I am satisfied.'

I darted towards the spot from which the sound proceeded; but the devil eluded my grasp. Suddenly the broad disk of the moon arose, and shone full upon his ghastly and distorted shape, as he fled with more than mortal speed.

I pursued him; and for many months this has been my task. Guided by a slight clue, I followed the windings of the Rhône, but vainly. The blue Mediterranean appeared; and; by a strange chance, I saw the fiend enter by night, and hide himself in a vessel bound for the Black Sea. I took my passage in the same ship; but he escaped, I know not how.

Amidst the wilds of Tartary and Russia, although he still evaded me, I have ever followed in his track. Sometimes the peasants, scared by this horrid apparition, informed me of his path; sometimes he himself, who feared that if I lost all trace of him, I should despair and die, left some mark to guide me. The snows descended on my head,

adjuration Earnest appeal.

and I saw the print of his huge step on the white plain. To you first entering on life, to whom care is new, and agony unknown, how can you understand what I have felt and still feel? Cold, want, and fatigue, were the least pains which I was destined to endure; I was cursed by some devil, and carried about with me my eternal hell; yet still a spirit of good followed and directed my steps and, when I most murmured, would suddenly extricate me from seemingly insurmountable difficulties. Sometimes, when nature, overcome by hunger, sunk under the exhaustion, a repast was prepared for me in the desert, that restored and inspirited me. The fare was, indeed, coarse, such as the peasants of the country ate; but I will not doubt that it was set there by the spirits that I had invoked to aid me. Often, when all was dry, the heavens cloudless, and I was parched by thirst, a slight cloud would bedim the sky, shed the few drops that revived me, and vanish.

I followed, when I could, the courses of the rivers; but the daemon generally avoided these, as it was here that the population of the country chiefly collected. In other places human beings were seldom seen; and I generally subsisted on the wild animals that crossed my path. I had money with me, and gained the friendship of the villagers by distributing it; or I brought with me some food that I had killed, which, after taking a small part, I always presented to those who had provided me with fire and utensils for cooking.

My life, as it passed thus, was indeed hateful to me, and it was during sleep alone that I could taste joy. O blessed sleep! often, when most miserable, I sank to repose, and my dreams lulled me even to rapture. The spirits that guarded me had provided these moments, or rather hours, of happiness that I might retain strength to fulfil my pilgrimage. Deprived of this respite, I should have sunk under my hardships. During the day I was sustained and inspired by the hope of night: for in sleep I saw my friends, my wife, and my beloved country; again I saw the benevolent countenance of my father, heard the silver tones of my Elizabeth's voice, and beheld Clerval enjoying health and youth. Often, when wearied by a toilsome march, I persuaded myself that I was dreaming until night should come, and that I should then enjoy reality in the arms of my dearest friends. What agonising fondness did I feel for them! how did I cling to their dear forms, as sometimes they haunted even my waking hours, and persuade myself that they still lived! At such moments vengeance, that burned within me, died in my heart, and I pursued my path towards the destruction of the daemon, more as a task enjoined by heaven, as the mechanical impulse of some power of which I was unconscious, than as the ardent desire of my soul.

What his feelings were whom I pursued I cannot know. Sometimes, indeed, he left marks in writing on the barks of the trees, or cut in stone, that guided me, and instigated my fury. 'My reign is not yet over' – these words were legible in one of these inscriptions – 'you live, and my power is complete. Follow me; I seek the everlasting ices of the north, where you will feel the misery of cold and frost, to which I am impassive. You will find near this place, if you follow not too tardily, a dead hare; eat and be refreshed. Come on, my enemy; we have yet to wrestle for our lives, but many hard and miserable hours must you endure until that period shall arrive.'

Scoffing devil! Again do I vow vengeance; again do I devote thee, miserable fiend, to torture and death. Never will I give up my search, until he or I perish; and then with what ecstasy shall I join my Elizabeth and my departed friends, who even now prepare for me the reward of my tedious toil and horrible pilgrimage!

As I still pursued my journey to the northward, the snows thickened, and the cold increased in a degree almost too severe to support. The peasants were shut up in their hovels, and only a few of the most hardy ventured forth to seize the animals whom starvation had forced from their hiding-places to seek for prey. The rivers were covered with ice, and no fish could be procured; and thus I was cut off from my chief article of maintenance.

The triumph of my enemy increased with the difficulty of my labours. One inscription that he left was in these words: – 'Prepare! your toils only begin; wrap yourself in furs, and provide food, for we shall soon enter upon a journey where your sufferings will satisfy my everlasting hatred.'

My courage and perseverance were invigorated by these scoffing words; I resolved not to fail in my purpose; and, calling on Heaven to support me, I continued with unabated fervour to traverse immense deserts, until the ocean appeared at a distance, and formed the utmost boundary of the horizon. Oh! how unlike it was to the blue seasons of the south! Covered with ice, it was only to be

distinguished from land by its superior wildness and ruggedness.
The Greeks wept for joy when they beheld the Mediterranean from
the hills of Asia, and hailed with rapture the boundary of their toils.
I did not weep, but I knelt down, and, with a full heart, thanked
my guiding spirit for conducting me in safety to the place where
I hoped, notwithstanding my adversary's gibe, to meet and grapple
with him.

Some weeks before this period I had procured a sledge and dogs,
and thus traversed the snows with inconceivable speed. I know not
whether the fiend possessed the same advantages; but I found that,
as before I had daily lost ground in the pursuit, I now gained on
him, so much so that when I first saw the ocean he was but one
day's journey in advance, and I hoped to intercept him before he
should reach the beach. With new courage, therefore, I pressed on,
and in two days arrived at a wretched hamlet on the sea-shore.
I enquired of the inhabitants concerning the fiend, and gained
accurate information. A gigantic monster, they said, had arrived the
night before, armed with a gun and many pistols; putting to flight
the inhabitants of a solitary cottage, through fear of his terrific
appearance. He had carried off their store of winter food, and,
placing it in a sledge, to draw which he had seized on a numerous
drove of trained dogs, he had harnessed them, and the same night, to
the joy of the horror-struck villagers, had pursued his journey across
the sea in a direction that led to no land; and they conjectured that
he must speedily be destroyed by the breaking of the ice, or frozen
by the eternal frosts.

On hearing this information, I suffered a temporary access of
despair. He had escaped me; and I must commence a destructive and
almost endless journey across the mountainous ices of the ocean, –
amidst cold that few of the inhabitants could long endure and which
I, the native of a genial and sunny climate, could not hope to survive.
Yet at the idea that the fiend should live and be triumphant, my
rage and vengeance returned, and, like a mighty tide, overwhelmed
every other feeling. After a slight repose, during which the spirits
of the dead hovered round, and instigated me to toil and revenge, I
prepared for my journey.

I exchanged my land-sledge for one fashioned for the inequalities
of the Frozen Ocean; and purchasing a plentiful stock of provisions, I

departed from land.

I cannot guess how many days have passed since then; but I have endured misery, which nothing but the eternal sentiment of a just retribution burning within my heart could have enabled me to support. Immense and rugged mountains of ice often barred up my passage, and I often heard the thunder of the ground sea, which threatened my destruction. But again the frost came, and made the paths of the sea secure.

By the quantity of provision which I had consumed, I should guess that I had passed three weeks in this journey; and the continual protraction of hope, returning back upon the heart, often wrung bitter drops of despondency and grief from my eyes. Despair had indeed almost secured her prey, and I should soon have sunk beneath this misery. Once, after the poor animals that conveyed me had with incredible toil gained the summit of a sloping ice-mountain, and one, sinking under his fatigue, died, I viewed the expanse before me with anguish, when suddenly my eye caught a dark speck upon the dusky plain. I strained my sight to discover what it could be, and uttered a wild cry of ecstasy when I distinguished a sledge, and the distorted proportions of a well-known form within. Oh! with what a burning gush did hope revisit my heart! warm tears filled my eyes, which I hastily wiped away, that they might not intercept the view I had of the daemon; but still my sight was dimmed by the burning drops, until, giving way to the emotions that oppressed me, I wept aloud.

But this was not the time for delay: I disencumbered the dogs of their dead companion, gave them a plentiful portion of food; and, after an hour's rest, which was absolutely necessary, and yet which was bitterly irksome to me, I continued my route. The sledge was still visible; nor did I again lose sight of it, except at the moments when for a short time some ice-rock concealed it with its intervening crags. I indeed perceptibly gained on it; and when, after nearly two days' journey, I beheld my enemy at no more than a mile distant, my heart bounded within me.

But now, when I appeared almost within grasp of my foe, my hopes were suddenly extinguished, and I lost all trace of him more utterly than I had ever done before. A ground sea was heard; the thunder of its progress, as the waters rolled and swelled beneath me, became every moment more ominous and terrific. I pressed on, but in vain. The wind arose; the sea roared; and, as with the mighty shock of an earthquake, it split, and cracked with a tremendous and overwhelming sound. The work was soon finished: in a few minutes a tumultuous sea rolled between me and my enemy, and I was left drifting on a scattered piece of ice, that was continually lessening, and thus preparing for me a hideous death. In this manner many appalling hours passed; several of my dogs died; and I myself was about to sink under the accumulation of distress when I saw your vessel riding at anchor, and holding forth to me hopes of succour and life. I had no conception that vessels ever came so far north, and was astounded at the sight. I quickly destroyed part of my sledge to construct oars; and by these means was enabled, with infinite fatigue, to move my ice-raft in the direction of your ship. I had determined, if you were going southwards, still to trust myself to the mercy of the seas rather than abandon my purpose. I hoped to induce you to grant me a boat with which I could pursue my enemy. But your direction was northward. You took me on board when my vigour was exhausted, and I should soon have sunk under my multiplied hardships into a death which I still dread – for my task is unfulfilled.

Oh! when will my guiding spirit, in conducting me to the daemon, allow me the rest I so much desire; or must I die, and he yet live? If I do, swear to me, Walton, that he shall not escape; that you will seek him, and satisfy my vengeance in his death. And do I dare to ask of you to undertake my pilgrimage, to endure the hardships that I have undergone? No; I am not so selfish. Yet, when I am dead, if he should appear; if the ministers of vengeance should conduct him to you, swear that he shall not live – swear that he shall not triumph over my accumulated woes and survive to add to the list of his dark crimes. He is eloquent and persuasive; and once his words had even power over my heart: but trust him not. His soul is as hellish as his form, full of treachery and fiendlike malice. Hear him not; call on the **manes** of William, Justine, Clerval, Elizabeth, my father, and of the wretched Victor, and thrust your sword into his heart. I will hover near, and direct the steel aright.

---

manes Spirits of people who have died.

WALTON, *in continuation.*

August 26th, 17–.

You have read this strange and terrific story, Margaret; and do you not feel your blood congeal with horror, like that which even now curdles mine? Sometimes, seized with sudden agony, he could not continue his tale; at others, his voice broken, yet piercing, uttered with difficulty the words so replete with anguish. His fine and lovely eyes were now lighted up with indignation, now subdued to downcast sorrow, and quenched in infinite wretchedness. Sometimes he commanded his countenance and tones, and related the most horrible incidents with a tranquil voice, suppressing every mark of agitation; then, like a volcano bursting forth, his face would suddenly change to an expression of the wildest rage, as he shrieked out **imprecations** on his persecutor.

His tale is connected, and told with an appearance of the simplest truth; yet I own to you that the letters of Felix and Safie, which he showed me, and the apparition of the monster seen from our ship, brought to me a greater conviction of the truth of his narrative than his **asseverations**, however earnest and connected. Such a monster has, then, real existence! I cannot doubt it; yet I am lost in surprise and admiration. Sometimes I endeavoured to gain from Frankenstein the particulars of his creature's formation: but on this point he was impenetrable.

'Are you mad, my friend?' said he; 'or whither does your senseless curiosity lead you? Would you also create for yourself and the world a demoniacal enemy? Peace, peace! learn my miseries, and do not seek to increase your own.'

Frankenstein discovered that I made notes concerning his history: he asked to see them, and then himself corrected and augmented them in many places; but principally in giving the life and spirit to the conversations he held with his enemy. 'Since you have preserved my narration,' said he, 'I would not that a mutilated one should go down to posterity.'

Thus has a week passed away, while I have listened to the strangest tale that ever imagination formed. My thoughts, and every feeling of my soul, have been drunk up by the interest for my guest, which this tale, and his own elevated and gentle manners, have created. I wish to

imprecations Curses.
asseverations Emphatic assertions.

soothe him; yet can I counsel one so infinitely miserable, so destitute of every hope of consolation, to live? Oh, no! the only joy that he can now know will be when he composes his shattered spirit to peace and death. Yet he enjoys one comfort, the offspring of solitude and delirium: he believes, that when in dreams he holds converse with his friends, and derives from that communion consolation for his miseries, or excitements to his vengeance, that they are not the creations of his fancy, but the beings themselves who visit him from the regions of a remote world. This faith gives a solemnity to his reveries that render them to me almost as imposing and interesting as truth.

Our conversations are not always confined to his own history and misfortunes. On every point of general literature he displays unbounded knowledge, and a quick and piercing apprehension. His eloquence is forcible and touching; nor can I hear him, when he relates a pathetic incident, or endeavours to move the passions of pity or love, without tears. What a glorious creature must he have been in the days of his prosperity, when he is thus noble and godlike in ruin! He seems to feel his own worth, and the greatness of his fall.

'When younger,' said he, 'I believed myself destined for some great enterprise. My feelings are profound; but I possessed a coolness of judgment that fitted me for illustrious achievements. This sentiment of the worth of my nature supported me, when others would have been oppressed; for I deemed it criminal to throw away in useless grief those talents that might be useful to my fellow-creatures. When I reflected on the work I had completed, no less a one than the creation of a sensitive and rational animal, I could not rank myself with the herd of common projectors. But this thought, which supported me in the commencement of my career, now serves only to plunge me lower in the dust. All my speculations and hopes are as nothing; and, like the **archangel who aspired to omnipotence**, I am chained in an eternal hell. My imagination was vivid, yet my powers of analysis and application were intense; by the union of these qualities I conceived the idea, and executed the creation of a man. Even now I cannot recollect, without passion, my reveries while the work was incomplete. I trod heaven in my thoughts, now exulting in my powers, now burning with the idea of their effects. From my infancy I was imbued with high hopes

archangel who aspired to omnipotence Satan, the fallen angel who rebelled against God in Milton's *Paradise Lost.*

and a lofty ambition; but how am I sunk! Oh! my friend, if you had
known me as I once was, you would not recognise me in this state
of degradation. Despondency rarely visited my heart; a high destiny
seemed to bear me on, until I fell, never, never again to rise.'

Must I then lose this admirable being! I have longed for a friend; I
have sought one who would sympathise with and love me. Behold,
on these desert seas I have found such a one; but, I fear, I have gained
him only to know his value, and lose him. I would reconcile him to
life, but he repulses the idea.

'I thank you, Walton,' he said, 'for your kind intentions towards
so miserable a wretch; but when you speak of new ties, and fresh
affections, think you that any can replace those who are gone? Can
any man be to me as Clerval was; or any woman another Elizabeth?
Even where the affections are not strongly moved by any superior
excellence, the companions of our childhood always possess a certain
power over our minds, which hardly any later friend can obtain.
They know our infantine dispositions, which, however they may
be afterwards modified, are never eradicated; and they can judge
of our actions with more certain conclusions as to the integrity
of our motives. A sister or a brother can never, unless indeed such
symptoms have been shown early, suspect the other of fraud or false
dealing, when another friend, however strongly he may be attached,
may, in spite of himself, be contemplated with suspicion. But I
enjoyed friends, dear not only through habit and association, but
from their own merits; and wherever I am, the soothing voice of my
Elizabeth, and the conversation of Clerval, will be ever whispered
in my ear. They are dead; and but one feeling in such a solitude
can persuade me to preserve my life. If I were engaged in any high
undertaking or design, fraught with extensive utility to my fellow-
creatures, then could I live to fulfil it. But such is not my destiny; I
must pursue and destroy the being to whom I gave existence; then
my lot on earth will be fulfilled, and I may die.'

September 2nd.

MY BELOVED SISTER,

I write to you, encompassed by peril, and ignorant whether I am
ever doomed to see again dear England, and the dearer friends that
inhabit it. I am surrounded by mountains of ice, which admit of no

escape, and threaten every moment to crush my vessel. The brave fellows, whom I have persuaded to be my companions, look towards me for aid; but I have none to bestow. There is something terribly appalling in our situation, yet my courage and hopes do not desert me. Yet it is terrible to reflect that the lives of all these men are endangered through me. If we are lost, my mad schemes are the cause.

And what, Margaret, will be the state of your mind? You will not hear of my destruction, and you will anxiously await my return. Years will pass, and you will have visitings of despair, and yet be tortured by hope. Oh! my beloved sister, the sickening failing of your heart-felt expectations is, in prospect, more terrible to me than my own death. But you have a husband, and lovely children; you may be happy: Heaven bless you, and make you so!

My unfortunate guest regards me with the tenderest compassion. He endeavours to fill me with hope; and talks as if life were a possession which he valued. He reminds me how often the same accidents have happened to other navigators, who have attempted this sea, and in spite of myself, he fills me with cheerful **auguries**. Even the sailors feel the power of his eloquence; when he speaks, they no longer despair; he rouses their energies, and, while they hear his voice, they believe these vast mountains of ice are molehills, which will vanish before the resolutions of man. These feelings are transitory; each day of expectation delayed fills them with fear, and I almost dread a mutiny caused by this despair.

September 5th.

A scene has just passed of such uncommon interest, that although it is highly probable that these papers may never reach you, yet I cannot forbear recording it.

We are still surrounded by mountains of ice, still in imminent danger of being crushed in their conflict. The cold is excessive, and many of my unfortunate comrades have already found a grave amidst this scene of desolation. Frankenstein has daily declined in health: a feverish fire still glimmers in his eyes; but he is exhausted, and when suddenly roused to any exertion, he speedily sinks again into apparent lifelessness.

I mentioned in my last letter the fears I entertained of a mutiny.

auguries Omens that fortell the future.

This morning, as I sat watching the wan countenance of my friend —
his eyes half closed, and his limbs hanging listlessly — I was roused by
half a dozen of the sailors, who demanded admission into the cabin.
They entered, and their leader addressed me. He told me that he
and his companions had been chosen by the other sailors to come
in deputation to me, to make me a requisition, which, in justice,
I could not refuse. We were immured in ice, and should probably
never escape; but they feared that if, as was possible, the ice should
dissipate and a free passage be opened, I should be rash enough to
continue my voyage, and lead them into fresh dangers, after they
might happily have surmounted this. They insisted, therefore, that
I should engage with a solemn promise, that if the vessel should be
freed I would instantly direct my course southwards.

    This speech troubled me. I had not despaired; nor had I yet
conceived the idea of returning, if set free. Yet could I, in justice, or
even in possibility, refuse this demand? I hesitated before I answered;
when Frankenstein, who had at first been silent, and, indeed,
appeared hardly to have force enough to attend, now roused himself;
his eyes sparkled, and his cheeks flushed with momentary vigour.
Turning towards the men, he said —

    'What do you mean? What do you demand of your captain? Are
you then so easily turned from your design? Did you not call this a
glorious expedition? And wherefore was it glorious? Not because
the way was smooth and placid as a southern sea, but because it
was full of dangers and terror; because, at every new incident, your
fortitude was to be called forth, and your courage exhibited; because
danger and death surrounded it, and these you were to brave and
overcome. For this was it a glorious, for this was it an honourable
undertaking. You were hereafter to be hailed as the benefactors of
your species; your names adored, as belonging to brave men who
encountered death for honour, and the benefit of mankind. And
now, behold, with the first imagination of danger, or, if you will,
the first mighty and terrific trial of your courage, you shrink away,
and are content to be handed down as men who had not strength
enough to endure cold and peril; and so, poor souls, they were
chilly and returned to their warm firesides. Why, that requires not
this preparation; ye need not have come thus far, and dragged your
captain to the shame of a defeat, merely to prove yourselves cowards.

Oh! be men, or be more than men. Be steady to your purposes, and firm as a rock. This ice is not made of such stuff as your hearts may be; it is mutable, and cannot withstand you, if you say that it shall not. Do not return to your families with the stigma of disgrace marked on your brows. Return as heroes who have fought and conquered, and who know not what it is to turn their backs on the foe.'

He spoke this with a voice so modulated to the different feelings expressed in his speech, with an eye so full of lofty design and heroism, that can you wonder that these men were moved? They looked at one another, and were unable to reply. I spoke; I told them to retire, and consider of what had been said: that I would not lead them farther north if they strenuously desired the contrary; but that I hoped that, with reflection, their courage would return.

They retired, and I turned towards my friend, but he was sunk in languor, and almost deprived of life.

How all this will terminate, I know not; but I had rather die than return shamefully – my purpose unfulfilled. Yet I fear such will be my fate; the men, unsupported by ideas of glory and honour, can never willingly continue to endure their present hardships.

September 7th.

The **die is cast**; I have consented to return, if we are not destroyed. Thus are my hopes blasted by cowardice and indecision: I come back ignorant and disappointed. It requires more philosophy than I possess, to bear this injustice with patience.

September 12th.

It is past; I am returning to England. I have lost my hopes of utility and glory; – I have lost my friend. But I will endeavour to detail these bitter circumstances to you, my dear sister; and, while I am wafted towards England, and towards you, I will not despond.

September 9th, the ice began to move, and roarings like thunder were heard at a distance, as the islands split and cracked in every direction. We were in the most imminent peril; but, as we could only remain passive, my chief attention was occupied by my unfortunate guest, whose illness increased in such a degree that he was entirely confined to his bed. The ice cracked behind us, and was driven with

die is cast What Julius Caesar is reported to have said as he led his army across the Rubicon River and began a civil war against Pompey and the Roman Senate. It means that an irrevocable choice has been made.

force towards the north; a breeze sprung from the west, and on the 11th the passage towards the south became perfectly free. When the sailors saw this, and that their return to their native country was apparently assured, a shout of tumultuous joy broke from them, loud and long-continued. Frankenstein, who was dozing, awoke and asked the cause of the tumult. 'They shout,' I said, 'because they will soon return to England.'

'Do you then really return?'

'Alas! yes; I cannot withstand their demands. I cannot lead them unwillingly to danger, and I must return.'

'Do so, if you will; but I will not. You may give up your purpose, but mine is assigned to me by Heaven, and I dare not. I am weak; but surely the spirits who assist my vengeance will endow me with sufficient strength.' Saying this, he endeavoured to spring from the bed, but the exertion was too great for him; he fell back and fainted.

It was long before he was restored; and I often thought that life was entirely extinct. At length he opened his eyes; he breathed with difficulty, and was unable to speak. The surgeon gave him a composing draught, and ordered us to leave him undisturbed. In the mean time he told me, that my friend had certainly not many hours to live.

His sentence was pronounced; and I could only grieve, and be patient. I sat by his bed, watching him; his eyes were closed, and I thought he slept; but presently he called to me in a feeble voice, and bidding me come near, said –

'Alas! the strength I relied on is gone; I feel that I shall soon die, and he, my enemy and persecutor, may still be in being. Think not, Walton, that in the last moments of my existence I feel that burning hatred, and ardent desire of revenge, I once expressed; but I feel myself justified in desiring the death of my adversary. During these last days I have been occupied in examining my past conduct; nor do I find it blameable. In a fit of enthusiastic madness I created a rational creature, and was bound towards him, to assure, as far as was in my power, his happiness and well-being. This was my duty; but there was another still paramount to that. My duties towards the beings of my own species had greater claims to my attention, because they included a greater proportion of happiness or misery. Urged by this view, I refused, and I did right in refusing, to create a companion for the first creature. He showed unparalleled malignity and selfishness, in evil; he destroyed my friends; he devoted to destruction beings who possessed exquisite sensations, happiness, and wisdom; nor do I know where this thirst for vengeance may end. Miserable himself, that he may render no other wretched, he ought to die. The task of his destruction was mine, but I have failed. When actuated by selfish and vicious motives, I asked you to undertake my unfinished work; and I renew this request now, when I am only induced by reason and virtue.

'Yet I cannot ask you to renounce your country and friends, to fulfil this task; and now that you are returning to England, you will have little chance of meeting with him. But the consideration of these points, and the well balancing of what you may esteem your duties, I leave to you; my judgment and ideas are already disturbed by the near approach of death. I dare not ask you to do what I think right, for I may still be misled by passion.

'That he should live to be an instrument of mischief disturbs me; in other respects, this hour, when I momentarily expect my release, is the only happy one which I have enjoyed for several years. The forms of the beloved dead flit before me, and I hasten to their arms. Farewell, Walton! Seek happiness in tranquillity, and avoid ambition, even if it be only the apparently innocent one of distinguishing yourself in science and discoveries. Yet why do I say this? I have myself been blasted in these hopes, yet another may succeed.'

His voice became faint as he spoke; and at length, exhausted by his effort, he sunk into silence. About half an hour afterwards he attempted again to speak, but was unable; he pressed my hand feebly, and his eyes closed forever, while the irradiation of a gentle smile passed away from his lips.

Margaret, what comment can I make on the untimely extinction of this glorious spirit? What can I say, that will enable you to understand the depth of my sorrow? All that I should express would be inadequate and feeble. My tears flow; my mind is overshadowed by a cloud of disappointment. But I journey towards England, and I may there find consolation.

I am interrupted. What do these sounds portend? It is midnight; the breeze blows fairly, and the watch on deck scarcely stir. Again there is a sound as of a human voice; but hoarser; it comes from the cabin where the remains of Frankenstein still lie. I must arise, and examine. Good night, my sister.

Great God! what a scene has just taken place! I am yet dizzy with the remembrance of it. I hardly know whether I shall have the power to detail it; yet the tale which I have recorded would be incomplete without this final and wonderful catastrophe.

I entered the cabin where lay the remains of my ill-fated and admirable friend. Over him hung a form which I cannot find words to describe: – gigantic in stature, yet uncouth and distorted in its proportions. As he hung over the coffin, his face was concealed by long locks of ragged hair; but one vast hand was extended, in colour and apparent texture like that of a mummy. When he heard the sound of my approach, he ceased to utter exclamations of grief and horror, and sprung towards the window. Never did I behold a vision so horrible as his face, of such loathsome, yet appalling hideousness. I shut my eyes, involuntarily, and endeavoured to recollect what were my duties with regard to this destroyer. I called on him to stay.

He paused, looking on me with wonder; and, again turning towards the lifeless form of his creator, he seemed to forget my presence, and every feature and gesture seemed instigated by the wildest rage of some uncontrollable passion.

'That is also my victim!' he exclaimed: 'in his murder my crimes are consummated; the miserable series of my being is wound to its close! Oh, Frankenstein! generous and self-devoted being! what does it avail that I now ask thee to pardon me? I, who irretrievably destroyed thee by destroying all thou lovedst. Alas! he is cold, he cannot answer me.'

His voice seemed suffocated; and my first impulses, which had suggested to me the duty of obeying the dying request of my friend, in destroying his enemy, were now suspended by a mixture of curiosity and compassion. I approached this tremendous being; I dared not again raise my eyes to his face, there was something so scaring and unearthly in his ugliness. I attempted to speak, but the words died away on my lips. The monster continued to utter wild and incoherent self-reproaches. At length I gathered resolution to address him in a pause of the tempest of his passion: 'Your repentance,' I said, 'is now superfluous. If you had listened to the voice of conscience, and heeded the stings of remorse, before you had urged your diabolical vengeance to this extremity, Frankenstein would yet have lived.'

'And do you dream?' said the daemon; 'do you think that I was then dead to agony and remorse? – He,' he continued, pointing to the corpse, 'he suffered not in the consummation of the deed – oh! not the ten-thousandth portion of the anguish that was mine during the lingering detail of its execution. A frightful selfishness hurried me on, while my heart was poisoned with remorse. Think you that the groans of Clerval were music to my ears? My heart was fashioned to be susceptible of love and sympathy; and when wrenched by misery to vice and hatred, it did not endure the violence of the change, without torture such as you cannot even imagine.

'After the murder of Clerval, I returned to Switzerland, heartbroken and overcome. I pitied Frankenstein; my pity amounted to horror: I abhorred myself. But when I discovered that he, the author at once of my existence and of its unspeakable torments, dared to hope for happiness; that while he accumulated wretchedness and despair upon me, he sought his own enjoyment in feelings and passions from the indulgence of which I was forever barred, then impotent envy and bitter indignation filled me with an insatiable thirst for vengeance. I recollected my threat, and resolved that it should be accomplished. I knew that I was preparing for myself a deadly torture; but I was the slave, not the master, of an impulse, which I detested, yet could not disobey. Yet when she died! – nay, then I was not miserable. I had cast off all feeling, subdued all anguish, to riot in the excess of my despair. **Evil thenceforth became my good**. Urged thus far, I had no choice but to adapt my nature to an element which I had willingly chosen. The completion of my demoniacal design became an insatiable passion. And now it is ended; there is my last victim!'

I was at first touched by the expressions of his misery; yet, when I called to mind what Frankenstein had said of his powers of eloquence and persuasion, and when I again cast my eyes on the lifeless form of my friend, indignation was rekindled within me. 'Wretch!' I said, 'it is well that you come here to whine over the desolation that you have made. You throw a torch into a pile of buildings; and when they are consumed, you sit among the ruins,

Evil thenceforth became my good Reference to *Paradise Lost*, in which Satan says, "Evil be thou my good."

and lament the fall. Hypocritical fiend! if he whom you mourn still lived, still would he be the object, again would he become the prey, of your accursed vengeance. It is not pity that you feel; you lament only because the victim of your malignity is withdrawn from your power.'

'Oh, it is not thus – not thus,' interrupted the being; 'yet such must be the impression conveyed to you by what appears to be the purport of my actions. Yet I seek not a fellow-feeling in my misery. No sympathy may I ever find. When I first sought it, it was the love of virtue, the feelings of happiness and affection with which my whole being overflowed, that I wished to be participated. But now, that virtue has become to me a shadow, and that happiness and affection are turned into bitter and loathing despair, in what should I seek for sympathy? I am content to suffer alone, while my sufferings shall endure; when I die, I am well satisfied that abhorrence and **opprobrium** should load my memory. Once my fancy was soothed with dreams of virtue, of fame, and of enjoyment. Once I falsely hoped to meet with beings who, pardoning my outward form, would love me for the excellent qualities which I was capable of unfolding. I was nourished with high thoughts of honour and devotion. But now crime has degraded me beneath the meanest animal. No guilt, no mischief, no malignity, no misery, can be found comparable to mine. When I run over the frightful catalogue of my sins, I cannot believe that I am the same creature whose thoughts were once filled with sublime and transcendent visions of the beauty and the majesty of goodness. But it is even so; the fallen angel becomes a malignant devil. Yet even that enemy of God and man had friends and associates in his desolation; I am alone.

'You, who call Frankenstein your friend, seem to have a knowledge of my crimes and his misfortunes. But, in the detail which he gave you of them, he could not sum up the hours and months of misery which I endured, wasting in impotent passions. For while I destroyed his hopes, I did not satisfy my own desires. They were forever ardent and craving; still I desired love and fellowship, and I was still spurned. Was there no injustice in this? Am I to be thought the only criminal, when all human kind sinned against me? Why do you not hate Felix, who drove his friend from the door with **contumely**? Why do you not **execrate** the rustic who sought to destroy the

opprobrium Criticism, reproach.
contumely Rudeness, insolence.
execrate Curse or condemn.

saviour of his child? Nay, these are virtuous and immaculate beings!
I, the miserable and the abandoned, am an abortion, to be spurned
at, and kicked, and trampled on. Even now my blood boils at the
recollection of this injustice.

'But it is true that I am a wretch. I have murdered the lovely and
the helpless; I have strangled the innocent as they slept, and grasped
to death his throat who never injured me or any other living thing. I
have devoted my creator, the select specimen of all that is worthy of
love and admiration among men, to misery; I have pursued him even
to that irremediable ruin. There he lies, white and cold in death.
You hate me; but your abhorrence cannot equal that with which I
regard myself. I look on the hands which executed the deed; I think
on the heart in which the imagination of it was conceived, and long
for the moment when these hands will meet my eyes, when that
imagination will haunt my thoughts no more.

'Fear not that I shall be the instrument of future mischief. My
work is nearly complete. Neither yours nor any man's death is
needed to consummate the series of my being, and accomplish that
which must be done; but it requires my own. Do not think that I
shall be slow to perform this sacrifice. I shall quit your vessel on the
ice-raft which brought me thither, and shall seek the most northern
extremity of the globe; I shall collect my funeral pile, and consume
to ashes this miserable frame, that its remains may afford no light
to any curious and unhallowed wretch, who would create such
another as I have been. I shall die. I shall no longer feel the agonies
which now consume me, or be the prey of feelings unsatisfied, yet
unquenched. He is dead who called me into being; and when I shall
be no more, the very remembrance of us both will speedily vanish.
I shall no longer see the sun or stars, or feel the winds play on my
cheeks. Light, feeling, and sense will pass away; and in this condition
must I find my happiness. Some years ago, when the images which
this world affords first opened upon me, when I felt the cheering
warmth of summer and heard the rustling of the leaves and the
warbling of the birds, and these were all to me, I should have wept to
die; now it is my only consolation. Polluted by crimes, and torn by
the bitterest remorse, where can I find rest but in death?

'Farewell! I leave you, and in you the last of human-kind whom
these eyes will ever behold. Farewell, Frankenstein! If thou wert

yet alive and yet cherished a desire of revenge against me, it would be better satiated in my life than in my destruction. But it was not so; thou didst seek my extinction, that I might not cause greater wretchedness; and if yet, in some mode unknown to me, thou hadst not ceased to think and feel, thou wouldst not desire against me a vengeance greater than that which I feel. Blasted as thou wert, my agony was still superior to thine; for the bitter sting of remorse will not cease to rankle in my wounds until death shall close them for ever.

'But soon,' he cried, with sad and solemn enthusiasm, 'I shall die, and what I now feel be no longer felt. Soon these burning miseries will be extinct. I shall ascend my funeral pile triumphantly, and exult in the agony of the torturing flames. The light of that conflagration will fade away; my ashes will be swept into the sea by the winds. My spirit will sleep in peace; or if it thinks, it will not surely think thus. Farewell.'

He sprung from the cabin window, as he said this, upon the ice-raft which lay close to the vessel. He was soon borne away by the waves, and lost in darkness and distance.

THE END

The natural world

Much of *Frankenstein* is set in a world of mountains, ice, and glaciers. In giving her book settings like these, Mary Shelley adds greatly to the impact of her story. But she is doing more than provide a dramatic natural backdrop against which terrible events unfold. Before her time, few people appreciated scenery such as mountains, rocks, and forests. These wild places were thought to be uncivilized and ugly. People were much more likely to admire scenes such as gardens and other places that had been tamed by human activity. What changed this was a movement in art and literature called Romanticism.

The Romantic movement

Romanticism began in mainland Europe, with writers such as the German Johann Wolfgang von Goethe (1749–1832). Frankenstein's Creature reads Goethe's novel *The Sorrows of Young Werther* (1774) and is impressed by its "lofty sentiments and feelings." This book, about a young man who commits suicide because he is unlucky in love, started the Romantic movement in continental Europe, which valued the imagination and emotions of the individual (see pp.172–173) over logic and reason. By the time Mary Shelley was writing *Frankenstein*, the Romantic movement had spread to England. Poets such as William Wordsworth looked on natural scenery with new eyes. Instead of ugliness, they saw in mountains like the Alps a new kind of beauty, a beauty created by the vast scale and grandeur of the scenery and by the very fact that it was produced by nature alone, without any contribution from mankind. They called this new kind of beauty the "sublime," and they found it in rocks, rough seas, lakes, cascading waterfalls, and shady forests, as well as among the snowy peaks. They found the sublime

Romantic traveler
This painting, Traveler Looking Over a Sea of Fog, *is by the German artist Caspar David Friedrich. The rocks, mountains, and fog make this a typically Romantic scene.*

in extreme weather, too, such as storms, thunder, and the rainbows that came afterward. Mary Shelley shows her love of this kind of dramatic scenery at many points in the novel. She mentions the "majestic" setting of Frankenstein's Swiss house, the "sublime" mountains, and a storm "so beautiful yet terrific." At many points the characters express their enjoyment of this kind of scenery. This love of the sublime transformed both writing and painting in the late 18th century.

The Romantic poets

England's first Romantic poets were William Wordsworth (1770–1850) and Samuel Taylor Coleridge (1772–1834). Wordsworth lived in the English Lake District, an area visited by Frankenstein on his British trip. He wrote movingly about its landscape and people. In 1798, Wordsworth and Coleridge published jointly a book of poems called *Lyrical Ballads*. Their idea was to write poems in the language of ordinary people, not in the kind of heightened poetic style used by previous writers. One of the poems included is *The Rime of the Ancient Mariner* by Coleridge, a poem mentioned by Mary Shelley in *Frankenstein*, and a work set, like her book, in cold, icy scenery. Poets such as Mary's husband, Percy Shelley, and his friend Lord Byron continued the Romantic tradition, writing poems set all over Europe.

Painting the sublime

Artists were enthusiastic about the sublime, too. The German art of the late-18th century—especially the painting of Caspar David Friedrich (1774–1840)—is full of landscapes with mountains and forests. Slightly later, British painter J. M. W. Turner (1775–1851) used such settings both as backdrops for dramatic subjects such as shipwrecks or marching armies, and as stunning scenery in their own right. Like Percy Shelley and Byron, Turner traveled widely in Europe, introducing British people to many places unfamiliar to most travelers of the time, from the European Alps to the English Lake District.

A backdrop to tragedy

The dramatic scenery of ice and mountains in *Frankenstein* plays several different parts in the story. Its sublime features seem inspiring and provide an atmospheric backdrop as Frankenstein, a lonely scientist, pursues his huge ambition. But the cold and gloom also hint that Frankenstein is doomed. At the end of the book, the scenery even takes an active part in the story, when Frankenstein, chasing the Creature, comes close to catching him. At a decisive moment there is a great crack beneath his feet and Frankenstein is left stuck on a floating island of ice. With "a tumultuous sea" rolling between him and his enemy, he is almost overwhelmed by the sublime landscape around him.

Islands of ice
A polar landscape like this is the setting for the final part of Frankenstein.

GLOSSARY

absolution
Release from punishment for a person's sins; in the Roman Catholic Church, a priest may declare absolution after sins have been confessed.

access
Here, passionate outburst.

acme
Highest point.

adjuration
Earnest appeal.

aerial
Here, imaginary, ideal; (also: to do with the air).

affability
Courteousness, openness of manner.

aiguilles
Peaks.

albatross
A reference to Samuel Taylor Coleridge's *The Rime of the Ancient Mariner* (1798). In this narrative poem, a ship is driven off course by a storm and reaches Antarctica. An albatross leads the crew out of danger, and then a mariner, for unknown reasons, shoots it. As a result of this action, supernatural spirits pursue the ship.

Albatross

Albertus Magnus
Or Saint Albert the Great (1193–1280), a theologian and natural scientist who applied Aristotle's philosophy to Christian doctrine. After his death he was sometimes portrayed as a magician or occultist.

Detail of Magnus's *De Natura Rerum*

alloy
Literally, a mixture of two metals, or of metal with nonmetal. More generally, an adulterated substance.

ameliorate
Improve, make better.

amiable
Good-natured; having a pleasant and friendly disposition.

Angelica
Heroine of Ariosto's epic poem, *Orlando Furioso* (1516).

animation
Life.

antipathy
Aversion, strong dislike.

apothecary
A druggist or pharmacist. Or, more generally, one who keeps a shop selling items such as drugs and spices.

appertain
To belong naturally or relate.

approbation
Approval.

arbiters
Judges, those whose opinions are authoritative.

archangel who aspired to omnipotence
Satan, the fallen angel who rebelled against God, a central character in Milton's poem *Paradise Lost.*

Archangel
English form of Arhangelsk, a town on the northern coast of Russia.

archfiend
Principal devil, in other words, Satan, the former angel who rebels against God in *Paradise Lost.*

Ariosto
Ludovico Ariosto (1474–1533) an Italian poet.

Arthur's Seat
Hill on the edge of the city of Edinburgh, giving panoramic views of the city and Scottish coast.

Arveiron
A river near Mont Blanc.

ass and the lap-dog
A reference to one of the *Fables* of the French poet Jean de La Fontaine (1621–95), in which an ass (donkey) tries to copy the affectionate behavior of his master's dog, but gets beaten rather than rewarded.

asseverations
Emphatic assertions.

asylum
Place of refuge.

augmented
Made greater.

auguries
Omens that fortell the future.

augury
Knowledge of future or hidden things.

ballots
Here, counters used in a court to indicate the judges' or jurors' decision; black ballots indicated a verdict of guilty; (also: system of voting, especially one using printed papers or machines).

beaver
Here, adjustable piece of armor attached to a helmet, to protect the lower part of the face.

benevolent
Kindly; charitable.

benignity
Kindness, generosity.

Suit of armor, including beaver

bestowing
Giving.

bourne
Literally, stream; here used figuratively to mean the course of Frankenstein's travels.

brake
Here, overgrown area or thicket.

buried with the dead
In *The Thousand and One Nights*, Sinbad the Sailor is trapped in a tomb during one of his voyages.

cabriolet
Two-wheeled, one-horse carriage with two seats and a folding roof.

cabriolet

calamities
Troubles, misfortunes.

campagne
Country house.

capitulated
Yielded, surrendered.

Capulets
From Shakespeare's *Romeo and Juliet*. The Capulets were Juliet's family.

causation
The bringing-about of effects.

celestial
Heavenly.

chaise
Lightweight open carriage.

chamois
Wild antelope that inhabits the loftiest parts of the Alps and other mountain ranges of Europe and Asia.

Chamounix
A valley at the foot of Mont Blanc. Percy Shelley describes the valley in *History of a Six Weeks' Tour.*

Charles I
(1600-1649), King of England, Scotland, and Ireland from 1625 until his execution in 1649. He advocated the "Divine Right of Kings" principle and tried to levy taxes without Parliamentary consent. He also married a Roman Catholic at a time when England was staunchly Protestant which resulted in the English Civil War. After the royalist forces were defeated, Charles was executed for high treason.

Charles I

charnel-houses
Places where corpses are stored.

chastise
Punish.

chimeras
From Greek mythology, fire-breathing monsters. Thus, figuratively, unreal creatures or fantasies.

Chimera

chimerical
Fanciful, imaginary.

circumstantial evidence
As distinguished from direct evidence, evidence that can be deduced from the facts of a case.

Columbus and his egg
In Washington Irving's story *Christopher Columbus* (1828), a courtier asks Columbus if he had not found the New World might another man have done so. "To this Columbus made no immediate reply, but, taking an egg, invited the company to make it stand on one end. Every one attempted it, but in vain; whereupon he struck it upon the table so as to break the end, and left it standing on the broken part; illustrating in this simple manner, that when he had once shown the way to the New World, nothing was easier than to follow it."

condescension
Here, acting kindly towards one's inferiors; (also: looking down on someone, acting in a patronizing way).

confessor
In the Catholic Church, the priest who hears a person's confession of their sins.

Constantinople
Former name of the city of Istanbul, Turkey.

contumely
Rudeness, insolence.

Cornelius Agrippa
(1486-1535) A German occult writer, astrologer, and alchemist.

cot
Cottage.

culled with the choicest art
Carefully selected.

Cumberland lakes
Group of lakes in north-western England, in the region known as the Lake District, an area especially dear to the country's Romantic poets.

Ullswater in the Lake District

daemon
Evil spirit.

Dante
Dante Alighieri (1265–1321), Italian poet, writer of the *Divine Comedy*, the most famous part of which, the *Inferno*, describes the torments of the damned in hell.

Dante Alighieri

Darwin
Erasmus Darwin (1731–1802), scientist, writer, and grandfather of the more famous Charles Darwin, originator of the theory of evolution

debility
Infirmity, weakness.

declamatory
Having the elaborate quality of a public speech.

delineate
Describe or portray.

demoniacal
Like a demon or evil spirit.

deposed
Here, gave testimony; told her story; (also: removed someone from office or a position of power).

derange
Disturb or destroy the order of.

despondency
Dejection; feeling of hopelessness.

desponding
Dejected, lacking in hope.

die is cast
What Julius Caesar is reported to have said as he led his army across the Rubicon River and began a civil war against Pompey and the Roman Senate. It means that an irrevocable choice has been made.

dilatoriness
Tardiness.

dilatory
Slow, tending to cause delay.

diligences
Stage coaches.

discover myself
Here, reveal, expose to view.

disquisitions
Carefully written accounts.

diversity
Quality or state of being varied.

divine
Discover, make known.

doated
Bestowed love or fondness.

dogmatism
Stubborn or arrogant assertion of an opinion.

dôme
French: literally, dome; term used to describe summit of mountain or hill.

dross
Refuse, waste matter.

dun-white
A dull or dingy shade of white.

efface
Obliterate, wipe out.

elemental
Here, relating to the powers or spirits of nature; (also: relating to any kind of element).

elementary principles
basic rules.

elixir of life
Imaginary potion that would make the drinker live for ever.

emaciated
Thin, wasted away.

encomiums
Praise.

enervating
Weakening, exhausting.

ennui
French for boredom or dissatisfaction.

enounced
Uttered.

enunciation
Utterance.

ephemeral
Short-lived, transitory.

epithets
Descriptive words or phrases.

eulogy
Speech in praise of someone or something.

Evil thenceforth became my good
Reference to Milton's poem *Paradise Lost*, in which Satan says, "Evil be thou my good."

evinced
Displayed, exhibited.

excommunication
Exclusion from a religious community; especially, banning from Holy Communion in a Christian church.

exculpated
Freed from blame.

execrate
Curse or condemn.

execration
Utterance of curses, expression of hatred.

exordium
Introductory part of a speech.

exotic
Here, plant introduced from a foreign country; (also: anything from another part of the world or having the qualities of the foreign or unfamiliar.)

exploded
Here, rejected or brought into disrepute.

expostulate
Argue, plead, or remonstrate.

Exotic plants

eyry
The nest of a bird of prey. Here, figuratively, a lofty or high-perched retreat.

Eyry

Falkland
Lucius Cary, second Viscount Falkland (c. 1610-1643) Secretary of State to Charles I.

fastidious
Exacting in taste, difficult to please.

feint
Deceptive action.

fervent
Showing great warmth of feeling; extremely devoted or earnest.

fetter
Restraint.

florins
Here, Dutch coins each worth one guilder; (also: several different historical coins, including examples from Britain and Italy).

Florins

forbear
Here, refrain, hold back; (also: forgive or be patient).

foreign service
Diplomatic or military service.

galvanism
Electricity produced by chemical action (as in a battery), or the application of electricity to the body for medical purposes. After Luigi Galvani (1737-98), an Italian scientist who argued that an "animal electricity" exists in nerves and muscle tissue.

garb
Clothing.

Genevese
Native of Geneva, Switzerland.

glut the maw
Overfeed the stomach; the creature is imagining death as a living being who he is feeding with his murder victims.

Goring
Lord George Goring (1608 – 1657), a general who alternated his support between the royalist and Parliamentary armies during the English Civil War.

George Goring

grated
Here, fitted with bars.

ground sea
Ocean swell, which occurs in calm waters, without apparent cause.

guile
Deceit, treachery.

Hampden
John Hampden (1594–1643), a statesman and central figure at the start of the English Civil War. He fought for the Parliamentary cause and was mortally wounded at the Battle of Chalgrove.

harem
Women's quarters in the palace of a Turkish sultan.

Havre-de-Grâce
A fortified harbor in Normandy.

Galvani experimenting with frogs

immured
Walled in.

immutable
Unchangeable.

imperious
Urgent, overbearing.

imprecations
Curses.

incommoded
Troubled.

incredulous
Unbelieving, skeptical.

indefatigable
Untiring.

indolence
A state of torpor or ease without pleasure or pain.

inestimable
Too great to be properly measured or appreciated.

Inexorable
Unyielding.

infidels
People who do not believe in a particular religion; here, those who are not Christians.

inglorious
Disgraceful, shameful.

innumerable
Too many to be counted.

insatiate
Incapable of being satisfied.

integrity
Uprightness; honesty; sincerity.

interment
Burial.

intoxicating draught
Literally, an alcoholic or stupefying drink. Figuratively, something which causes exhilaration beyond self-control and leads to delirium.

intuitive
Having to do with immediate or instinctive understanding

irradiated
Here, lit up; (also: exposed to radiation).

irresolution
Indecisiveness.

irrevocably
In a way that cannot be undone; unalterably.

Isis
Alternative name for the River Thames where it passes through Oxford.

Jura
Heavily forested mountains that run along the border between France and Switzerland.

The Jura

keeping
Here, in painting: setting down with attention to proper proportions and harmony.

languid
Weak with fatigue.

lassitude
Weariness.

laudanum
A narcotic consisting of an alcohol solution of opium.

Lausanne
Capital of the Vaud canton on the northern shore of Lake Geneva.

Lausanne

league
A distance of about three miles.

Leghorn
Old-fashioned English name for the town of Livorno, on the north-western coast of Italy.

liberal education
Form of education designed to develop the mind for its own sake rather than to give the pupil specific knowledge.

lineaments
Features.

loathing
Hatred; intense dislike or disgust

Lord Byron
George Gordon, Lord Byron (1788–1824) a major English poet and a leading figure in the Romantic Movement. Byron's best-known works include *Don Juan* and *Childe Harold's Pilgrimage*, both narrative poems. Like Shelley, he was famous not only for his art, but for his extravagant and unconventional lifestyle.

Lord Byron

Lycurgus
(c.700–c.630 BC) According to legend, a lawmaker from Sparta (in southern Greece) responsible for Sparta's militaristic and communal social code.

machinations
Plots or schemes, usually with evil intent.

Mahometan
Muslim.

maladie du pays
French for homesickness.

malignity
Deep-rooted ill will, hatred.

mandate
Right to rule or wield power.

manes
Spirits of people who have died.

Mont Blanc

masquerades
Masked balls, assemblies in which the guests wear costumes.

meed
Reward, result.

melancholy
Depressed, brooding.

metaphysical
To do with the basic principles of nature.

mien
Appearance, demeanor.

miniature
Here, a very small portrait, often painted on ivory.

minutiae
Small details.

Miniature

Mohamet
Muhammad, the great prophet of the Islamic religion. According to Muslims, God's last messenger or prophet.

Mont Blanc
The highest peak in Europe; it marks the border between France and Italy. Mary and Percy Shelley visited Mont Blanc in 1816 and Percy Shelley wrote a poem about it.

mutability
Changeability; the quotation is the last part of Percy Bysshe Shelley's poem *Mutability*.

mutable
Changeable.

my husband
Percy Bysshe Shelley (1792–1822) a major English poet associated with the Romantic Movement. His *Ozymandias* and *Prometheus Unbound* are widely considered to be among the greatest poems in the English language. Percy Shelley is also famous for his unconventional lifestyle. He was expelled from Oxford University in 1811 after publishing a political pamphlet entitled *The Necessity of Atheism*.

Percy Bysshe Shelley

myriads
Countless numbers, hordes.

natural philosophy
Physical science—the study of nature as distinguished from social science, the study of human behavior and society.

Newton, Sir Isaac
British scientist (1642–1727), author of ground-breaking works on mathematics, optics, and the theory of gravity.

Sir Isaac Newton

nicer
Here, more careful, discriminating, perceptive.

noisome
Foul-smelling, disagreeable.

Numa
The second king of Rome (r. 715-673 BC) who succeeded Romulus (see below). He instituted four priestly orders: the pontifices, the salii, the fetiales, and the vestals. The Fetiales were peacemakers.

obdurate
Stubborn.

'old familiar faces'
The Old Familiar Faces is the title of a poem by poet Charles Lamb (1775–1834).

opprobrium
Criticism, reproach.

Orkneys
A group of about 70 islands off the coast of northern Scotland.

'palaces of nature'
Quotation from Lord Byron's poem Childe Harold's Pilgrimage.

palpable
Tangible, something that can be touched or handled.

palpitation
Quivering, throbbing.

Pandaemonium
Reference to John Milton's epic poem, Paradise Lost (see p. 130). Pandaemonium is the capital of hell, a palace built by fallen angels.

panegyric
Speech of praise.

Paracelsus
Philippus Theophrastus Aureolus Bombastus von Hohenheim (1493–1541), a Swiss physician, alchemist, and occultist who thought human beings could be produced through alchemy, without a mother or father. The name "Paracelsus" means equal or greater than Celsus, a Roman encyclopedist.

Paracelsus

Orkneys

Paradise Lost
An epic poem in blank verse by John Milton (1608–1674) published 1667. Broken up into 12 books, the poem relates the temptation of Adam and Eve by Satan and their expulsion from the Garden of Eden. In Book 1, Milton states that his purpose is to "justify the ways of God to men."

paradisiacal
Heavenly.

paroxysm
Fit, sudden outburst.

parquet
Flooring made of wooden blocks laid in a pattern.

partiality
Bias; taking one person's side over another.

pedantry
Showy display of learning.

pensive
In deep thought

penury
Poverty, destitution.

perambulations
Strolls, leisurely walks.

perceived
Grasped mentally; observed.

perdition
Spiritual damnation, hell.

perfectionate
Bring to perfection.

pertinacity
Obstinacy.

phantasm
Apparition or ghost, a figment of the imagination.

philosopher's stone
Imaginary substance that alchemists hoped would enable them to transform low-value metals into gold.

physiognomy
Facial features or expression.

physiology
Science of living things and their parts.

plain work
Simple needlework.

Plainpalais
A promenade south of Geneva.

she plaited straw
She wove strands of straw together to be used in basket-weaving or in the manufacture of hats and other fashion accessories.

Plaited straw

Plutarch's Lives
Mestrius Plutarchus (46–127) a Greek historian and essayist. His *Parallel Lives* (c.100) contains 23 pairs of biographies, each pair consisting of one Greek and one Roman.

Polidori
John Polidori (1795–1821), traveling companion and personal physician to Lord Byron.

portmanteau
Traveling bag.

Portmanteau

precarious
Insecure; uncertain.

preceptors
Tutors, teachers.

precepts
Rules of conduct.

precipitate
Cast down violently, throw over.

predilection
Preference.

professions
Here, open declarations of love or friendship.

prognosticated
Indicated, foretold.

purloined
Stolen.

recapitulation
Summary, brief repetition of main points.

recompensing
Compensating for a loss or injury, making amends.

remorse
Deep regret or guilt felt for a wrong one has done.

replete
Plentifully supplied .

republican institutions
During most of the 18th century, Switzerland did not have a centralized government. The Swiss Confederation was composed of semi-independent regions called cantons.

requisition
Demand, request.

retrod
Literally, retraced. Thus, figuratively, re-investigated.

reverie
Daydream.

Romantic
Person who values freedom, originality, and individuality in the arts; a follower of the Romantic movement championed by writers such as Byron and Shelley.

Romulus
(c. 771–c. 717 BC) According to legend, Romulus slew his twin brother, Remus, in order to take control of the area we now call Rome. He is said to have created the Roman Senate and the Roman Legions.

Romulus killing Remus

Roncesvalles
A village in the Navarre province of northern Spain where Basque tribes defeated Charlemagne's troops. Roland, Charlemagne's chief warrior, died during the battle. The 12th-century *Song of Roland* recounts Roland's last stand.

rustic
Typical of country people or the countryside.

sallies
Bounding leaps. Alternatively, clever remarks.

salubrious
Healthful.

Samuel Taylor Coleridge
(1772–1834) an English poet and philosopher. One of the founders of the Romantic Movement, he is best known for the poems *The Rime of the Ancient Mariner* (see p. 21) and *Kubla Kahn*.

Sanchean phrase
Words like those of the character Sancho Panza in Miguel de Cervantes' novel *Don Quixote*. Mary Shelley and her husband were reading *Don Quixote* in 1816.

Don Quixote

sanguinary
Bloody, bloodthirsty.

Sanscrit
Ancient literary language of India; now usually spelled *Sanskrit*.

satiated
Satisfied fully or to excess.

schiavi ognor frementi
Italian: slaves always trembling; referring to the plight of the Italian people when ruled by Austria in the 18th and 19th centuries.

scion
Heir, descendant.

sedulous
Diligent, persistent.

serenity
Calmness.

siroc
Usually called sirocco, a hot, dust-laden, wind blowing from North Africa.

slaked
Quenched or satisfied.

slough
Muddy area or marsh.

solemnisation
Performance of a ceremony or rite.

Solon
(c. 638–c.558 BC) an Athenian statesman and lawmaker. He is said to have written the Athenian constitution.

sophisms
Deceptive, misleading arguments.

Sorrows of Werter

The Sorrows of Young Werther, a novel published 1774 by Johann Wolfgang von Goethe (1749–1832). It was an important work in the *Sturm und Drang* or "storm and stress" movement in German literature, which emphasized extreme emotion as opposed to rationalism. *Werther* also influenced the Romantic Movement.

Spanish Armada

Fleet of ships sent by King Philip II of Spain as part of a failed attempt to invade England in 1588.

Spanish Amarda

spectres

Ghosts, objects of terror.

St Bernard's Well

Elegant building housing a pump that brings up water from a hot spring near the Water of Leith, a river that flows through Edinburgh and on to the coast at nearby Leith.

St Paul's

St Paul's Cathedral, London.

St Paul's Cathedral

sublime

Inspiring awe or admiration through grandeur or beauty.

succour

Help, assistance.

suppliant

Person who makes a humble request.

syndics

Government magistrates.

tapers

Wax candles.

Tartary

Old European name for a large area of eastern Europe and western and central Asia, inhabited by Turks, Mongols, and other peoples.

Tay

A river in Scotland.

temperature

Here, temperament.

The Vicar of Wakefield
A novel by Oliver Goldsmith (1730–1774) published 1766. It is most often described as a "sentimental novel" promoting belief in the innate goodness of all human beings.

Theseus
A legendary king of Athens credited with slaying the Minotaur, a mythological creature that was part man, part bull.

Theseus   Minotaur

Tilbury Fort
A fort built by the side of the Thames estuary in England, to protect London from invasion by sea.

timorous
Frightened, apprehensive.

torpor
sluggishness.

Tower
The Tower of London, a huge medieval castle in Britain's capital city.

Tower of London

transitory
Short-lived.

true Swiss
A patriotic citizen.

tyros
Novices.

undulations
Wave-like movement, rising and falling.

unhallowed arts
Ungodly or unnatural scientific activities.

University of Ingolstadt
A Bavarian University (1472–1800). During the 18th century, the University was associated with the Illuminati, an Enlightenment secret society with humanist, anti-church attitudes.

vacillating
Unsteady.

vale
Dale or valley.

'very poetry of nature'
Quotation from The *Story of Rimini* by English poet Leigh Hunt (1784–1859).

viands
Provisions, items of food.

vivacity
Spiritual or mental vigor, liveliness.

Volney's Ruins of Empires
Constantin François de Chasseboeuf, comte de Volney (1757–1820), a French historian, philosopher, and politician. His *Ruins of Empires* (1791) describes the rise and fall of ancient empires and advances the idea that all religions share an underlying common truth.

William Wordsworth
(1770–1850) A major English poet. His *Lyrical Ballads* (1798), published jointly with his close friend Samuel Taylor Coleridge (see p. 60), a collection of poems written in vernacular or every-day language, helped launch the Romantic Movement.

William Wordsworth

DISCUSSION QUESTIONS

Letters 1-4 and Chapters 1-4

1. In the opening pages of the novel, how does Mary Shelley use a frame story, or a story within a story?

2. Why has Robert Walton organized his expedition to the Arctic?

In what way is Walton similar to Victor Frankenstein?

3. What do the details about Victor's parents show about the type of home in which he was raised?

4. How does Shelley create suspense at the end of Chapter 2?

5. At the university, which two professors does Victor meet?

How does Shelley contrast these characters?

6. As Victor becomes more and more interested in scientific subjects, what question continues to preoccupy him?

7. In Chapter 4, what reason does Victor give to Walton for not revealing the secret of how he brought his creature to life?

Chapters 5-8

1. What atmosphere is created by the setting at the beginning of Chapter 5?

Why is this setting appropriate?

2. When the monster approaches Victor's bedside, how does Victor react?

3. How does the story of Justine Moritz offer a parallel to the story of Elizabeth?

What theme is developed in these narratives?

4. What horrifying news does Victor's father reveal in his letter in Chapter 7?

5. What conclusion does Victor reach about who is responsible for the crime?

Why doesn't he tell the authorities?

6. What is ironic about Justine's situation in Chapter 8?

Chapters 9-12

1. In Chapter 9, how have the deaths of William and Justine affected Victor?

What restrains him from committing suicide?

2. Toward the end of Chapter 9, where does Victor go to find consolation and peace of mind?

What do you think of this decision?

3. When Victor meets the monster in Chapter 10, what biblical allusions does the creature make?

Why do you think Shelley includes these allusions?

4. Why does Victor agree to listen to the monster's story?

5. Starting with Chapter 11, Shelley uses an extended flashback.

From whose point of view is this narrative told?

Why do you think Shelley chose this point of view?

6. Why are the cottagers-the old man, Felix, and Agatha-not entirely happy?

Chapters 13-16

1. In Chapter 13, what event occurs to lift Felix's spirits?

2. In Chapter 13, what paradox, or seeming contradiction, in human nature does the monster begin to confront?

At the end of this chapter, what internal conflict does he experience?

3. What is revealed about the history of the cottagers in the flashback in Chapter 14?

4. In Chapter 15, the monster has learned to read. What three books make a powerful impression on him?

How does the discovery of Victor Frankenstein's journal affect him?

5. What are some conflicts, both external and internal, that occur in Chapter 16?

Chapters 17-20

1. In Chapter 17, what does the monster demand that Victor do for him?

How does Victor react?

2. Who accompanies Victor to England?

3. How does Victor feel as he works to create a second monster?

4. How does Shelley use foreshadowing to create suspense in Chapter 20?

Chapters 21-24

1. What horrifying discovery does Victor make in Chapter 21?

2. What do you think Victor means when he says at the beginning of Chapter 22, "William, Justine, and Henry-they all died by my hands"?

3. What major event occurs in Chapter 23?

Do you think that this event is the climax of the novel?

4. Explain how the reader is reminded in the novel's closing pages that this has been a frame story.

Briefly explain your reaction to the outcome of the plot.

(c) Pearson Education, Inc.

FURTHER READING

Other Works by Mary Shelley

History of a Six Weeks' Tour (1817, with Percy Bysshe Shelley)

Mathilde (1819, published 1959)

Valperga: or, The Life and Adventures of Castruccio, Prince of Lucca (1823)

The Last Man (1826)

Perkin Warbeck (1830)

Lodore (1835)

Falkner (1837)

Rambles in Germany and Italy (1844)

Critical works

Maurice Hindle, Mary Shelley's *Frankenstein* (Harmondsworth: Penguin, 1994)

Miranda Seymour, *Mary Shelley* (London: John Murray, 2000)

David Stevens, *The Gothic Tradition* (Cambridge and New York: Cambridge University Press, 2000)

ACKNOWLEDGMENTS

The publisher would like to thank the following for their kind permission to reproduce their photographs:

(Key: a-above; b-below/bottom; c-centre; l-left; r-right; t-top)

Aalborg University: Carsten Hammer Andersen/Lars Christensen/Mads Orbesen Troest 122-123b. **Alamy Images:** David Noton Photography 40-97; ImageState/Pictor International 103-159; Karl Johaentges/LOOK Die Bildagentur der Fotografen GmbH 246bl; Lebrecht Music and Arts Photo Library 10, 72, 238; Joshua Roper 98. **The Bridgeman Art Library:** Louvre, Paris, France, Giraudon 246br; Museo Nazionale del Bargello, Florence, Italy, Alinari 240; National Portrait Gallery, London, UK 246t; Private Collection 249c; Private Collection, Photo © Rafael Valls Gallery, London, UK 250cl; Plaza de Espana, Madrid, Spain, Ken Welsh 249bc; Wordsworth Trust 252. **Corbis:** 172; Tiziana and Gianni Baldizzone 243; Stefano Bianchetti 242bl; Gianni Dagli Orti 236cr, 250tr; Michelle Garrett 25-39; Wolfgang Kaehler 235; Frank Lukasseck 244-245b; Rick Price 173; Lynda Richardson 241br; Gustavo Tomsich 15-22, 58, 245crb. **DK Images:** Blists Hill Museum, Ironbridge, Shropshire 248; The British Museum 251cl; Judith Miller/Rogers de Rin 245c; Rough Guides 239tl; Wallace Collection, London 237. **Getty Images:** The Bridgeman Art Library/Caspar David Friedrich 234; The Bridgeman Art Library/David Roberts 251tr; The Bridgeman Art Library/Thomas Phillips 59, 244tr; The Image Bank/Walter Bibikow 244cl; Stone/Arnulf Husmo 4-5; Stone/Kim Westerskov 13; Stone/RGK Photography 165-232; Stone+/Sune Wendelboe 6-7; Taxi/Richard Price 1. **The Granger Collection, New York:** 160, 161. **Mary Evans Picture Library:** 238cl, 242cr, 248br. **National Portrait Gallery, London:** John Opie 11; Miss Roberts/Thomas Kearsley 73. **PunchStock:** Digital Vision 2-3; image100 8-9; Thinkstock 123tr. **Wikimedia Commons:** 99tr.

Jacket images
Front: **Alamy Images:** Lebrecht Music and Arts Photo Library tr; Dale O'Dell bl; **DK Images:** The Science Museum, London br. *Spine:* **Alamy Images:** Lebrecht Music and Arts Photo Library. *Endpapers:* **Mary Evans Picture Library.**

All other images © Dorling Kindersley
For further information see:
www.dkimages.com

DK team credits

Editorial Lead **Heather Jones**

Project Art Editor **Clive Savage**

DTP Designers **David McDonald, Nicoline Thilert, Pankaj Sharma, Harish Aggarwal,** and **Tarun Sharma**

Production Manager **Silvia La Greca Bertacchi**

Project Manager **Nigel Duffield**

Fig.2.

Fig.1.

A

a

b

Fig.5.

a

a

b

Fig.6.

Fig.13.

Fig.14.

B

Fig.12.

B

A

Fig.9.

B

B

B

B

A

Fig.11.

B

b

c

a

Fig.18.

b

b

c

Fig.

c